OUTLAW

A SCI-FI ALIEN COWBOY ROMANCE

THE MIDNIGHT SEVEN
BOOK 1

A.G. WILDE

DEDICATION

This is a work of fiction. It is in no way meant to be real. But if something like this should come to pass, give me a cup of coffee and an outlaw by my side.

We'll make the world burn.

BEFORE YOU READ!

There are sensitive topics in this book, including but not limited to allusions to/mention of sexual abuse, sexual abuse trauma, and alcohol abuse. There is a character suffering from a terminal illness and, in chapter 24, there is a tragic event involving a child. Though I handle it with care, I know even the slightest words can bring memories and experiences we'd rather hold back. Mental health is important and I would rather that you know this beforehand so you can make your own decisions. If chapter 24, is too much for you, feel free to skip past it to 25 where things get much better. Or, if all of this sounds like something that will affect you negatively, it's fine to pass on this book. I have many others you might like to read.

Otherwise, I hope you enjoy Elsie and her outlaw! Their story is full of love and a fight for what is right.

Happy reading!
 AG

CHAPTER ONE

Elsie

I grip my satchel tight and dip my chin, gaze averted as I make my way down Comodre's main street. There's hardly anyone out here. Our colony's once-thriving business district is deserted. The few shops I pass that should be open have their doors closed. And the houses, even with the heat and dryness of Ivuria 10, all have their windows closed, curtains drawn.

There are few resources here. Hardly enough to stay alive. The destroyed buildings are now dilapidated ruins. Comodre is like a ghost of what we all imagined it would be. The town is dead. And that's just as well. There is no life here. Not anymore. No joy. The wonder and hope that rose after landing on this desert planet and finding our place here have long faded. The hope of a rising new city built by us survivors is gone.

All that's replaced it is fear.

I can almost feel it in the wooden walls of every building I walk past. Every shop. Every cabin. It bleeds through the walls of the cured wood, straight into the sandy road under my feet. Almost as if it will go up through the soles of my boots and sink into my skin. Take me whole.

But I can't allow it. If I do, I'll give up and if I give up, I'll have lost everything. All I have is here in Comodre. Just like everyone else living in this gods-forsaken colony, I have no other life but this one.

So I swallow hard and keep on walking. Not wiping the sweat gathering on my brow from the offending heat of the blinding sun. Ignoring the wisps of sand flying in the air, embedding into the blonde strands I've tied into a braid that settles along my spine.

The deep orange sky above me has thin pink clouds that float aimlessly into the horizon and on another day, before all this *fear*, I would have stopped to look up at them. Stopped to appreciate the beauty of this place that saved me and the others. But I can't.

As I walk, a sound causes my gaze to shift upward. It's only to see the haunted eyes of a woman just like me. Settler. Colonist. Hopeful. But all that hope has disappeared from her eyes. She shuts her window with a haunting slam before pulling her curtains closed and disappearing from view.

I pause for a moment before hastening my steps. Maybe she's smarter than I am. I shouldn't have come outside. Not when the Nirzoik are due to come collect their dues. The bread and cream fruit could have waited until later. I should have done like the others and stayed inside like I usually did. Left the credits the Nirzoik want in a satchel at my front door so they could collect it. Worst they'd do then is probably smash a window or maybe take a piss on my wall. But now I'm outside, unprotected, and if I don't get back in time, I'll have to see them face to face. And do I really want that?

No. No, I did not.

Nobody wants to meet the Nirzoik face to face. Only someone completely insane, unhinged, would wish for such a meeting.

The skin on my back burns, the scars from our last encounter heating up as if drawing energy from the blazing sun. I gulp back a grunt and the urge to touch the very reminders of what can happen if you stand up to the Nirzoik. It's enough proof that I should be afraid. I should be *very* afraid.

But even as I think this, my shoulders set with an almost painful stubbornness that makes me lift my chin. The quiet wind whips loose grains of sand to tangle in my skirt as I walk quickly, all the while trying to appear as unaffected as I can manage. Brows diving, I hold my head high. This place is my home. The only real one I've known. I should be free to walk within it as I please. Free to live, even if I risk getting beaten for it.

Only, despite what I know is true deep in my heart, one fact remains. And that one fact could never be clearer as I stop short in my tracks.

I'm not free.

The dust cloud approaching is the first thing I see. That, followed by the undeniable sound of rocket bikes zooming across the rough terrain.

They're here.

Panic hits me immediately, all bravery and stubbornness momentarily forgotten as my head snaps in the direction of my little cabin. Not far now. If I run, I can make it inside before they arrive. I can get to safety.

Another window slams shut not far from where I stand, but I don't even turn to see who it is. I already know what I'll see on their face. The terror. The hopelessness.

And so I run.

The thin linen skirt whips around my legs before I lift it

with one hand, satchel in the other as I pick up the pace, boots thumping against the loose sand as I push all my energy into my legs. My heart thumps hard in my throat, breaths coming in full force as I push my body to move, running past the *endolo* tree sitting at the center of the colony and taking a sharp right.

The heightened sound of the rocket bikes increases, and I almost stagger and fall into the dirt as fear shoots up my spine. I push my legs harder, running down the street, my cabin in view. Just as the sounds get almost deafening, my hand closes on the doorknob to my home. I swing the door open, throw myself inside, and slam the door shut. Back pressed against the warm wood, my breaths come with heavy heaves that make my entire body rise and fall.

I can hear them laughing as the rocket bikes come to a stop. They sound much closer than they should be. Usually, they start collecting dues from the center of town and make their way outward, but, from the sounds of it, that's not the case today. They're doing something different this time, and any change is a cause for concern.

I hear the first of their boots hit the ground as they get off their bikes and I stiffen. There are only five cabins on this little offshoot street, not nearly enough to warrant a whole band of Nirzoik. Just one of those brutes sends enough fear through us all and, by the sounds of it, at least three have alighted their bikes in just this little area.

A soft wind rustles my curtains and my gaze shifts to the window. I drew my curtains but didn't pull the window all the way closed. Couldn't. Have to keep the house as cool as I can and with no extra credits to pay for a cooling system, it's the best I can do. My throat feels tight as I stare at the moving curtains now, almost as if they're beckoning the brutes to come closer. Almost as if I'll see one of their claws poking through the thin linen curtain, reaching inside.

The possibility holds me frozen, breath stopping in my chest, only a thin trickle of sweat running down my brow, crawling so slowly, it feels like it's alive.

I could move. Crouch and pull the window shut. But my feet won't let me. They're rooted to the spot. Maybe some of that fear that threatened to overtake me in the town *did* get to me after all.

Forcing the lump down my throat, I barely breathe as I listen.

Heavy boots hit wooden deck as they walk up to someone else's cabin and then there's a hard thump that I know well. The heavy butt of an energy rifle hitting wood.

"Open up, *kinchi*."

Their word for *bitch*. It's a guttural snarl, one that booms through the air as if the speaker is right outside my door, and for a moment, I wonder if I was mistaken. That they are really outside *my* house and not at another.

There's silence once more before the air suddenly cracks with the shattering of glass. A window, no doubt blown in. The tinkling of glass falling and then being crushed under boots is distinct.

Fuck.

"*Wherrre arree youuu?*" The Nirzoik says it singsong and my heart hits hard against my ribs. He's not talking to me, but it feels like he's talking to all of us who he knows no doubt are in our houses listening. I don't dare to breathe, holding my breath as if my very lungs will betray me.

There are only three of us women on this offshoot of Comodre. Me, Estella, and Viv. The other two houses belong to men who arrived with us. Craig and James. Humans like us. Afraid just like us.

"Someone's been cheating on their dues," the Nirzoik says and I don't have to see his face to know he's sneering, his ridged nose pulling back on his boxy face, flaring as it usually does whenever a Nirzoik is pissed. "Filling the bottom of their satchel with rocks, thinking we wouldn't notice."

The words make my body go cold.

A death sentence. They've punished us for far less. The scars on my back burn like evidence.

To purposely cheat them? I can't imagine it. It must be a lie. Another way to control us. Make us work for these credits even harder. Make us their slaves.

"Come out, *kinchi*...or your other little friends will pay."

There's another smash and more glass shatters. Whoever's house it is, both front windows are now gone.

For a moment, there's silence, and my hand trembles as I grip my satchel tight, the bread and cream fruit inside feeling like they weigh a thousand tons.

When there's suddenly the hard thud of a door being kicked in and the resulting scream, my body suddenly kicks into gear.

I move to the window, eyes wide as I see the scene before me. Not three, but four Nirzoik are at Estella's. Two lean nonchalantly on the beams supporting her roof overhang, one smoking a *cantri* root, the other popping *cagri* crystals into his mouth. I can hear them popping on his saliva even from here. Neither is paying attention to what the other two are doing. As if this is nothing to them. Just another day. Just another job.

The ridges on the first one's nose crinkle as he puffs on the *cantri* root, narrowing before opening as he breathes out the toxic smoke. The wisps rise through the narrow slits in the ridges, before escaping through his nostrils and mouth. Even without visibly threatening us, just that one action is terrifying. Maybe because Nirzoik look like one of the great predators from Homeworld Earth. We humans of Comodre tremble in fear at just the sight of these shark men.

As there's another scream from inside the house, the Nirzoik grins, sharp blackened teeth baring as he finally glances in the direction of the scream.

Estella.

She screams again as the floor thumps hard with the footsteps of the Nirzoik hauling her from within. The moment he appears, more blood drains from my face. He's bigger than the others. Hulking shoulders underneath the dark leather they wear. Silver scales glistening in the sun's light. Even from here, I can see how dry, thick, and impenetrable they are. He's gripping Estella by the skull as he drags her from the house, his strength against hers making her look like a rag doll being pulled by a child. I can see the pain on her face as she tries to fight off his grip.

"Do humans go deaf after a few sols?" He tilts his head at the one smoking the *cantri* root. The smoker shrugs and the Nirzoik sneers at Estella before tugging her hard. "Don't think so."

"Let me go, you bastard!"

The Nirzoik grins right before he throws her off the deck. She falls with a thump into the sandy ground, right at the feet of the other two Nirzoik.

Something clenches in my chest, my entire body tingling, and I know I'm about to do something I'll regret later.

But I need to help her. I can't just hide like the others and watch. That could be *me* out there. That could be any of us.

I move before conscious thought can tell me to stay where I am, turning from the window so quickly that I knock down a candle from the small table set beside the window. It's unlit and it rolls underneath the cot pushed against the wall right beside it.

The sound isn't loud, but I glance up at the short flight of stairs that leads to the loft above me and swallow hard. But there's no sound up there. Nothing to give away that there rests the one other person I care about in this whole new world. The one person stopping me from packing up and leaving this settlement to take my chances in the wilds. Because I can't.

She *needs* me.

Swallowing hard, I steel myself, shoulders setting.

"You've been robbing us, *kinchi*, haven't you? Been putting rocks at the bottom of your satchel to add weight. Think we wouldn't notice, mm?" The Nirzoik's voice floats through my open window as I hurry over to the small, makeshift kitchen at the back end of the cabin. The knife I was going to use to cut my bread sits there on the table. Sharp and glinting as if it's looking at me.

Without a second thought, I set the satchel with the food down on the table, grip the knife, and stuff it in the folds of my skirt.

"Answer me!" There's a dull thud, a soft cry, and when I fling my door open, freezing on my deck, four sets of eyes snap to me immediately. The three Nirzoik standing outside Estella's house, and the one now leaning on her door frame. All four look my way and, for a moment, I want to turn around. To go back inside. To keep myself and the person I'm supposed to protect safe. But at the sight of Estella on the ground, the dark bruise already forming on her face, the blood on her lips, and my feet move me forward.

The big Nirzoik rises from where he is crouching over her, and I force myself to look him in the eyes.

"Well, well, well..." he says, that unnerving dark gaze that all Nirzoiks have moving over my frame in such a way that makes my skin crawl. Maybe because it's like looking into a human's eyes. Maybe it's because of that uncanny feeling it creates. He takes a step toward me and I halt. He takes another and I take a step back. He grins. "Come to save your little friend, human?"

My tongue swells in my throat. I must be going mad. Willfully putting myself before them. But as Estella grunts on the ground, I know if time turned back, I'd do it all over again.

"Whatever she owes you," I keep my voice as steady as I can, "I'll pay her debt."

My hand tightens on the knife still hidden in my skirt. If he comes closer, if he tries anything, I'll bury it as far as I can into his chest. I might hardly hurt him, but if I can make him bleed even just a little, it will be worth it. Because once he comes at me, I'll be punished; whether I decide to fight back or not.

He stops just a few inches from me and I stare up into a face I wish I would never have to see again. Just like all the others I've ever seen of his kind, his skin is hairless, with a faint metallic sheen. His eyes, completely focused on me, are slightly too far apart, his ridged nose flattened, his mouth a lipless slit.

The Nirzoik could have been our allies. Can't they see we're not that different from them? That we're just trying to survive?

"You'll pay her debt, you say?" He grunts, taking another step forward, so close now that he brushes against me. "If you have extra, maybe we're not taxing you enough."

My jaw clenches as I try to remain still, even though his hot, raw breath assaults my nose. "You know damn well that you are."

My fist tightens as he makes a sound like he's pulling air through his teeth. The truth is, I *don't* have money to pay Estella's debt. But I can buy us time till she can get the credits they think she owes. It's the least I can do.

"Better watch your tone, kinchi." The Nirzoik lifts a coarse finger to my jaw, tracing a light pattern. The sensation of his touch is one I can't withstand, and I shift, snapping my head to the side and out of his reach. Bad decision. I sense it the moment he pauses, his hand hovering midair like evidence of my insult. "Seems to me you might need some reminding of just who's in charge."

My heart thumps hard in my chest, fingers tightening on the blade. The odds of something happening to me before they leave just went up by a hundred percent. "I'll pay her debt. You can take your credits and then you can leave."

"Elsie, don't..." My gaze snaps to her as Estella groans and crawls onto her knees. Once more, my hand burns on the handle of the blade as I see the full extent of the blow she'd received. One eye is already swelling up, the whole half of her face turning black and blue.

Something swells inside me akin to hatred as I shift my gaze back to the Nirzoik and the moment he sees the look in my eyes is the moment I know he's about to do something terrible.

"Search her dwelling," he says, not shifting his gaze from mine. "And burn the other one to the ground."

I hear Estella's horrified gasp and my heart does one large thump before it falls inside my chest. Search my house? They... they can't. I can't allow them to.

Panic swells inside me as the Nirzoik's companions move without further instruction. At the same time, I hear the screams and sounds of altercation rising from the center of town where the rest of his crew must be collecting dues.

It's always like this. Every time they come, it's like this. Ever since the first day they descended on our little colony. Never have we lived in peace since that first moment.

Estella screams, rushing after the Nirzoik who turns back toward her home, begging for mercy while he flips a fire cube in his palm. One spark from that thing and the whole cabin will go up in flames. I've seen it before. I've seen families lose everything in an instant.

Meanwhile, another of the Nirzoik shifts past us, heading toward my cabin, and my heart seizes in my chest. I can't allow them to go in. They will see her. They'll know my secret.

The world suddenly comes back into focus. Time speeds up. My lungs work again.

"No! Stop! Wait!" But they don't stop. My words mean nothing to them, because they only speak one language. My brain screams at me to do something. *"I'll give you double!"*

That causes them to pause, almost as if time has stopped, and I realize it's because the big Nirzoik before me has signaled them with a finger in the air.

Estella's horrified gaze snaps to mine, a plea mixed in with disbelief and fear. Swallowing hard, I hurry on. "I'll pay you double next time. Please..." I swallow my pride and shift my gaze back to the Nirzoik before me. "Please...spare us."

I can almost feel Estella screaming at me, asking why I'd promise such a thing. One week working in the mines digging for the precious ore these Nirzoik want hardly provides enough credits to survive much less pay the dues they come to collect. To promise double is like asking for death.

The big Nirzoik moves faster than I can move. Fist closing around my throat, he pulls me up till I'm on the tips of my toes, and snarls at me.

"Double," I force out, eyes watering as I meet his stony gaze. My throat burns with the effort to speak. "I promise."

When he says nothing, I wonder if the offer isn't good enough. Surely they'll bite. They want credits; it's the only thing they react to.

"Mom?" Even in the heat of Ivuria 10, it feels like a cold draught of air shifts across my spine. I freeze, praying above all else that I didn't just hear that little voice. "Mama, are you okay?"

Kiana.

The tremor in her little voice hits me as clear as day and I stiffen in the Nirzoik's grasp. The panic I felt before is nothing like the utter terror I feel now.

She must have woken up. Seen me surrounded by these brutes.

She knows better than to come out in the open when they're around. I've taught her to hide. But I know what it feels like when someone you love is in trouble. The pure urge to do *something*, even when you know there is little you can do.

It's the reason I'm out here in the first place.

The reason why, despite the fear, I'm face-to-face with a Nirzoik.

He chuckles, the sound like knives scraping against zinc. "What do we have here?"

He releases me without concern and steps around me. Pulling air into my starved lungs, I reach for the hulking bastard without thinking. The moment my fist closes on his scaly arm, pure dread shoots through me.

But I can't do anything else. And he stops. The brute stops to look at the hand against his arm. The fact that I'm touching him. It is as shocking as the fact that I don't pull my hand away. Because if I fear one thing, it's what he'll do if he goes closer to the source of that little voice. I fear it more than I fear losing my own hand.

The Nirzoik leans down, his lips coming close to my ear. "Hiding another resident, are you? It seems you owe us double the credits already."

I swallow hard, pulling my arm away from his.

"Mom?"

"I-it's okay, Kiana. Everything's going to be okay." I still can't even turn to look at her, still praying that maybe this is all a dream and she's still asleep in the loft. Safe. Away from all this.

"Come here, little one." It's the Nirzoik that was eating *cagri* crystals that speaks. The one who'd been about to search my cabin and discover Kiana anyway. At his words, I spin to face them, my heart almost breaking in two as I spot the little five-year-old standing on the deck, still in her nightclothes. Her inky black hair is like a frazzled nest on her head and her clothes are a tad too big. She's smaller than she should be. Skinnier.

She shifts her gaze to me, understanding in her little eyes, before she shakes her head slowly and the Nirzoik growls low.

"I said come here, *little one*," he repeats.

My hand trembles on the blade as Kiana's gaze shifts back to mine. Slowly, she takes a hesitant step forward. Then another. And another till she's about a foot away from the Nirzoik. He crouches, opening his palm, and my hand tightens on the blade some more.

What kind of mother watches her child walking straight toward danger and does nothing about it? The thought almost makes my knees buckle. The only thing keeping me standing being the fact that she needs me. Needs me to be strong.

In the Nirzoik's palm is a *cagri* crystal and my throat tightens as I stare at it. I can see Kiana's hesitation as she shifts her gaze back to me and the uncertainty underneath the hope and fear in her gaze almost brings tears to my eyes.

When was the last time she's had a treat? I can't remember. Can't afford it.

And now this thug is holding one out to her. Her favorite too.

The big Nirzoik by my side leans close to me once more. "I wonder what will happen if she *doesn't* take it..."

Adrenaline makes me want to shake and scream. Makes me want to run. This unknown territory sets my heart on a race course that feels like it leads to certain destruction. I nod but it comes out in a jerky motion, as if my body is fighting the movement.

"It's okay," I whisper and Kiana blinks, focus shifting back to the Nirzoik with the treat. With breath held, I watch as she takes the candy from the Nirzoik's hand, her small one looking dwarfed by his.

It only takes that moment for his hand to close around hers and in one smooth movement, he lifts the child by the arm.

Kiana screams.

"Kiana!" I move toward them, but I'm suddenly held back by the Nirzoik by my side. One heavy hand on my shoulder and I can't move. Almost as if he plants my feet into the ground below me with just the power of that one arm.

As I watch Kiana hanging there, the helplessness that swims around Comodre, the *hopelessness*, it floats around me, filling me like water filling an empty well.

"Look at that," says the Nirzoik, holding me still. "Seems these *kinchi* are always trying to trick us." He leans in close so only I can hear. "Next week, you will give us *triple* your debt... or we will take the child." He chuckles as my eyes widen at his words.

"Burn it down." He flicks a wrist and Estella's scream is all I hear as my heart hammers hard in my chest.

Triple payment.

There's no way I will be able to afford that.

I hear the flick of the fire cube, the first spark of a flame, and Estella's scream. The sudden heat of fire eating through wood and Estella's continued screams echo through the still air.

"Foolish humans!" The Nirzoik releases me as the other sets Kiana down and the child runs into my arms. She wraps her small arms around my legs as I grip her against me, the terror of it all making everything around me feel unreal. "You seem to forget who is in charge here." The Nirzoik lifts his voice so all can hear. "Double payment for all on our next collection!"

I'm hardly aware of the thugs climbing back on their bikes, their laughter filling the air even as more screams and blaster fire sound from the center of town. The one that gripped Kiana gathers a glob of spittle from the back of his throat and spits at the ground at my feet before popping the candy he'd been offering the child into his mouth.

Kiana trembles and I hold her tighter.

All I can see are her sweet little eyes as she looks up at me. All I can see is the knowledge of the fact that I have failed her.

I've failed us both.

CHAPTER TWO

Elsie

I wipe the sweat from my brow with one hand, probably smearing soot over my skin as I grab the multi-tool and try tightening the bolt on the machine before me one last time.

"Even if you get it to work, Elsie, that thing won't get you to Calanta and back in one piece." Estella leans against my front door, all smeared in soot from the fire, her hair a mess, her clothes ragged, probably a mirror image of me.

We'd tried to save as much as we could from the fire, which turned out to be nothing at all. Once the spark was lit, it ate everything in a matter of seconds. The only thing that we managed to save was an aluminum mug. The same one she was holding now, clasping it as if it were the key to life. Her life. And probably that's exactly what it was.

The cup survived, and so would she.

I keep my back turned to the skeletal remains of what was Estella's cabin and focus on fixing the rocket bike before me. I'd found the wreck of it abandoned out on the plains and had hauled it back home months before. After many days, we'd managed to get it working, but it had been abandoned for a reason. It didn't run for long. Was unreliable. But it was the only thing I had that could get me out of here.

"It's too dangerous, Elsie."

My shoulders stiffen at Estella's words and I force my gaze to the pale cream-colored bike before me, brown rusting metal in too many patches speckling its frame. She was right, of course. Who the hell would take this thing out into the plains all alone?

Me. That's who.

Because there's no other choice.

"I *have* to go."

Estella doesn't say a word and I know that deep down, she knows I'm right. I *do* have to go. Apart from dying the next time those Nirzoik return and I don't have triple the dues they want, this is the only other option.

"We could work together in the mines. Get the gems. Take shifts sleeping. Split the haul and bust our ass to pay the credits when the Nirzoik return."

My shoulders stiffen again and, for a moment, I can't see. It's only then I realize my vision's gone blurry because of tears I'm refusing to let fall. I fight them away, tilting my head back so they seep right back into my skull.

"We're already doing that, Estella." I meet her gaze and try not to flinch. The wound on her face and eyes is even worse now, like necrosis on her otherwise perfect sun-kissed skin. "We already work together. We already take shifts sleeping. We're already doing everything we can to get as many of those gems as we can, and it's not enough. It's *never* enough."

She opens her mouth to say something but I lift my hand to stop her.

"No, we can't do more. Even less sleep and we'll both go insane. And we need to be...*I* need to be..."

"Alive so she can be," Estella finishes for me.

I push a hard lump down my throat as I shift my gaze from hers and give her the barest of nods.

Kiana needs me. *Us.*

"Is she sleeping?" I whisper. Through the corner of my eye, I see Estella nod.

Good. Kiana needs all the rest she can get. All the energy she can save so she can get better.

For a few moments, I turn my attention back to the rocket bike before me, unscrewing one of the control panels to fix the lights, which seem to only remain lit for a few minutes before conking out.

"Did you do it?" I finally whisper.

Estella doesn't answer and after a few more moments, I lift my head to look at her.

And she doesn't have to answer. I see it there in her eyes, even though she's averted her gaze and is looking out across the darkening skies of Ivuria 10.

"*Why*, Estella?"

Again, she doesn't answer. Instead, her shoulders rise and fall with a heavy sigh. With a grunt, I watch as she sets her cup down and heads across to her yard, bare feet stepping on burned sand grass that dissipates into dust as soon as she steps on it.

Crouching, she begins to dig. For a moment, I don't know what she's doing and when she continues digging, I finally rise from the bike I'm working on to go stand by her side.

I see it the moment she uncovers it. A satchel buried in the ground.

She lifts it and the tinkling of credits catches my ears.

"Estella?"

Sitting back on her ass, she sighs again before thrusting the satchel toward me. But I can only stare at it as if it's a snake ready to strike out at me.

"Take it."

"I—" I shake my head, still staring at the satchel in disbelief. "You had the credits?! Then why on Ivuria did you try to cheat those bastards? Why didn't you—"

"Because you need it more than I do."

Her utterance makes me stop short, the implications almost too much for me to consider.

"You and Kiana need it more than those fools. *She* needs it. She won't get treatment if you can't ever save enough to take her to get it done. It's the least I could do."

Something like an inflated bag of emotion rises in my chest, making my ribs feel tight and blocking my airways. I stare at the satchel before shifting my gaze to Estella, fighting to push past the emotions threatening to consume me.

"She's not just your weight to carry, Elsie. She's all of ours."

I can't speak. I can't even cry. My mouth opens but all that comes out is a wordless sort of whimper.

"Don't cry. You'll make me cry and I don't do that weak shit." But even as she grins up at me, I see the tears in her eyes.

"But your house..."

"We can build it again. I'll stay with Viv until I do."

"All your things..."

"Didn't have much anyway." She shrugs. "I'm alive, thanks to you, Elsie. Those bastards would have done worse if you didn't come out to save me."

I shake my head. I didn't save her though. Everything's just gotten worse than before. Now Kiana's in danger, I owe triple the credits for however long they'll demand I pay it, and the dues of the whole colony have been doubled for at least one fortnight. We're screwed.

Estella thrusts the satchel toward me again. "Take it. Use it when you get to Calanta. Gods know you won't get a mercenary to bite with the few credits you have."

I swallow hard again before tentatively taking the satchel. The weight of the credits in my palm brings with it a wave of pure guilt.

But Estella is right, of course. This whole plan of mine—to head across the plains to the city in search of a hired gun—will require credits. It's a reckless idea I've tossed around before, but always put off because of the risk. I'd be putting our lives in the hands of a complete stranger. But...I have no choice. Things truly can't get much worse than watching my home die slowly. Of watching Kiana suffer because I never have enough credits left over for food or worse, the medicine she so desperately needs. So if hiring a mercenary is what it takes to have even a sliver of a chance of survival, of fighting back, the risk might finally be worth taking.

"How'd you know that's why I'm going to Calanta?" I whisper, still staring at the satchel.

Estella grins then winces with the pain. "Because you're not the first one who has thought of doing the same thing. I have too. Only way to get these assholes off our back is to give them a taste of their own medicine, and gods know our men can't do it."

My gaze shifts to the other cabins nearby. I spot one of the males in our little offshoot sitting there on his deck. Eyes on us. James. He doesn't say a word. Didn't even move to help while Estella's cabin burned to a crisp. To them, it's all hopeless.

"We need someone to help us." Estella rises and grips my hand that's holding the satchel. She gives it a hard squeeze, closing my fingers around the little bag. "If anyone can do it, Elsie, it's you."

Her faith in me seems almost misplaced. If anyone could do it, I'd give her the job. But she's injured and, as far as I know, no one else in this town is brave enough to go against these Nirzoik.

It's either I do it, or we die.

I grip the satchel, meeting Estella's gaze. Maybe her encouragement and faith were the exact things I needed. With a nod, I lift my skirt and stash the satchel in the custom pockets I'd made to strap against my legs. Strapped to the other leg is the blaster I'd acquired the second sol after the Nirzoik arrived. Its weight against my leg is like a comforting reminder that I can do this.

Heading back to the bike, I flip the wires and give the handle a turn. There's a choking sound and the twin rockets at the rear of the vessel backfire before the bike comes online, the lights flickering on. Guess that's a sign I have to do this.

Slamming the control panel shut, I screw it back in place and flip the multitool back in the toolbox under the seat.

One last look at Estella and I grab the pack with the little bread and cream fruit I'd saved from dinner, bottles of water, and my wayfinder. Hopping onto the bike, I tie the bag in front of me so it doesn't fall off and grab my coat from the ground at my feet. Like what Earthmen used to call ponchos, it slides over me in one smooth movement.

Bike helmet and sand shield on, I'm ready.

Estella limps over to the bike and rests a hand on my shoulder.

"Be safe out there," she says.

Safe. I muster a smile. "Kiss her for me, when she wakes up?"

Estella nods.

As I rev the engine and the bike sputters before taking off, I know today might be the last time I see them both. Because where I'm going is everything but safe.

Calanta is a city filled with thugs, murderers, and outlaws.

And I'm hoping to bring one home.

CHAPTER THREE

The Outlaw

This drinkery has far too many patrons and not enough brew.

I lean back, chair tilting to the wall against the dark corner in which I sit, exactly diagonal to the exit. Nothing behind me. Nothing I can't see either directly or through the corners of my eyes. I'm aware of the four walls that enclose the room, and every single fool who has come in here hoping to drown in their failures.

It's loud, but I don't mind. The chatter tells me two things. These males are comfortable. There is no threat. But that can change in a second.

My fingers twitch around the still-full flask of drink clasped loosely in my hand. The condensation rolls down the outside, wetting my fingers like ice melting against the pressures of the hottest desert sun. For even though this drinkery is in the underground of one of Calanta's seediest districts, the sheer amount of beings in this place and the cooling system can barely keep up.

It's the perfect place to disappear. Fade into the shadows. Somewhere I can watch and not be seen. Not be known.

Only, I'm not working. Haven't been for a while.

Leaning back some more, I bring the drink to my mouth, eyes narrowing slightly as the flask touches my lips. The scent of the booze wafts into my nose and my nostrils flare as I hesitate.

Once upon a time, I'd have finished at least three flasks by now. What is wrong with me?

But the scent of the drink only makes me want it less. Almost as if my tongue wants something else. Something...more?

Food?

When's the last time I had a good meal that wasn't synthetically fabricated by the food processors on some random outpost? I can't remember when. It's been a mighty long time then...

I let the flask hang between my fingers, debating whether I should shoot it back or set it down. Maybe it's time to move on again. Find a new planet. A new city. Somewhere I can get a decent meal and a drink that doesn't turn my stomach. Or maybe this restlessness isn't because of that at all. Maybe I'm just bored.

The last few jobs have been incredibly far from exciting. Mundane. Predictable even. It's time to retire. Put my blaster away. Pack up. Go find something else that satisfies my soul. Because my *ayahl* screams for something *more*.

And that's why I've committed to doing only one job after this. A grand finale. Maybe I'll choose something worthy— something to end my legacy and make all other jobs pale in comparison.

Setting the flask down, I'm about to drop a few credits on the table and take my leave when something in the air makes me pause. Call it my seventh sense, but something is here that shouldn't be. Or maybe *someone*. Nefarious? I'm not sure. Just an...anomaly. It makes my *ayahl* rise within me like a wave, catching its attention and holding it there. My chair slowly falls back into regular position, feet hitting the floor as I scan the establishment.

It's dimly lit in here, but I have no problem seeing through the shadows. My gaze sharpens, flicking over every face one by one until I frown. The chatter hasn't stopped. There's nothing *different* about the males around me. No new patrons have entered the establishment. So what am I sensing? What's that zing in the air that's made my ears perk and my *ayahl* writhe underneath my skin?

When my fangs descend, I know something's not right. I only ever get this feeling when I've come close to some great bounty, and as far as I know, none of these males hold enough credits worth my trouble.

My fingers brush against the flask still resting in my hand as I scan the room again. I trust my instincts more than anything else. I'm never wrong about things like this. Never—

The moment the whole room suddenly goes silent is the moment I know I'm right.

I see him a moment later.

A thin, small male. Species: unknown. And that's probably because he's covered his head with the strange hooded coat he's wearing. Why him? Why has he gotten my attention out of everyone else? He's a traveler, a poor one, judging from his strange well-worn attire. Baggy clothing that still betrays his thin frame. Long skirts that swish as he moves. Certainly not someone who should warrant the buzz rising in my *ayahl*. Even so, I track him as he moves, frown deepening, not sure why I'm not looking away. But I'm not the only one.

He makes his way from the entrance, seeming oblivious to

the dozens of eyes tracking him. Or maybe not. His shoulders look like sharp blades underneath his thick coat.

"Eh, sorry stranger, but no disguises allowed in here," the barkeep's voice cuts through the silence. "Gonna have to lose the hood if you want to drink."

A pause. No, *a stiffening*. The stranger looks caught in a trap. Slowly, reluctantly, he moves and I glimpse smooth skin and delicate fingers when he reaches out with a slender hand and slowly lowers his hood.

No. Not a him. Far too small and delicate to be any male from Ivuria 10. A *her*? A *female*? Yes. I'm sure of it. A female, but from a species I've never seen before. Pale, scaleless skin. Light-brown filaments pulled back into a braid at the back of her head that runs down her spine. Rosy red lips pressed into a thin line under a straight, ridgeless nose. No horns. No spikes. No hackles. And no *ayahl*. I reach out without thinking, but no *ayahl* answers back. I sense...nothing. Just piercing blue eyes that look straight through me.

What's a female of any sort doing in a place like this? And an off-worlder no less.

She shifts through a crowd that parts for her automatically, and the corners of my lips curl upward. If she knew the power she holds, parting a mass of lowly males like this. I track her as she makes her way to the front of the bar. Shoulders still set in a harsh line, she climbs up on a stool that's suddenly and strangely available, all while the eyes of every single male in the establishment are at her back.

"Give me a drink," she says to the barkeep. "The strongest you got."

Soft, melodious voice with a strange inflection. Definitely not from here. My *ayahl* perks up some more.

As the drink is slammed down before her, she lifts the flask and takes a swig big enough to rival the males around her.

That takes the edge off things.

Someone grunts and then there's laughter before the chatter starts up again and the female's shoulders visibly sag with relief.

My eyes narrow, head tilting back a little more than I usually do just so I can lean my chair back again and watch her from underneath the rim of my hat. Guess I'm staying here a little longer.

Two flasks later and I'm still sitting here. Same position. Same place. The only difference is that I'm no longer scanning the establishment. Every being has faded into the background. The only one I can't pull my eyes away from is that female.

She's still sitting at the bar, back straight, shoulders rigid as if she's scared to even breathe...or look around. I can sense her uncertainty from where I sit, and even though the other scumbags in this shithole are back to their usual merriment, I can tell they're all as acutely aware of her presence as I am.

After her first big swig of the drink, her nose crinkled in the strangest fashion. Something she quickly disguised as she set the drink down but still kept a firm grasp on the flask. She's brought it to her lips after, several times even, but I can tell she isn't drinking.

She's pretending, and that's interesting.

What's her game plan? Why is she here?

She's scanned everything at her front. The bar with the shelves and shelves of brew. The Nizeki barkeep with his several tentacles serving the patrons, keeping them happy. Even the empty flasks all being set down beside her once drinks are finished.

Finally, she scans to her right, then her left. The moment she sees the bounty board is the moment I see a light in her eyes, even from where I am. So...she's looking for a bounty? She doesn't strike me as any type of hunter I've ever seen. Maybe she's new?

Negative. Sweet little thing doesn't look like she could even kill a sand flea. But she's staring at the bounty board with such an intensity I wonder if I'm wrong.

Rosy lips disappear into her mouth and my eyes narrow some more, slipping down the angle of her long neck as her throat moves. What *is* she? With scales and an *ayahl*, she would look almost Zamari like me. But despite her differences, she's also smaller than our females. More...delicate.

She doesn't belong here.

My *ayahl* zings again and my eyes sharpen on movement to her left. An Ulturion hunter leans against the bar at her side, outside of her peripheral view. He leans in, close enough to sniff the filaments on her head, and even from where I sit, I see the thin hairs along her arms rise.

Curious. No *ayahl*, but she must have something else.

"What's a human like you doing in this part of Calanta?"

Human? I catch the Ulturion's words without even trying. Fek. I can focus on nothing apart from what's happening to her. I've tuned everything else out. The chatter fades into almost silence as I wait to hear her response.

"Looking for somebody," she says and her voice floats over me in a way that makes a ripple go through my scales. Strange.

Enticing.

"Maybe I can help..." The Ulturion makes his words trail off with suggestion and my right eye twitches as I wait to hear her response. Ulturions are only known for two things. Robbery. And murder. Not that we Zamari can look down on their kind. But something tells me this little *human* isn't looking for that kind of trouble. No, she's here for something else entirely.

Her throat moves again and I follow the line of her neck right back to her lips before she turns her head to face the Ulturion. That slight stiffening of her shoulders, the way one of her hands moves discreetly to the long skirt she's wearing.

She has a weapon. I'm sure of it. And she's smart not to trust the Ulturion. Smart to reach for it. But this is a "no arms" zone. One of the few places where unworthy men like me can come to unwind. No weapons allowed. But even the slightest hint that she has one makes a slight smile curl my lips again.

"Are you looking for work?" she says. It's almost a whisper, not even loud enough to filter through the chatter, but my *ayahl* tells me every single patron is listening. And that makes me slowly lower my chair back to the ground.

"What type of work?" the Ulturion leans back against the bar, his nonchalance as fake as the grin on his shadowed face. "Any male you find in here, they won't do anything for free..." His gaze slips past the female's shoulders. "But I'm sure you can find a way to pay." He grins wider. "What do you want, human? Need some repairs done on that scrap ship of yours?"

Her ship? So he's been watching her from before. I lean forward a little at the same time that the human's eyes harden. She's not a fool this one. She's presumed the same.

"Where can I find someone who can do that?" She points without looking at the bounty board and now a few other patrons stop feigning mindless chatter to look her way.

The Ulturion grunts. "Something like that will cost a lot of credits, soft thing..." He leans closer, not hiding the fact that he's smelling her hair this time and she hops off the stool to get out of his reach, nearly bumping into another patron who has moved to stand at her back, practically caging her in. The Ulturion chuckles; a sound that makes my muscles tighten and prime for a fight.

"I am willing to pay," her voice is tight, that melodious note now edged with acidity, "the right man...*male*...for the job."

There it is. Her fire. That spark.

The Ulturion takes a step toward her, and I almost intervene. Something I never usually do. I've seen pretty faces before and I've never acted rash. So the fact my *ayahl* almost pushed me to stop this has my brows diving toward my nose.

I don't know this female. This isn't a job of mine. I've seen worse things happen before and I've walked away. That's just a part of the job. Get too involved and you risk a stupid death. For all I know, this human, or whatever she is, could be working with this Ulturion. I've seen it before. Too many times to count. Their game plan? No fekking clue. Do I want to find out? Fek no. Wild trust is a fool's game.

And yet...

The female takes a step back, her brows diving, all pretense of keeping it cool thrown out the window when her back meets the patron who stands behind her while the Ulturion approaches, blocking her in further. Some of the other patrons pretend to ignore what's happening, downing their drinks and gambling away their credits while some others watch from the corner of their eyes. No one messes with an Ulturion once he has his eye on a prize. Built like tanks, those monsters take what they want, whenever they want. And right now, that little human is his prize.

As she shifts from the male at her back and turns her back to the bar instead, choosing the barkeep as her lowest threat and facing the others head-on, I close my eyes and release a smooth breath.

Okay, maybe she's not working with the Ulturion. Maybe this isn't some ruse to lure in some rookie hunter into whatever messed-up plan they've concocted.

Fek.

I should have left this shithole when I'd been prepared to.

CHAPTER FOUR

Elsie

The hard metal of the bar at my back and two sneering meatheads at my front.

My heart thunders in my chest, panic swirling in my gut, but I'm prepared for that feeling, at least. It's not like I didn't know something like this had been highly possible. These males aren't in the higher echelons of society. Even Ivuria 10 society. They operate in the darkness, in the underground, and that's exactly why I need their help. I need their help, but I would be crazy to hire these ones. Their intentions are already clear.

They both look like Nirzoik minus the ridged nose and I bet they're a branch of the same evolutionary vein. Probably even allies. I've been discreetly checking out every single one of these men in the mirror behind the bar. Saw how they were all shooting covert glances my way. Watching me while pretending not to. Could have cut the tension with my bread knife if I'd carried it with me.

But even though I don't have that, I have something else. The blaster strapped to my thigh burns insistently and I hesitate to draw it. It's the reason I wore my skirt. With the weapon hidden underneath it, I look more vulnerable than I already am. It's my only trick card. But if I don't put my foot down now, I'll be robbed or, worse yet, taken advantage of in the worst way possible. And it's clear this fool has been watching me from before I even entered this place. He mentioned my rocket bike and I'd parked it several sectors away. That means I've been watched from the moment I entered this part of the city. Or even from before.

The fact makes a shudder threaten along my spine. A sort of vulnerability I don't want to acknowledge taking root.

I've heard the stories.

There's a reason females are not known to visit this part of Calanta.

Fuck.

What are you going to do, Elsie?

Time ticks like an analog clock in my head as I meet the gaze of the first meathead. Can't make any sudden movements. Can't upset him either. Don't want to give him the impression I don't respect him, but I also need him to drop his guard.

Dipping my head, I release a shy giggle. "Y-you're scaring me, mister. I'm just looking for a strong, daring male just like yourself...that's all. I'm sure you can help me..."

The sound of a chair scraping against the floor at the back catches my ears and I suppose it's another of these thugs rising to come and scam me out of the few credits I have.

A part of me wanted to leave the credits hidden on the bike, but that would have been foolish. I had to take the satchel with me and there's no way I'm just going to let this bully take it away.

"Hand it over, soft thing."

I grit my teeth at the nickname he's given me but lift my head with the sweetest smile I can muster. "Hand over what?"

The meathead grins and steps closer, sharp teeth glinting. "How many credits you got? Don't make me have to check..." His gaze drops to my bosom and I get the distinct impression he believes that's where I've hidden the credits.

I smile again and his gaze shifts to my lips, but there's a hardness there that almost makes my smile freeze. I'm not dealing with regular males. These thugs have been hardened by the life they chose. Even if I could smile and sway my hips to make them drop their guard, it wouldn't work for long. Not that I'm going to lean on feminine wiles. Couldn't pull it off even if I wanted to. But that doesn't mean I'm not going to try.

"What do you mean? Are you just going to take them from me?" I bat my eyelashes and pout a little and the meathead grins wider.

"There, now you get it." He steps closer. "Pretty little human like you don't belong in a place like this. So far from your colony." His gaze shifts down me again and that spot of vulnerability that I feel increases. "Could get yourself hurt carrying around credits for the taking. Take this as me...helping you out. Just give them to me...quick and easy, and I'll tell these other males to leave you alone."

Ah, so he's helping me, is he? Doing this out of the goodness of his nonexistent heart?

I smile at him, soaking my voice in sugar. "You're so nice."

He grins again, gaze shifting to his companion as if to say 'told you it would be easy'.

"If you keep the credits, will you help me?" I bat my eyelashes again.

"Sure thing," he says, but even someone blind could see through that lie.

"And maybe I could even..." I slowly lift my skirt, revealing inch after inch of my skin, "...help you with something else, seeing as you're helping me." I bite my lower lip only to ground myself even while knowing it comes off as flirtatious when I meet his gaze. I want to puke.

He glances at his friend again, hairless eyebrows rising. What an idiot.

The moment my hand closes around the hilt of the blaster is the moment I pull it free. Both hands gripping the weapon I lift it fast, pointing the business end directly at Meathead #1's skull. His eyes widen slightly, just a moment before a blur of movement erupts behind him.

My heart slams into my chest, the only thing betraying the panic that suddenly fills my soul as about ten different blasters are pointed my way. Behind me, the barkeep exclaims something in a language my translator chip doesn't know. Flasks of booze crash to the floor as he loses his hold on them.

"No weapons! This is a weapon-free zone! *You all know the rules!*" he shouts.

"Shut the fek up, Gridwald," Meathead One snarls before shifting his gaze back to me. In the background, I can hear the barkeep releasing a slew of profanity as he desperately tries to clean up the mess he made.

I clench my teeth, hands trembling only slightly before I steady the blaster once more.

Oh, my fucking, god. I'm going to die. This was a mistake. I'm going to die and Kiana will not get her treatment. The Nirzoik will return and burn my cabin to the ground, leaving her homeless. The whole of Comodre will suffer and I'd have failed, left to rot in some unmarked grave in a seedy district in Calanta.

It all races through my mind like a blinding flurry of thoughts. Almost so loud I don't hear the meathead speak.

"Give. Me. The credits," he growls. His eyes flare red, his

teeth sharpening into points right before my eyes, and I can't pull my gaze away from the monster. "And maybe I'll let you go free. Hmm, no... I think I'll take you up on your offer first..." He growls, stepping forward to press his skull into my blaster. The audacity sends a chill down my already frozen spine. "*Then* I'll kill you."

There are chuckles from his comrades even as they all stay focused on me. The entire bar, filled with chatter before, is now silent.

It's the only reason I hear the sudden hum. Like something charging. So soft but yet so distinct I can tell the moment the meathead hears it too.

We both shift our gazes to the far corner. It's dark there, so dark I didn't see the male sitting on a chair all alone at the single table set in that corner. His feet are on the table. Thick leather boots, each with a spur at the back, pointed and deadly enough to do damage. He leans back in the chair, tilting it back to balance on its two back legs so effortlessly it looks like it was meant to be used that way.

His curved hat is pulled down low over his face, casting his features in shadow, as if the darkness of that one corner isn't enough. But two singular lights are shining from underneath that wide brim. His eyes. I almost gasp as it hits me. He's staring right at *me*. Unblinking. With unnerving intensity.

I realize almost with secondary awareness that something else should have caught my attention first. The blaster in his hand. I've never seen one like it before—not that we have state-of-the-art weapons in Comodre. But even from this distance, I can tell it's deadly. A red light shines from it like a seeker and I follow the line, eyes widening even more when I see the red dot lit dead-center in the meathead's skull.

"I wouldn't do that if I were you..." The words move from the dark corner, like a vibration that spreads outward. The stranger's voice is a low rumble that is said so softly it shouldn't have any effect on me at all. Except it does. My ears perk and something within me shivers enough that I have to grip the blaster tighter in my hand.

I don't know what the hell is happening but the other patrons who have not drawn arms slowly rise and back away. For a moment, I think they're backing away so they don't get hit if blasters begin firing. But then I realize they're all only looking in one direction, as if the host of weapons drawn in the room is of no consequence except the one the stranger is holding. They back away almost as if they're creeping out of sight, most pressing against the far walls and those closest to the exit quickly taking their leave.

I force myself to breathe. These are known thugs and if they're afraid, where the fuck does that leave me?

"Come here, Firespark," the stranger's voice washes over me again and I swallow hard. Firespark? Is he...is he talking to me?

No. Why would he? I don't know this male.

"What is this to you, Zamari?" The meathead growls, taking a step forward, a tinge of annoyance in his voice that even I can hear. His comrades shift their gazes from him to Zamari in the corner. No, *the* Zamari. Somehow, I get the sense that isn't his name at all. "This business is not yours."

The Zamari tilts his head back, letting it touch the wall as he watches us down the line of his straight nose. I can see more of his face now. The angles. The shadows making them look sharper than they should be. As if he has a face that was sculpted by the Ivurian gods themselves.

"It is...when you're messing with my bounty."

There's a moment of silence as his words land. His bounty? Wait, he's talking about me? But I have no contract with this stranger.

His declaration not only throws me but the meathead and his minions who suddenly look completely lost. But that shock mixed in with confusion only lasts for one second. The meathead's teeth elongate in a way that should send fear right through me if I wasn't staring at the stranger, a myriad of thoughts churning like a roaring river in my head. If he's just another greedy thug looking for easy pickings...

But even as I think this, my eyes narrow. Squinting, I try to make out just who or *what* he is. But all I can see is the light of those piercing eyes and the fact that they haven't left me, not even once. I can't read a thing in his gaze. Not greed. Not hunger. He looks almost bored, but there's a hardness, a coldness in those eyes hovering over something else simmering just underneath.

Violence.

Call it a dying instinct that tells me danger is close by. That I should tread carefully. That this thug is not like the other meatheads in this place.

"Yours?! This human doesn't belong—"

"*Come here, Firespark.*" Three words that cut through the air and silence the meathead.

It isn't a request anymore. It's an order, and the meathead's furious gaze snaps to me, probably to see if I will comply. Or probably he's just as shocked and mortified as I am.

The room's gone so quiet a drop of water would sound like a pitcher crashing to the floor and though I can't drag my gaze away from that all-consuming stare of the stranger, I can feel the eyes of every single being in this establishment glued on me.

I have to do something. And despite that, I can't tell whether this stranger is trying to help me or help himself to my credits, I get the distinct impression that whatever I do next will determine if I step out of this city alive.

Holding my breath, I keep my blaster trained on the

meathead as I take my first step toward the dark corner. As I move, some of the meathead's comrades keep their guns trained on me while the others shift theirs almost reluctantly to the stranger.

Walking backward, each step is slow, each thud of my boots against the smooth floors like a heavy thump as I take one step and then another toward the darkness. I have my back turned to the stranger and yet, I can feel him. *Feel* his gaze. Feel it along my spine, every bone and nerve ending tingling with the pressure of his stare.

Swallowing hard, I brave a look over my shoulder only for a lump to stop in the center of my throat as my breath hitches. He's right behind me now, those eyes boring into mine as if they are lasers that could go through my skull.

His weapon is still trained on the meathead, but those intense eyes burn with an intensity as if he can only see me. There's a light in them, almost as if they're glowing in the dark, and as I step closer, I wonder why I'm even heeding his command and moving over to his side. I don't know him.

I tighten my fingers on my blaster, ready to turn the barrel his way if he tries anything. But he does nothing. Doesn't reach for me, doesn't turn his weapon my way.

Confusion must flood into my gaze because just slightly, I see one of his brows cock almost as if he finds my reaction humorous. That makes my brows dive. But I continue moving the few feet left, reducing the distance between us.

Friend or foe, he's taking the heat away from me and for the moment, I have to go with it. It's either that or be robbed, raped, and killed. Not much of a choice.

In one smooth movement, the stranger swings his feet off the table. The chair's lowered next as he sits with his legs planted on the floor and wide apart, all while his weapon remains steady on his target. The red dot doesn't even shift slightly from its mark in the center of the meathead's skull.

The stranger's big. That I can tell. All muscle underneath the thin shirt, leather vest, and trouse that he wears. The dark leather blends into the shadows like he does because the only things I can see are those eyes.

When I'm finally just about two feet before him, he cocks his head slightly. He doesn't expect me to come closer, does he? Does he think I'm just going to trust him and close all the distance between us?

"Sit."

I can only stare over my shoulder at him. Sit? Now isn't the time for sitting, is it? There are guns pointed at my skull *and* his, but he doesn't even seem to notice them.

Sit? Seems simple enough. But what I really want to do is get my ass out of here. A second passes as I try to think of my next move. On my way from Comodre, I'd gone over countless scenarios in my mind. None of them prepared me for this.

Knowing that the wrong move could cost me my life, I wish I had a few more seconds to think. I have people depending on me back in Comodre. I can't afford to make a mistake. But the whole damn establishment is watching us, almost as if not one of them is breathing. Am I breathing? I don't even know.

I guess the only option is to sit.

I glance at the table, but there's only one chair. Heat flushes straight into my cheeks the moment I realize just *where* he wants me to sit.

I open my mouth to scald him with a few choice words but any retort dies on my tongue.

The stranger cocks his head some more, those piercing eyes almost daring me to not comply. I can feel the eyes boring into me from all sides. The weapons pointed directly at us.

My gaze hardens as I stare him down. The brute doesn't flinch.

Moving backward two more steps, I intend to sit just on the tip of his leg so my back is toward his chest when a strong arm snakes around at my waist. I jerk in the sudden grasp, swallowing my tongue and the yelp of fright bubbling up my throat, but the stranger takes the moment to spin me around so I'm facing him. His hold on my waist is firm, the heat of his arm like a furnace.

Now that we're so close, it feels like he's whispering to me so only I can hear. As if the whole establishment has faded into the background and it is only me and him in the room.

"Sit."

Gods know my legs must buckle because I comply.

Straddling just one of his legs, I immediately feel the strength within it. Pure, raw, power and I can't help the shudder that moves through me. Not from fear. But from something else entirely. Anxiety? Anticipation? I don't know what the hell to expect next.

"Good," he says, and when my wide eyes meet his, I see that his pupils are indeed glowing. Luminescent in the dark even though his eyes are the coldest green.

He doesn't say a word. Doesn't seem to have to. For when he finally shifts his gaze to the meathead behind us, I hear the moment the fiend lets out a growl of frustration. I risk a glance over my shoulder to see his cronies lowering their weapons and the band of them storming out of the establishment, knocking down stools and booze as they leave, the whole room holding its breath. A pregnant silence is left in their wake.

Only then does the stranger lower his weapon. He slides the fancy blaster into a holster on his hip before shifting his gaze back to mine.

"That's one problem sorted," he muses. "Now, what to do with you?"

There's a glint in his glowing eyes. It's like he's looking deep into my soul and even when the chatter picks up back around us, I find I can't look away, no matter how much I try to.

CHAPTER FIVE

The Outlaw

There are three things I didn't expect when I first saw this female.

First: that she would draw a weapon and on an Ulturion, no less. The brute will hold a grudge. Not against me. He'd be a fool to. But her? She's got a target on her back now. The idiot's been embarrassed in front of his men, and maybe that's my fault.

Fek. Here comes that sense of duty.

If I didn't step in, they'd have robbed her and used her as they pleased, but then she'd have been free to crawl back to whatever poor outpost she's wandered from. Far from this place, I'm sure, or I would have seen her kind before. Her pride and possibly her physical being might have left this ordeal wounded. But she'd be free.

Now, not so much.

And then there's the second thing. I didn't expect that she would be so utterly mesmerizing up close.

This...creature is not like any other resident of Ivuria 10 that I've seen before and for a moment, I wonder if she's from one of the colonies on Ivuria 11. The planets circling the dark star Ivuria are known to be the home of stray, homeless species. It's the reason it's so lawless. The reason beings like me can survive.

But she...she's nothing like the females I've seen here in the city. Not roughened by the desert sand of Ivuria 10. At least, not yet. If she's from here, her settlement is new. And the longer I look at her, the more I think this is true. She is no traveler. She is from a colony. A new one.

Travelers don't start fights with random fools unless they have something to fight for. And I can already tell she has something she needs to protect. Herself?

No...more than that.

Her skin is so pale I can almost see the threads of lifeblood pumping in her veins. The sight of it makes the tip of my fangs burn and now, this close, a unique scent of xyleen oil and... smoke...wafts into my nose. For the first time in a long while, I wonder what it would taste like. What it would feel like to pierce her soft neck with my fangs and taste her true essence.

Her scent and this sudden urge is a combination that makes me stiffen, my cock hardening in my trouse as she balances on my leg.

Her body is so soft, my grip is almost too tight. And that little yelp of surprise that dies in her throat, the barest sound of that melodious voice...I want to tell her to scream just so I can hear it again.

I did not plan for this. Any of this.

My *ayahl* reaches out almost on instinct, searching for hers again but coming up empty. She is not Zamari. I know this. So these urges shouldn't be there either.

Wide blue eyes stare back at me like the seas on the coast of

East Calanta. The warmth of her soft body under her layers of clothing almost beckoning. And that brings me to a third thing I didn't expect.

Right where she sits on my knee, the spot burns almost like there is a furnace between her legs. It's a different kind of heat, one that moves through my trouse as I pull her further up my leg. My cock hardens some more. What would she do if she knew I could feel the muscles in her center clench as she tightens herself? What would she do if she knew it was making my *ayahl* go crazy?

The bar disappears from around us as I stare into this strange being's eyes. Searching for...I wish I knew what. Certainly not this thrumming insistence that is building in my *ayahl*.

Her heartbeat quickens and only then do I acknowledge the blaster she has pressed into the center of my chest.

"If you're aiming for my blood organ, you're aiming at the wrong place."

Her eyes widen only slightly more before she schools her features.

"I'm sure if I pull the trigger now, it would still kill you."

The barest of grins twitches my lips. She obviously doesn't know who or what I am.

"What do you want from me? I have no business with you." Her throat moves as she speaks before she shifts her gaze, taking in the room quickly before focusing all her attention back on me. There's a thin line of perspiration on her brow and I almost lift my thumb to it. The urge to taste it—some part of her—is almost overwhelming.

Her throat moves again and I realize it's a tell. Despite that the blaster is steady in her hand. Despite that she holds herself so rigidly, her focus not waning, she is nervous. Scared. That building beat of her pulse, so strong I can feel it vibrate through that heat at her center and onto my leg, directly results from her fear.

I lift a hand and she tenses. The blaster presses harder into my chest. I don't have to look at it to know it's an old model. Almost an antique. Doesn't fire quickly. Recoil is a kinchi. And reloading is a pain in the fangs. Wouldn't choose it unless there was no other choice. But she holds it well. Well enough that I know she's used it before...and isn't afraid to use it again.

I watch that soft throat move as she shifts her gaze to my hand, watching as I motion to the barkeep before resting my palm flat on the table. My other hand is still at her waist but I hold it so still she must have forgotten it's there.

My gaze shifts to her weapon.

"It's a weapon-free zone. You're breaking the rules."

Her mouth falls open before she slams it shut. "You know damn well every piece of shit in this place has a weapon hidden somewhere. Including you. Weapons-free my ass."

It's been a while since anyone's spoken this freely with me. There's always the ghost of fear and distrust. The element of zero connection.

A ghost of a smile threatens on my lips once more as I tilt my head back slightly, taking in more of her face and allowing her to see more of mine.

I see the moment her pulse quickens. That feathering of movement underneath her skin as she looks at me.

"Perhaps," I concede. "But you're the only one brazen enough to press a barrel to my chest in full view." I pause, gaze flicking downwards. "Though I can't say I mind the position overly much."

The strangest thing happens to her skin. Her cheeks become filled with lifeblood like a magnet that snaps my attention. Again, there's an insistent ache in the tip of my fangs. When was the last time I drank directly from a source? I can't recall. Such pleasures have been lost on me for a long time. I've had no appetite for it.

I pull my gaze away from the strange sight just as her lips flatten into a thin line. The blaster digs deeper into my chest.

"I'm not some pleasure doll you can toy with."

My lips quirk this time. She dares to insult me even though she knows she has no power here.

"You think I use pleasure dolls..."

"I really couldn't care less." Her gun presses deeper even though I can see that slight beat of fear underneath her pulse. She has a weapon to my chest and I'm not responding to it. I could pretend to care, give her some confidence that she could take me down with one shot, but something tells me the moment I lie she will know.

Again, I reach out with my *ayahl* but I sense none within her.

"What do you hope to gain from helping me?" That blue gaze of hers searches mine. There is coldness there. Fear. And... pain. I inhale again, taking in that edge of smoke mixed in with the xyleen oil on her skin.

Only colonies on the outer region have easy access to xyleen oil. She's probably from there. But the scent of smoke...I can't tell where that's from or what's caused it.

When I don't answer her question, she shifts, ready to rise, but I'm not ready to let her go. Not yet. In that brief moment, when her round behind lifts off my leg and the heat of her cunt disappears, I almost growl.

I *did* growl.

I can see the shock in her eyes, sense the eyes shift from the patrons who have been pretending to ignore us.

I tighten my hand on her waist and settle her back down.

"Put away your blaster. I'm not going to hurt you."

Her throat moves again and my eyebrow twitches, eyes

shifting to hers as she glances around the room. It's the same moment that the barkeep arrives with two flasks of drink grasped in his tentacles. His gaze shifts to me briefly before he sets them down without a word. The female's mouth opens the moment he looks at her, almost as if she's about to ask him for help. But he averts his gaze immediately and hurries away.

No help there, Firespark. I told you I'm not going to hurt you.

But this desert flower isn't so easily convinced.

Good. I'm not a male to be trusted anyway.

CHAPTER SIX

Elsie

The stranger watches as I lift my skirt, slowly letting the fibers ride up my bare leg. The brute doesn't even avert his gaze and I fight the sensation of a shiver that goes down my spine at the intensity of those eyes.

I don't know his game plan. Have no clue what he's playing at. He wants something. Everyone on this cursed planet does. Nothing is done for free and I know I already owe him. My satchel of credits. My life too maybe. It's a debt I'll have to repay, and I have no doubt he will soon call to collect.

As I slip the blaster back into its holster high on my thigh, the corners of the stranger's lips quirk as if there's something he was going to say but thought better of it. Good. I don't really want to have a conversation with him...and yet, some traitorous part of me...is intrigued by this male.

There's a fluttering in my chest that started and hasn't gone away from the moment I set eyes on him in this very corner. It's uncharacteristic of me, something that's scaring me as much as sitting on a stranger's leg is.

But he said he wouldn't hurt me.

As far as words go, I take it with a grain of salt, as my grandmother used to say. She'd been a child when she left Homeworld Earth and she'd never made it to Ivuria 10. When our ship finally set down on the planet, all of the original group who had boarded back on Homeworld Earth had already passed away. Can't say it wasn't for the best. The dream world they all set out for didn't turn out to be much of a paradise after all.

The stranger's hand on my hip is like a weight I'm constantly aware of. From the moment he touched me there, he hasn't moved it. Hasn't held me tighter. Hasn't pulled me into him. Just silently holding me there, preventing me from rising. And underneath me, the hardness of his thigh presses into my core.

It's overly intimate and yet cold at the same time. Apart from staring at me, there's an air of wariness surrounding this whole interaction. Maybe it's just me, but I can't read this stranger. Not when I was on the other side of the room, far away from him, and not when I'm this close, face to face.

His gaze remains on me as he reaches for a flask of booze and hands it to me before taking the other for himself.

There are three other empty bottles on the table, telling me he's either drunk them all himself or he had company before. But apart from the two of us in this corner, it seems the entirety of the rest of the room has shifted away slightly. As if to put space between them and this stranger. As if he's here alone. And I'm yet to figure out what he wants from me.

But I'm not going to let that fool me. The meathead had approached me alone before a whole band of misfits had backed him up.

Aware of every slight movement of this male that's far too close to me, I remind myself he's just playing a game. I have to figure out the rules, and quick, before I lose.

Releasing a breath, I try to ignore the hardness between my legs as I throw my head back and take a swig of the booze. It hits my throat with an icy tang and I resist the automatic reaction to screw up my nose.

When I face the stranger again, those eyes glint as he slowly lifts his flask and takes a sip.

Fuck, it's unreal, the angles of his face. High cheekbones, a jawline cut from stone. A defined brow, piercing eyes set over that straight ridgeless nose. His lips aren't thin like most other residents of Ivuria 10 and I'm not sure I've ever seen his kind before. His ears are slightly pointed, short dark hair peeking from underneath his wide-brimmed hat.

Now that I'm close, I can see the scales on his arms, on the skin that disappears underneath the vest at his neck. They look soft and almost as if they're shifting in the light, changing color before shifting back to a shade of bronze.

And those eyes, the luminescence within them is almost enthralling.

"We leave after you finish your drink," he suddenly says, abruptly enough that I jerk, cheeks flushing at the fact I'd been staring at him, taking him in the entire time that he'd been watching me.

I blink at him, his words taking effect. "We can leave *now*."

I move to set my drink down when he stops it with the bottle in his hand.

"Drink," he says. "You're being watched."

That makes my spine stiffen, that cold wary feeling that's been hovering there heightening at his utterance.

Bringing the booze stiffly to my lips, I don't even react this time with the tang hits my tongue.

"Where?" I whisper.

His eyebrows move slightly. He's not even looking around the room, how does he know people are watching us?

"Your little friend has eyes in here. I wouldn't be surprised if they're waiting to see what you do. If you really have a bounty for me. If you're here alone... As soon as you step out of this drinkery, you'll be taken."

I swallow down a hard gulp of the booze, for once appreciating the way it feels like it's setting fire to my insides.

"Finish your drink. And then we leave."

We?

I eye him over the rim of the flask, watching as his eyes twinkle as he takes another sip of his drink.

"You're helping me escape this."

He shrugs so slightly it's almost unnoticeable.

"Why should I trust you? How do I know this isn't just some ploy and you're in league with them?"

Setting his flask down, he meets my gaze. "You don't."

That's it. No more explanation. Not even an effort to convince me otherwise. And yet—probably because of that—I'm inclined to think that I can trust him. That I *have* to.

Fuck.

Taking another big swig, I down the contents of the flask and set it down on the table. It sways a little with the force at which I put it down before it steadies at the same time that the Zamari sets his flask down too.

He sets his down far too gently for a male his size. As if he's used to dealing with things delicately, even though the muscles that flex in his arms betray the power he possesses. There's not a sound as his flask touches the table, and when I glance back at him, my spine tightens again.

For the first time since he held me, he releases his hold at my waist. My heart thumps far too hard as I rise, much less gracefully than I would have liked, and straighten my skirt. My gaze shifts to the other patrons remaining in the room and just as I suspected, the chatter has stopped once again. The hairs along my arms rise as I turn my attention back to the stranger just in time to see him set a credit down on the table.

I stand here not knowing what to expect as he rises and I try to school my expression. I was right about him being big. The male towers over me, putting the top of my head at just the center of his chest. Standing tall now, his face is once again in shadow and I only see the moment his eyes shift to the door.

Giving him a slight nod, I turn and head in that direction, pushing back the urge to look over my shoulder to see if he's following. But when a shadow falls over me as soon as I reach the door, I know he's there. How a big guy like him moves so silently is hard to believe.

My chest tightens as my hand hovers over the hidden blaster on my thigh. The door slides open and the dark streets of Calanta's lower district are right in front of me. I search the shadows of the alleyways, but I can't see anything directly out of the ordinary. The street is busy. Citizens zooming by on their rocket bikes, loud laughter from different drinkeries, males leaning against the walls of different buildings, white wisps of cantri smoke going up into the dark night.

After what the stranger said, that spot of vulnerability makes me hesitate for just a moment, but then I'm stepping out of the drinkery and onto the street.

"Thank you." I look over my shoulder to find those luminescent eyes on me.

He doesn't reply, simply watches me and I wonder if there's more. Does he want me to pay him?

The satchel filled with credits feels heavy against my thigh, but no way I'm taking it out here in the open. I'll have to cross this part of the city off my list and head to another section to find a mercenary who will help me. And I need to preserve as many credits as I can until I get there.

I study him for a moment more. The way he stands with his arms hanging loosely at his side. He looks nonchalant, but I'm not convinced. If the reaction of those males in the bar says anything, he is not what he seems.

"Follow me," he suddenly says.

I expect him to leave. Certainly don't expect him to walk ahead of me as if expecting me to follow.

I hesitate again.

If he's working with that meathead...

My reservations are strong but, somehow, my stiff legs press forward and soon I am hurrying in this outlaw's wake.

"Where are we going?"

"My ship."

I almost stop short, but I can feel the covert stares of the thugs lining the streets. Before, when I was heading to the bar, their presence almost derailed me. Back then, I'd been covered with the poncho. But now I'm completely visible, it's even worse. Now that my plan's been shot out of the water, I'm even more out of my element. It's the only reason I grip my skirts and continue after the male before me.

"Do you really think you can abduct me and I will willingly crawl into your vessel?"

He makes a sound like a grunt of laughter. "So untrustworthy."

"Shouldn't I be?"

"Yes."

My lips tighten into a thin line as I glare up at him, at the same time that I realize males on our side of the narrow thoroughfare seem to press themselves against the walls of the wooden buildings almost as if they're trying to stay out of his way while maintaining some semblance of agency.

Their gazes shift to me and I up the pace.

He stops at the side of a building where several rocket bikes are parked. I try to figure out which one is his before one suddenly blinks alive, almost soundless as its smooth engine comes online. I'm almost jealous. Mine sounds like a dragon farting when it starts up compared to this fine-tuned beast.

The bike is pitch black, almost blending into the night except for the gold accents that shine in the dark, much like the owner's eyes. Twin rocket engines adorn the back, flaring to life with white-hot fire from the engines. He hops on, straddling the beast before looking over his shoulder at me, with the exact same look he gave me when he told me to sit on his leg.

"Where are you taking me?"

"Where do you want to go?"

My throat tightens as I glance behind me. Several thugs are now watching us with interest.

"What's your plan?"

He shrugs. "I'm heading home. And if you know what's good for you, you'll do the same."

So...he isn't trying to rob me by some elaborate trick. At least, it doesn't seem like it. Fine.

Moving over, I climb up on his machine. It's bigger than mine and I have to spread my legs wide just to straddle it. My skirt rides all the way up, my creamy legs like a white contrast against his dark leather. The engine hums underneath my ass, the vibrations shifting me closer to him as he turns it down the road, and I have no choice but to tighten my legs and hold on.

The wind whips with the sudden speed, and without my visor I can hardly see or breathe. I'm left with another thing I have no choice but to do and I press my face into the stranger's back, wrapping my arms around his chest just to hold on. There's a movement in his chest, one that vibrates through my arms as if he grunts...or growls...I can't be sure. Maybe he doesn't appreciate me holding on to him like this, but he's the one ripping down the road as if he's late for something.

Fuck, maybe he just wants to get home for real. Maybe he has a wife there. A family waiting for him? Do thugs like him even have liabilities like that? Connections that are more than surface level?

"Where are you taking me?!" I shout over the roar of the bike and the wind.

"Your ship." It's surprising how clear his voice is through the noise. Or maybe it's because I can feel the rumble of it in his chest. But it's not what he says but where he says we're going that makes me stiffen.

He's riding like he knows where I parked. And if he's not in league with those thugs that accosted me in the drinkery...how does he know where I left my rocket bike?

The implications heighten my awareness in ways I don't expect. I sense the strength of his frame between my thighs. Strong enough to snap me in two if he likes. The plane of his hard back against my face. The waft of a musk I can't place but one I know definitely comes from him, embedded in the very fibers of the leather he wears.

And then there's the bike itself. How he handles it with dexterity and power, the massive machine bending and swerving to his slightest will. If he knows where I parked, he'd been watching me all along as well. Followed me to the drinkery? No. That doesn't make sense. I'd have noticed him if he'd entered after me...but then again, I hadn't noticed the meathead entering.

Maybe they have people on the outside who sent the word in.

Shit.

I try to slow the hammering of my heart as I release my grip on the stranger, shifting my hand down to the blaster on my hip and I grip it in its holster.

I don't know why I hesitate.

Maybe I'm praying I've got it all wrong and this outlaw isn't like the others. He's helped me so far...or maybe he was just helping himself. I hesitate because I want to believe I could have achieved this mission. That I could have found someone to help me...Kiana...Estella and all the others...to help Comodre. But the longer I stay in this city, the more that hope dwindles.

So I grip my blaster, my faith in this stranger dwindling the moment I spot the parking compound where I'd paid to leave my rocket bike.

My heart drops.

So he *does* know where I parked. I don't bother trying to figure out how or why. As soon as the bike grinds to a halt in the dimly lit parking sector, I swing my leg and hop off, blaster in hand, just as a shadow shifts from behind the many parked ships there.

CHAPTER SEVEN

Elsie

It happens so fast, my brain is slow to catch up.

I swing off the bike, rolling onto the floor as I pull the blaster from where it's strapped on my thigh. I land on my shoulder, pain rocketing through the bone. Pain that makes me grit my teeth, eyes watering with the ache, but I keep my gaze on the Zamari before me.

Shadows shift around us, and my heart sinks even more.

They were waiting for us. For *me*. I'm in an even worse spot than I was in the bar, only now I'm pretty certain of the outcome.

I'll lose the credits. I'll lose Comodre's chance at liberation.

Blaster fire reaches my ears before I roll out of the way, just for the spot where I was lying in to singe, the wisp of smoke from the residue of blaster fire making my eyes widen.

Shit.

Momentarily forgetting the stranger, I scramble to my feet and rush behind a parked hovercraft. More blaster fire and my heart thumps so loudly I can hardly hear. But the blaster fire isn't coming my way anymore.

Eyes wide, I shift enough that I can see from behind the hovercraft, and what my eyes land on has me forgetting how to breathe.

The outlaw is airborne as he sails through the air in a move that defies gravity. In one hand, the red sight of his blaster finds a target in the shadows. In another second, the target goes down. One single, piercing shot to the head.

There's a flurry of blaster fire that misses his body as he does a somersault midair, landing on another parked hoverbike with almost feline balance as he points downward at someone hiding there. One more shot. The target's dead.

A lump rises in my throat as I watch him move, jumping from that hoverbike just as green blaster fire shoots in his direction. It's almost as if he knows just when and where they'll fire. As if he can sense the danger before it occurs.

He fires into the far dark recesses of the parking sector and I hear someone wail in pain before their body thumps hard to the ground. One more down. Without even looking behind him, he flicks his blaster in his hand and points it over his shoulder, firing into the dark. Another hard thump. Another one down.

He's like an angel. An angel of pure destruction as he moves. Eyes shifting through the dark, wherever his gaze lands, his blaster fire follows next and I hear a dull thud.

Above where I hide, someone cries out as the blaster fire hits them. Their body shakes before they fall from the roof support, and I have just a moment to shift out of the way before their deadweight lands, almost crushing me. Scrambling on the back of my elbows, my wide eyes fall on the body of the thug who'd stood up with the meathead in the bar. There, in the center of his skull, is a deep red burn. The scent of burned flesh fills the air. His dark, soulless eyes stare up at me, unmoving. Dead. Not that I expected him to survive a hit like that.

Fuck. My mind's a swirl of emotions.

So the outlaw was right. They'd planned to converge on me here. But if he's working with them, why's he killing them? Shit. I don't know what to think, and as the sound of blaster fire and more bodies falling fills the space, it's hard to even concentrate when I know time is ticking down.

One of them will win this war. I'll be left to fend for myself in just a moment.

It only takes a few seconds before the last body falls and the parking sector is filled with silence.

If we were in some law-abiding city, beings would rush to see what the commotion was all about. Offer some help. Stop the killing. But I hear no one coming to check what's going on. Outside is just about as quiet as it is in here.

There, still crouched, hidden with a thug's dead body lying just before me, I slam my free hand over my lips, not daring to breathe lest I make a sound.

Is the stranger dead?

I doubt it. From what I saw, he was the one taking them all out, even though he was outnumbered. Shit. Just who the hell is he? He's obviously more deadly than any other male that had been in that drinkery. And now he's ready for me.

But there's complete silence. Enough that I slowly peer over the hovercraft I'm hiding behind. My breath hitches again the moment I find those luminescent eyes on me, as if he knew exactly where I was hiding and that I was still alive this whole time.

When he doesn't move or say a word, I force the shudder away from my bones and rise, slowly stepping over the dead thug. White, luminous eyes track me as I step out in the open and lift my blaster. There isn't even a spot of fear in those eyes as they look at me and I hate the fact that my hands tremble as I point the weapon at him.

He doesn't say a word. Doesn't even move and I hesitate again. He's not doing anything I expect him to do and it's all throwing me for a loop. But just as I begin to convince myself that I've got it all wrong, that he's helping me and he really isn't meaning to do me any harm, there's a sudden movement of his arm.

He lifts his blaster pointing it in my direction.

My heart stops.

Elsie, you foolish, foolish girl.

It happens as if in slow motion. I see the spark coming from his blaster, heading right for me. Cutting through the air like a fiery line at the same time that I release one of my own. I see the moment he dodges my blast, just tilting his head to the side as if it's nothing. My shot goes straight past him and hits the wall at the far back. Dying and dissolving into nothingness as I am about to be.

But I don't go down. Instead, there's a heavy thud at my back as something massive falls to the ground behind me. The sound tugs at the threads of reality and I suddenly realize that I'm still alive. Still breathing. Glancing over my shoulder, my eyes widen even further the moment I see the meathead on the ground there. His body spasms, death seizures wracking his frame as the threads of darkness close in on him. Blood gurgles in his throat from the hole that was just burned right through his neck and all at once, my dread and confusion turn into sudden understanding.

The stranger hadn't been aiming at me. He'd been aiming at *this bastard*. The meathead who had crept up behind me and I didn't even hear.

I step away from the large shuddering frame of the thug still shaking on the ground, disbelief and pure terror still rushing through my veins. The only thing keeping me connected being the warmth of the blaster's barrel.

He just...killed him.

Heck. I know this. He's killed all of them. I saw him do it. But this guy had been right behind me, and judging from the blaster that is lying on the ground near his fingers, he'd been about to place a blast straight through the back of my head.

My fingers tremble as I take another step back, the fact that I've come so very close to death repeats like a beating gong in my head.

The stranger's boots are almost soundless as he walks over, crouching to look down at the dying meathead before us. His blaster dangles loosely within his fingers as he uses the barrel to turn the meathead's head from one side to the other.

"I'd tell you to run and tell your master to fek off...but you'll bleed out before then," the stranger says, but I know he isn't talking to me. "You Ulturions don't know when to take a loss." He shakes his head slowly, feigning pity even though he was the one to sear that hole in the meathead's neck. "I was going to pretend I didn't see you hiding there...but you just had to come out and try to kill her."

There's a sick feeling in my stomach and another shudder goes through me as I take one more step backward.

The Ulturion uses his last energy to snarl, sharp teeth stained red with his own blood. "Fek...you...Zamari."

The stranger chuckles. It's the first time I've heard him laugh and it's now. In this situation...

I watch in a sort of cold terror as his eyes seem to flash in the darkness as he watches the light die in the meathead's eyes. Then he lets out a low breath from between his teeth.

Using his blaster, he pushes at the Ulturion's pockets before opening one and taking out a satchel that's no doubt filled with credits. He glances up at me next.

"Search the others. Take what you need...or what you want." He shrugs like he doesn't really care. "Make it quick."

I'm so stunned I can only stare at him in silence. But then I move. More like a puppet being ordered than of my own volition. My legs are stiff as I head back to the meathead's crony who'd almost fallen on top of me. My hands shake as I hold them over his body. Is this really right? Looting the dead. Even males like this...no, *especially* males like this. But the stranger's next words echo in the now quiet parking sector.

"You take it, or someone else will." *And it looks like you need it.* Those are unsaid words. Words I hear echoing in the silence, anyway.

I swallow hard, shifting my attention back to the dead thug before me. Quickly, I search his pockets. There's a navigation device that makes my wayfinder look like a historical artifact, a few credits, and some data discs. I take the first two before moving to another dead thug, almost as if I've done this before.

By the time we've searched them all, I have enough credits to bump up the amount I have stashed on me quite a bit. I turn to find the stranger staring at me. Or rather, watching me. Tracking me? The blaster's still in my hand and his gaze shifts to it.

"You going to put that away, or are you going to try to blast my head off again?"

I cringe a little, wanting to pretend I'm busy with something like getting ready to leave or actually leaving. But there's about seven feet between us and he's blocking the path to my rocket bike.

"In my defense, you aimed at me and pulled the trigger."

Even from where I stand, even with the shadow his hat casts over his features, I see his lips twist in a ghost of a smile.

"You should get going."

I nod, forcing a lump down my throat as I take one step,

then another, toward him. He shifts just out of the way, slightly. Only enough that I have to brush against him to climb on top of my hoverbike. That alone tells me he knew which one was mine. And with that realization comes back all the confusion and uncertainty concerning this stranger.

As I climb up on the bike, there is silence between us. Silence from him, but I feel his gaze on my back. When I get out of this place, I'm going to remember this night for a long, long time. This stranger. The bizarreness of this all.

Resisting the urge to look back, I sheathe my blaster and reach for my visor, clipping it onto the helmet before pausing. My shoulders are stiff as I stare down at the helmet in my hands.

"Why did you help me?" I finally whisper, certain he's still there. Certain he's still listening.

But there's no response. It's so silent, I have to look over my shoulder and I see him standing there, just watching me. But even with me looking at him, he still doesn't answer.

"Go home, female," he finally responds. "You don't belong here. Go back to where you're safe."

He turns and steps toward his rocket bike and there's a sudden, almost erratic panic-filled beating in my heart. Because the fact of the matter is that going home won't make me safe. I came here to hire a mercenary who can help me. Help my people. I can't go back empty-handed.

"I want to hire you!" The words slip from my mouth with ease, falling on the dead silence that fills the parking sector as soon as he stops walking.

His back is turned to me and I have no idea what he's thinking. He's just suddenly...frozen.

"I'll pay you whatever you charge if you can help me."

"You can't afford me, Firespark."

My throat feels dry and every convincing argument I had fails to come to my tongue.

"Go home."

His words sound final, so why am I climbing off my rocket bike? Why am I walking to stop about three feet behind where he stands? Why does it feel like I *have* to get him to agree to help me or everything will be for shit?

"Please," I say. Every possible convincing argument I devised to get a henchman on my team doesn't seem good enough. I can't pander to his emotions. Males like him have none. And still, I try. "I need your help. We all do."

His head tilts back slightly as he looks up into the dark roof. "We?"

"My people...our colony...we need protection..."

He lets out a wry laugh, already shaking his head, and desperation fills me.

Reaching for the satchel tucked safely against my leg, I pull it out and thrust it toward him. The credits jingle against each other and his head turns enough to the side that I see his profile.

Of course, I knew it would catch his attention. Emotions won't get to males like this. But credits will.

"Come with me. Help us. And I'll pay you double what's in this bag."

His gaze shifts down to the satchel and I follow the light of his eyes as they lift back to mine.

But he still doesn't look convinced. He's still not biting.

"Fine. Three times. I'll pay you triple this. I promise." There's a note of desperation in my voice that I know he can hear. But I can't go back empty-handed. I just can't.

A beat of silence passes between us before the stranger suddenly turns to me and takes the satchel from my hand, his fingers brushing against mine.

My tongue darts out and wets my lips as I watch him pocket the credits.

If he takes the bag and leaves now, I'll be royally screwed.

He probably reads the thought in my eyes because his lips twist slightly.

"Get on your bike," he says. "Lead the way, *Firespark.*"

CHAPTER EIGHT

The Outlaw

Only the gods know why I'm even entertaining this female. One last job...and this is the one I choose. This is the one that will mark the end of my fekking career.

I tell myself it's just another contract. Protection in exchange for credits. Nothing I haven't done countless times before.

But why her?

If I know anything since being without a base for so long, it's that beings like her that draw trouble to them like a magnet are beings to stay away from. My life's already been more chaotic than most. I don't need more trouble.

But there's a spark in her eyes, a light that didn't appear till the moment I semi-agreed to help her. I've seen that look before. It's hope. As familiar in her strange eyes as if looking into the eyes of a female from my own species. And I want to tell her that looking at a male like me with hopeful eyes is the last thing she should do.

Males like me are dangerous. We are attracted to pure little things and give nothing good in return.

My eyes narrow slightly as I watch that spark in her eyes grow. An almost pep in her step as she heads back to her rocket bike. I might rip degenerates' throats out without even a moment's hesitation. But the thought of ripping away her hope? I...cannot.

So I watch her hurry back to her ship. Watch how she takes a deep breath, chest swelling with anticipation and those blue eyes shining with that same hope as she climbs on top of the vessel.

I thought her blaster was outdated and not fit for use, but her ship is worse. Leaning on my rocket bike, I watch as she puts on her helmet, the visor sliding down to protect her eyes from Ivuria 10's sands. And then she opens the storage compartment and pulls out a woven sack. A bottle of what I assume is water is retrieved and she tilts her head back, exposing that thin graceful neck to the light of Ivuria's moon.

I should turn away, but I cannot. Her neck is slender, silhouetted against the moonlight, and for a split second, I forget where I am. My fangs ache again and I force myself to focus.

"—some?" Her eyebrows are raised as she looks my way and I can only blink at her. Not usual for my surroundings to fade in the background. Foolishness like this would have already gotten me killed.

"Do you want some?" she repeats.

I shake my head and she shrugs. Stashing the water into the sack and then returning it to the compartment, she pulls down her visor and starts the ignition of her bike. It takes several tries before the system comes online and even then, the poor thing sputters as if it is alive and has the sickness.

I must have been wrong. She couldn't have come from far. Not on that thing.

Jerking her head toward the exit, I understand that's her way of asking me if I'm ready. Over the sound of her sputtering engine, she probably thinks I won't hear her if she speaks.

I mimic her movement and hop onto my bike, the warmth of the satchel she'd given me in my palm. There aren't enough credits in here to pay any worthy hunter. With this amount, she'd attract only cutthroats hungry for a quick job or, if lucky, a novice who wouldn't get the job done. Weighing the satchel in my palm, I hesitate before tucking it into my trouse, gaze shifting back to the female as she guides her bike backward and lines up with the exit.

"Try to keep up!" she shouts over her shoulder before holding down on the accelerator.

I watch her disappear out the parking sector's gates, a cloud of soft dust glistening in the night air, and in the silence left behind, there's a moment's clarity. Am I really going to do this? As my wrist tightens on my bike and the systems come online, the beast beneath me revs with power I've become used to.

As it shoots through the gates, I take off in the female's wake.

Guess I'm doing this.

We zoom through the narrow streets of Calanta toward the western side of the city. The female leading the way and me close behind. The denizens of this place turn to nothing but blurred shapes with the speed. Soon the buildings thin and we're met with other travelers like ourselves, some heading in and others like us, heading out. On the road like this, we're mainly just beings trying to survive in this wasteland, the blinding lights of the hovercrafts differentiating little.

The higher we go, the tightly packed buildings of the

Calantan underground begin to thin, soon giving way to bustling market stalls the moment we reach the surface. The female shoots past those too, flooding her engine with enough juice that she would fly if the vessel had wings. I keep up, barely noticing the number of market stalls thinning, the way ahead only dotted with sparse structures on the outskirts of the city. The noise and chaos of Calanta fade behind us, replaced by dusty roads that are barely visible underneath loose brown sand.

We ride for several minutes. Now and then, the female looks over her shoulder, blue eyes finding me before she turns back to face the road and continues on. Now, only occasional hovels dot the barren plains, stretching toward the horizon. The arid desert wind of Ivuria 10 whistles around us, sending dust and sand flying in clouds that swirl, almost blocking visibility completely. My eyes adjust, the protective membrane sliding across them to keep the particles at bay while allowing me to keep my eyes wide open. I can see fine, but it's clear the female before me can't.

Her pace slows as her head dips against the wind, even with the visor on. But she keeps going, glancing behind her every few minutes to check if I'm still there before pressing on. Soon, the last signs of so-called civilization disappear behind us entirely.

I ease forward, upping my speed till my bike keeps steady pace beside hers in this vast endlessness. I notice how she's gunning her throttle, then easing off before the bike chokes—a delicate balance that's almost undetectable. A dance between her and the machine, each push and pull of acceleration flowing seamlessly to keep her engine surging at the highest edge without cut-out. Otherwise, the thing would have given up already. Her subtle manipulation is probably the only reason it hasn't died yet. When she turns her head and our gazes meet, I expect her to look away, but she doesn't. She meets my gaze, everything passing behind us in a blur, the only constant being the steadiness of our locked eyes.

I wonder what she's thinking.

She's taking me, a stranger, back to her settlement. And, from the looks of it, she is no fool. What sort of trouble could her people be in that they've resorted to hiring a stranger to solve their problem? Nothing I'd usually concern myself with, that's for sure.

As I watch her, the questions burning in my head, she finally pulls her gaze from mine and turns her attention forward. But even then, I can tell she knows my attention hasn't waned. I can't pull my eyes away from the spectacle that is her. This strange female who walked into a drinkery full of scum with only a single blaster and a stash of credits strapped to her thighs.

I wonder if there are others like her...but I know that can't be true. Because if her people are anything like her, she wouldn't have needed to crawl to Calanta for help. Something isn't right about all this and I don't need my *ayahl* to point that out. I'll find out soon enough.

Leagues pass, the road stretching beneath our hovercraft as we zoom into the unknown, and she decides she won't look at me. Something about the way she sets her lips. How she stares straight ahead, her gaze not shifting as if she's forcefully pointing it there. When her eyes start to stray, shifting in my direction, her gaze hardens, her chin pointing forward from underneath her visor.

Endearing.

She can look at me if she likes. It's pitch black out here in the plains. Only the light of the rocket bikes piercing this darkness. That and the luminescence of my eyes. I've purposefully not cloaked myself from the moment she met me till now. If not for her, my eyes would have already dimmed, the slight shimmer in my scales quieted, and my ship would be in stealth mode. No lights, and certainly no sound.

Well, that's not entirely accurate. Her lights don't stay on for long, cutting in and out at random intervals. But she hasn't completely killed them. And her bike, it's noisy.

To ride out here without those basic adjustments tells me two things. She's new to Ivuria 10. And she can't see in the dark. Out here, her lights are like a beacon calling all sorts of scum. Surprising she made it all the way to Calanta in one piece.

We ride for a few oras. Enough that I know for sure now that wherever she came from, it wasn't close to Calanta. For we're heading out to the plains. There's nothing out there. Again, my *ayahl* stretches toward her. *Seeking*. But there is no in response. The female's *source* is completely quiet. Just like most other non-Zamari species. But with her, I don't know whether that's impressive or fekking terrifying.

When her bike makes a strange keening sound and she suddenly falls back in speed, I wonder if this is the end of our trip. But she urges the machine on. Talking to it. *Begging* it. As if she believes it is sentient. She squints ahead, trying to make out the way as her lights flicker on and off in quick succession before dying completely. The machine will be next.

The shadow of a small cropping of large, hollow rocks appears about two leagues ahead, and she slows down further. They're large enough to hide a band of maybe five beings, but a quick extension of my *ayahl* and I know the spot's empty. We slow to a crawl, reaching the rocks just as her engine hiccups and makes a gurgling sound that has no place coming from a machine. Maybe I'm wrong and the thing is actually alive and has the sickness.

I hop off my bike as hers comes to a halt and she lifts the visor from her face. With some struggle, she climbs off the bike and guides it over to the side of one of the rocks.

"We rest here for the night." She's breathless as she braces her hands against her hips and looks at me. "I only left Calanta in a hurry because..." Her lips tighten and she releases a heavy breath. "Well, you know why."

I eye the rocks.

It's an obvious spot to hide in. One where scum like that fool back in Calanta would check for unsuspecting travelers. We can't stay here for long, and even though the female turns away from me as she focuses on her ship, the tension in her shoulders tells me she knows this.

Leaning against my bike, I watch her run her hands over her arms before she releases another breath. Shoulders still stiff, she eyes the darkness before opening the storage compartment on her bike. The thing she retrieves is a multi-tool and a small light. Placing the light between her teeth, she crouches at the bike's control panel and unscrews it. My eyes narrow slightly as I watch her from under the brim of my hat.

She messes with the wires, adjusting a few, taking some out only to reinstall them in different spots. She's diverting power from the lights back to the engine.

She plans to wait out the darkness here.

Shifting my gaze to the horizon, I can tell that we have three, maybe four oras till dawn.

Four hours of standing still like a target in just one spot. I don't like it.

"Well?" she suddenly asks.

When I don't answer, she looks at me over her shoulder.

"Aren't you going to ask me what type of job it is or what I want you to do?"

Her question falls right through my consciousness, as all I can hear is the sound of her voice.

Does she know she's the first female in what feels like eons to have caught my attention in any sort of way? Even now, as she speaks, the light of the moon catches the fine hairs standing on that exposed bit of skin at her shoulder. Her cheeks are flushed a warm red from the cold, and that rouge extends to her ears, her lifeblood on tantalizing display.

"Or doesn't it matter to you?" Her gaze scrutinizes me, shifting from one eye to the other as she tries to keep me in focus.

I force my attention away from the distracting flush of her skin. "I don't care about the details of the job."

She frowns, squinting at me before turning back to the console and messing with a few more wires. Finally satisfied, she closes the console and sets the multi-tool and light away.

Her gaze shifts to me once more, mouth opening and closing as if she wants to say more but isn't sure just how to voice it.

"My town..." she finally says. "Our colony..."

Pushing off from where I lean, she stops talking, stiffening as I circle behind her, drawn like gravity. Her entire frame goes rigid, but she doesn't shrink away, and I'm reminded of how close she'd been, sitting on my leg in that bar. Of the heat of her core on my thigh. A glorious warmth I never expected.

Up close, that scent of xyleen oil teases my senses even through the sterile night air. Those delicate veins pulse in her neck and I lean a little closer. Once again, the thought of how she might taste floats into my brain and my *ayahl* rises at the prospect, my cock hardening in tune.

With effort, I stop just shy of contact.

What could possibly tempt a sweet female like her to brave these wilds on her own? Travel with a male like me all alone? What she's doing is highly dangerous. Only desperation could have tempted her to this.

"Keep it on a need-to-know basis, Firespark. Your little colony matters not to me. The less I know, the better."

She tilts her head to look up at me, eyes hardening. "You just kill for sport then?"

I bare my teeth in a slight smile and I see the moment her gaze lands on my fangs. "No."

Her eyes widen as she stares at them and I can read her thoughts like recorded script. The danger she sees. The fear. And then an almost complete erasure of those thoughts as her lips thin.

Her throat bobs in a swallow and I have the sudden urge to dip my lips there. Taste her skin. Puncture her neck with my fangs. Drink her blood. See if she'll still be as brave with my fangs deep inside her.

And then, the thought of piercing her brings other images. Images of maybe piercing her somewhere else, too. A soft growl, almost like a purr rumbles in my chest and I let it thrum. I've never been one to resist my basest of desires.

"Then why?" she whispers, and a shudder goes through her that has nothing to do with the cold. She shudders because it seems, for the first time, she realizes something that didn't cross her mind before.

She is alone. Out here in the wilderness, there is no one but me.

And while I might be one to hunt these lands...she is nothing but prey.

"Why do you do it?" she repeats, intent on keeping the conversation going. As if it will save her somehow.

I shrug, eyes narrowing slightly even as my *ayahl* reaches

for her again. Like an invisible cloud, it extends from me and wraps around her, searching for a response. A mate. Little dots appear on her skin at the contact, even though she cannot see or truly feel the essence of my being. But it's a response. The same response I saw that time in the drinkery.

She might not be able to sense it, but on some level, she *feels* it. Feels me calling to her.

"I hunt because it's in my blood to give chase," I lean closer. "I am Zamari, little human. We corner frightened things. And tear them apart."

A visible shiver goes through her slight frame at my words. But still, she does not cower. This female is either very brave, or very stupid. Judging from the events of this night, I still can't decide and I find myself intrigued to discover just which it is.

Silence descends between us again, but her wide eyes tell me everything. My words have shaken her. That delicate skin at her neck moves once more before she takes a step away from me. Tightening the large cloak over her frame, she averts her gaze.

"Alright. I'm going to rest there." She gestures to the open hole of the largest rock. "If there's trouble—"

"There won't be trouble." She doesn't have to worry about that. Not as long as I'm here.

This will probably be the safest night she'll have in these plains.

She nods, her chin jerking to her chest twice before she tugs the fabric thing around herself and goes to sit within the rock. She pulls her legs up underneath the cloak, shielding herself from the cold as much as she can, and as soon as she settles, silence descends completely. The night air is as still as the unmoving grains of sand beneath our feet.

Silence. Until I hear a soft murmur.

"What kind of hunter doesn't care what he's hunting?"

Her whisper is quiet but I hear it anyway. It comes straight to me through the stillness. Those piercing blue eyes are focused right at me and for the first time I grin.

What kind of hunter doesn't care what he's hunting?

Only the kind that's solely concerned with the thrill of the chase.

CHAPTER NINE

Elsie

He's out there, in the darkness somewhere.

I try to remain awake, for even though we've traveled out here together with no incidents, and even though he's saved my life twice, I still don't fully trust this male. And perhaps that's because he isn't actively seeking my trust at all. He doesn't care what I think. For the first time in my life, I encounter someone who is indifferent to whether I see him as a scoundrel or my savior. Someone who isn't trying to bullshit the fact that in this existence—at least, here on Ivuria 10—it's every being for himself.

Including me. I can't forget that.

Offering him three times the amount in that satchel, desperation had hooked me and made me a slave to its whims. Every being for themselves? I could see the future if I didn't get his or someone else's help. I'm doing this for my own survival.

I don't know what it says about me, hiring a mercenary for

protection. Hiring him to *kill*. Because I have to face it. Scaring the Nirzoik alone won't work. Blood will have to be spilled.

I never thought I'd ever be led to such a thing. And yet, here I am.

My hand lifts to my throat, my fingers brushing against my skin as if to release some of the unease churning within me.

Even with Estella's addition and the coin I looted from those corpses, the sum I gave this stranger amounts to little. Months of saving and it still wasn't enough. But did I have a choice?

I'm pretty sure my offering to triple the credits is the only reason he's here with me now. I did what I had to do. Even if when we arrive in Comodre I'll have to sell everything in my cabin just to pay him back, borrow funds from the other settlers, and work three times as hard in the mines, I'll do it. If he can help me, help *us*, it will all be worth it.

But I can't think about all that. I just have to get him to Comodre first.

My hand falls from my neck as I rub my fingers together to put some warmth into them, the cool night air getting colder by the minute. It's frigid out here with the dark sun hiding on the other side of the planet. Cold enough that my toes have gone numb. Shivering, I search the quiet darkness outside the hole in which I've settled, my eyes hardly picking up a single detail in the vast wall of black.

That's when I realize, if the outlaw is out there, I can't see him anywhere.

There's no light out here in this cold wasteland. Not even the light of the moon pierces the thick blanket of darkness. And he must have moved from where he was leaning on his bike.

Has he slunk off? Or maybe he's just resting in one of the other holes on the other side of the rock. I mean, we're traveling together but that's about it, right? No need for us to be in each other's space.

I shift, trying to force my body to rise to go search for him, just to be sure. But movement causes the little warmth I've cultivated within the poncho to ebb, and I decide to settle back down. He hasn't left. I'd have heard his hoverbike if that was the case and somehow he doesn't strike me as the dishonest type.

A stone-cold killer? Yes. But a petty thief? No.

I stare at the darkness for a few more moments. He's out there somewhere. Yet, there's an almost chilling stillness...as if I'm completely and utterly alone.

That thought heightens every single one of my senses.

I can hear my own breathing. Every slight shift of my skin against the clothes I wear. The beat of my pulse in my ears. The smooth breaths releasing through my nose.

There's a strange sort of terror that awakes out here in a place like this. A strange reckoning within the depths of isolation. Terror...and then peace.

When we first arrived here, it'd been like this. Behind the sound of the fire, the ringing in my ears, the pain in my limbs, the blood, the sounds of screaming, the smell of death, the terror...behind it all, there'd been silence.

Stillness.

Me standing on the hot brown sand, looking across a vast plain just like this, while behind me...

I stop the thoughts because I know where they're heading. I don't want to think about the mothership or what happened to it. I don't want to think about the past at all. And so, I force myself to take a deep breath, pulling the cold air into my lungs and focusing on the crispness of it as it fills my head. Exhaling, I steady my lungs and do it all over again.

I don't know how long I practice simply breathing. How

long I sit there in the cold, forcing my body to relax and pushing back against the thoughts of that time—of our arrival to this world. I just know that soon my eyelids begin to droop, the increased oxygen in my system making me a bit dizzy, and a yawn threatens to force its way past my lips.

Three days' travel from Comodre and I'd been too paranoid to sleep. Too afraid to shut my eyes for even a second lest some less-than-honest traveler come upon me. Now that I've taken a moment to just sit down, the tiredness is catching up to me. But I still can't rest.

For the next few minutes, I keep my ears and my eyes open, scanning the darkness before me and keeping watch. But the harder I try to keep my eyes open, the more I catch my eyelids drooping. I readjust myself, my body aching against the biting cold and the hard rock. But I fight the sensation.

I have to stay awake. Alert.

I *cannot* fall asleep.

I don't know when I doze off. Only that something shifts in the air and when my eyes fly open, luminescent green orbs, shining so bright they look white, are right above me. I startle just as the stranger presses a finger down on my lips.

"Firespark...don't make a sound."

I freeze, breath lodged in my throat, instant panic making my eyes go wide as I stare up at the stranger.

I fell asleep. *Fuck.*

A swell of self-disappointment wells within me. It's followed right behind by unease. What's he doing so close?

I try to shift, to put some distance between us, but that's futile. He's pressing into me hard enough that I can't move.

More panic ensues. Swinging my arm upward to push him back so I can move, he moves quicker than I can. My arm stops midair, his fist tightening around my wrist as he catches my hand without even looking.

His finger presses harder against my lips, silencing me as that strange gaze of his bores into mine. "Careful, Firespark," his voice is a low murmur that's only meant for me to hear. "Slamming your pretty little fist in my jaw will hurt you more than it will hurt me."

Cocky fucking bastard. I wasn't aiming for his jaw. Maybe I should have been.

I stiffen, heart beating hard as uncertainty mixes in with the panic I've tried hard to ignore. I'm alone in the wilds with a mercenary. This had always been a risk and I've run through similar scenarios in my head a thousand times.

I wait for him to make his next move. Wait for him to do something so I can respond. I can't see for shit, but if he tries anything, the tip of my blaster should be pointing directly at his cock. Mercenaries like him like precious things. Pretty sure those jewels won't be worth much once shattered.

But he doesn't say anything. Doesn't try to advance on me. Doesn't release my wrist. Doesn't lift his finger from my lips either.

He's staring at me, but then his head tilts slightly and I realize...he's listening to something. Behind the rapid beats of my pulse in my ears, I find enough clarity for my ears to perk. It takes a few moments before I hear what he must be listening to. It's a low sound. Far away. But it sends vibrations through the air that increase each second that I'm focused on it.

I stiffen again, heart rate increasing.

I know that sound. I know it, simply because it can't be anything else. It's the steady growing hum of an engine.

Something big. Far bigger than any rocket bike or regular hovercraft.

An airship.

Sometimes we see airships far away on the horizon off Comodre. The darn things are notoriously expensive to run, the fuel that powers them rare and usually bought off-world. Only two species I know use airships on this part of Ivuria 10. A hooved, horned species called the Beh'ni'nites and the scourge that won't leave my people alone, the Nirzoik.

Both unfriendly.

Both scum.

My heart thuds against my ribs as the sound grows consistently louder. It's coming closer. I stare up at the stranger, unmoving. He wasn't intent on taking advantage of me. He was here to warn me of the ship's approach.

"Sand scrapers," he rumbles low.

I swallow underneath his finger. Scrapers?

"Large, low-floating ships run by the Beh'ni'nites." Even though he's explaining all this, there is little to no reaction in his eyes. As if he's merely stating facts from the back of his mind and not talking about one of the most fearful species that roams this planet. It's so strange, it holds my attention, pushing away the panic, the anger, and the new fear that the Nirzoik might have found us.

He's not afraid of them. Not even slightly.

"Beh'ni'nites scrape the desert floor, searching for scraps." His head tilts a little more and I know he's listening to the sound out there. "Their nets have caught more than one careless wanderer."

Like me. I fell asleep, and he crept right up to me without me hearing. The thought makes me suddenly aware of how easy it would have been for him to slit my throat if he'd wanted to.

Swallowing hard, I lick my lips, eyes widening a little more when my tongue brushes against his finger. There's a distinct coarseness to his skin that makes me blink before I realize what I've just done.

I freeze and I feel the moment he does, too. I thought he was still before? Unmoving? Alert as he listened to the airship approaching? I was wrong. He goes *rigid*, as if he's no longer breathing.

What. The fuck. Did I just do?

The air crackles between us and I wonder if it's just an effect of the airship getting closer and not an extension of my pounding heart. I don't dare to move as his gaze slips down to my lips, his attention only making me more aware of them, and my mouth goes dry for reasons I shouldn't think of. The instinct to lick my lips again is so utterly at odds with my predicament and, at the same time, almost overwhelming. Somehow, I keep still, watching as he *drags* his gaze back to mine.

My eyes are wide discs as he stares at me, and even with the approaching rumbling, I can't say a word. I can't read his expression. Can't even see his face. Can't tell if he's disgusted or annoyed. Angry or surprised. Because those eyes, though lit, tell me nothing.

It hits me then that there is a big difference between us two. This stranger...he can see my face, the entirety of it. This close, his gaze moves over my skin like a machine taking note of every detail.

Unlike me, he was made to traverse the night. This dark, soulless desert is his domain. Meanwhile, I'm hardly surviving in it. As soon as we get to Comodre, I have to sit him down with Estella. Have a meeting. Maybe just two more days on the bikes...

"The bikes!" The thought comes to me and it slips right past my lips, brushing them underneath his finger again. His gaze follows the motion, eyes lingering on my mouth once more.

This time, there's an answering rumble in his chest, one that comes before he even speaks. One that I feel against the pit of my belly. Something clenches between my legs, an almost involuntary response, and I force myself not to focus on it. Or on myself. Because I must be going insane to have any sort of reaction at all.

"The bikes?" He finally asks. "Safe."

I nod, chest burning with the fact that I've held my breath without meaning to. My gaze shifts to where his finger is and another rumble moves in his chest. It vibrates all across my center, running up my midsection till the vibrations end at my neck. It's only then that awareness dawns on me at the fact that this huge male is straddling me, his thighs on either side of my body as he leans over me. I can feel the hard muscles in his legs, pressing into me in a way that shouldn't be any sort of comforting at all.

"If the bikes are safe," my voice comes out as a hoarse whisper that I hope doesn't betray the direction of my thoughts, "why'd you come in here?"

There's a glint in his eyes.

For a moment, he says nothing. And then... "There are scanners on the bottom of that ship that pick up even the slightest movement." His head tilts a little as his gaze slides down the side of my face, following my jawline straight to my chin. Then moving to my lips. My nose. Like he's following a slow invisible path. "If they see us, they will descend, and I'm not in the mood to kill a Beh'ni'nite." He pauses, that glint returning as his gaze snaps to mine. "Unless you want me to."

I shake my head a little too quickly and this close to him, I feel the rumble of a silent laugh in his chest. He releases my wrist to press his palm into the ground at my side as he braces himself up.

Outside, the engine sound draws closer and with it, the sound of something jangling on the ground all around us. The rock we're within vibrates so hard, bits of stone and dust fall down around us and the thought that the whole thing might collapse flashes through my mind. It's enough to make me focus above me as my palms flatten on the rough ground. More dust falls as the sound gets louder. Like huge pieces of metal being slammed and scraped together. It sets my teeth on edge, my eardrums aching. The ground shakes, the sound getting louder and louder till I can feel it vibrating in my skull.

Above me, the stranger slowly removes his finger from my lips. I can feel his attention, those eyes watching me with a sort of interest I cannot place. But as the flashing lights of the scraper ship break the darkness around us and the sound outside grows louder, I can't focus on him. Instead, something else grabs my attention. Steals it away. The sound all around is loud enough that it pulls me back to that one place I don't want to return to. A place that remains only in my nightmares.

I grit my teeth, knowing exactly what's happening and praying at the same time for it not to.

Fuck. Shit. Not now. *Not now!*

I tremble, fingers raking against the hard rock beneath me as I try to regain some control. Gritting my teeth, I fight against my own mind. *Gods help me.* I thought I was over this. I haven't had a panic attack in public in a long time. I've learned to hide away from my fears. So why now? Why here?

But I know why it's happening again. Now, of all times. There's a pounding in my head. A war between my will and that part of my mind that's shattering.

That drinkery. Those thugs. And because of what happened afterward too. I almost died. *Twice.* In just a short time, I've had to face my mortality. Again. And it seems, on this world, Ivuria 10, having to constantly face one's mortality has one great side effect. For me, it's the nightmares. Vivid terrors rehashing those moments that led to my people's arrival on this planet.

Only, I'm not asleep now. This hasn't happened before when I'm wide awake!

As the jarring sound increases, the ground beneath me shaking, the flashing lights of the approaching ship merge into a memory of other flashing lights. Images come to the fore of my mind, cutting off my view of the present. I fight against them, knowing none of them are real. But I fail.

I'm suddenly weightless. The desert of Ivuria 10, the stranger, the scraper ship, all gone. The familiar walls of the mothership on which I spent my first two decades of life are all around me.

The warning lights in our ship flash in repetitive sequence, the alarms blaring as the whole vessel shakes. I scream as the weightlessness suddenly ceases and I slam into the floor, only for the gravity control to go off again and my body to float, weightless once more. All around me, items hang in the air that shouldn't be there. Heavy items. Light items. Large ones. Small. The magnetic locking clips that held them tethered have failed. The ship's entire system is down.

In front of me, a trail of blood floats in small globules and, like in slow motion, I lift my hand to my bloody nose.

That's when the lights start flashing with blinding urgency as chaos erupts. The ship shudders, metal groaning as if being twisted by some great force. Muffled shouts and alarms echo from all directions.

Another bone-jarring impact slams me to the ceiling before the failing grav-system sends me spinning weightlessly again. I catch flashes of the corridor—debris flying, wires sparking, oxygen masks dangling useless from the walls. The stench of burning plasmold chokes the air.

Over the pandemonium I hear it—the distinct boom and hiss unique to only one thing. An explosion.

We've been breached.

I hear a voice that doesn't match up with my memory. A voice that tries to pull me from the terror of my own pain.

"Firespark?"

The stranger. He's saying something to me, but even as I try to grasp onto his voice, try to hold on to it like a lead that can guide me back to the present, the sound all around us sends me further under.

I drown in the pain as our ship drops out of orbit, falling into Ivuria 10's atmosphere with no controls to stop us. Squeezing my eyes shut, my fingers feel wet as I lift them from the rocky floor and press my hands against my ears, trying desperately to stop the sound and along with it the memories I don't want to face. Not here. Not now.

I can't break down in front of a complete stranger. Can't show how vulnerable I am.

Even blocking my ears, I can still hear that the rumbling outside picks up. Large clouds of dust and sand fly into the small hole, reducing visibility, choking my air, and I curl into myself. Or, at least, I *try* to; but I can't. Not with the stranger's body braced over mine. His entire frame forces me to acknowledge his presence. Prevents me from curling up and hiding away from all this.

And then suddenly, it all slows down. The sound of the scraper ship diminishes. The memories it has resurrected fade slowly. And the warmth of two large hands pressing down hard over mine pulls me back.

Squinting through the dust and sand swirling in the air, my eyes flutter open to realize the stranger's hands are on mine.

Pressing down on my ears. Blocking the sound. I stare up at him, not understanding why he's helping me. Not quite believing he's actually doing it and this isn't some trick of my mind. But then in the flashing lights, I catch a glimpse of his face. Those shining eyes look down at me with a knowledge that has me transfixed.

He knows what's happening to me.

His face is inches from mine, so close, I can only see him. I have no choice but to meet his gaze. To focus on him and him only. To meet that deep, knowing gaze as his eyes bore into mine. He doesn't speak—just keeps my attention locked there, blocking out the outside world with his hands pressed hard over mine.

This strange, nameless male keeps me focused on him. Compassion I could have never expected from a being so lawless. One so lethal he shouldn't even have a heart.

It gets louder out there, the sound picking up so much that it cuts through the barrier of both our hands. I tuck my chin down, a whimper escaping before I can stop myself.

There's an answering rumble.

He leans closer, pressing in against my legs. Pressing into *me*. My forehead hits his chest as he leans in, taking the brunt of the flying particles and allowing me a moment to breathe. Tucked against him, some of that fear encroaching through my memories dissipates. I get a moment to think, to ward away the thoughts that threaten to swallow me whole. I get a moment to be present even as the sound outside grows louder.

It takes a while for the ship and the net it pulls to pass, and through it all, I'm held close as if we're more than mere strangers brought together through an offering of credits and the chance of bloodshed.

I stiffen the moment the sound of the ship begins to die, waiting for him to pull away and yet, hoping, just a little bit, that he won't. Because if he does, he'll see the terror still lingering like a specter behind my eyes. He'll see that I'm weaker than I pretend to be. He'll know I'm vulnerable. And out here, the vulnerable are used. Abused. Killed. Discarded.

A minute passes after the sound of the ship dies down completely, and another before the stranger finally releases me. I can't look at him. Don't have it in me to lift my gaze.

Our mothership crashed to Ivuria 10 a whole decade ago. I should have gotten over it by now. The nightmares. The trauma.

I keep my gaze averted as the stranger releases me fully, and for the first time, I'm truly thankful that he doesn't speak much. I don't have to explain what the hell just happened and I'm glad he doesn't ask either. Because I'm not sure I could explain even if he did. Not even Estella knows about the nightmares. I've never let anyone else see me break down like this.

I am, frankly, ashamed.

The stranger shifts and rises, stepping out of the little cave and disappearing into the darkness. For a moment, I just lie there staring into the night.

The entire floor of the little rock cave is now filled with a thick, fresh layer of sand. It's in my hair, embedded in my clothes. There are still particles even on my tongue. And yet, I can't move. Time passes as I just stay there in the dark, letting it swallow me for a bit. Letting the darkness within me leech out into it.

When I don't hear anything outside and the stranger doesn't return, I rise on shaky legs, pulling my poncho tight as I step out of the little shelter.

I don't see him—I can't see anything, but as I move I almost stumble over uneven ground. I pause, using the tip of my boot to feel the ground before me. There are furrows—deep lines dug into the sand about two inches apart. They weren't there before and I can only assume they're because of that ship. I step out farther, using my feet to count a few and I stop when I get to ten, not wanting to stray too far from the rocks. Even then, I can tell there are more.

If my bike had been where I left it, it would have been trawled and pulled up into that ship. Just that thought, and I turn my head to where it was parked. Slowly, I feel my way over there and, sure enough, the bike's gone.

He said he'd move it, but where? And where the hell is he?

"Zamari?" I whisper, using my hand to feel my way around the rock. It's so cold out here that I shiver even in the poncho.

"Zamari?" I call again and almost jump out of my skin when a heavy hand closes on my shoulder.

I spin to face...darkness, and a scream bubbles in my throat just before two eyes suddenly light up right before me.

His eyes.

Words stop in my throat as the skin on his neck and arms shimmers for just a moment before it goes all dark again.

"The bikes?" I clear my throat. It's hard to face him after I practically sucked on his finger and then proceeded to lose my mind right in front of him.

"Over here." His voice is level, unaffected, and I scold myself again. Who am I to him? He probably doesn't even care.

He must realize I can't see for shit because he reaches down and takes my elbow, his touch far gentler than it should be as he leads me slowly to one side of the large rocks. There, in a smaller cave, the bikes sit alongside each other.

He moves over to his and fidgets with something in the storage compartment and I watch him with words on my tongue that I don't know how to say. I end up going for the obvious.

"Thank you."

Whatever he's doing, he stops. His gaze finds me and I think he's going to say something that will throw me for a loop like he usually does. Instead, he says nothing. He finishes getting whatever he was fidgeting with and returns to take my arm.

"It's okay, I can find my way back."

"This is quicker."

I open my mouth to argue but he's right, so I press my lips together and let him lead me back to the little cave in which I was resting. I step inside and I expect him to do what he did before—disappear again. Only this time, he follows me in.

Light suddenly pierces the darkness and I squint at the small lit-up hexagonal disk that he sets on the ground. The glow is just enough to light the small space between us and my breath hitches when I see his face. No shadows. No darkness to hide behind. I'm rendered mute as the light reveals his features in full for the first time.

The scales that seem to cover his body fade just halfway up his neck, disappearing into a smooth bronze that seems blended with colorful stardust. He is bronze, and yet I see shades of purple and pink blended into his skin depending on how the light hits him. And then there are the high cheekbones, the strong jawline, and the full lips that all come together in the light as if he were created by some great artist.

My eyes move over the elegant points of his ears, the strong block of his neck... He is utterly beautiful in an otherworldly way.

Muscles ripple subtly beneath his clothes as he moves and I'm suddenly hyper-aware of his physical presence in the small space. Suddenly aware of just the fact that he'd been pressing into me with that same body not long before. Heat blooms across my cheeks and I lower my gaze. Strange. I thought I was a lot of things. Easily affected by some male's mere physical appearance wasn't one of them.

I risk another furtive glance, my breath catching as those green eyes meet mine. Amusement flickers in their depths, as if he senses my discomfort.

"What is it, Firespark?"

Firespark? Why does he call me that?

That deep voice of his caresses my senses in ways it shouldn't. "Do you find me so hideous in the light?"

"No," I answer far too quickly and I want to bite my tongue for betraying my awkwardness. "You're not hideous at all." *You're a drop-dead gorgeous male specimen that makes even the males of my species quail in comparison.* But of course, I can't say that. I shouldn't even be thinking it.

The barest hint of a smile tugs at his lips and I know in an instant that he's toying with me. He moves closer and I freeze, pulse racing.

"Sit."

I grab the hem of the poncho and stare up at him. It's only the second time he's ordering me to sit and I realize it's becoming a habit. At least, he's not demanding I sit on *him* this time, and only for that reason do I comply. Lowering myself to the floor, I sit on the ground, the fresh layer of sand providing some cushioning against the cold, rocky surface.

"Shouldn't you turn off that light?" I ask, gaze shifting to the hexagon between us. "Won't it draw attention?"

Surely with that Scraper ship not far gone, they might spot the light in the distance. Though, I don't know how far the light spreads, or if they'd truly be able to see it so far up. The last thing I want is for them to turn around and head back this way to investigate. And I certainly don't want my own brain to betray me again and have me whimpering in the arms of this stranger.

He shifts, pulling me from my thoughts as he kneels so we are on eye level, and a lump rises in my throat at the same time. I avert my gaze, for if I look him in the eyes it's like he can read every thought that passes through my head. And the thoughts that are forming there...

Fuck. I never considered this before leaving Comodre. It hadn't been something to consider. But how long has it been? How long has it been since I...pleasured myself?

Too fucking long for me to be reacting like this.

"Attention is easily handled," he says, those four words reminding me I'd asked him a question. With that simple sentence, he brushes away my fears. Attention is easily handled?

In other words. Whoever comes he can easily take care of them. Confident words that shouldn't increase my comfort. He's talking about possibly killing any interloper. But that's exactly what I'm paying him to do.

Arm flexing, he sets down the thing he'd been carrying in his hand all along. Something I'm only just noticing because I've been so transfixed by his existence. A little trunk. Just bigger than his hand. Metal. I find myself staring at it, waiting for him to open it so I can see just what he's hiding in there.

"It will be better for you if you can see what I'm about to do."

I frown slightly, a question in my eyes. What *is* he about to do?

When he opens the trunk, it reveals several different small bottles with labels I can't read. And gauze. Lots of gauze.

My eyebrows shoot up as he rests his elbow on one knee, his arm stretching toward me, palm upward, and waits. I can only stare at him, confused.

"Your hands," he says. His head's lowered enough that his gaze pierces me from just under the brim of his hat, making my heart beat at a tune it shouldn't. Making it feel like that one look is stripping me bare. As if I should grab my poncho just to make sure it's still there. Wrap it around myself to hide every vulnerable bit of myself.

"M-my hand?" I stutter, lifting my hand from where I'm still gripping my poncho. Only then do I see the red stain. Only then do I see the fact that every single one of my fingertips is scraped off and bloody.

I blink at the blood, not immediately reconciling what I'm seeing with actual reality. I'm...bleeding?

My gaze shifts back to the stranger in time to see his nostrils flare. His jaws clench and there's a rumble in his chest that cuts off the moment I look at him. For what feels like a very long time, we're both frozen. With what appears to be great effort, he pulls his gaze from my fingertips and I swallow hard when I see something that should make me scream and run. Something that should make instincts kick in. The need to preserve myself coming before all others. And yet, I remain frozen. Hardly breathing as I look at this being before me who looks more like a dangerous creature than anything else.

His beautiful green gaze has gone completely dark. Black. All-consuming. Like the void that surrounds us.

I wait for him to do something. To snarl at me. To pounce. To attack me like I know the bloodlust in his eyes is telling him to.

But...he doesn't.

Rigid he remains.

Between us, there are no words, and yet it feels like a thousand things are being said. For what dangerous creature kneels before the thing it's about to rend? What dangerous creature doesn't move an inch as if waiting for my permission to even react?

I force another lump down my throat as I look into those

strangely dark eyes. I expect to feel the frigidity of that stare. To feel raw, uncontrollable fear. All that happens is wonder.

"You hurt yourself," he finally says. His voice has dropped an octave, almost guttural now, as if he's finding it difficult to speak, and my gaze shifts back to the blood on my fingers. "Damaged them on the rock when the Beh'ni'nites passed by."

I blink at my fingers. I'm not sure what to say. I...I didn't feel the pain. Still don't feel it. My brain wants to focus on other things. Like the way I can see the imprint of his fangs behind his lips as he clenches his jaws tight.

My breath feels like a hard block in my chest that I can't push through my airways.

He has scales. Fangs. Pointed ears. No tail. Claws, though they aren't extended right now. He can see in the dark. Hear quite well too. And his eyes bleed to black.

He's nothing like the Nirzoik, Beh'ni'nites, or any of the other species on the pyramid of this planet. I was right. Whatever he is, he's not from here.

Whatever he is, he's dangerous.

And maybe that's the key to this mission actually being successful.

"Here." He reaches for my hand, taking it in his in the same gentle way in which he'd held my arm just before. Too gentle. As if he's afraid to even touch me. It's all so strange, that at the contact of his skin on mine, goosebumps run in a lightning trail from my fingertips to the tips of my ears. I force myself not to move as he takes one of the little bottles and pops the lid, wetting gauze and wiping the first fingertip.

Again, his nostrils flare and he exhales so forcefully I can hear it. He can smell my blood? Or is it the antiseptic? I don't get to ponder what's causing the different reactions because just a moment later, the pain from the antiseptic shoots through my finger.

It stings and a hiss escapes through my teeth. My hand jerks in his, the reflex to pull my hand away too strong. But he holds me tighter, and a blast of gentle cold air blows over the wound, cooling away the heat of the pain. Those dark eyes shift to mine and again, I'm speechless. I try to not react as he lifts my hand closer to his lips and does it again. A cool blast of air from his lips as our gazes lock. With his breath, he chases away the pain.

"Better?"

That lump in my throat grows ten times larger and all I can manage is a silent nod.

One by one, he tends to the other fingers, blowing on each one while he pins me with that stare, and soon, every single finger's been cleaned and bandaged with thin gauze.

As soon as he's finished, he releases me and rises. He moves so quickly, I don't even get to speak. Reaching for the little trunk, he closes it with haste, and a moment later, the light goes off as he deactivates the hexagonal disc. I open my mouth to thank him for what he's done. But I don't get to. One moment he's packing up. The next, he's gone. Darkness descends and I'm alone again.

Releasing a shaky breath, I once again stare out into the dark unknown before me, the heat in my cheeks probably enough to warm the entire desert as I listen to his footsteps retreat.

What the hell just happened?

I can't understand it, but there's one thing I do comprehend. The flutter in my chest. The unsteady beat of my heart. Things I might not be able to continue ignoring.

I release another shaky breath as I lean against the rough rock, mind reeling.

He's gone for a while, and I sit in silence till my eyes start to grow heavy again. By the time I hear him return, I'm still staring at the night sky with barely open eyes. Only a slight movement and the barest of visibility make me see his form as he moves to lean against one of the rocks nearby.

He remains there in the dark. Not disrupting the silence between us. Not saying a word.

"Zamari?" I whisper.

I don't think he hears me but a few seconds later, his eyes light up and I find that his focus had been trained on me all along. Fuck. I don't think I'll ever get used to that.

"Thanks," I say. "For helping me. Again."

There's only a moment before he replies, that deepness in his voice vibrating through the air and reaching me as if to caress my skin.

"You owe me, Firespark."

I nod, cheeks heating. "Right. Of course. Yes, I know I do."

Triple payment. I owe him more than half of what I've already paid. Of course, he'll make sure I live so I pay up. And yet, some silly part of me appreciates his help as if this relationship we have is suddenly more than that.

Silly, silly girl.

I stare at him through the darkness, allowing my mind to wander.

He's ruthless. I've seen him kill over ten males without even a second thought or any sign of regret. And yet, he tended to me with a gentleness that seems in complete contrast to the male he's supposed to be. It's a contradiction. One that makes me wonder just *who* he really is.

"I...don't understand you," I finally admit.

My words fall on the dead silence of the dark and I don't expect him to respond.

"Do you need to?"

A slight smile comes to my lips. He's right, of course. Do I?

The answer is no. No, I do not.

I'm getting ahead of myself. This...relationship, if I can even call it that, is simple. We both play our part and at the end we go our separate ways. Nothing more than that.

"Can you tell me one thing at least?" Weighing whether I should continue, I decide why not? "What's your name?"

More silence.

"Only a few have the pleasure of knowing my name," he says after a few moments.

I nod. "Of course." My gaze shifts back to the night sky. "Those you trust," I whisper. "Those you love."

I wait, but his name never comes.

"Guess I'll just call you 'Zamari' then."

"You, Firespark, can call me whatever you like."

I don't know why his words bring a smile to my lips when they shouldn't. There's nothing to smile about. Back in Comodre, people are depending on me. My, Kiana, and Estella's lives depend on this trip.

"I'm Elsie," I say after a few more moments as my head tilts back, my gaze scanning over the star-filled sky. Moments pass between us, a comfortable silence as I stare up at those worlds far away.

"You look at the stars..." he says after a while, "as if you want to go up there and not return home."

His words make a sad sort of smile hang on my lips.

"Up there...is the only home I know..." I whisper, pulling my gaze away from the view before my memories drown me again. "But that was before we fell to this cursed place."

I've shared a part of myself I didn't intend to. So much for keeping this strictly business. But I find not one part of me cares that I've revealed that much.

Probably because he's seen me at my most vulnerable. Probably because he's a stranger who doesn't know anything about me. It's easy to open up to him, because when this is over, I'll forget about him, and he'll forget about me.

The silence between us stretches, and I find myself settling back against the rough cave wall, wrapping myself in the poncho.

I plan to remain awake, but the night is long, and soon my eyelids grow heavier. I slump even harder against the rock, sleep dragging me down, the weight of remaining conscious too much. Every time I startle awake, those luminous eyes are settled on me and finally, I allow my lids to close. Because, for the first time since landing on this forsaken rock, I feel something within me that I'd almost forgotten. Something that was chased away a long, long time ago.

I feel...safe.

CHAPTER TEN

Elsie

I wake with a start.

Bright light shines within the little cave, making me squint. Ivuria's already risen, coming over the horizon with her usual blazing power. The glowing line that surrounds the dark sun glistens in the clear, cloudless sky. It's a spectacle to look at. Probably the strangest yet most beautiful thing about this planet. Far off in the void, I can see the dim shapes of the three closest planets in this star system. They say they're just as arid as number ten. Some even worse.

My gaze immediately shoots to the spot where the outlaw had been standing when I dozed off, but he's no longer there. Deep in my chest, there's something that feels oddly like disappointment.

Something must be wrong with me.

Rising, I stretch, pushing sleep from my aching bones as I stand and brush as much of the sand as I can from my clothes.

Two steps out from the cave and I stop short. Before me, rows and rows of furrows are dug deep into the sand.

Last night I'd counted ten. Now that it's daylight, I realize just how far off I was. There must be hundreds. Just how big had that ship been? If the Zamari hadn't been here with me last night...or worse...if those scrapers had passed me on my way to Calanta, I might not have even made it to the city.

I shiver despite that the air's warming up and wrap my arms around myself. My fingers brush against the poncho and the strange sensation brings my attention to my fingertips. The gauze is black, wrapped neatly around the tip of each finger with almost robotic precision. It looks more like an accessory than something protecting my wounds. It's a strange type of gauze that I've never seen before. Blocking all trace and sight of my blood.

Probably for the best.

My gaze shifts over my shoulder as I search for the Zamari, but he's still nowhere to be seen.

The way he'd looked at me last night. The way his eyes turned to utter darkness. The memory makes me shiver again but this time for whole other reasons unrelated to the temperature.

There's movement in my periphery and I startle, attention snapping in that direction.

He's standing there, as glorious as he was last night when the light shone on him. Only now, his hat is set low and I can barely see his features. So how can I feel his gaze traveling over me, moving over my skin even though I'm clothed?

I clear my throat. "You're up early."

His gaze is green today, but not any less consuming. Those eyes don't shift from me as he lifts a hand and gently tips his hat. It's not even sexual. Why's that one action so damn attractive?

My cheeks heat. "I just need to...uh..."

I glance toward the rocks and I'm sure he understands. My cheeks flame some more as I hurry out of his line of sight to relieve my aching bladder. Nothing like crouching over sand so hot it steams when you pee on it. I tell myself that brush of steam is why that little nub between my legs engorges and throbs and that it has nothing to do with the Zamari.

When I fix my clothes and step from behind the rock, he's still standing in the same spot.

I clear my throat again, brushing down my skirt. "Ready?"

There's only a slight movement of his lips. The ghost of a smile.

"Lead the way, Firespark."

That nickname again. It sounds overly intimate. As if he's known me for years. I try to pretend it has no effect on me.

Lifting my chin, I nod before walking to the other side of the rocks where he'd led me the night before. He's already set the bikes up for departure. Opening the storage compartment of mine, I grab a drink of water before glancing his way. But the Zamari is already climbing on his bike, gaze scanning the horizon. I shrug and hop on mine. I don't know if he slept last night. I haven't seen him eat and he certainly doesn't seem like he wants a drink either.

"Let's go." I jerk my chin and start up my engine. It struggles, choking a few times, the engine starting up then dying out shortly after. I try again, but it doesn't even budge the second time. Trying once more, my gaze shifts to the Zamari to find him watching me, a frown so slight it's almost not really there on his brow.

"Don't worry, it'll..." At least, I pray it will. How will I get back to Comodre without it? I give him a tight smile, embarrassment coloring my cheeks as I try to get the bike online. He must be wondering how the hell I'm going to pay him when I don't even have a ship that moves.

"Fuck." I'm about to hop off and open the control panel when the bike does a wheeze and roars to life. Relief sets my soul on fire and I look over at him triumphantly, a grin on my lip. "See!"

I swear I see a huff of a laugh release from his nose.

Putting just enough juice in to coax the engine, we set off.

For leagues, we travel. Me in front, the Zamari behind, and the closer we get to Comodre, the more I play scenarios in my head. I'm asking him to risk his life to protect me and Kiana, and he doesn't even know the details of it all yet. What if he changes his mind when he gets there? What if it's too much for him to deal with alone?

The Nirzoik are terrifying. I've seen many of our settlers die at their hands for the slightest disrespect.

Worry plagues me. So much so that I don't immediately notice when the Zamari's bike comes closer to mine till we're riding at the same pace side-by-side.

I glance over at him, wondering why he's pulled up next to me when he's traveled the entire time behind. But his gaze is focused straight ahead, giving no indication.

I pull my visor up so I can shout loud enough for him to hear without the speed pulling my words out into the wind. "What is it?"

His gaze shifts to me then, a sort of hardness in his eyes that I've seen before—when he killed those males in the parking sector. "There's a storm," he finally says. "Several leagues out."

"A storm?"

I blink at him, momentarily confused before I turn my gaze forward. Scanning the horizon before us, I see nothing. It looks as dead and lifeless as ever out on this endless plain.

"Slow down," he says, and for some reason, I automatically

comply as if it's second nature, my hand loosening on the accelerator so suddenly that my bike hiccups and almost stalls.

"Shit!" I manage to stop it before it does. I'm not sure it will start again if the engine cuts out.

His bike reduces speed in synchronicity with mine, slowing down to a crawl before stopping.

I slip my visor up, squinting at the cloudless sky above us. Nothing. At least, nothing out of the ordinary. Off in the distance, thin pink clouds are floating aimlessly by. Everything seems normal.

"There." He jerks his chin forward and I squint again. Nothing.

My gaze flashes to him, but the complete seriousness in his gaze, hardening his features, is the only thing that tells me he's not joking. He hops off his bike then opens the storage compartment and takes out a bottle I don't recognize. Moving to the back of the ship where the rockets are, he opens the bottle and splashes some of the liquid inside, coating the chamber.

It's a strange scent that wafts into the air. One I've smelled before. On the Nirzoik. I eye the bottle, unease in my throat.

"Zyka fluid," he says, not looking at me as he moves over to my bike and does the same. "Nonflammable. Will protect anything from a flame. But will also stop your rockets from being clogged with sand."

Zyka fluid. I've heard of it before. A passing merchant tried to sell it to us in Comodre, saying it would protect our cabins from the Nirzoik's wrath. His cost? A year's worth of gems from the mines. Needless to say, this magic fluid has coated no cabins in our colony.

My eyes widen as I watch the Zamari splash the fluid so generously I could choke. It's like watching the gems I've bled to dig up from the unforgiving rocks being thrown away without care. I frown as I watch him. There's already a mechanism to stop sand from clogging the rockets. These things were made for the plains. It's almost like he's preparing for a catastrophe.

Turning back to the view ahead of us, I narrow my eyes and focus. I still don't see anything and I'm about to say the same to him when a thin gust of breeze brushes lightly across my exposed skin.

I pause, lifting my arm as I watch the thin fibers running along the poncho move in the slight breeze.

Wind? Out here?

My gaze snaps back to the view, throat tightening as the outlaw puts the zyka fluid away and hops on his ship once more.

I see it then. So small it looks like a thin wall blending into the ground that meets the horizon ahead. "That's—shit."

The line grows larger the longer I look at it, just as another soft wisp of wind flows over me.

"Sand devil," I whisper. My gaze snaps back to his. "It's the seventh month. Those don't usually form until the first, in the new year." At least, not after the rainy season passes and the plains dry again. And we haven't had the rainy season yet.

His gaze hardens a little, jaw ticking as he clenches his teeth.

I'm right, of course. It's not the season for those storms. It's one of the reasons I risked taking this trip now. Now's supposed to be the safest time to traverse the plains. When the plains are calm. Before the rains come.

"Seems this one's coming early."

Fuck.

I swallow hard, turning back to face the thing approaching. It's so far ahead, I still wouldn't have spotted it until I was much closer, but even in the few seconds it's taken me to acknowledge its presence, that line has gotten thicker. Larger.

It's moving fast.

My heart hits hard against my ribs as my gaze snaps to either side of us. We need protection. Shelter.

Sand devils are the one phenomenon in which I don't want to be caught out without cover. Massive sandstorms carrying not only grains of sand moving so fast they're like miniature bullets, but small bits of sharp metal pulled up from the loose surface. It's a death sentence to face something like that head-on.

As my breaths come harder, I glance behind us. Our safest bet is to backtrack, head in the opposite direction. Find the rocks we sheltered in the night before. Hope we get there before the storm reaches us.

The hum underneath my butt makes me whisper a silent prayer, thanking the gods that my bike hasn't cut out yet. We can turn back.

"Won't do, Firespark." His words make me pause. He's looking at me as if he's read my mind. "That thing's too big for us to shelter in simple rocks. You'd get sliced and diced." Then his gaze dips to my neck. "Can't let that happen."

I swallow hard as he guns his engine. "Follow me."

He turns off our course, heading into territory I don't know, and for a moment, I just sit there watching him go. More wind flies around me, this time bringing bits of sand with it, and I turn my gaze back to the approaching storm. That line's even bigger now, rising from the horizon like a solid brown wall that stretches as far as I can see. And if I can see it already, it means the thing's a monster.

Heart hammering an unsteady beat, I gun my engine, my bike backfiring before I get it to shoot in the mercenary's wake.

He's not going fast, slow enough that I catch up with him in about half a minute.

"This isn't the right way!" I shout over the wind. I mean, I have my wayfinder, but going off course brings more worries than simply getting lost. Ivuria 10 isn't the most forgiving of places.

"Have to change your course. Either that, or..." He lifts one eyebrow and I get the insinuation. Either that or risk dying in a demon storm that's come out of nowhere.

"But where are we heading?!"

He shrugs. "Bone territory. Where wanderers go to die."

I swear my eyes bug out so large I feel the pressure in my skull. "Maybe we should go the other way?!"

"Worse."

What the fuck can be worse than the place you go to die? Maybe we should just face the storm, since there's a chance we're going to die, anyway? But just the thought and something in the center of my chest aches.

I have to get back to Comodre in one piece. People need me there.

"If we get lost out there, can you find the way back?"

He doesn't answer for a few moments, but he goes faster and faster because I have to pump more and more energy into my engine to keep up. Panic sets in as I pray the old machine doesn't fail me now. One glance to my left, and I see the storm as clear as day; no need to squint. He's trying to outrun it. My heart thumps harder. He's trying to outrun it, but that wall of brown seems to stretch forever. I don't see the end.

"If anything happens," I say, turning my gaze back to the outlaw beside me, "head to a place called Comodre. Find a woman named Estella. She will pay you the rest...after you do what we need you to do."

He's been looking straight ahead, but suddenly his gaze shifts to me.

"What are you doing, Firespark?"

I gulp, the wind picking up around us and it has nothing to do with the speed at which we're going. "Just in case," I say. It's not loud. Probably even a whisper. But he hears anyway.

"Don't worry. I won't let anything happen to you."

His words make my heart clench with an unexpected ache and I stare at him, unable to look away. His gaze shifts off to something behind me and I know he's watching the storm. I still can't understand how he knew it was coming and I note it in the back of my mind as something else I'll have to thank him for.

"Faster," he growls, his voice deeper than before.

I engage my thrusters, the fire igniting in my rockets as I shoot forward, almost too fast to see the outlaw keeping pace at my side. For a moment, I look his way and our gazes meet. We're going too fast. One mistake, and we're dead.

Bits of sand hit against my visor hard enough that I can hear them and the wind beginning to whip around us. Holding on to the rocket bike, I try to keep it level because it sways, leaning one way with the push of the wind as I swing my body in the opposite direction. I'm surprised it's even keeping up with the speed but thanking the gods at the same time. I clench it between my thighs, gripping it for dear life as I put all my faith in the old machine.

"We have to find shelter!" My scream goes off in the wind, just as the sky darkens above us, swirls of airborne sand blocking out the sun. So thick, visibility plummets.

Shit, even riding this fast, we can't outrun it. We're still going to end up within the damn thing and it's going to hit us hard if we don't find somewhere to hide soon.

"There!" I hear him shout, but I can hardly see in front of

me now. I reduce the thrusters, slowing down against my better judgment. It's one thing to go so fast everything around you becomes a blur. It's another to do so when you can't see a thing ahead of you.

"Where?!" I yell.

He appears and disappears in the swirling gusts, his figure flickering in and out of sight ahead of me, a phantom in the swirling maelstrom. I can hear the wind coming. Already feel the sand particles battering my helmet and my clothes.

I thought this storm was a monster? It's a frickin' behemoth.

Now I understand why he used that zyka fluid.

Suddenly a dark-clad arm shoots out of the gusts and grips one handle of my bike. It careens, almost flinging me one way as it goes another, but the Zamari steadies it.

Eyes like big discs behind my visor, shock has me in a chokehold as he controls my bike and his, one hand each. He appears and disappears from view a second later and I duck my head against the wind.

"Come!" The Zamari's voice sounds close to my ear as he guides me to whatever shelter he's found. As the bikes come to a stop, he hops off his as I scramble to do the same.

In the middle of the swirling brown clouds before me, I see bits of white. Stark against the sand that surrounds us.

"You go in first!"

I nod, pulling up my skirts as I run toward the white thing. Wind batters me, like a physical thing doing a wrestling match with my entire body. I push and strain against it, my boots sinking into the loose sand as I force one foot in front of the other, pressing toward safety. I'm only a few meters away when enough of the swirling sand clears and I see just what I'm heading towards. I am nearly overpowered by the gusts with how suddenly I stop moving.

A huge white cage stands before me. Ribs. Half of them

buried in the sand. A spine like a thin, narrow roof holding them together in the air. They're huge, dwarfing me, and for a moment, I stare in horror before the storm cuts off my view again.

"Bad news, Firespark." The outlaw is suddenly beside me, close enough that his body presses against my side, his mouth close to my helmet so I can hear. "We're going to need to leave one."

I swallow hard. "One of what?!"

"Yours...or mine." He gestures to where the bikes are. "Preferably yours. Mine will get us to your little town. Yours won't."

Fuck. No. I can't lose the rocket bike. It's one of the things I was thinking of selling just so I can afford to pay him what he's due.

But there's no time to deliberate. The storm's coming and there are things worse than being stranded. I barely nod to him and then he disappears again.

"Head towards the skull!" His voice finds me through the wind and I grip my skirts tighter. Marching toward the giant ribs, the outlaw appears behind me a second later, hands on the handlebars of his bike as he guides it along. The wind picks up, blinding me again and I reach out with one hand, trying to find the massive jail of bones that I know are before me.

But I can't. It feels like I'm still a thousand miles away, even though I know it's there somewhere before me.

I stagger, stretching, whispering a silent prayer as I force one foot before the other, the swirling wind now starting to scream around me.

"Here!" He appears again, this time grasping my arm, pulling me toward him. I feel the strength in his grasp and for a blinding moment, I'm suddenly not alone. There is someone here with me. I don't have to be strong all on my own.

I relax my arm, allowing his grasp to guide me as we press toward the cage of bones. I can see nothing before me. Only the knowledge that we're somewhere close to where we need to be. Beside me, the outlaw pushes forward but now his head is bent too, bracing against the wind, his hat the only protection from the swirling sand. I don't know how he can even see. I'm wearing a helmet that's protecting my eyes, mouth, even my ears and nose from all this sand, and I'm still struggling. Still, we press forward; me trusting he knows where he's going. Trusting he knows what he's doing.

But it's not the first time I've had to trust him, is it?

The wind dies down for a moment as we hit a patch of dead air and I see the bones not far in front of us. He pulls me closer toward him, guiding the bike at our back as we step into the bony cage.

"This way." I don't know how I hear his voice over the scream of the wind as it picks up again. But I do and I follow his command, turning with him as he guides us through what was once the chest cavity of some creature. I see the white walls next. A dark cavern with smooth white walls I shortly realize is actually sun-bleached bone. The head of whatever massive creature this was.

It towers over us, the sand flashing and curving around it as we enter its depths. The force of the wind is cut in half as we step inside.

Large sharp teeth decorate a powerful jaw that now lies shut, half of the entire skull buried deep in the sand, leaving only one small opening for us to squeeze through—where the neck would have been.

It's a tight fit and the Zamari guides me in before him. I turn as another gust of wind picks up, just in time to see him disappear once more.

Shit.

The wind screams now, the storm getting closer still. It's almost here. I can tell from the bits of metal I hear battering the outside of the skull, scraping against it like a creature with a thousand claws is trying to get in.

My fist tightens on my skirt as I squint from where I stand, waiting with my heart in my throat. It's getting worse out there, bad enough that bits of sand and metal are flying into the little shelter. I should press farther inside, as far away from the opening as I dare, but something's stopping me from rushing away and hiding from all this.

Him.

He's out there. And I can't move. Not until he comes in.

More sand. More metal. The wind screeching like a banshee now and I shift back to the mouth of the skull cave. He left his bike there, set just inside the neck of the cave, and I scramble over it.

He's been gone too long.

My heart hammers in my chest as I wait. Every second feeling like a minute. Every minute feeling like an hour.

As the storm screams louder, drawing ever closer, I know I can't wait any longer. With a deep, steadying breath, I step back into the ribbed walkway. Sand swirls all around me immediately, blocking my vision, and sounding like a million little projectiles hitting my helmet all at once. I press forward, one hand reaching outward to guide me when a sudden, piercing pain lances through my palm. I flick my hand back out of pure reflex, but not before another sharp pain cuts through it. I can feel my blood running without being able to see it. Hissing with the burn of the wound, I grip my wrist, wincing as I fight to see through the swirl.

It's too dangerous. The metal is flying too fast. If I go out there, I risk getting sliced some more. And that can only mean one thing. He went to get my bike, and that means he's getting killed. Sliced and bleeding. How can I just stand here helplessly while that happens?

As I step back to the entrance to the little cave, something twists in my gut. That same feeling I had when the Nirzoik took Estella's house down as I stood there, unable to do anything.

It's a feeling that's bitter in my gut. A feeling that shatters every confidence I've built, only bringing me back to those times when I could never do anything.

When the mothership fell...

When the Nirzoik came...

And here now, with the Zamari out there in the storm.

But fuck that.

With another deep steadying breath, I wrap the bleeding hand in my skirt, not bothering to look at how deep the cuts might be, and I step out again. I only make it a few steps when, this time, a sharp piece of metal flies past my visor. It's a split second, just a blur, but the sound the plasfilm makes as it's cut into is like a deafening screech in my ears. My eyes widen at the deep groove that's suddenly set into the visor, stopping me in my tracks. I follow the groove with a sort of panic-filled disbelief as I stare at it in shock. A long piece of metal sticks out at the edge of the thin line. Some sort of blade in its other life. One sharp end embedded in the plasfilm and jutting out dangerously. If the visor wasn't there...I'd be...

Fuck.

I'm so stunned that for a second, the swirling sand and all of its dangers are forgotten because I cannot move. But then I do. My body's suddenly grabbed, a muscular arm wrapping around my waist as I'm taken backward in one swift movement into the skull cavern.

My chest heaves as I grip the Zamari's arm, gaze turning to find him so close beside me.

He huffs, dragging something behind him, and I hear when it collapses. My bike. It makes a dull thud underneath the screech of the wind. I only catch a short glimpse of it before a shower of sand claims it.

The storm rages, blowing inside the cave and I hear a growl as I'm carried farther back, away from the small hole that is our only exit, farther in where it's safe.

My back hits a hard incline of sand as twin luminous eyes are set above me, and for the first time, I see some real emotion in them.

Rage.

His gaze shifts to the piece of metal jutting from my visor and another growl leaves his chest.

"What were you thinking, human?"

He's alive. My eyes squeeze closed for a moment as I let that fact settle in my head. He's alive. I let out a breath of relief that's quickly disturbed as both my shoulders are grabbed and I'm not-so-gently shaken. My eyes fly open to his fiery ones.

"What...were you thinking?"

I blink at him. I don't know what he means. Or maybe I've missed part of his question, for the storm's shrieking so loudly now, I want to cover my ears and curl in on myself.

That thought makes another type of panic beat in my chest and I bite down hard on my lower lip, forcing myself to focus. I can't break down in front of him again. Not again.

I gasp as he snatches my hand from where I still have it gripping my skirt. He lifts it between us, and blood drips from my palm. His lips pull back so viciously, a deep snarl leaves his throat. His fangs descend—one smooth, quick movement—and I'm frozen as I stare at them. So sharp, the tips glint in the dim light.

All around outside, there's a tremendous screeching. The

storm's upon us now, darkening the skies, blocking out the light, but all I can focus on is the fire in the Zamari's eyes.

My gaze slips to my hand and I see why he's so enraged. The gashes the metal dug are two deep grooves from which my blood flows. It looks worse than it feels. Or maybe it's just the shock of this all.

The Zamari releases me suddenly, a slight hiss on his lips as he backs away and turns from me. Even in the barely there light, I can see his shoulders heaving. I open my mouth to say something, but words fail me. But then he moves. Rising, he closes the short distance to his bike. There, he brushes away sand that's already burying it as he fumbles with something. I can hear the bike being battered with sharp bits of metal and pebbles that have made their way inside, and I can't imagine what's happening to my bike that's even farther outside the hole. Adjusting myself on the sandy incline, I freeze again when the outlaw turns and heads back over to me.

This time, there's nothing slow or tentative about how he grips my hand. The hexagon lights up the little cave as he drops it on the sand beside us and sets my palm upward on his knee. Without a word, he grabs his first-aid supplies that he set beside him. But his face says it all. There might be no expression, not even a slight furrow of his brow, but those eyes tell me everything. When he glances up at me, I see his gaze has bled to black again.

It's nothing like the first time that I saw it happen. Back then, I'd been frozen in shock, staring at something so unreal before me. Now, it's all different. Now there's an intensity there that has my throat tightening as I wait.

My palm aches, more blood oozing from the cuts, and his nostrils flare at the sight. So, I wasn't imagining it last night then. It wasn't the antiseptic. He can smell my blood.

I'm not sure what I should do with that information. If I

should be scared, or cautious, or intrigued. I accept that something is wrong with me, because there is no fear at all when there clearly should be.

Silently, he takes out some gauze and a small bottle of what can only be antiseptic. He wets the gauze, soaking the sand beneath it before he puts away the bottle.

"You don't have to do this," I whisper. "I'm well enough to bandage it myself."

"You have no supplies."

My mouth opens and closes as I look at him. How did he know that?

It's just one problem in Comodre. With the Nirzoik's presence, we're blocked off and dependent on what they allow us. The few merchants that come in do so only because they let them and most of us can't afford to waste credits on things like gauze and fancy first-aid items.

My lips thin. I call them fancy, but they're basic. We can't even afford basic first-aid items. This is why I have to succeed in this.

I hiss as he presses the gauze into my palm. It burns like hell, bringing water to my eyes. It's an effort to keep my hand steady and he must realize that because his fist closes around my wrist, keeping my hand there on his knee. He leans in and, just like he did before, his cool breath chases away the pain. I grit my teeth as I watch him blow on my palm, trying to place the male who seems more dangerous than anyone I've ever known with the male before me who's *tending* to me.

"*Never* do that again." His voice has taken on a tone I can't place. It's a warning, but it's one I can't exactly follow.

"Never do what? Disobey you?"

His dark gaze flicks to me and I'm rendered speechless once more. I feel like I'm testing fate when I really shouldn't. It's like his gaze is swallowing me whole. Does he have any idea how terrifying he looks with his eyes all black like that? And shouldn't I be more afraid of just that fact?

"Never come after me like that again."

His response makes something akin to defiance tighten in my chest. "You went out into the storm for *my* bike. I couldn't just... I thought—"

"That what? You could save me?!" He barks. The change in his tone is so sudden that I jerk in surprise. There's an immediate look in his eyes, one I can't read before he dips his head and focuses on my wounded hand once more.

My throat feels tight, words not coming easily as I think of how to respond.

"I was trying to help you."

"Don't." A growl. An order. A *reprimand.*

Brows diving, I try to pull my hand away but he holds it steady, almost forcing me to make him tend to my wounds. When I realize he isn't letting go, I allow my arm to hang limp in his grasp with a heavy outward breath.

"I was only worried..." I begin and that dark, inky gaze snaps back to mine. But his reactions, his words, they make whatever explanation I had dry up like the arid sands swirling around us.

"That's not your place. A female like you...females like you..."

My jaw tightens and he shifts his dark gaze back to my palm. Taking a metal tool from his trunk, he spends the next long minutes taking grains of sand, one by one, from my wounds. It's slow, meticulous, and the tension between us grows with every minuscule grain he removes.

The silence between us feels louder than the screeching wind on the outside. Every minute that passes as he tends to my hand, cleaning it and then wrapping and bandaging it with that strange black gauze, feels like a heavy weight grows heavier on my shoulders.

When he's finally done, he kneels and reaches for me. I stiffen and the movement, or lack thereof, is obvious. His jaw ticks as he closes the distance and uses his tool to dislodge the piece of metal that was still stuck in my visor. His jaw ticks some more as he stares at it, gaze growing more cold and murderous. Turning, he flicks the tool and the piece of metal into the trunk, slams the little box shut, and deactivates the hexagon as he rises and heads back to his bike in silence.

But I can't just ignore what he said.

It makes something inside me harden. Makes my blood boil.

I run my fingers over the bandage he just made, wondering how he can be such a mixed bag of contradictions.

"Females like me?" I finally ask, gaze cutting to him like those shards cutting through the air. I can feel the disappointment in my gaze. The fire sparking within it. Taking off my helmet, I frown at him. "What's that supposed to mean?"

Back still turned to me, he stiffens briefly. And then he looks at me over his shoulder.

"Don't do it again." His words are a dismissal that hurts more than it should. And I fire right back.

"You helped me. I thought I could help you, too!"

He moves quickly. Far too fast for me to react and then he's suddenly upon me. My back presses into the sand as he leans over me. Caging me in.

I can't see his pupils. Can see no form of humanlike emotions in those eyes that will tell me what he's about to do. And as he leans in, fangs bared, he comes in close. Close enough for me to catch a whiff of his musk. Close enough for the tip of his nose to touch mine.

"*Never*...do that again," he growls. "Never come after me. Never worry about me. *Never care.*"

I gulp, pushing down the lump in my throat. He's right, of course. This is just a business arrangement. I shouldn't care more than that. But something about the way he speaks makes me think he's not just referring to business. And I can't stop myself. Can't stop the fire sparking inside me at him, at the situation, at the fucking state of my life.

"*Why?*" I growl right back. "Because 'females like me' aren't good enough to be of any use?"

The words taste bitter on my tongue, but I force them out anyway.

"No," he growls, leaning ever so closer. His lips brush against mine and I forget how to breathe. "Because females like you are far too good to be worrying about brutes like me."

CHAPTER ELEVEN

The Outlaw

I shouldn't do it. And yet, the soft brush of her lips against mine feels like some kind of beckoning from the gods themselves.

Elsie.

She told me her name, even though she has yet to know mine.

A name holds power. It can command. Rip you back to the core of yourself. Uttering it can conjure the very essence of a person. The vessel that holds their identity. The key to their soul.

To share it is an act of trust. An offer of vulnerability.

And she has entrusted me with hers. *Elsie.* I roll the syllables in my mind, savoring them.

There is something about this female, of the species "human". She is the first of her kind I have encountered and, possibly, that is the reason for this strange calling. This...magnetism.

Maybe it's the scent of her blood, how I can almost taste it, feel the power of it. The power within her. One taste, and I might not want to stop. One taste, and I might drink her dry.

I can hear it now. Her pulse hammering through her veins. Feel her life organ pressing against her chest. She has only one. Only one chance to live. And yet, the hammering beat is so strong, I wonder if she knows I could hunt her just from that sound alone.

Only one life organ...and she risked it for me.

I want to pull away. Know that I should. This is a job I should have never taken, and yet, I can't do the most basic thing that comes naturally to me. Leave.

A Zamari's solitary life should not be compounded by complexities. Troubles. And everything about this female spells just that.

Her chest heaves as we both freeze, only her breaths causing her body to rise and fall against mine, and I shift, spreading her legs in one movement. I settle between them like I was made to fit there, and a gasp pulls in air through her lips, brushing over mine, bringing me closer to the edge of this insanity.

I should move. Get away from her. Put space between us. But just like the first instance when I called her over to me, forced her to sit on my leg, felt her hot little center burning through my trouse, I refrain from doing what I know I should.

There is more here than pure need.

She is exactly what I call her. A firespark. Igniting something within me that shouldn't dare to see light in the first place. Something I've kept buried for a long, long time.

I've seen her fire. Seen her fear. Seen her bravery. Seen how she dares.

This female without an ayahl. This female with nothing else to protect her but her own wit and strength.

Does she even know how ludicrous her mission is? A lone

female with no defenses traversing the plains to hire an outlaw. Whatever drew her to this must be worth her life, for she is incredible in her hope.

And I am crazed.

"What if I want to?" she whispers, lips brushing against mine with every word. Her voice pulls me back from the claws slowly closing around me.

I don't hold back my growl. Her daring hits a spot deep inside me that draws on respect for her bravery. But at the same time, it hits something else, too.

I was right when I said a female like her shouldn't worry about a brute like me. I am nothing to her but a hired weapon. How foolish of her to even consider me as more. To *care*. To risk her life for an unworthy stranger like me.

I know my gaze has gone dark. I can't help it. And yet, she's still here. Doesn't run. Has no idea what this darkness slowly overtaking me even means. Has no idea it's a sign she *should* run. Get away from me. That I'm a beast that wants to consume her.

Her being. Her essence. Her *everything*.

Beneath me, she glows like an ember. The heat from her body lighting up in my gaze like a beacon outlining her form. She is prey in the darkness consuming me. And I must put distance between us. For her sake.

It's her that moves first.

While I war with my senses, her soft lips shift under mine, so tentatively yet so daring that I go rigid. It's not clear what she's doing. The movement repeats and I wonder if it's some kind of exploratory thing her kind does. Or if it is some type of greeting? If that's the case, we're far past introductions. But as her lips brush against mine once more, the sensation sends a surge of need straight to my cock. It twitches under the firm fabric of my trouse and I have to clench my teeth. *Hard.*

Her mouth movements continue, those soft lips of hers brushing against mine in a dance that I am quickly learning. I remain rigid as she continues teaching me this greeting, struggling to understand exactly how I am meant to respond.

For we Zamari do something similar, though not with our lips. But rubbing one's nose against the delicate neck of one's mate occurs only during mating. And it has deep meaning. It is a symbol of intention. Of need. And of acceptance. Just that simple act can drive a Zamari wild. The scent of his mate. Her delicate neck just inches away from his fangs. But this... This thing this human is doing...

It's different, and yet it generates the same response in my being. My cock hardens almost painfully, arching against my trouse as if to spear it. Its presence is a clear warning that this should stop, a warning she must feel, but her lips shift again, rolling against mine. Testing. Feeling. Investigating.

Another soft breath leaves her mouth and with that single brush of air, my *ayahl* goes feral. I try to hold back but I growl anyway, only able to pull back my fangs in time before my lips crash against hers.

This mouth rubbing is strange. But it's intoxicating. A dance of our lips in a space suspended in time. Her lips roll against mine, her mouth opening to take my lower lip between hers as she sucks lightly and my hold on reality lapses for a moment. The sensation makes my lifeblood roar in my ears louder than the storm raging outside.

She releases my lip to tilt her head back, a gasp brushing against me as her little pink tongue grazes the seam of our joined lips. And then she gasps again, her body shuddering as if a lightning spark has gone through her.

Fek.

My cock goes so stiff, my trouse becomes a prison. My ayahl distorts at the edges like a thick, dark, inky cloud around me as that one sensation of her little wet tongue travels right through me.

I lose hold on my restraint, my tongue diving into her mouth at the same time that my *ayahl* rushes toward her, surrounding her, seeking hers, seeking a *mate*. And even though she can't interact with it, she shudders in my grasp, a slight tremble going through her frame as she opens her lips to mine.

I join in her strange dance even though the steps aren't clear. I sway to her rhythm, anyway. Just tasting her like this is so unexpectedly pleasurable, I press her harder into the sandy floor. She shudders against me, thighs tightening as she pulls me in. Her unwounded hand finds my jaw, the tips of her fingers gripping me tight as our tongues crash and play. And when her fingers find the brim of my hat, digging underneath into the filaments on my head, she pulls me even harder against her still.

Insatiable; it is like a beast is lying dormant within her, ready to come to the fore. Her thighs press in tighter, as if she wants to consume me, and I revel in the taste of her, the feel of her, this aspect of this female I could have never seen coming.

The scent of the sweet xyleen oil on her skin, her beckoning warmth...

I...want her.

A little whimper escapes her lips, dying against mine as her thighs tighten even more, digging into my side as she presses her pelvis against mine. Grinding her heat against me as if she's seeking something she just can't reach. Fek. I growl again, but then she freezes. By the gods, she stops.

Reluctantly, my lips slip from hers, my breaths unsteady as I ease back and look down at her. The growing horror in her eyes isn't something I'd wished to see, but one I should have expected.

Because this cannot be real.

She has realized what she's doing, *what she was about to do*, and she has finally come to her senses. I want to tell her not to worry. That I would have stopped before she did something she'd regret, but I am too far gone by whatever just happened between us. Something has risen in me now that I can already tell will be fekking difficult to tame.

But I should know this firespark often does the unexpected.

That look of horror grows as the arm gripping my skull is lifted, so slowly I see the slight tremors going through it. When her gaze shifts to it and gets larger, the horror almost palpable, her hand shakes hard enough that I shift my gaze to her palm just to see what's caused her to look at her own hand in such a way.

Thick, dark lifeblood coats her entire hand. *My* lifeblood.

Gods. I resist the urge to groan. I was supposed to take care of that later, when she fell asleep.

"I-it's blood. Y-you're bleeding." Her utterance makes her shake, her gaze shifting to where she'd been holding my head before her eyes widen with even more horror. "You're hurt. You've been hurt."

Her gaze shifts down and I realize she's scanning me for more injuries. I can only kneel there, watching her look at me as if I'm someone she should care about. And yet, although I'm not, despite that I don't deserve any of this, I can't seem to move away. Can't seem to deny the attention. Can't seem to deny that I...like it. Want it?

Poor, foolish, Zamari.

What the fek is wrong with me?

Her breaths come hard enough that her chest heaves, her gaze flying around as she blinks. The sound of the storm, where we are, all coming back into focus.

At least I wasn't the only one lost there for a moment. Consumed by need and want. It brings little consolation.

She scrambles backward, putting space between us before she rises, almost stumbling as she walks on unsteady legs back to my bike. Feverish, delicate hands brush the sand away as she ducks from the wind entering through the little hole.

"Where is it? How do you open your storage compartment?" The words float over her shoulder, reaching my ears just fine. They twitch at the sound, but that's all the reaction she receives from me. All I can manage. For she's scraped the sand from my bike and has opened the storage, pulling my supplies from within before slamming the thing closed again.

Stumbling, her feet sinking in the sand, she turns back toward me, a strange sort of determination in her eyes as she heads back my way.

My gaze shifts to the supply trunk then back to her.

"I can fix it myself."

"Sure as hell you will," she snaps, and it makes my brow rise slightly.

She is...angry?

Just moments before, she was anything but that. This same female that was whimpering, lids half-closed as her tongue swirled with mine, is now looking at me with her fists clenched, her mouth in a thin line, and fire in her eyes again.

She returns to where she was sitting, where I pressed her into the sand and spread her wide, and adjusts the long skirt she wears over her legs. Brows dipped, that same fire in her eyes, she pats one knee.

"Down."

My brows lift, my *ayahl* swirling around her, trying to understand what the fek is happening. It wants to mate. This is not the direction it intended. She's ordering me like I'm a subservient creature. "I'm not a beast—"

"Put your head down." Clipped. Terse. No room for arguments.

I don't know why I comply. Why I turn my back toward her before leaning down to rest my head on her thigh.

Bad fekking decision.

My head rests right near her hip. A slight shift and a turn and my nose will be buried in her center. I inhale, her scent filling my senses. Yea. Bad, bad idea. And still I remain there. I don't even adjust the tent in my trouse.

But my hat shifts, those delicate hands on the brim as she pulls and I catch her wrist.

Her eyes are no longer fiery when I snap my gaze to hers.

"I need to take it off," she whispers.

I stare at her for a few moments. No one removes my hat. It's as much a part of me as my ayahl...and yet, my hold on her wrist softens. I feel her chest move as she releases a breath, those blue eyes of hers flicking to the hat as she slowly lifts it and sets it down on my chest.

For a moment, she does nothing, only stays looking at me.

She doesn't comment as she pops the trunk open at her side. Doesn't say a word as she turns my head slightly, tilting my nose in the exact direction she should keep me away from.

"Which one of these is the antiseptic?"

"Every single one of them." Even to my ears, my voice has gone guttural.

Control. Need to control myself.

"This is going to hurt."

I grunt.

I hear when she pops the lid off one of the bottles before her tentative fingers brush over the wound at the back of my head. Her breath hitches and a soft sound escapes from her chest, but she doesn't say a word. It's almost like a whimper. As if this pure little thing is sorry to see me hurt.

I can feel the tremor in her fingers as she uses the picker tool to remove the grains of sand stuck there. One by one, like I did for her.

It's a strange sort of thing. One that has me stiff, unable, or unwilling, to move lest I break the spell.

She is *tending* to me. Unexpected warmth bubbles in my chest, extending through my *ayahl* which wraps around her like an invisible cloak.

Since we're not mating, it has settled for this. And maybe I am too. It's almost like stepping into a territory I have not yet explored. One I'm finding I do not hate.

She shivers slightly as my ayahl writhes around her in a calming wave. Not consciously aware of it, and yet her body responds. I watch it, knowing fully well what that means. That somehow, I've stumbled upon a potential mate. That my *ayahl* thinks I can knot this human and create viable young. Not going to happen. As with all the other times, I will reject this urge.

I might be heartless, but I am not selfish. A female like this doesn't need the trouble a male like me brings.

It takes a while, but eventually, I relax.

The wind is screeching outside and we are slowly being blocked in, sand rising at the entrance. But here I am, head on the soft thigh of a sweet-scented female. The last place I would have imagined to find myself after entering that drinkery. I still don't even know why I went there...or maybe now I do. A soft growl rumbles in my chest as I allow myself this one moment. To forget who I am. To forget *what* I am. And to just feel.

Just a little.

I will not lose control.

Leaning in, I press my nose into the skirts at her center,

another unashamed growl rumbling in my chest. I can scent her musk through the fibers.

She stops moving, and I hear her throat move in a swallow. But I remain where I am. Here, in this spot, where I can smell her essence. A scent that's slowly imprinting on my mind as she tends to me as if I'm worthy of her care.

I shift, throwing my arms around her waist in an embrace that presses me even closer against her, and she stops moving again. Freezing. Immediately, I think she will push me away. Tell me to tend to myself like the brazen fool I am. For what the fek am I doing? I don't *embrace*, much less relax in the lap of strange females.

But she does nothing. Doesn't push me away. Doesn't say a word. The tension between us rises as her fingers move again, tending to my wound before a breath shudders through her.

She tends to me, mending my wound and maybe a little part of my insides, too. This whole scenario is so much like a dream that I wonder if I should show her the other lacerations across my back and sides. Would she tend to them too? Would her delicate fingers brush over my skin, stained with my lifeblood, while she cares for me in a way I haven't been in as long as time can tell?

No Zamari female would do this. My wounds would be mine to mend and mine alone. Any weakness, and I would be struck off as a potential mate. Or maybe, that's just it. The human doesn't see me as a potential mate.

And yet...

The scent of her heat says something different.

Not wanting to break the spell, my gaze shifts up toward her face almost reluctantly. But she does not see. She is focused on cleaning the wound.

There is no derision twisting her lips. Firespark is...genuine.

I shift my gaze back down before our eyes meet. For little does she know, this moment is worth the whole triple payment of credits she offered me. This single moment is one a male like me is destined to never have. For the gods to grant me this, for even a short time, is like torture and sweet pleasure at the same time.

For a female like this can never be mine.

And so, maybe I am selfish. For I will take her pity and her care...even though in the end, I will have to leave before I break her.

CHAPTER TWELVE

Elsie

I finish gluing the wound at the back of the Zamari's head and I take a few moments to just look at him. He must deal with injuries a lot to have all these supplies. The gauze. The antiseptic. The medical glue. There's more too. More than I initially thought. The small, unassuming trunk is deceptively well-stocked—far more than meets the eye upon first glance.

I shift, squinting a little. I can hardly see now, the light so dim in the little cavern that everything is cast in shadow. Outside, the wind still screeches, the constant scrape of metal against bone telling me it's still deadly out there.

Deadly and dark.

I would have asked him to lend me his light source, but the hexagon wasn't in the supply box, and, even as visibility diminished, I couldn't find it in myself to rouse him.

He's been still, silence enveloping us from the moment I began. A comfortable silence that feels like it's wrapped around us like a cozy blanket. I almost don't want to break it.

But his nose is pressed against my pussy, only the thin fabric of my skirt in between. I can feel it like a firm little nub against my clit and every inhale and exhale he makes sends a lighting spark to my core.

I try to hold back, to control this whirlwind of feelings that seem intent on controlling me, but with each second that passes, I slip farther into insanity.

This shouldn't be happening. I don't know this male. So why am I so comfortable around him?

I lift my hand, the dark stain of his dried blood still on my fingers, and a lump rises in my throat. I should clean my fingers. But I can't move.

Or maybe, I just don't want to.

Tentatively, I lower the same hand, my fingers playing with the short, dark hair strands adorning his head. They're silky smooth underneath my fingertips. The type of hair I could run my hand through for days.

Another breath shudders through my chest, even though I try to release it smoothly. Is he asleep? He hasn't moved since he threw his arms around me. Even after I worked out how to use the glue and worked my way through closing the wound. It was a deep gash, even deeper than the ones in my hand, and I shudder to think that I was right about all this. That he might have been sliced open out there.

I know I didn't force him. That he's here of his own volition. That I'm *paying* him to be here. But even though he's a male I hardly know, even though he must have questionable morals, the thought of him dying out here because I dragged him into my problems is a load I don't want on my chest.

That may all be true. But I also can't deny that there's something else. Something that's caught my attention and keeps pulling me toward him. Maybe it's the question of it all. The fact I know nothing about him and yet it doesn't quite feel that way. Or the fact that behind the ruthless killer, I've seen glimpses of something else that's attracting me like a moth to a flame.

And then there's the taste of his lips. My bottom lip pulls into my mouth as I take it between my teeth.

That kiss. It was...like fire. Hot. Scorching. And oh so fucking dangerous.

I resist the pull of the memory of his lips on mine. Of the pure electricity that flooded through me and made me forget who I am.

A groan rumbles underneath the screeching of the storm outside and the Zamari shifts. Not away from me, but closer. His arms tighten around my waist as he presses his face deeper into the center of my thighs. My eyes widen as I freeze, hardly breathing as he inhales deeply before going still again.

He *is* sleeping. And I guess he should. We've been traveling for two days now with no rest and I have a feeling he was up all night keeping watch while I recklessly slept.

But the position of his nose. His face...

Heat rises in my cheeks as I run a hand through his hair again, taking liberties I shouldn't.

Without his hat and that glint in his eye, he looks like just another male. Not a killing machine. He looks almost... vulnerable. That stops the movement of my fingers as I blink at him in the dim light, a soft laugh making my chest rise and fall.

"What's so funny, Firespark?" His breath is hot, seeping right through the linen to spread across my clit and it's so intense I wonder why my underwear feels like it's nonexistent.

I stiffen at the sound of his voice, preparing myself for him to rise and face me, but the outlaw remains with his face tucked into my crotch. It's so inappropriate, so naughty, that in awkwardness I don't know how to respond.

I don't hate it.

I certainly shouldn't *like* it.

"You have no *ayahl*," he suddenly mutters, the vibration rumbling against my core.

I gasp a little before being able to contain the sound and his head shifts so his eyes find mine. They're lit now. No longer bled black like the last time he looked at me.

Forcing down the lump in my throat, I try to pretend that this whole situation, that the position he's in is normal and that it doesn't affect me at all. He's not human. He probably doesn't even know that he's at my most erogenous spot.

"Ay-al? I don't know what that is."

His gaze narrows a little as he watches me and I am instantly jealous of the fact he can see me, see every emotion my face betrays, while I can hardly see a thing.

"Where did you come from? Your people are not from this world...or mine."

I can't help the slight smile that floats with my words. "This is on a need-to-know basis?"

He shifts again slightly, just so he can take me in. The movement takes his face away from my clit and I release a breath of some relief. At least now, I can focus.

"No," he responds. "But I'll break this rule...for you."

My heart thumps hard and I force myself not to think too hard on his words.

"I'm from up there." I point above us. "The stars."

His eyes narrow a little more and I know I have to explain.

"I was born on a ship called the Voyager Genesis 311. The mothership. Three thousand humans from Homeworld Earth. Three thousand people seeking a new home." There's an immediate ache in my chest as I utter the words, and they fall on silence. When my gaze shifts down to the outlaw with his head still rested in my lap, I find his intense focus remains on me.

"I don't know of that planet."

He says it like he's traversed the stars far and wide...and then I realize he might have. I know nothing about him. I only know that like me, he's not from Ivuria 10 either.

A breath shudders through my chest as I continue. "You won't know of it. It's not in this star system."

I can almost feel his frown. "You said you were born on your mothership?"

Swallowing hard, I nod. Keeping the memories at bay is hard. Keeping the pain away even harder. I ache inside, and I try not to let him see.

"There was a problem. The...the life support that kept the cryopods working malfunctioned a little over seventy years before they were meant to arrive here."

"Here?" His tone is as if to say 'this cursed rock?', and a sad laugh huffs through my nose.

"They thought it was a utopia. They were wrong. But that wasn't the worst problem. The ship couldn't make the entire journey. Before I was born, over half of the people in cryo died before someone's pod malfunctioned and they actually woke up. My grandfather." I gulp again, pushing back at the pain. "He woke up the rest of them that were still alive. Found out the systems were failing. Diverted the remaining energy, hoping to keep everyone alive for the next seventy or so years."

The Zamari waits for me to continue and I take another breath and push on.

"And he did."

I gulp hard now, but the lump is stuck in my throat. I can't continue. Can't speak out loud the exact thing that rules my nightmares.

The Zamari's gaze shifts away from me to focus on the small hole now where a bank of sand is blocking the exit, only a narrow space left to mark where we can exit.

"Your people have no home like mine," he finally says.

I sniff, hating that I'm once again vulnerable before him. All the while realizing at the same time that he is making it easy for me to do so. There's no judgmental glare. No contradiction of the feelings coursing through me. No interruption of this unending process of grieving.

He is allowing me to feel. A stranger. Doing more for me than my own people ever have.

I swallow hard, looking away from him as I wipe away the tear that's escaped from my lids. "Where are you from?"

For a moment, I wonder why I bothered to ask. He's not going to tell me. Need-to-know basis and all that. Just like his name, this too will be a secret he keeps close. And that's to be expected. A male like him can't spill his secrets to every traveler he takes a job from. It would be bad for business.

"Kelon 4." His words make my attention snap back to him. "The third planet in a cursed system like this one."

Surprise has me hesitating before the words stumble from my lips. "Kelon 4? But you said—"

"That my people have no home?" His gaze shifts back to mine. "We don't. We travel the stars. Vagabonds at the mercy of our own desires."

"No home..." I pause, but my tongue is less wise than my brain. "No family either?"

His gaze travels over mine and I know he definitely won't answer that.

"None. Once a Zamari matures enough to procreate, he leaves to make a life of his own. I know not whether my brethren are alive. Whether my progenitors are still breathing."

He says it like he doesn't really think about it. Meanwhile, it's all I can think about. My mother. My father. The family I lost.

"Sounds lonely," I whisper and then, realizing what I said, I squeeze my eyes shut, silently berating myself. Who am I to comment on his way of life? It certainly seems to be working for him and his people. And, based on what I've seen so far, no Nirzoik could walk into a colony full of Zamari and turn them into slaves. Just a few oras and I already know that.

Silence falls between us, the storm the only sound breaking the lull.

"I have traveled for a long time," he finally says. "Through places worse than this."

Thank the gods he wasn't offended. "That's why you're so adapted to this place while I am..."

"Too delicate for a world like this."

I don't know whether it's a criticism or a compliment and more silence stretches between us. But I find it doesn't bother me. It's not like he isn't speaking the truth. It's the whole reason Comodre is in this predicament. We're not tough enough. The Nirzoik bend and break us like we're nothing.

Pulling air into my lungs, I lean back and stare into the darkness, his words repeating in my head.

"You're right," I whisper after a few moments. "I don't know why I've survived this long. I don't know why I survived from the start at all." *And a part of me feels guilty about that.* There were other, more useful people on that ship who would have done more for the colony. But I can't tell him that. I can't tell him because the words are stuck in my throat.

He doesn't reply. Just waits for me to continue. And the weight of everything I've been holding back from Kiana, Estella, even myself, presses hard against me.

"Something large hit our ship when we reached Ivuria 10's orbit. Breached us. Ripped a hole so large, the ship lost control. I remember my mother screaming..." My whisper stops short. I'm surprised I'm even uttering the words, but his silence is like a blanket filled with nothing but zero judgment, and I can't help myself but go on. "I remember her calling out my name as she and my father searched for me." My heart aches, but I press on. "I remember the mothership shuddering as the gravity controls came back online and I crash into the floor, only for the controls to go again and for my body to fly toward the ceiling." That lump in my throat grows larger, filling my windpipe, making it hard to speak. "I saw them." My throat gets tight. "I saw them as I floated there. My father. My mother. They were together. He was holding on to her while he tried to grip something in case the gravity came online again. She was frantic, calling for me and then she turned."

My voice cracks and for a moment, I stop.

The Zamari doesn't say a word. It's like he's not even there. And somehow that's exactly what I need. To talk about this to someone who will just listen. I don't need him to say anything. I've screamed at myself for too many nights. Gone through the scenario over and over again. And the guilt is always there. I don't need to hear him say it, too.

"My mother turned. Floating there, she saw me. I can't...I can't explain the look of relief in her eyes as she stretched for me. And then..." I pause again. The lump swells in my throat. "The gravity came back. Pulling everything with it. Everything, including all the untethered storage that had gone loose. A storage cabinet shot between us, pulled down by the stabilization."

The images are like a horror movie being replayed right before my eyes. I still remember the gray of the cabinet. The colorful drawings that were on it. Drawings I had made as a kid. We'd made the mothership our home.

"The cabinet...it moved faster than I could blink. One moment my parents are there. The next, I see that cabinet shooting through an airlock, pushing them along with itself, just moments before the airlock is torn off and emergency lockdown seals me behind the doors."

I shudder, the memory too vivid and too great. The sound of the storm outside melds with the screams in my memory, becoming almost deafening. I squeeze my eyes shut, forcing myself to continue. Knowing he doesn't need to hear any of this, but also realizing I've needed to do this for a long time. To tell this story to someone. To scream at the world and let out some of my pain.

"We fell to the surface. Only about one hundred of us survived." I can feel a tear making its way down my cheek and I let it run. I let some of the pain leave me. "And we've been trying to survive since then. Only…"

I sniff, opening my eyes as I wipe away the tear. He's said he didn't want to hear about the colony or the job but when my gaze falls back to his, his focus is still on me. He doesn't tell me to stop. In fact, he's so silent, his gaze so intense, that I get the sense he wants me to continue.

So I do.

"Our colony is small. We called it Comodre. One hundred or so settlers set up homes there in what we thought was free land. And we lived that way for about seven orbits. Now, only about thirty of us remain." I release another heavy breath. "There are sansa gems underneath the settlement, and we didn't know about it until an orbit or two ago. That's when the Nirzoik came. Claimed we built on their lands. Claimed we owe them for the seven orbits we've lived free." I pause, the anger I've felt over these rotations coming back to the fore. "They've set up outposts around Comodre. Track what's going out and coming in. We have few supplies. Little food. Little water. No medicine. No tech. They keep us dependent on them and force us to work the mines, mining sansa in exchange for credits that they collect." My lips press into a line as I pause again, waiting for the implications of what I said to sink in. "We can't survive for much longer. The whole future of Comodre... my species...it's...it depends on *me*. We have to do something."

A part of me is rigid, waiting for him to say "fuck this" and cop out of our whole agreement. Another part of me is desperate for him to say he'll still help.

"A single mercenary can't take down a whole legion of Nirzoik." His rumble sends a shiver through me even though his words aren't ones I want to hear. But then he lifts his hand, his finger tracing my cheek down to my jaw, brushing away the remnants of a tear, right before he eases up on his elbows and rises. "That's asking for death."

My heart drops as he takes up the little trunk that was still rested at my side, sets his hat on his head, and walks toward where his bike is buried underneath the sand.

Those luminous eyes find me and my pulse quickens as if some expectant thing is hanging in the air.

"Good thing you found me."

CHAPTER THIRTEEN

The Outlaw

One last job.

Guess I chose a good one.

I've never liked the Nirzoik, but hearing the human... hearing *Elsie's* story, I have a new reason to despise them. Ivuria 10 is infested with scum. The Nirzoik being just one set I'd be happy to put down.

Clearing as much sand as I can from my bike, I find the compartment I'm looking for. There are scratches all over the metal, some with deep grooves I'll have to pay attention to later. Even with pulling the bike in as far as I could, I still couldn't protect it. I can only imagine hers is in a much worse state. But we'll deal with that later.

Pulling the flat square of woven *frah* from where it's neatly folded in its compartment, I grip it in my fist before pausing, gaze shifting to where her bike's buried under the sand. I can't see it now with the heavy layer on top of it, but I know where it is. The entrance wasn't big enough to pull both bikes through and hers is still where the wind and all the danger that it brings can reach. That close to the storm, I risk getting cut by some stray metal shards if I venture too close.

And yet still, I move toward her bike anyway.

With the wind and flying particles, it takes some time to uncover the vessel and then some more to find the compartment where she hid her container of water. I grip the flask as soon as my fists close around it and step back, the freshly sliced wounds that have been dealt to my skin burning with the movement.

I snarl a little, but it's a small price to pay. I have not seen her eat a thing, and though her long garments hide much of her frame, I can still tell she hasn't been eating enough. Females need food. A warm nest. Zero stress.

It seems she has had none of that. At least, not since her kind fell here.

Her story about her colony, Comodre, is just confirmation of my suspicions. Something made her desperate enough for a journey like this. No matter the job, it always boils down to one thing: survival.

Turning, I head back to her. Her eyes are large as she widens them, possibly trying to see me better, and I activate and drop the light disc near her. It lights up the space and those blue eyes squint before adjusting to the glow.

I stretch the *frah* toward her with one hand, her water with the other, and her brows rise as she stares at the two objects. I watch her blink at them, those long pale lashes fluttering as thoughts as clear as the solar flares that escape Ivuria flick across her eyes.

"For me?" She whispers, as if she can't believe—no, as if she can't *comprehend* the kindness.

She takes the water first, taking a drink as color rises in her cheeks the longer she looks at the *frah*. With a slight tremble in her fingers, her cheeks growing redder, she takes the *frah* as well.

I can only stare at her. The increasing redness in her skin is concerning.

She's not ill. At least, I don't think so. Angry? But as she shifts and tugs the *frah* over her, I realize it's neither of those things.

She refuses to meet my gaze. Her cheeks are red...because she's embarrassed?

By what?

I try not to think on it. As a matter of fact, I force myself to move a few strides away from her, putting some distance between us. For her sake.

I took far too many liberties while she tended to my wound and it's haunting me now.

I can still feel the shadow of her lips, the sensation of her tongue, my *ayahl* is still unsettled, and my cock...

Fek, can't think about my cock.

Sitting on the inclined sand, I lean back, trying to ignore the female who, though silent, is pulling every bit of my attention.

Her lips...her tongue. That was no simple greeting. The way her hips bucked and pushed against me. Fek. Just the thought and I want to do it again.

It was a mating ritual. Had to be. And dead gods of Kelon 4 watch me, I can't let it happen again.

"So, what's the plan?" Her whisper finds me and I try not to look her way. For I know if my eyes settle on her, I will leave my position and all pretense of resistance will be forgotten.

"Plan?"

"Yea..." She pauses. "For the Nirzoik?" She pauses again before hurrying on. "I know it's a lot to ask. But I just want you to scare them off. Stay in Comodre for a little while. Make them think we have some protection. I-I meant to hire more mercenaries but until we can keep most of what we mine and I can afford..."

I shift my gaze to her then, at the same time that the light disc fades, the cavern going dim before lighting up again.

"It needs charging," I say in response to the worry in her eyes.

She nods. But she's not worried about the light. Even a fool would know that. She's worried about her people.

For a male who has never really cared about his own kind, it's a strange sensation watching her stare at the light, seeing the horrors pass through her memory.

Humans are communal, it is clear. Zamari are not.

But that doesn't mean I don't understand her pain. Because despite that my kind never settle in one place for too long, there's always that need...that pressing need that drives all Zamari to take to the stars, searching.

Searching for...*something*.

Only, I don't know what the fek I'm searching for.

"So?" she whispers after a few moments. Those eyes turn to me, worry and hope combined in their depths, and I wonder if I had a choice in the first place. When I first saw her in that drinkery, did the fates bring her there?

How can I say no to a being like this?

That look in her eyes, and all I want to tell her is that I'll make it all go away.

But I can't.

I *shouldn't*.

I can't become involved. At least, not more than this.

"Are you worried?" I ask, not betraying that I obviously know the answer.

Her smile comes but it's one etched with sadness. "A little. I have people that need me."

A family then. A mate?

I clench my teeth in annoyance I shouldn't feel.

"I'm offended." For the first time, I grin at her and her eyes fasten on my lips. Immediate thoughts of corruption and debauchery flash through my mind. I am no better than the Krykrill who thrive on fountains of perversion. "There's no need to worry, Firespark. I am here now."

The light disc flashes again before the light dims to less than half the usual glow. The cavern is suddenly cast in shadow and I catch the female still looking at me, eyes fastening on me as if she's using the last bit of light left just to see me.

Then she smiles, grips the *frah*, and wraps it around herself before settling down into the sand. Outside the wind screams as the light disc dies.

"Thanks for the blanket," she whispers and I assume she's referring to the *frah*.

There's no need to respond.

Dimming my eyes so she can't see their glow, I keep my gaze on her, my focus glued to her face as I watch her stare into the darkness above us, a mountain of thoughts on her mind. I watch her shamelessly, knowing she can't see me, and yet, this violation of her privacy does not weigh on my conscience. For I cannot pull my eyes away.

Not from her strange, entrancing face, or from the myriad of thoughts flashing through those eyes.

I watch as she slowly falls asleep, a yawn stretching her pretty lips before her lids begin to fall. And in the final moment, just before she falls asleep, her eyes settle on me and I see it clearly.

That worry? It's gone.

She's looking my way now, and I see hope.

CHAPTER FOURTEEN

Elsie

I wake to a soft scratching sound that makes me frown. There's a dull huff, and my eyes flutter open. I'm met with stark white walls and a mountain of sand around me. Only one thing is missing. The screeching sound of the storm.

We made it? It's over?

Another soft scratching sound and I rise on my elbows to see the Zamari at the cavern entrance. He's been up, probably hours before me, if he actually did go to bed. There's a path through the sand now, banks risen on either side of the cavern as he clears a path for our exit. He's just about finished pulling his rocket bike from underneath the heavy layer of sand when he speaks as if he knows I'm staring into his back.

"Time to go, Firespark."

Great. Two seconds awake and my cheeks are already warming at the utterance of that name.

I nod even though his head is still turned away from me, just because words can't come to my lips just yet. I yawn, pushing the sleep from my bones with a stretch that has the blanket surrounding me shifting. I look down at it, the dim light playing over the brown threads that were used to weave the fabric. I was warm and comfortable last night just because of him.

Gripping the thing, I rise and fold it before snatching up my water bottle and helmet from where I'd carelessly discarded them the night before. I slip the helmet on, and by the time I'm done, he's already cleared a path to the small exit. The sand looks considerably higher than it did the day before, and I realize I can't see my rocket bike anywhere.

When I move closer, I see that the dark metal of his bike is filled with scratches and scrapes that will take a long time to buff out. The pristine machine looks battered, and I can't imagine that mine even survived.

Something clenches in my chest.

I knew this would happen, he warned me yesterday, but the reality is still hard to face. That bike was the most expensive thing I owned.

I swallow hard, pushing away the tremor and holding my chin up. I can do this. Kneeling, I fall beside the Zamari as I set his blanket and the water bottle out of the way. Digging my hands into the sand, I work to help him clear a path for us. He stops working immediately and even though he doesn't look at me, I can tell he has something to say.

As if he doesn't want me to help him.

"My hand's fine. You bandaged it well," I say. "Plus, it's faster this way."

I reach forward again to dig my hands into the sand when his arm flashes out so quickly, I jerk. His fist curls around my wrist in the next second.

"It's sharp." His voice sounds...strange, and my brows furrow a little as I try to see his face, but he's not turning toward me. "The last thing you need, is me scenting your lifeblood right now."

My mouth opens and closes, not quite sure what to say. His words add more questions than they do answers. He shifts then, blocking the place where I was digging, his large frame making me feel small even though he's crouched.

The muscles in his back shift underneath his clothes as he works, and all I can do is rise and watch him finish the job. He does it quickly, much faster than I ever could have, and soon there's a groan and a shudder of sand as he pulls my rocket bike from under where it was buried.

He pushes it out first before turning and heading back for his, and all I can do is walk slowly to the thing that got me here in the first place.

The bike's mangled. Deep grooves cut into and bent the metal casing that's there to protect the engine. Some wires are exposed, and many are sliced in two. The rockets at the back look choked with sand, despite the zyka fluid. But even if I could clear them, the injector that leads from the engine must have been knocked off at some point because it's missing.

I step over to the thing, hand trembling slightly as I touch it. It's...gone.

There's a sound behind me and I pull my hand back, faking a smile as the Zamari exits the cavern. My breath stops in my throat as my gaze lands on him properly for the first time since I woke. His eyes have bled to black and once again, I'm transfixed by the dangerous beauty of this male.

His nostrils flare as he passes me, walking through the giant ribs of the creature that protected us last night, and as soon as his back is turned, I tilt my head and do a quick sniff of my armpits.

Do I stink? All I can smell is the xyleen oil that we use as moisturizer back in Comodre. Lifting my hand, the bandages are still intact. It can't be my blood. My gaze shifts back to him as he sets his bike up and fires on the engine. A blast of sand shoots out the back, but otherwise, the vessel hums a happy, almost silent sound, ready for departure.

Right. We have to go.

With a deep breath to steady myself, I take the last few moments to gather all the things I had in my bike. All that's worth tugging along with is the satchel that holds the morsel of food I'd been saving, and the navigation device I stole from the dead thug. I grab that and hurry to where the Zamari sits on his bike, waiting for me.

He watches me approach, that dark gaze not revealing a thing and yet I can feel it moving over my entire frame. I stop walking once I reach the bike and it hits me that I'll have to straddle him. He watches me, nose flaring again and I glance back at where my rocket bike rests.

It looks like a pitiful piece of mangled rubbish. Definitely won't get it to work. It wasn't even working well before.

Biting my lower lip, I push past the voice screaming in my head and climb on top of the Zamari's bike.

It's fucking big. Bigger than mine. Wider. And I almost feel cheeky as I slide down on the seat, my legs spreading to fit on either side of his thighs as I try to adjust myself. The seat on his isn't like mine was. His is slanted and no matter how I try to sit with a little space between us, my butt slides down the small decline, pressing my core right into the small of his back.

I gulp when his voice rumbles in his chest before he reaches back and grips my arm.

Without a word, he pulls my hand, forcing me forward. My chest hits his back, my legs tightening on his thighs as he reaches for my other hand and wraps them both around his chest.

"Hold tight."

That's all I hear before his bike shoots off. I can only squeal as my visor slides down and I press my face into his back. His bike moves fast. Faster than it was moving when we'd been traveling on separate vessels, and I realize that's because he'd been keeping pace with me all along.

We shoot across the plain and as soon as I can breathe again, I open my eyes.

Above us, the orange sky is clear, as if nothing happened the night before. Thin pink clouds float peacefully above us, and the air is clear and crisp. I squint as we go, trying to pick out just where we are now, but I have no clue. There are shapes in the distance, but we're too far for me to make them out.

"Do you know which direction to take?" I ask over the wind.

There's a rumble against my palms pressed into his chest and I swallow hard, trying not to think about the vibration, or that it travels right through me, skating a path down my arms to my breasts before shooting straight to my center.

"We have to take a detour." He turns his head slightly so I can hear. "These are the barren lands."

I glance around us. Everywhere on Ivuria is barren. For this to be called *the* barren lands...

But then I see just why a moment after. Those shapes I saw in the distance? The closer we get, the more I can tell what they are. Soon, we're passing them like a bullet cutting through the air.

Skeletons. Dried bone standing in the sand. We pass several and then some more. Enough that I unintentionally grip the outlaw harder, as if his strength is a surety that I can count on to not end up like the things that died here.

If there are skeletons out here, then there are creatures. And if there are creatures that are living, then that means they're the reason for the skeletons.

"These things...they died because of storms like the one that passed?" I hope my words carry a bit forward in the wind and I'm happy when he turns slightly, dark gaze finding mine.

"No."

His single utterance is enough to make me swallow hard.

When we zoom past a skeleton that's just as large as the one we sheltered in the night before, I begin to worry. Shifting one hand from his chest, I lift the navigator still in my hand. It takes me a few moments to punch in Comodre's coordinates and when I finally do, the green light from the navigator tells me we're heading in the right direction. Steadying my breathing, I try not to focus on the skeletons we're passing by, even when that number increases until we're flying over a sea of half-buried bones.

"Shouldn't we have gone back to the path we were taking before the storm?"

He shakes his head. "Not after the storm. Scavengers will be hiding along the paths now. Waiting to pounce on injured travelers. Unless you want a trail of blood leading back to your settlement, I advise against us turning around."

His meaning is clear, and I nod. Pressing my face into his back, I go silent and pray that we don't end up with the skeletons surrounding us.

I'm rigid the entire time the bike shoots across what can only be classed as a graveyard and when the sands finally turn clear again, free of a sea of bones on the surface, I let out a breath of relief.

Lifting the navigator, I see we're still going in the right direction. I allow myself to relax, at least, as much as I can. The bike moves smoothly, no hiccupping or jerking, no stalling or coughing, but still I'm pressed against the hardness of his body and now that we're not in direct danger, my mind is going to other things.

I try to think of something else. Not the way every slight movement rubs my core against the base of his spine. Or how my breasts are squashed against the hard planes of his back. I try not to even breathe because each breath feels like I'm writhing all over him. And that only brings back thoughts of the night before. How good he felt as his tongue dived into my mouth.

I didn't expect him to kiss me back. Didn't expect him to understand or even know what I was doing. And I certainly didn't expect it to feel so good. Pulling my lower lip between my teeth, I close my eyes and try to purge my thoughts.

My core clenches anyway.

Shit. Fuck. I should really think about some alone time with my fingers and some candlelight as soon as I can. It's not right for me to be reacting this way. But...

I bite my lip hard as I release the tension in my shoulders and lean into the Zamari some more. I almost groan. The planes on his back, each muscle sculpted and hard. I could oil myself and writhe all over him with zero hesitation. The bike jerks as we go over a mound of sand that pushes my core even harder against him. I squeeze my eyes tight.

If he knew what I was thinking right now, he'd probably think I'm such a pervert. But...gods...I've never been affected by any man like this before. Sure, I've had fantasies, but the Zamari is like a wet dream come true. Dangerous. Forbidden. And yet tender in a way I could not have expected. The bike jerks again, pressing me harder against him and my core throbs.

It's the kindness, isn't it? He's drop-dead gorgeous, dangerous, and he's kind. Fuck me.

I tell myself I'll allow the thoughts this once, and then I must get my shit together. That's when there's a rumble in his chest that makes my eyes fly open.

I don't know what it is. He's rumbled in his chest before.

It's not the first time I've felt it and yet, something about this instance makes me suddenly alert.

"What is it?" I glance on either side of us, taking in the view as far as I can see. The plains look empty. Dead as they usually are.

"We're being followed."

He says it so simply, so matter-of-factly, that a shiver goes down my spine.

My head turns sharply as I look behind us. There's a small sand cloud following in our wake, but I can't see any other bikes through it. I look to our left, our right, nothing. That's when I spot the first wreckage.

Part of an old rocket bike, half-buried in the sand. We zoom past it before, not long after, there's another.

"Crashes?" I ask. "Engine trouble maybe?" Then a chill goes down my spine. "Scavengers?" I look behind us again, squinting to see through the dust cloud, but I can't see or hear any other bikes.

"Worse."

His utterance does nothing for the mounting panic warming up in my gut.

"What?" I feel stupid asking, but fear wins over my tongue anyway.

"Hold on."

If I thought we were going fast before, I was wrong. The Zamari amps the power and there's a boom like an actual bullet is shot from the rockets at my back. They fire blue before we move so fast, the world blurs around me before my brain can catch up with the speed.

If anyone's coming after us, there's no way they can—

But then I hear it. Over the rush of my pulse and the sound of the wind against my helmet, I hear it. I almost don't want to turn around. Almost don't want to believe that sound is coming from a real thing.

Turning slowly, I look over my shoulder, pure, unbridled terror shooting right through me as I see something erupt from the sand.

A scream lodges in my throat as I hear the Zamari shout my name.

"Elsie!" He reaches behind him, gripping my ass with one hand as he holds me steady a moment before the speed amps up again. "Hold on!"

I can only stare at the horror unfolding behind us. A monster that could have only originated from someone's nightmares.

The worm is huge, its mouth a terrible, tooth-filled orifice that spreads wide as it roars at us. It's so tall, we fall in its shadow as it rears back and bellows. I cling tighter to the Zamari, feeling the rumble of the bike beneath us as he pushes it to its limits.

As the monster behind us crashes back down, its head disappears into the sand as its body curves, running like a train, segments disappearing as it burrows back into the ground. In that moment, I think it's gone. I *hope* it's gone. That's right before the dust cloud behind us erupts again, sand shooting everywhere and showering down on us as the thing shoots from beneath the sand once more, closer this time.

The landscape blurs into a streak of brown and orange as we dart across the barren terrain, and still the beast is managing to keep up. I can see its grotesque teeth, each one as large as a man, gnashing in anticipation. Its mouth closes suddenly, the flaps coming together like the petals of a flower as it dives under the sand again.

My heart constricts in my chest. It's going to do it again.

The last time it dived, it came up even closer behind us. This time, it will be right on top of us. Fuck!

"We're not going to make it." It's a whisper to myself, even as the realization settles within me. "But we *have* to." I know what we need to do.

I release my hold on the Zamari, letting go of my little satchel with food and the navigator too. There's no time to stash them away properly. My hand goes to my skirt, gripping my blaster and pulling it from its holster. Over his shoulder, the Zamari's gaze meets mine, a look in his eyes I can't quite read as I put my trust into his one arm still holding my ass pressed against him.

Some kind of understanding passes between us as I twist in his grasp.

It's perfect timing.

The beast behind us roars as it exits the sand just a few feet behind us. The hoverbike destabilizes for a moment and I would have lost my balance if not for the pressure of that hand holding me steady.

Raising my blaster, I look down the sights as I pull the trigger.

The blast knocks me sideways and I bump into the Zamari's shoulder.

"Again," he orders, but he doesn't have to tell me twice.

The weapon charges again and I release another blast, hitting the worm in its long neck. It screeches and I think that will be enough to at least scare it away, but the bastard doesn't budge. It gets angrier.

A blob of fluid I don't want to know the origins of falls on us as the thing screeches above us. It dives and in just one moment, I realize it's not diving into the sand again. It's diving for *us*.

Desperate, the blaster charges just in time for me to fire off another round.

I see the teeth descending from above, the blobs of saliva falling from the air to land on us, and I see...death.

And still, I can't give up.

It happens in slow motion, that moment where you see death coming for you and the whole world slows down. And if the death lord was here, I'd tell him to fuck the hell off.

People are depending on me. I can't die like this.

The blaster burns in my hand as I force it to charge again, my fists trembling with how hard I pull down on the trigger. I'm knocked back again as the laser shoots from the mouth of my weapon, going straight into the creature's mouth.

"Fuck you," I whisper, the breaths fogging up my visor. And I think that's it. It's dead now.

Wrong.

The Zamari swerves suddenly, throwing us into a dizzying turn, just in time for the worm to crash into the spot that we just were. For a moment, the world is a chaotic spin of sky and sand and then we're racing in a new direction, the worm's thunderous roars still chasing us.

It disappears underground and I stare at the spot, not believing the creature is still alive. Its body vanishes underneath the sand like some great snake once more and I hold my breath.

That's when an arm snakes around my midsection.

I screech in surprise as I'm lifted, the Zamari taking me in front of him in a movement I can't even understand. One moment, I'm behind him, thighs fastened against his, the next, we've switched positions. His thighs squeeze mine as he settles me in front of him. Gripping both of my hands, he places them on the handlebars of his bike.

I watch as he punches buttons on his control panel, his face right beside mine and a hardness is in his gaze that I haven't seen before. When he finally looks at me, a chill goes down my spine.

"Ride," he says. "Don't stop. No matter what happens."

My stomach lurches as I hear the roar behind us and the Zamari releases me. With wide eyes, I look over my shoulder to see him stand on the back of the bike, blaster in hand, a wicked blade in the other. He crouches slightly, knees bent as the creature bursts through the sand once more.

We sway with the sudden disturbance but I manage to keep us steady. Not worried about the bike stalling like mine would if I tried to push it too hard, I press more power into the engines, forcing us even faster.

One look behind me again and I see the worm towering above us. It dives again and I scream for the Zamari to hold on. I only manage to swerve, barely missing the beast before my world stops.

I see it happen, but I don't believe it. See the sand showering down as the worm dives. Feel the moment the bike jerks as the Zamari launches himself into the air. And the moment he's airborne as I swerve. The same moment the worm dives, mouth open, sharp teeth glinting.

They collide. Or rather, the worm's mouth opens wider as it takes him whole. Swallows him. In one bite.

"No!" Something in my chest shatters at the sight and I lose control of the bike, spinning into a dizzying cloud of sand as I hold on to the handlebars with all I can.

I'm thrown from the bike, hitting the ground hard with sand raining down on me. My helmet makes a dull thud that reverberates through my skull as it hits something hard and the visor becomes useless with the amount of small cracks suddenly threading through its surface, making it hard to see.

Pain shoots through my entire being and for a moment, I wonder if I'm still alive.

Struggling with the helmet, I manage to pull it off my head, a deep breath pulling into my nose as I take in sand-filled air. I cough, something that tastes like dirt and blood in my mouth as my lungs protest the particles.

I can hardly see as I first rise on my hands and knees before making it to my feet.

The entire area is filled with a thin layer of dust and I cough again before slapping my hand over my nose and mouth. Staggering forward, I move in the direction I think is the right one. Off to the side, I see the dark shape of the rocket bike where it landed and I shift my gaze from it back to the surroundings, eyes squinting as I search for something, anything, to say the Zamari is still alive.

But there's silence. As the sand settles and the air becomes clear some more, there is complete, deafening silence.

My chest hurts as I force myself to breathe. Force myself to not give up hope.

I stagger on, turning in slow circles as I try to orient myself. There are not even furrows in the sand to tell me where the creature went down. But I don't stop. Don't stop looking until I feel it. A tremor in the sand beneath me.

My heart's thundering in my chest, so much that as I stare at the thin layer of sand vibrating underneath my feet, at first my brain can't understand just what the hell is happening. Not until the vibrations become harder and it's clear.

The worm.

It's coming back for more.

I scatter, my legs pushing me to move out of the way and not stumble as I run. I hear it the next moment as it rises, a shower of sand raining down on me as a roar splits the air at my back. I turn to see the towering creature swaying above me, its head turned to the heavens, petals wide open and teeth gnashing as it lets out another mind-shattering screech.

I stop running as something within me changes. Something I don't expect or understand. My fear disappears only to be replaced by the one emotion that has floated underneath it all. Anger.

I look at the fucking thing as it twists, turning to face me and for a moment, it's just me and it. One human female against this giant menace. I see my past. I see the mothership. I see me and the others struggling to make a home on this cursed rock. And then I see little Kiana. I see her face. Those big brown eyes set into that angelic face framed by her unruly raven hair. And I see the hope in those innocent eyes.

I'm fucking tired of not being able to just live!

The rage flows through me like fire and I grip the blaster still in my hand, a throat-ripping scream leaving my being as I aim at the thing before me, point and shoot.

It screams, the first blast hitting one of its petals, and sways with the impact. I don't fucking stop. My blaster is slow to charge but I overheat it anyway, ignoring the burn against my palm as I hold down the trigger, forcing it to unload shot after shot. Pain shoots through my palms, but I don't stop. Not when my wrists start shaking with the pain, not when the blaster begins to glow red in my hands, not even when my vision goes blurry from tears running down my face. Tears I'm not strong enough to hold back.

The worm sways, screeches cutting through the air and probably alerting scum as far as a thousand leagues from here. But I don't stop. I unload everything until the blaster fizzles in my hand.

That's when I see it. Something that isn't quite right. Through the blurred vision caused by my tears, I see the neck of the worm distort. At first, it's slight, slight enough that it could be nothing. But then it happens again and suddenly a fist with a sharp blade punches through.

My heart stops, my whole being freezing as I stare up at the thing in disbelief.

That's why it hasn't dived yet. Its last meal wasn't quite successful. The Zamari is still alive!

With renewed determination, I continue aiming for the head, unloading blast after blast as I watch that fist disappear inside the worm's body only to reappear again as he slices through another spot. He's slicing it apart from the inside out and the thing sways in the air, unable to dive underneath the sand to protect itself or get rid of the creatures attacking it.

It twists downward and my heart lurches into my throat as it heads right for me. The pain in my palm as I grip the blaster, firing one last desperate shot, is nothing compared to the rush of adrenaline that shoots through me. I dive at the last second, rolling on the hot sand as a heavy thump sounds at my back.

The creature crashes into the ground, a cloud of dust and sand rising as I scramble to my feet. Blaster still in hand, I shudder as my eyes lock on the worm's massive body. It's not moving.

One step then another, I force myself forward even as my knees want to give out. The blaster in my hand hurts, but I don't manage to let it go until I round the worm's head. The petals are huge and limp, the jagged teeth still visible as I walk around it. But there is zero movement.

It's...dead.

Relief shoots through me at the same time that I suddenly drop the blaster, letting it fall from my fingertips even though holding on to it for longer would have been no use. That last shot it managed to give was the last time I'll ever be using it. The barrel's spent. And so is the skin on my palms.

Panic mixing with hope, my heart hammers against my

chest as I run, following the body of the creature until I spot him. He's lying in the sand, half of his body still within the animal, the other half coated with thick, transparent slime.

I fall on my knees in the sand beside him, hoping beyond hope that he's really still alive. The moment I fall there, that green gaze of his finds mine.

"Firespark," he says, and I choke on a sob or a laugh, I'm not sure.

But then he grins. This foolish, foolish male grins and for some reason, it lights a flame within me.

His gaze shifts to the heavens and his chest shudders. For a moment, I think he's having a seizure before I hear the rumble in his chest. His mouth opens, and a deep rich laugh leaves his lips. I ease back, sitting on my legs, for I can only watch him in shock.

He laughs, the notes rich and wonderful as they float on the still air.

It's a sound so full of life, so utterly unexpected in the face of our recent brush with death, that it's almost surreal. I watch him. I sit there, barely believing what just happened, and I watch him laugh. Soon, the tension and fear that had gripped me moments ago start to melt away.

His laughter becomes contagious, and despite the absurdity of our situation, a smile tugs at my lips. And then I'm laughing too. It starts small. A giggle. And then my shoulders shake and laughter escapes my lips. Soon, my head tilts back and I glimpse the peaceful clouds above us, floating in all their glory, the whole planet oblivious to what just happened. We almost died, and the world keeps turning.

I laugh. Because it's all so absurd.

When my laughter finally dies down, I sober to find the Zamari's green gaze on me. Studying me. Watching me in such a way that I become aware of myself.

Our gazes lock and remain there, neither looking away first.

I don't know why I do it. Why I reach out, fingers shaking as I brush away some of the slime that coats his face.

"You're a mess," I whisper, but my tone is gentle. Gentle in the way that only Kiana has ever heard me speak.

His gaze travels over my face like a scanner collecting data. "But not hideous, right?" he teases, and I can't help but smile.

"Not hideous."

He breathes a soft laugh through his nose before he eases upright on his elbows, gaze shifting to the creature before his focus moves to the sky.

"This is far too much meat."

For a second, I have no clue what he's referring to till he crawls the rest of the way out of the thing. There are squelching sounds and I almost puke in my mouth. Standing, he runs a hand along the side of the worm, studying it.

"Meat? Don't tell me you're considering eating that thing."

He chuckles and the sound is warm. "Not me." He looks above us again. "But others will. And they will come." His face suddenly grows serious. "Such bounty is rare in these lands."

His words sober me up too, and I try not to brace on my hands as I rise. I might be able to block most pain, but my palms are raw.

"We need to find shelter," he says, gaze scanning the plain. "Water."

I nod again.

"The bike?"

I point to where the bike tumbled into the sand on the other side of the carcass and he jerks his chin in a nod.

"Lead the way, Firespark."

I nod again, turning and walking off, my heart beating an unsteady rhythm. It feels surreal, stepping past the large head of the creature that almost killed us, but as I move I know that's not the reason the thin hairs at the back of my neck stand on end.

It's not because I almost died...again.

It's because something's shifted between us, and even as I lead him to the rocket bike I can feel it. As sure as the dark sun above us I feel it. As sure as his gaze that tracks my every movement.

The unspoken bond that's forming between us hangs in the air, almost like a new force of nature. We just survived the unthinkable, and it makes me think we have a good shot at surviving whatever the Nirzoik throw at us.

I feel his presence behind me, a steady and reassuring force amidst the chaos of this unforgiving world.

When we reach the bike, I pause to glance back at him. Our eyes meet, and in that silent exchange, there's an acknowledgment of everything that's unsaid.

"We should get going," I finally say, breaking the moment.

He nods, a slight smile playing on his lips as he lifts the bike and steadies it. One swing of his leg, and he straddles the big machine, those green eyes finding me again. "Ready, Firespark?"

There's a glint in his eyes. An invitation. And as I climb onto the bike, wrapping my arms around him this time without even being prompted, I realize something I didn't expect to feel when I left Comodre on this journey.

I know this is a job and that his only loyalty to me is the credits I promised to pay him...but even then I know...with him by my side, I feel like I can take on whatever comes next.

I feel like I can take on anything.

CHAPTER FIFTEEN

The Outlaw

Sweet mercy is the moment Ivuria hides behind a cloud that isn't a mere wisp in the sky.

The shadow cast down on us eases some of the pressure of the heat, and allows me a moment to breathe.

We've been traveling for oras in the wrong direction, but I haven't the guts to tell the female. She's exhausted, half-starved, and dying of thirst. I'd seen it while she slept. That only her will alone was what she was surviving on. But now, after that fight with that sandworm, the last of her energy has been spent.

Even though her arms are around me, they grow slack as the leagues pass beneath us. Her head lolls against my back and I know she's trying to keep it together. To not let me know she's struggling in the heat without water and food. Her only focus is on getting back to her colony and whatever supplies she had were to last her until then. But now she has no supplies and I can't take her back like this.

That would be like walking into a trap we've set ourselves.

So I follow my *ayahl*. I let it lead me and as the clouds above us grow thicker, I know it's taking me the right way. The terrain slowly changes from sandy plain to jagged outcroppings of rock rising toward the sky.

I inhale, pulling the warm air into my lungs. Water. It's close by. I can taste it on my tongue. And we can't reach it soon enough. Dried sandworm saliva has turned flaky on my scales, a constant reminder of what we just endured.

When I'd launched myself toward that thing, a sort of thrill that shouldn't have been present shot right through me. I was facing death. My existence finite. And yet...I'd never felt more alive. But there was something else. Something that also spurred me into that insane move to kill the beast. I frown slightly, watching my bike eat the distance between us and our destination.

This is above being paid for a job. I didn't jump into the mouth of that beast out of loyalty to my task or the promise of credits.

I did it because if I didn't kill the thing, it would have gone after *her* next.

Fek.

The warmth at my back pulls my thoughts back to the female, and with it comes another slew of emotions I'm not allowed to feel.

She came back for me.

I told her to go. She has no debt of loyalty to me. She could have taken my bike. Escaped with it. Sold it for more credits than she realizes it's worth. She could have left me to die in that beast. But she returned.

This stranger who doesn't need me more than the service I can provide, my protection, came back for me.

Either she's more desperate for my help than I realized, or...

My jaws clench, refusing to continue that train of thought. Instead, I push the bike to continue onward. To get us where we need to go.

"Almost there, Firespark," I whisper over my shoulder, the same moment I turn to see exactly what I'm searching for.

A cave hidden far within the rock. One that's difficult to spot, nestled in between a series of large outcroppings. I guide the bike toward it, taking care that we fit.

"Wh-where is this?"

I can sense when she lifts her head, looks around. Feel when she stiffens against me.

"Water." It's all the explanation she needs, and I feel the moment she perks up a little. Now, I can really taste it on my tongue and I follow my *ayahl*, letting it lead me to the source.

The moment we enter the cave, I know we've found a bit of paradise.

It's cool within, a stark contrast to the blazing heat just outside its walls. The water sits quietly in a little rock pool, rays of light shining on its surface from a natural hole in the rock right above it. There's a small pool that empties into the big one and above that, berries grow on a bush sticking out from the rock. Just the sight of that alone and I'm transfixed.

Nothing grows on Ivuria 10.

There's a mumble as the female shifts behind me and lifts her head. Her eyes widen and she's suddenly more alert.

"Where are we? This place is..."

I stop the bike, steadying it and she hops off, taking a few steps forward, wide eyes on the water in the pool not far from us.

"How did you find this?"

I lean the bike against the rocky wall, killing the engine,

before I turn to face her. How can I tell her it's because I can smell the water? Taste it. That my *ayahl* led me to this place like there was a beacon calling me to it. That the reason she has not seen me stockpiling water and resources, the same reason I hardly drink or eat, is because I haven't been hungry for many sols...and worse yet, my drink of choice is the very thing running in her veins.

My gaze slips to her neck now, to the soft skin there, and to the vein throbbing so enticingly beneath. Her throat moves, catching my attention next and it takes everything within me to drag my gaze back to her eyes.

"Luck," I finally say.

She smiles. "You seem to be a very lucky male."

She has no idea.

I can't pull my eyes away as she steps closer to the pool. It's safe. My *ayahl* hasn't alerted me to anything dangerous, so I let her go. Watch as she crouches at the edge, skimming the surface with her fingertips before she winces and pulls her hand back.

She's hurt.

I take a step forward before stopping myself.

This isn't my business. She's not mine to take care of. Never will be. It's doing things like this that makes the lines blur. And so I plant my feet on the ground. Clench my teeth. Force my *ayahl* to shut the fek up.

"Hey," she shoots a glance over her shoulder, and I plant my feet harder onto the sandy ground. The light coming in from that hole in the ceiling plays over the flying strands of her hair, making them shine gold...like she's some kind of goddess descended from the star itself.

Have I dreamt her up? Is any of this even real?

"Do you think it's safe to drink?" Her cheeks color as if her question warrants embarrassment. "It's just...my water's gone and—"

I jerk my chin toward the smaller pool. "Drink from that one. You can bathe in this." I point to the bigger one. Her cheeks color again. Gods...I need to leave. I need distance. "I'll keep watch."

She nods at me, those wide eyes tracking me as I leave the hole to get some air. Fek me. What in Ivuria is going on?

Stepping outside the cave, I scan the outcroppings. It's so silent and still out here that I can hear every single sound the female makes inside the cave. The almost silent shuffle of her boots against the sand. I track her as she moves, even without looking in to see her. Know she's taken a few steps around the rock pool. Certain of the moment she holds her breath, a slight shuffle of sand telling me she's kneeled and is looking into the water. And then another shuffle when she stands. There's that soft release of breath, and then I hear the rustle of fabric as she removes her garments.

Clenching my teeth, I step farther away, forcing my back against the rough wall as I stare up into the sky. And still, I can't force away the image being drawn in my mind.

Is she pale all over, too? Does she have scales underneath those garments? A tail? Ridges along her spine? Fur? There are mounds on her chest. Felt them pressed tight against me while we were riding. Try as I might, I can't pull away from the thought that she's now completely bare in there. Even focusing on the dead sky above me, my cock hardens once more in my trouse and the agitation in my ayahl grows.

I plant my boots harder into the sand. I will remain here. I. Will. Not. Enter.

I keep my promise, reaching for my blaster and twirling the thing around one claw. Beautiful machine. But my thoughts keep drifting back to the female. I hear the moment she dives into the pool, the soft gasp and then the moan that leaves her throat and my teeth clench again. Sliding the blaster back into its holster, I remain rigid against the rock. Can't move because I'm sure I'll do something that's simply insane.

I'm only outside for about half an ora when I hear a scream. My life organs drop.

I move quicker than lightning, darting back inside the cave, gaze bleeding to black the moment I enter. I pick up two life signs immediately. Her warmness glowing in the center of the pool and a smaller thing down in the water.

I don't think, I just move, using my *ayahl* to guide me as I dive.

The water's just the right bit of cool against my scales and they ripple, flashing color before snapping back down. I reach her in the next instant. She's thrashing, trying to get out of the water and when I wrap my arms around her, she shrieks and thrashes some more. A well-aimed kick hits me right in the gut and I grunt in surprise.

"It's me, Firespark." I pull her against me, treading the water as my gaze lights up, scanning the depths for whatever she's trying to get away from. I feel the moment she calms, no longer fighting to get away from me as she realizes I'm not some monster who has come to consume her.

Ha. She would not like that experience. Getting swallowed by *any* creature is not one I would recommend. But she should still beware. Because I *can* consume her. In other ways. Ways that would make her writhe and scream in ecstasy. By the gods, only a thread of control is preventing me from doing so. I could almost grunt in laughter, but all sense and decorum leaves my mind when her arms wrap around my neck.

Wide-eyed, she presses into me and I suddenly become aware of *everything*. Her legs wrapping around my torso. The softness of her entire being.

Heat blooms right through me as I ignite against her body heat.

She's bare. Utterly and completely bare. And that soft, pale body is flush against mine.

"There's something in the water," she pants, and I finally see her face.

Rivulets run down from her wet hair. No longer in its braid, it hangs down her shoulders. Her pink lips look rosy and swollen from the water's cold. Her skin's been washed off of all the dirt, sand, and blood. I see now the little dots that decorate the skin on her nose like an inbuilt marker I never noticed before.

"We have to get out." She glances around the surface, legs tightening around me, and my brain goes hazy. This has never happened before. No female has ever simply touched me and made me go straight to basic instinct. I have to focus.

She doesn't realize what she's doing. Too caught up in whatever fear has gripped her. Her wide eyes flick over the surface before her legs suddenly tighten again, pulling me in against her center as she screeches, writhing against me.

"It's there!" She points behind me, legs jerking even though she's tied herself to me. "It touched me! I felt it!"

I turn in the water slowly, eyes glued to her face even though she doesn't realize.

My *ayahl* isn't concerned with whatever's making her scared. All it's concerned about is reaching out to her. That only means whatever's gotten her so afraid is harmless. It wraps around her now and she shivers again.

She's so focused on whatever's in the water with us, her fear is causing her to ignore the hard rod pressing up through my trouse against her center.

I can't pull my eyes away from her. Can't focus on anything except that soft heat pressing into me.

I want her.

She jerks again, eyes wide. "There!"

When I turn, I see the thing floating just beneath the surface.

I lower us in one short dive and she screams again, wrapping tighter around me. A rumble goes through my chest, the sensation so pleasurable I'm unable to stop myself from what happens next.

One hand snakes down, gripping her naked ass and another growl goes through me. It's soft. Grippable. Zamari females are not like this. This complete softness on the entirety of her frame? Human females are incredibly delicate.

Is it bad that I enjoy it?

I growl, a rumble in my chest as I grab the little creature and take it back up to the surface with us.

I've never questioned my morals before. There was never a need to. My *ayahl* has never led me astray. It is a perfect judge of character, guiding me ever since my birth. Why would it betray me now?

But with this female...

I balance her with one hand, steadying her as she pulls in a deep breath of air, trying not to enjoy the feel of her hot skin against my palm or the roundness of her behind in my grasp. Bringing the other hand around, I lift my arm so we can both see.

The creature in my hand wiggles and thrashes just like the female in my arms was, its big eyes wide with terror as it struggles to get away. Thin tentacle arms wrap around my wrist, sending minute shockwaves through my skin as it tries to harm me. I could almost laugh.

"This?" I rumble.

Her wide eyes stare at the thing. "*That's* what it was?" Pink lips move as she speaks, threatening to take all my attention and

I can't help but wonder what she tastes like now, with the cool water on her lips, her hot breath just underneath. The contrast must be godly.

"It's an octo—" She squinches her brows. "My grandmother told me what they used to call those things on Homeworld Earth. A pooze? Octopooze?" She shakes her head. "Doesn't matter. I thought it was something else. It felt...bigger."

Her cheeks slowly color as she suddenly goes still. Wide eyes turn to me before slipping down from my eyes, moving to my nose, my lips, my chin... Her gaze travels to my jaw, down my throat, my chest, until it meets those delectable round mounds on her chest. Another thing Zamari females don't have. They're squished against me in the most delectable way, and her eyes widen even more at the sight.

"Oh gods!" Her wide eyes fly to mine. "I'm so sorry. I—"

She detaches herself, arms releasing from around my neck, legs from where they're wrapped around me and I growl a warning, hand tightening on her rump.

She stills.

I allow my gaze to travel over her face as I lift the little creature higher into the air. "What do you want me to do with this?"

She blinks at me. "Don't kill it, if that's what you're asking me. This is probably its pool and I swam in it. It was probably just trying to defend its territory, that's all."

"Something you admire?"

She pulls her bottom lip into her mouth, gaze averting. She doesn't answer for a few moments, but her gaze shifts to my arms as I release the torturous little creature, still busy trying to shock me with all its strength. She watches it swim away to the depths of the pool, quickly getting away from us.

"I admire a lot of things." Her lashes dip as she looks up at me through them, and my cock throbs hard in my trouse.

I tread water for a few moments, not sure I want to break the tension between us, but knowing the moment will come all too soon.

"Are you finished washing?"

She nods and I tighten my arm around her some more. As I move toward the pool's edge, she holds on to my shoulder, keeping her legs around me, but doesn't meet my eyes again. I climb out with her still in my grasp and the tension mounts between us. Walking over to my bike, I grab the frah and shake it out before setting it on the ground. When I kneel and she slides from my grasp, I watch those cheeks grow red again as one hand rises to cover those mounds on her chest and the other settles at the apex of her thighs—as if every other part of her isn't visible. As if she's not mesmerizing either way.

Bare in every sense. No fur. No scales. No ridges. Just soft, pale skin.

"I, uh, I washed my clothes," she says. "So I have to wait. You didn't have to get your blanket wet. They'll dry soon enough."

My brows rise. Impressed. I'd only been gone for half an ora.

Rising, I put some distance between us, allowing her some space to breathe. No, really, I'm putting some space between her and the predator in her midst. Maybe a dip will calm my nerves, but her gaze snaps to mine as I release my vest.

"Um, what are you doing?"

I shrug. "I need to wash too."

Her cheeks color again. "Ok. Um, I'll...give you some privacy." She wraps the *frah* around her frame and makes to rise. But I'm already moving toward the water, my tunic in my hand.

I unfasten my trouse next, letting it fall from my hips as I reach the pool. Grabbing my hat, I let it fall right at the pool's edge, just as a little gasp comes from behind me, making my lips twitch. I dive into the pool next, the sight of her wide eyes on me all I needed to see.

She's watching me...just like I couldn't take my eyes off her. And suddenly, that's all I need.

CHAPTER SIXTEEN

Elsie

He's underwater for far too long before his head suddenly breaks the surface.

I startle, breath pulling sharply into my nose.

I don't know how he does it. How his gaze immediately finds mine at every instance. As if his senses fixate on me alone whenever I'm near. An automatic homing reflex.

Not like I'm his home or anything, or that I have any claim on his male.

I bite my lip, trying to ground myself. I'm getting ahead of myself. But what's worse than that is that his gaze makes something inside me respond. My heart beats a little faster. My pulse quickens. My throat goes dry. And every nerve ending on my skin feels activated and alert.

He watches me with only half of his head above the surface, the water hovering just below his eyes. He looks like something dangerous waiting for me to make some mistake so he can pounce. Why doesn't that freak me out? Why does it make threads of electricity skitter across my spine instead?

Can he breathe under water? I don't even know. Can't even ask because my tongue's currently stuck in my throat.

I should look away. Maybe in Zamari culture, staring has no social implications. Stare at a human too long and they get uncomfortable. Stare at a human male too long and he thinks you want to fuck him. Is that what the Zamari thinks I'm saying to him now? That I want to fuck him? Do I?

The question makes me swallow as if to cool my insides, which have suddenly gone alight. And still, I can't pull my gaze away.

We kissed. Well, *I* kissed *him,* and he responded. He responded, and it felt so good. But even in the haze of the moment, the rational part of me knows this fiery attraction sparking to life between us spells only trouble. He's an outlaw and I'm...I'm just a girl from Comodre. And though he may not seem like the dangerous male I've hired, I can't forget that's exactly what he is.

I repeat that in my head like a mantra, even as my body continues to betray me. I can't pull my eyes away as he dips his head under the water before rising again. He does it so effortlessly, it doesn't even look like he's treading the water. Running a hand through his slick hair, his eyes find me once more. This time, I can see his entire face. The rivulets of water that run from his hair down his jaw. The way they move over the contours of his cheekbones then jaw.

I repeat the mantra harder, pressing my lips together to refrain from licking them. To refrain from so obviously displaying my thirst for flesh.

But gods know...

I freeze as if caught doing something illegal when he

suddenly rises from the pool. All senses fade as I'm momentarily shocked into just sitting there, staring at him.

The water slides down his scales in a way that makes each drop look like it's a wanton, sentient thing caressing his skin, not wanting to let go but cling on forever. Now, in this warm glow coming from the hole in the top of the cave, his scales change in color right before my eyes. Like a wave of purple and pink stardust sliding across his skin, his scales release the water before turning bronze once more and suddenly he's dry. I should look away now.

If only. I have no self-control. I can't pull my eyes away because there is an even more interesting thing than the color change in his scales. Something still holding my focus.

He turns and walks off to the side of the cave, reaching into the smaller pool there. With his hands cupped, he gathers some water and turns back toward me.

Rippling muscles shift and move as he steps my way, his chest like something carved by a higher being, the power in those thighs making me think of darker things, and the rod hanging between them...

My lips go dry. My throat. My mouth. My tongue darts out, wetting my lips as I fight to pull my gaze from the monster hanging between his legs.

I've never seen a cock like that before. Never seen something so frickin' large, even when flaccid. It's like a thick bronze shaft that rises the longer I stare at it, right until it's staring me in the face and I realize he's standing right in front of me.

Why am I not telling him to go get dressed?

I swallow hard, unable to lift my gaze to his.

The tip of his cock is smooth and slightly curved as it leads down to a wide ridge. It tapers slightly there before it gets thicker and thicker. There's a set of muscles that I can see underneath his skin, wrapping all around the shaft to produce a slightly widened band before the shaft thickens some more, widening to another set of muscles, another band underneath his skin. The ridges that run on the underside of those thicker sections look like carvings set in the muscle itself, and I can't help but wonder about their purpose. I can't help but wonder how they *feel.*

I pull in a deep breath, daring to lift my gaze to his and immediately wonder if that had been the wisest decision. His gaze has bled to black and I remember immediately that they weren't black in the water. Now there's a strange look in those darkened pits that sets my soul on fire.

He kneels before me, clasped hands moving forward and I realize the water he'd gathered is still in his hands. He brings them to my lips, slowly and with enough care that the moment his fingers brush my lips, a shock of electricity travels from the spot right through me.

I tilt my head, accepting the water, feeling the coolness of it as it soothes my dry mouth and throat, quenching some of my thirst yet unable to touch the fire blazing within me. When I finish, he pulls his hands back but doesn't move. The air crackles between us as I see my reflection in those darkened eyes. As the power of this male washes over me even though he has not moved another inch.

I'm a fool for doing this. For letting the blanket slip from my shoulders. For licking my lips again as if I can taste the tension surrounding us.

He doesn't move, only stiffens even as his cock jerks in my peripheral vision. The seconds that pass by seem inconsequential. As if all that matters is whatever's happening right here, right now. No words pass between us but the conversation is raging in my head.

Does he want this? Do *I* want this? Should I do this? Is this wise? Am I a fool for letting basic urges cloud my judgment?

But...I do want this. Even if I'm denying it to myself. Even if I know it won't lead to anything.

I swallow hard as he watches me, never letting his gaze shift as I ease back on my elbows. Just like back in the cave when I told him my life story, he's allowing me to make the decision. No coercion. The power is all mine. And I realize I want this moment more than anything, even though I know I shouldn't have it.

I can't breathe as he finally shifts, moving closer. Setting his palms down on the blanket, he leans in, crawling over me like I'm some prey, and all I can do is lie there completely still, too afraid to move because this both thrills and terrifies me, but also wanting to see what will happen if I stay.

"Firespark." That same rugged, guttural tone. The same one I've heard before. The one that makes it sound like he's trying his damnedest to control some instinct of his.

"Yes?" I whisper.

It only takes that one moment. That one sound before he dives in, stopping just short of his lips crashing against mine.

My hands move up, fingertips brushing against his slick wet hair as his nose brushes against mine. His hair is so frickin' soft. More like tiny soft feathers than anything else, and a shudder goes through me as I brush my fingers through it again. His chest heaves as he pants and waits, as if he's fighting the same urges I am. As if he's also telling himself this isn't right but can't seem to release himself from this electric storm raging between us.

When I think he's about to pull away, he moves closer, lips brushing against mine. I wait for it, my whole being anticipating it, but all he does is brush his lips against mine again.

"That...greeting," he rumbles.

"Greeting?" I pant.

"The one with your lips."

Realization dawns. "You mean...when I kissed you?"

There's another rumble in his chest. "Do it again."

His command makes me throb between my thighs as I shift my chin upward slightly, just enough to brush my lips against his. There's a deep groan before a large hand cradles my skull and I'm pressed into him.

His kiss is brutal. As if he wants to draw everything I can give and take it into himself. His lips crash against mine, a growl and rumble vibrating on his tongue as it slips into my mouth, swirling with mine, dancing.

I whimper at the force of his kiss. The sensation of his desperate need, and my legs fall open between us. He settles there, his large frame spreading my thighs as he pushes against me, spreading me on the blanket as his kiss consumes me.

I whimper into his mouth, a cascade of feelings I didn't know I was holding back coming crashing down like they're released by some tsunami. Every inch of my body that presses against his bare one sends electric sparks through my being. I tremble against him, my arms wrapping around his neck, pulling him even further in.

Something thick and hot slides against me, traveling up through the valley at the center of my thighs, igniting sensations through my core. I shudder, a gasp against his lips as he freezes. Those dark eyes find mine as he growls into my mouth and I melt. The power of that sound, the vibrations going down my throat and spreading through me. My pussy clenches, need wetting my core.

He slides back, before pulling away just enough so he can look between us, so he can see just what he's doing. And then he slides forward again, running that thick rod right through my folds one more time. My eyes dim, my back arching at the sensation of his hardness against my clit. There's a rumble, but I can't see. My eyelids flutter as he pulls back and does it again, and again, until I feel like I'm grinding myself on him and it's not the other way around.

It feels so fucking good that in a matter of moments I'm trembling, unable to control the fireworks setting off in my being, only able to grip him hard, my fingertips digging into his shoulder as he lifts his gaze to mine again.

I thought he looked crazed before. I was wrong. Now the look in those dark eyes is downright predatory. His lips crash against mine once more as he rams his dick up through my folds, the tip reaching my belly button before he pulls back and does it again, and again, and again. Those thick bands are like textured ridges that roll through my heat. It's wet and hot. A delicious combination of his pre-spend lubricating my folds as he grinds against me.

I don't know if he knows what he's doing. If he knows he's stimulating that bud between my folds and that it is driving me wild. But when I look up at him, I see those eyes on me. Taking everything in. His hips tilt and adjust as if reacting to every whimper, every moan.

Desire consumes me as I reach a peak I didn't expect. My legs stiffen as I muffle a scream into his shoulder, tremors wracking my frame as my body experiences a high that's so amped up, all my energy drains to my toes.

That's when he finally slows down. His head snaps up, watching me with an intensity that only makes me shudder some more. Watching me as if he's documenting every second of this.

As the shockwaves finally pass and I settle back down, I look up at him through hazy eyes. There's a tickle on my belly and my gaze slips down on its own. His cock jerks the moment my eyes land on it between us. His pre-spend is a thin milky white that's dripping from his tip, but that's not what draws my attention.

The first widened band of his cock seems to be darker now, as if there's a lot of pressure focused there.

"What..." What's happening?

He pulls his gaze from me, looking between us too.

"Human males do not have these?"

I shake my head and when I pull my gaze from the band, I find he's still studying me.

"You do not know what it means then..."

I shake my head again.

The moment snaps and he leans in, fangs baring right in front of me. He is almost terrifying. Almost. Because what I feel is not fear. Only need. A skittering need that runs over my spine like warm honey before exploding through every nerve ending like a firework.

"It means," he rumbles, lips brushing against mine as he speaks. "That I am aching to fill you with my seed." He pauses, pressing his hands harder against the blanket as if to steady himself. "That my cock wants to form a knot deep inside you... I do not want to scare you, Firespark...but if I do not stop now..."

Another tremor goes through me, my body reacting to his words. Reaching up, I grip the back of his head, coming close enough that there's just a breath between us. Slipping my tongue between his lips, I slowly lick one of his fangs.

The groan he utters is so masculine my pussy throbs.

"Who said anything about stopping?"

There's a beat between us, one where I can see the look in his eyes grow more intense before he growls.

He slides back, that hot rod sliding through the center of my sensitive folds once more as my fingers dig into his nape. I brace myself, squeezing my eyes shut, knowing this will be painful before it even starts getting good, but when I feel the first press of his head against my entrance, there is no pain.

I look up to find him focused on me, and I can't pull my gaze away.

He takes his time, pressing the head with a steady force that slowly spreads me. My breathing picks up, chest heaving as our gazes remain locked and his cock continues to push against me. I'm so fucking wet, and yet it feels like he's too big to get in.

I see him grit his teeth, jaw clenching as he leans down, bracing on his arms over me before pausing.

"This will hurt you if I continue." His voice is thick, filled with the same need coursing through me. And at his words, a sliver of panic shoots through me. I shake my head, wiggling my hips as I bite down on my lip.

"I want this. Don't stop now."

Another growl, but even though he's stopped moving, he doesn't pull back. I wiggle my hips again, pressing against that delicious burn and he growls, a tremor going through his arms before he presses into me. A tinge of pain is chased away by indescribable pleasure as he breeches my entrance, and when the head pops in, a deep groan rumbles in my ears.

I'm not sure if it's him or me who uttered the sound, only that he freezes again.

We're joined. The feel of him stretching me with just the head of his giant cock shouldn't feel this good. My pussy weeps, asking for more, but he eases back, dark gaze shifting over me as he takes me in, looking down between us to see where we're joined.

"Fek," he growls, and I'm transfixed. No one has ever looked at me the way he's looking at me now. His gaze sears with raw hunger that steals my breath and stops my heart.

Both hands clasp my jaw before they slide down, running

over my shoulders, and stopping at my breasts. He clasps them, fingers running over my nipples and I gasp, pussy clenching on his thick head. There's another rumble in his chest as he kneads my breasts and I can't help but move my hips. I press against him, taking him in some more, circling that rod that's impaling me, rolling my hips so I can take him some more.

Another rumble and he bares his fangs as his muscles go taut in his neck.

He's trying not to move. To allow me to take control and get used to him. And just seeing him like that, at the end of his restraint, only makes me want this more.

I pull my hips back, sliding over his tip, only to settle on it once more, this time taking more of him than I did before. I let the sensations settle for a moment before doing it again, and again, till his hands are gripping my midsection as he holds me there while I fuck myself on his rod.

It doesn't last long. Soon I'm being pushed back against the blanket and he's leaning over me again.

"You're so small, Firespark. I can't fit." His breath is hot against my lips and he leans his head down, forehead resting against mine. I've no choice but to look up into the eyes of this being that is so different from me. Even with this simple joining, even though he's hardly moving, I can feel the power in his frame. Know he could wreck me if he wanted to.

And that sets off some strange sort of desire within me.

"If you are hurting..." he continues.

I tilt my head, silencing him with my lips. "Not enough, outlaw. Not enough."

He growls against me and when I push my hips down harder against him, I feel when his control snaps. He steadies my waist with one hand before pulling back and surging forward. My channel stretches, trying to accommodate him, and I see stars.

It's nothing like when I was directing the movements, sliding myself over him. It's completely different when he's in charge. My eyes roll back at the power of his thrust, feeling myself open up to him as he surges forward. There's a stretch. An almost excruciating yet pleasure-filled stretch as I try to accommodate that first widened band of his shaft.

"Tell me if it's too much," he growls somewhere near my ear. "Tell me if you can't take it." His voice sounds so strained, as if he's still holding so much back and I clench around him, demanding more.

"Don't stop," I whisper.

My vision goes blurry as he pulls back and starts fucking me. His cock like a heated rod sliding in and out of me mixed with both our juices. My eyes roll back as, for the first time in how many orbits, I release all my worries and just feel.

It's intense. As he begins to pummel me, his cock pistoning in and out in a rhythm that has my entire body jerking, I feel myself entering a place of complete bliss. My hands flatten, gripping the blanket and sand beneath us as I open my body to him, allowing him to take me. Completely.

He growls, the pressure intensifying the deeper he goes, until he stops mid-thrust and focuses that pressure. My eyes roll over as that first thickened band of his cock spreads me wide before slipping into my heat. My pussy stretches to accommodate the shift in width and I groan, eyes rolling over as my head tilts back.

He stops there. Panting. I can feel his cock jerking inside me, and when I open my eyes he takes my lips again, leaning forward to capture my mouth in a kiss so slow and tender it makes me moan again. He keeps his cock steady, grinding it inside me, his pelvis rocking in a tortuous rhythm as he works his length into me, and I whimper into his mouth, body stiffening once more as I reach another peak.

His lips swallow my scream and I'm dimly aware that I've only taken half of his cock. But I'm full, so incredibly full. And I want more. I want him to reach his peak, too.

It feels like I'm losing my grasp on lucidity as I roll my hips, but his hand tightens on my waist, keeping me still as he grunts hard. Slow, deep thrusts and I'm lost again. My body trembles without my control, my grasp on my surroundings waning as he growls deep against my lips.

"So fekking perfect," he murmurs, pulling back so slowly I feel my pussy adjusting to each inch of his length before he slides forward again. "You're gripping me so tight, Firespark."

And then he trembles, too. His cock jerks, tugging at the soft flesh surrounding my entrance, making me clench and throb around him. He groans again before he grips my hips tighter and begins to move again. I am everywhere and nowhere. I am the sun, the moons, and the stars as his hips pull back and move forward. His pace is punishing, every corded muscle in his arms and chest tight. Those dark eyes stare into my soul as he thrusts into me, and I see worlds far away even though there is only us in this place. Me and him. Him stretching me and me taking every inch that he can give.

He growls, low and deep as he pulls back and thrusts deep, and my hands dig into the blanket beneath us, pain shooting through my palm at the extent of my grip. Pain that I hardly feel. The Zamari presses his forehead against mine as he groans, hot fluid filling me from within and I whimper at the feel of his release.

Chests heaving in sync, we take huge breaths together.

"This isn't good, Firespark," I think I hear. "If it wouldn't hurt you, I'd be tempted to make you mine."

His words whisper in the space between us, entangled in our labored breaths and the scent of our pleasure. And for a moment, everything is right with the world.

Until his voice changes, something in his tone making my awareness snap back. Something wild. Something dangerous.

"Firespark," he growls.

I blink, some sort of clarity reaching me through the haze. "What is it?"

His nostrils flare. His whole being stiffening.

"You're bleeding."

I blink. "What?"

CHAPTER SEVENTEEN

The Outlaw

Caught in the throes of something that I can only describe as mind-reeling, I didn't scent it at first. But now I do.

The scent of her lifeblood. Indescribable. Distinguishable from everything else. My fangs ache, and with my ayahl subdued from our joining, I cannot stop the change crashing through my being.

An utter lack of control. Primal instincts that I rarely let see the light of day.

And this couldn't happen at the worst possible time. I'm still within her. Still wrapped in her scalding heat that has given me pleasure I never thought possible. She is so incredibly soft and warm. *Everywhere.* To fall into her and never return to myself would be an existence worth living.

But I can't.

Growling, I stiffen, fighting the scent of her blood while trying to force my fangs to retract.

No good. My body isn't listening to me. Not when I've felt

her. Not when we've shared the unthinkable. I want her now. Every piece of her. Every last bit.

It takes every effort to withdraw myself from her channel and my cock jerks with indignation. It's still painfully hard, aching to return to her center even as my spend leaks from her core. But continuing what feels so good will only erase the last bit of clear judgment remaining in my mind.

Then I will really do the unthinkable. I will harm her.

We Zamari might be treacherous beings. But there's one thing we never do.

We never harm females.

Only...I just did. I hurt her. And yet still, that depraved part of my being can't control my reaction to her spilled lifeblood.

I can feel the darkness taking over as the scent of her lifeblood swims in front of me, even as I fight for clarity. I can taste it as strongly as if I have it on my tongue, running across my fangs as it goes down my throat.

"I hurt you." It's the only thing I manage to croak. I try to focus, try to calm myself as I study her flushed folds. I must have been too rough. She is soft, after all. Delicate. Something to be treasured. Something I should have taken my time with. Had I lost control? Did I thrust too hard? By the gods, I'd only been using a quarter of my power. I thought I was being gentle. Apparently not.

But I don't see the red stain. All I see is her soft, perfectly pink core, unhidden and glistening with our combined juices. I can't see where she's bleeding from, but I scent it. I stiffen, if only to prevent myself from moving and doing something stupid.

But even though I force myself not to move, she does. She moves. Shifts on the *frah* and looks down at herself. Looks down at the evidence of our mating.

"I'm not bleeding, am I?"

Yes, she is.

I stop my breath, the sweet scent of her blood making it difficult for me to concentrate on anything else.

She looks down at herself, a slight frown on her brow, her cheeks warming at the sight of her swollen center even as she fights to pretend all is well.

"I'm...not bleeding."

My lips pull back in a hiss I can't control, nostrils flaring. "You are."

Her cheeks flush, and not because of our joining this time. "Well, this is embarrassing." She averts her gaze. "It's not like I've never had sex before. I've used toys. I never thought..." She grows redder still. "Fuck. It's just...you're just...you're the first actual person..."

It must be the madness slowly overtaking me that's making her words incomprehensible.

"You're the first person I've done it with." She speaks the words hurriedly, her voice almost muffled. "But I shouldn't be bleeding."

The air chills, my whole world going silent.

"Firespark." It's a coarse growl, as if my tongue and my throat have forgotten how to form words.

"Don't worry." She offers me a faint smile. "I didn't feel any pain. And I don't see any blood, so you must be mistaken." She smiles again, cheeks warming some more. "It felt...*good*."

Her words repeat in my mind a thousand times, for I cannot believe what I'm hearing.

"I'm...the first..." I let them slip across my tongue. Testing, questioning whether I heard her right.

She averts her gaze again. "Yes. You are." And then a soft huff of a laugh expels from her nose. Her lips press into a thin line and there's a stiffening of her shoulders that I wish I could take away. For there's nothing for her to be embarrassed about. Nothing for her to be defensive about. She's just given me, an unlawful mercenary unworthy of her treasure, the greatest bounty a brute like me could ever hope for.

"I know it's strange. I'm a fully grown adult. Thirty years on this plane of existence and I've never..." She trails off, but I wait for her to continue. For her words are the only thing bringing me some clarity. Clearing the darkness. Fighting this primal thing inside me that wants to take her whole. "Back on the mothership, the kids like me who were born after the accident didn't really date. At least...*I* didn't." She huffs another laugh through her nose. "It was weird. We all grew up together. Like brothers and sisters, almost. Plus, since we were going to arrive on Ivuria 10 after a few years, it was mandated that the next generation was to be born here and not on the ship. New world and all. New hope. A new beginning." She releases a breath. "And...after we arrived here...those of us that survived the crash, that is...and then the Nirzoik after...have just been focused on staying alive." She pauses. "We also...don't have many males left." Her eyes met mine again. "They like to kill the men. We females are not as strong to do the mining, but they think we're easier to control. That we won't fight back as much. There are not many human men left in our settlement. Few options for dates."

She widens her eyes a little at the end of that statement and presses her lips together and keeps them there. Her words settle between us until that color in her cheeks returns and she shifts again, grabbing one end of the *frah* and bringing it to her core, wiping away her delicious juices, and mine, before I can react.

And then I see something else. The source of the lifeblood that's sweetening the air like an intoxicating concoction of drugs.

I snatch her arm, causing her to fall back against the

blanket as I lift her hand between us. A growl rumbles in my chest even more, my fangs lengthening again, need once again filling me for something other than her cunt.

Her wide eyes shift to her palm and she winces.

"Fuck."

She *is* bleeding. Only, the wound isn't where I thought it would be. The lifeblood's red against wounds that are spread across her palm. Gripping her other hand, I lift it to see similar damage. Another growl erupts inside me and my cock dies a little.

Even though it is not, I understand why her cunt would be bleeding. But her hands?

I bring them up higher and another growl rips through me.

"How did this happen?" I ask even though I know what's caused these wounds. I've had them before on my own hands. But the thought that she endured this...and the potential reason why...

"My blaster," she says. "When the sandworm had you, I..."

I force myself to breathe. To breathe through the delicious scent of her sated cunt and the intense concoction of her blood. To breathe through the darkness threatening to overtake me once again.

I knew she'd returned. After I sent her away, she'd turned the bike around. I just hadn't wanted to consider it. Or what it might mean.

This female...

She came back for me. *Again.*

Rage builds inside me that I fight to hold back. Rage at myself because the implications of her sacrifice are clear. She burned her hands using her blaster to *save* me.

I push my anger back, for though it rages inside me, she is not the true cause of it. *I am.* My failings. And that one true fear that lies deep in the soul of every outlaw like me.

"I'm going to do something..." Even to my ears, my voice is a rough mess. "Something that might scare you."

She studies my face, trying to read me but I know she gets nothing back. No *ayahl* to feel me out, tell if I'm about to be a threat or not. She relies on her eyes and that feeling in her gut. There's still a soft sheen of perspiration resting on her skin from the intensity of our joining, and I resist the urge to run my finger across her brow, put some more time between what I'm about to do and the fact that it might repulse her.

"Do it."

The utter trust. She has no idea how it beats against me, slowly breaking down the walls I've held around myself from my dawn.

It's the reason I'm here now. Why I was sheathed in her warmth. And I wonder again if she is something the fates intended for me to find.

Taking a deep breath, I fight the darkness as I reveal my fangs. Slowly. Ever so slowly, trying not to scare her. For many unravel into fear-filled beings when they see a Zamari ready to feed, and I know my fangs are dripping. I'm *making* them drip. Can feel them wanting to bury themselves in her skin. But I can't.

I won't.

Instead, I hover my lips over her palm, allowing my venom to drip into her wounds. There's a slight sting and her hand stiffens in my grasp. I know the moment the venom begins to work, numbing her wounds as she relaxes again, her puzzled gaze watching me as if bewitched.

"You did not feel the pain of this?"

The wounds are large enough that she should have been writhing in discomfort. No doubt we disturbed them when she pressed down hard on the *frah*, the friction opening her delicate skin.

"A bit," she breathes. "But it doesn't hurt that much."

Or maybe she can't feel the pain as she should. Blocked it somehow.

I push down at the darkness pulling at me, stopping my breathing again as I release some more venom and watch as it seeps into her wounds.

I only mean to numb it. To soothe her and then head back to the bike for the gauze. But when she releases a soft gasp, a little moan I shouldn't have heard, my control snaps. This close to her lifeblood, so close I can almost taste it, I'm unable to pull away.

I dip my tongue to her hand and she jerks in surprise before another moan bubbles from her lips. I groan in pleasure too.

It spreads across my tongue. Sweet. So incredibly sweet. *Intoxicating.*

Her lifeblood is exactly what I thought it would taste like, and so much more. The intensity of this nectar that flows in her veins is unlike any other I've tasted before.

I groan again, allowing my tongue to circle her palm and clean the blood away, telling myself I'm only doing it because my saliva will help her heal. She shudders in my grasp and when I set my eyes on her, her tongue darts out of her mouth, running over her bottom lip before she pulls the lip into her mouth, biting down on it.

I clean her hand, watching her battle with pleasure that confuses her. Pleasure stemming from my venom that's now seeped deep into her wounds. I know she can't understand it. Can't understand why the heat of my tongue, the wetness of it moving across her palm is making her clench her thighs together. Or why a groan is rumbling in my chest, my eyes darkening even more at the taste of her.

She swallows hard as I move to the other hand, giving it the same treatment, and the entire time I taste her lifeblood, I can't take my eyes off her. My cock rises, hot and hard again, and I know if I get the chance, I will take her again like this. My cock deep inside her. My fangs buried in her neck, her lifeblood on my tongue. Making her come over and over and over again like the occasion demanded the first time I took her.

If I had known it was her first time, I would not have fucked her so hard. Next time, I will...

I groan, pushing the thought away. There won't be a next time.

They say a Zamari should be careful of the females he drinks from, for some have the power to bind. And even as I drink, even as I taste her, I can feel those invisible threads pulling us together.

So why the fek am I not pulling away?

Why am I allowing myself to be drawn in?

I stop long after the lifeblood's been cleared from her palm. Long after I should have. And even I have to admit that I'm not doing this because of thirst. I'm doing it because of the reflection of need in her eyes. The same need that gnaws at me, even though I just had her.

When I finally release her hand, she pulls it back toward herself slowly, wide eyes moving from me to her palm and then back. And when I shift my hands to her legs, spreading them for me once more, she doesn't resist.

I dip between them and she gasps again the moment my hot breath brushes over her center. *So fekking sweet.* Her scent alone is driving me across the sands.

Patience is what I have to draw on as I let my fangs drip over her pretty folds. Watching my venom slide down the center, finding its way down to her core until her chest is shuddering with anticipation and want.

I dip my head, grazing my fangs along her delicate flesh so

lightly, it's just the shadow of a touch. The venom will soothe the shadows of any aches I've left behind…but I can't resist.

I swirl my tongue first, running over her in a way that makes me groan. The utter softness of her; it makes my fangs lengthen even more and I have to be careful I don't nick her. My moan drowns out hers as I lap against her, taking her juices and everything else she can give.

And falling deeper with every second of it.

I lose myself in her taste, her scent, her essence. Each flick of my tongue sends waves of pleasure through her, through *me*, and her body responds in kind, arching towards me, begging for more. So fekking responsive. My cock throbs, hardening even more, jerking with every moan that bubbles from her throat. I might spill here on the *frah* if I'm not careful. The intensity of her taste is too much for me to withstand.

Her hands find my hair, tangling in the filaments, pulling me closer, deeper, and I groan into her, the lingering taste of her lifeblood, the fresh taste of her juices, all like a siren call to my own primal needs.

She stiffens, grunting, pulling me closer and I can feel her nearing the edge, her body tensing, her breaths coming in short, ragged gasps. I intensify my movements, determined to have her shatter on my tongue and the moment it happens, the moment she screams, her juices cascading down on me, I wonder if I will ever be the same again.

No. I will never be the same again.

Ever.

I use my tongue to clean her. Taking every drop she gives before I lift my head, easing back on my haunches, my cock jumping and demanding more, my *ayahl* doing the same, and that primal thing inside me awakened now that I've gotten a taste of that red liquid running through her veins.

Hard breaths are shared between us as we look at each

other. My fekking cock is so hard, I know that if I take her now, I will knot her.

She doesn't ask what just transpired, even though I can tell she wants to. Even though I can see the unsurety flash behind the desire in her eyes as she tries to chase both away. She gulps, bracing up on her elbows before licking her lips again and I feel the need to offer some sort of explanation, even though she doesn't demand it.

"My venom will soothe the pain." I pause. How much should I tell her? How much does she know about my kind? "My saliva will help you heal." My lifeblood would do so much faster but unlike me, I'm sure she's not attracted to any part of my blood the way I am to hers. I pause, watching her, words at my lips that should be said but which don't come forth.

"Yes," she breathes. "I'm sure your saliva will really help... down there."

Cheeks growing warm again, she looks away, and there's an urge I never have to pull her into me and just hold her there.

Instead, I say something that I haven't had to say to anyone in a long time. "Thank you, Firespark."

Her gaze snaps up from where she'd averted it, moving to me in confusion.

"For what?" Then her countenance drops. "For the sex?"

I shake my head. "You have given me the greatest bounty." My gaze falls back to her center and I can see she resists the urge to squirm. To hide herself from me. "The sweetest treasure." I lean closer. "But I am thanking you for something else." I pause again. "I'm thanking you for coming back for me."

Her throat moves, her eyes searching mine.

"You would have done the same." And then, realizing what she's said, her cheeks color some more. So fekking endearing. Her species wears their thoughts on their faces, their skin, every body movement. "I mean, I'd think you would do the same. I—"

I grasp her gently by the chin, tilting her face up to mine. Looking at her like this, moments pass before I can even say anything. "For you, I think I would."

Her mouth opens slightly, her gaze still searching mine before a soft smile spreads across her lips.

We don't have to say any more. It's all there in the air between us.

Forcing my body to move, I rise, ignoring the lewd bob of my cock as it jerks hard, slapping against my pelvis as I stand.

I can't have her again. At least, not right now. I would surely make her bleed.

Walking over to the berries growing from the crevice near the drinking pool, I climb up on a ledge to reach them and retrieve a few. I taste one first, testing it with my *ayahl*, but nothing seems to alarm me. They're safe to ingest.

I pull a handful more, taking as many as I can carry before heading back toward her. She's pulled a part of the blanket around her, hiding herself, but the image of her bareness has already been imprinted on my mind. It's one I will revisit many times to come.

I settle beside her, leaning on my side as I turn to face her.

Her face is red from the heat? Embarrassment? Her eyes are glued to my still-hard cock and even though I'm trying to ignore it, her attention only makes it jerk again.

"Suck on this," I whisper, my voice more like a rumbled vibration than speech.

Her cheeks flame even more, eyes widening slightly as she pulls her eyes away from where her focus has been.

"Okay." She presses her lips together, cheeks still flaming. "Oh! You mean the berry." She snatches it from my outstretched fingers in one swoop of her hand, stuffing it into her mouth so quickly she almost chokes.

"What did you think I meant?" My cock grows harder just

thinking of being sheathed between her lips and when she shakes her head, pretending her mouth is too full for her to answer, I can't help but chuckle.

The berry fills her mouth, the red juices bursting at her lips like lifeblood marring her skin. I watch enthralled as she finishes it before turning to me, reaching for another. I pull my hand away.

Taking one between my fingers, I stretch it toward her. She swallows hard but leans into me, taking my fingers into her mouth, her breath against my skin as I set the berry on her tongue.

She eats it while looking at me, her eyes, for the first time, something I can't read.

"How much extra is this?" she whispers and a small smile quirks the corners of her lips.

I'm not sure if she says this in jest or not. What if I tell her that her satchel of credits means nothing to me. That I'm doing this purely because I decided she'd be my final job.

I have a feeling saying such a thing to a female like this might hurt her pride. She *wants* to pay me for my help.

So I grunt, allowing my gaze to soften. "Complementary. I aim to please."

Her little chuckle is enough payment and I soak up the sound like a male starved.

Time is insignificant as I feed her, her tongue swiping against my digits each time I set the food in her mouth. It's something I could do for oras without tiring, but when there's suddenly a rumble outside, enough to snatch our attention, I know it's time to stop.

Firespark's wide eyes turn to me as she freezes. The earth shakes and I can see the fear in her eyes. Setting the remaining berries down, I rise.

"Time to leave, Firespark."

She nods, accepting what I said without argument. Her trust in me is just one thing pushing me to see this final job through. The growing urge to protect her is just another.

Grabbing my trouse from where I'd washed it and set it to dry before finishing my swim, I slip it on. Beside me, Elsie is doing the same, hastily slipping into her tunic and then her skirt. We're dressed in a matter of moments and I head back for the *frah*, bundling and stashing it away by the time she reaches the bike.

The rumbling grows louder and as she climbs up on the bike, those wide eyes on me, I know she doesn't know what the sound is.

"Another worm?" she asks.

I shake my head, climbing on the bike as I lead it out of the cave. "Worse."

She stiffens as she wraps her arms around me, and I engage the engine, shooting the bike back down to the plain at the same time that we see the cause of the rumbling.

"It's..." Elsie's voice dies in the wind as we race around the outcroppings, heading away from the sight of the train shooting across the plain before us. "What's a train doing out here?"

The rockets that make the monstrous vessel hover make sand and dirt fly in massive clouds at its back. But it's the speed at which the vessel travels that's frightening.

"Supplies," I say.

"What type of supplies?"

"Food. Water. Medicine." I eye the vessel as we head in the opposite direction, away from it. And just like I expected, with that fekking supply train comes those that follow it, hoping for scraps.

Ahead, high on an outcropping, is a band of scavengers, just arriving as we're leaving. They spot us, would have no doubt found us in the cave if they'd decided to scout, but the train passing by is of more interest to them than we are.

As we fly by, they turn their gazes away from us at the same time that Elsie grips me tighter.

"Medicine?" She shouts over the wind. "For the sickness?"

I grunt in the affirmative.

Her hands tighten on me some more. "Are you sure?!"

I know what she's thinking. She said her people have nothing. She'd join the scavengers if she had the choice, hoping beyond hope that some brave fool hijacks the vessel and she can get some of the spoils.

It's what they all do. But no fool in eons has been brave enough to even attempt it. The speed of the train alone and one mistake would lead to death. Many have tried before. Their remains are left scattered across the plains.

I can almost feel the thoughts crossing her mind at lightning speed. The moment she settles on some decision is the moment she focuses on the task before us. The moment everything that happened in that cave is set aside and she's back to that female I first saw in that bar.

Focused. Determined. Ready to do anything to survive.

"How long till we reach Comodre?"

"Two rotations. One if we don't stop."

She nods, her chin brushing against my back. "Then don't stop."

CHAPTER EIGHTEEN

Elsie

We ride.

For hours upon hours we traverse the sandy sea, the rumble of his bike the only constant. But I don't tell him to stop. I don't tell him to slow down. I lose track of the setting and rising sun as we travel over sparkling dunes.

We stop only once when necessary—a quick stretch while he refuels his bike with solar chips. Wordless, efficient, then we are off again into the endless expanse.

My body stiffens, grows sore, then numbs to the unrelenting pace. Still, I do not ask him to stop. I cannot, when I feel the hearts of those counting on me with each blast of wind that whips my hair. We pass small trading posts nearly buried in the sands. Abandoned way stations where metal beams creak forlornly in the desert wind. Strange spiking rock formations and towering sand mountains that disappear in our wake.

Sometimes my heavy eyelids convince me to rest. I doze,

waking with a start whenever a particularly large bump jolts me back to full awareness. I cannot relax fully, anxious dreams plaguing any real rest. In those moments when my heart lurches, beating a little harder from some fear still haunting me, the strength of the male I lean on is like a soothing, calming presence that makes it all melt away.

I lose myself watching pink and golden bands stretch across the sky. The occasional cloud of sparkling dust kicked up by a roaming sandskimmer. The rhythmic pulse of the bike beneath me.

Worry fills me for the entire time that we ride. That we won't arrive on time. That there will be nothing left to save when we return. Even worry that we might encounter another storm. Or, worse yet, another one of those sandworms. But the going is steady. Sure.

The moment we near Comodre, my senses heighten. It's dark, night closing in, but even with the lack of the sun's light, I start recognizing things. Little bits of the horizon that always looked familiar from my view in the town, only now flipped as we approach from the opposite direction.

We shoot past one of the Nirzoik outposts and my shoulders are stiff with awareness. But this one stands empty. Whoever should be standing guard has probably left since nothing ever happens in Comodre. We are subservient. Docile. So, when there is no sound or alarm, I force myself to calm. To not freak out as we get closer. But my heartbeat gets more erratic the closer we get, knowing that this is really about to go down. For the first time, I'm about to fight back against the Nirzoik with the type of resistance that will get through to them. And even though I know it's my best bet, *our* best bet to freedom, I can't help the uncertainty still flooding through me.

As we approach the colony, I keep my eye out for any Nirzoik. They're not due to come back for dues, at least, not yet. But the terror of entering the colony to find them there, before we've had time to prepare, sets my nerves on fire.

The Zamari doesn't say a word, but the steeling of his jaw tells me everything. And through fresh eyes, I can see it from his perspective. Comodre looks more like a dump than a bustling settlement filled with hope for the future.

The few cabins left standing on the outskirts have either been burned to a crisp or have been long abandoned. When the Nirzoik first came, it was those homes that got the brunt of the destruction first.

It looks more like a graveyard than anything else and when the Zamari zooms past them, finally entering Comodre, a pain tightens in my chest as more of the colony is revealed.

Wind gusts through abandoned shacks with doors hanging off broken hinges. Shop fronts stand shattered, wares long ransacked. The saloon where us settlers once gathered for camaraderie and cheer echoes now with only the haunting call of wind flowing through its rafters.

Further in, many remaining homesteads bear scorch marks up their feeble wooden walls. Entire rooftops are gone. Hardly a building stands undamaged. Those still inhabited sit lonely amongst the rubble of their neighbors. Faint wax-light behind dusty windows barely keeps the darkness at bay.

The people who dare to sit outside on their decks have wide eyes as we fly past. Some rise to hurry back inside, thinking we might be the Nirzoik. Others are frozen in fear. And some are not able to do a thing as the Zamari doesn't even slow down to acknowledge their presence. They see us and it hurts me that their first thought is to run to safety.

When we first started building here and the Nirzoik came through, we greeted them with open arms and celebration, not realizing they would soon become our end. Now, there is no greeting for the Zamari at all. Just fear. My people are no longer used to anything but those thieving raiders riding through. Their broken spirits reflect on mine and I'm reminded why I have to do this. Why I can't just give up. I refuse to let us all die. For that's the end to all this. The Nirzoik won't stop till they bleed us dry. Either we reclaim our frontier from the scourge...or we wither to dust along with it.

I pull my gaze from the depressing buildings, facing forward as the Zamari continues on. It's only then that I realize he's going in the right direction. As if he knows exactly where I live. Something flutters in my chest as he swerves around the *endolo* tree sitting at the center of the colony and takes a sharp left, heading down my street.

"How do you know which way to go? How do you know the way?" I shout over the wind.

There's a grunt in his chest and I'm suddenly thrown back to that cave, to how my knees went weak when he made a similar sound in his throat while his lips were fastened between my legs.

"I don't," he replies, and yet there's a slight sensation that goes through me. Climbing up the soft hairs on my arms, exploding in my chest. Making me shiver. "I only follow my *ayahl*."

His *ayahl*. He mentioned it before. And as he mentions it again, there's something like a wave of thin silk that brushes over my skin at the sound.

He doesn't stop, doesn't slow down till we reach the husk of what was once Estella's cabin. Seeing the remains of her house, I'm pulled from my musings as my chest tightens again. The bike stops and I sway as I hop off, my muscles not used to the movement after sitting so long on the bike. A large hand steadies mine—the outlaw—and I glance up at him as he helps me stand.

Reality hits me like a brick.

We're here. I brought him to Comodre. This isn't all a dream anymore. I'm really pushing this plan forward.

As the words beat through my head, I don't get time to let the thoughts settle. The front door of my cabin flies open, a torch chasing away the darkness as Estella steps outside.

"Elsie! You—" She stops short, gaze immediately flying to the outlaw at my side. I see the moment she pauses. The way her shoulders straighten. How her gaze shifts to his hand steadying me. The way one arm has disappeared behind her, and I know she has her hand on her blaster. "You've arrived," she finishes, adding a smile of greeting that is obviously fake.

Her eyes don't leave the outlaw and when I glance at him, I realize he must look quite mysterious. Dangerous. An unknown standing beside me in the darkness.

His hat is the way it was when I first met him. Pulled down so low she can't even see his eyes. But he's not looking her way. His gaze is on me, his eyes lit as he helps me to balance until blood rushes back to my legs and the tingling within them stops.

"Elsie?" Estella's voice snaps me back from the void created by just looking into his eyes.

"Oh! Estella, this is—"

"Mom?" The little voice behind Estella is so soft, yet it breaks through the air, cutting through it as it reaches me and beats on the door guarding my heart.

I don't know why tears fill my eyes as Kiana steps from behind Estella. Those big brown eyes are on me and I can see the fear within them. She'd had Estella, but I'd left her for days. It's the longest we've ever been apart and I realize now, that even though my trip to Calanta and back had kept me busy, she'd been here waiting for me all along.

I'd been out there grinding on an outlaw's dick while she was here thinking I wasn't coming back.

Immediately, I feel like shit.

Kiana takes a step forward and Estella stops her with one hand, brows furrowed as she stares at the outlaw. She doesn't know who the hell he is. Doesn't trust him. She has a right not to. And I realize some silly part of me has abandoned all my reservations regarding this male.

I trust him. With my life.

"Mom?" Kiana's voice cracks again, fear lacing the soft utterance as her gaze moves to the Zamari and I'm immediately reminded of the scene she'd witnessed the day I decided to leave. Of the Nirzoik, what they did to Estella's house, and how they treated us right in front of her. All her life, I've tried to protect her, but I know that deep down she's come to learn that strangers are to be feared. And I can see that fear in her eyes now.

I release the outlaw's hand and fall to my knees, reaching out to her. With a nod of assurance at Estella, I beckon the child to come to me.

"It's okay, Kiana," I blink away tears I don't want to fall. I want her to feel safe. That there's nothing to be afraid of and me crying won't help. "I'm here now."

That's all she needed to hear. As soon as Estella moves her hand, Kiana hurries toward me. Her gait is jerky, slower than she should be at her age, but she comes toward me nonetheless. As soon as she's close, I pull her into my arms, showering her with kisses until she's a giggling mess.

"I missed you so much!" I give her a squeeze before my eyes find Estella. She smiles at me, a genuine one this time and I close my eyes for a moment, just reveling in the feeling of being home. This is why I put myself in danger. For *this*. Kiana deserves so much more than what life has sent her way. She deserves everything that was promised to us on that mothership,

I rise with her in my arms, gaze shooting to the outlaw. He's standing there, no readable expression on his face. I can't tell what he thinks, but there's something in the way he's looking at me.

"You have young," he finally says, eyes shifting to Kiana then back to me.

There's something I'm missing. Something I can't put my finger on. And then I remember. The bleeding. How I'd thought he meant I was bleeding from *there* and I'd tried to explain the cause...and how he'd cleaned me so thoroughly with his tongue afterward.

My core throbs and his gaze immediately falls to my pelvis, as if he can see through the fibers of my skirt. It takes everything within me not to squirm.

"Yes," I reply. It's all I can reply for now. If he cares to listen, I might tell him the story. But I doubt he will. Despite what happened to us out there on the plains, he'll be leaving after this job is done. Leaving once he gets paid.

And for some reason that grates on me, making me clench my teeth to press back a sudden surge of emotions I'm too coward to face right now.

"Come on in," I turn away, heading toward the door. "There's a lot to discuss."

His jaw ticks again and I wonder if he will follow me inside, but I keep my head forward, trying not to look at the fact that James, the human male that lives close by us, has exited his door and is watching us. But the Zamari must realize too. His gaze shifts ever so slightly before he disengages the engine on his bike and follows me in. Estella stands by the door, eyes pointed at him as she lets him enter before her. Her gaze bores into his back as she closes the door behind them, and when the door is shut, when the world outside is locked out and we are here in my space, my personal little haven, I turn to look at him.

The male who has come into my life and has me questioning things. The male who has stepped into my home and his presence seems to fill the place. Not choking. Not intrusive. But something else.

With him here, it feels like I've opened yet another part of me to him. His gaze flicks around, taking everything in, just in the same way I've seen those very same eyes scan every detail on my face. Sitting with Kiana on my lap on the little cot off to the side, I release a breath and pull out the one chair at the table before pushing it gently toward him.

His gaze flicks toward it, but he doesn't move. Meanwhile, at his back, Estella stays leaning against the door as if she's ready to spring into action at any moment.

The tension in the room is so thick I can feel it. I wonder what he thinks of this: my home. What he thinks of Comodre.

Those eyes of his light me up like I'm under searchlights. As if my every thought is coming under scrutiny. There's something in his gaze that's hardened and when he opens his mouth, it all becomes clear.

"Where...is your *mate?*"

CHAPTER NINETEEN

The Outlaw

I've known of settlements on the fringes in the west. The beings who live in these colonies on the free lands usually keep to themselves, only visiting big cities like Calanta to trade wares they can take back to their people. But this place...

Flying through the streets of the colony told me one thing. These beings out here are on their last hope. It is even clearer now why Firespark risked her life to get a mercenary like me on her side.

The risk of her journey was less than the threat to her and her people's survival. There was nothing to deter her. And now, I realize there was something else pushing her too.

My gaze slides to the *kiv* in her arms. A small little thing. Thin. Weak. And not because she is young. I can already tell she suffers from the sickness. I can see it in the way she moves. See the pain underneath her flesh, aching in her bones. She doesn't have much time left. And my *ayahl* senses it too, writhing in discontent as I use it to scope the room around me.

Firespark's nest.

The home is small. Barely big enough to hold all four of us comfortably, but clean. Tidy. And smells just like her. There's a dim glow provided by wax-light that warms the place.

I stop breathing just to give myself some more time to build up my resistance to the sweet scents in this space, and my gaze snaps back to the *kiv*.

"My mate?" There's confusion in Firespark's eyes as she looks at me. "I don't...oh..." Her cheeks color a little before she wraps her arms tighter around the *kiv*. "It's just us. I know you must be confused because of..." Her gaze shifts to the female standing quietly at the exit. "Well...you know what. But it's just me and Estella."

"A female pairing?" My gaze narrows. I did not expect this.

Firespark's eyes widen, cheeks reddening slightly even in the dim wax-light. "No. We're not together. Not like that." Then she smiles. A sad one. One filled with hidden pain and desolation. "We're both Kiana's moms. Viv helps out sometimes too. It's always...it's always just been us."

"Hmm." The sound rumbles in my chest as I turn my attention back to the room. So she's alone. With a *kiv*. While her world is torn apart around her. So why is there a sense of relief making my *ayahl* feel lighter at those first two things?

I have no right to feel such things. I have no claim on this female, even though each ora that passes makes me itch to mark her as mine. This is just a job.

I know that. She knows that.

Nothing more can come of this. No matter how good she tasted in that cave or how I could lose myself thrusting deep within her. No matter how sweet her lifeblood was running down my throat.

Grunting, I force my focus on the room around us. There's a section above us that looks like it's for storage. Unimportant and uninteresting if my *ayahl* couldn't sense the sickness. That single disease that rolls through the sands of Ivuria. The sickness is a blessing and a curse, taking both innocent and guilty. And the law? Hnghh. The Ivurian government will do nothing to stem its course. This planet is a lawless pit. Why stop the sickness when it's thinning the horde?

My gaze shifts back down, taking in the small food preparation area, the cot Firespark's sitting on, and finally, the table that stands beside it.

There's another door, one I assume leads to the washing area. One entrance. One exit, not counting the two windows. Nowhere to run. Nowhere to hide. And too small to defend. If anyone should come in, she'd have no choice but to fight back. If they send a missile into this place, it would all splinter. None would survive.

That has to change.

"Where do you keep your weapons?" My gaze shifts back to Firespark and there's a look of vulnerability in her eyes.

"We...don't..."

"Our blasters are all the weapons we have," the female behind me speaks. I may not have acknowledged her presence yet, but I've been aware of her every move. How her gaze has been boring in my back. How she still has one hand on the blaster she's hiding, the other on the door handle. How she attempts to appear relaxed even though the pulse in her veins is running wild. And how, when I shift, how her life organ beats just a little faster.

Estella. Her name flows like my Elsie's.

I glance at her over my shoulders and as soon as my gaze meet hers, her eyes widen slightly and she stiffens.

Brave, I think to myself, *but not as brave as Firespark.*

She's different too. Human like Firespark, I presume. They look to be the same species, but this one has darker skin. Her snout is a little wider. And her eyes are a deep brown that look black in the lack of light. The filaments on her head are different too. Thicker, and styled like the Tandoorians on Cessna I. Thick braids that are pulled back, revealing her face.

"Well, just one blaster now," Firespark says. "Mine's...lost."

"Fuck," Estella says, momentarily shifting her glare. "What happened?"

Firespark shrugs. "We...ran into some difficulty." Her gaze shifts to mine and I tilt my head, watching her.

She doesn't want to alarm them. Doesn't want to make her friend or the *kiv* worry.

"We'll need more weapons." I move and Estella jumps. I choose to ignore it as I step over to the door off to the side. Pushing it open, I see it's a small washroom, just as I thought. "When are the Nirzoik meant to return?"

"Next week," Firespark's voice reaches my ears as I shut the door, my attention moving to the loft above us. I move up the short stairs to get a better look and there is indeed a small bedding space hidden underneath empty baskets. She's been hiding the *kiv*. Why?

I step down, standing on the main floor again.

"Your people. How many weapons can they gather?"

Firespark's gaze shifts to her friend's and I see her throat move as a heavy silence lands between us.

"None," she finally says. "They won't want anything to do with this."

My eyes narrow some more.

Of course. They all skittered like sandskimmers as soon as my bike arrived.

"Wait, before you get to all that," Estella moves to my side and pops up in my peripheral vision, that dark gaze of hers still boring into me and her hand still at her back, grasping the blaster she has tucked into her trouse. "We haven't been introduced yet. Who are you? What's your name and how do we know we can trust you?"

I shift my gaze to her, and she steadies her feet on the wooden floor. Plants them even as her brain tells her to move away from me. I can see the battle in her eyes. Tell she's more scared than she's letting on. Even though I have been on my best behavior.

Hmm, maybe just as brave as my Firespark then.

"My name?" I tilt my head and her throat tightens in much the same way Firespark's does. "I'd have to kill you if I tell you that."

I hear when she inhales sharply. Hear the moment Firespark pulls the child tighter against her before letting out a laugh that's meant to soothe her companion.

"It's alright, Estella. He's on our side." She puts the *kiv* down on the cot. Pulls a *frah* over her to keep her warm. "Call him Zamari."

She shoots me a glare and my lips curve a little. I only told her friend the truth. But I hear the other female's whisper, anyway. "He's only one guy. Impressive muscles, sweetheart, but do you think he alone can take those brutes on?"

Firespark whispers back. "It's not like we have a choice but to try. We're out of credits."

"Does he know what he's getting himself into, though? What if he bails on us when he sees them coming?"

Firespark shoots a look over her shoulder before Estella takes a seat in the chair she'd offered me. "He won't."

Her trust in me is unfounded.

But she's right. I'm in this now, whether I like it or not. For I know I can't just leave her like this. Her situation is too dire. But more than that...I...don't want to leave her at all.

That's something that makes my *ayahl* rise and flutter around me, filling the space, invisible to their eyes. A nomad who wants to stay in one spot? I tell myself it's just for a little while. Just to get this job done. It is my final job, after all. I have to do it well.

Firespark gives me a tight smile before heading over to the food preparation area. A kettle is put on and she reaches into the single cupboard for the hard bread settlers on this side of Ivuria buy from the merchants. As she prepares the food, I turn my attention back to the two other females in the room. To the *kiv*.

"Her progenitor..."

"Dead," Estella supplies. "And he wasn't Elsie or my or Viv's mate. He was..."

"A guy Kiana's mom loved very much." Love? Another human concept that has no definition through my translator. When I shift my attention back to Firespark, her back is still turned to us, but there's a stiffening to her shoulders. "Her parents...they..."

"Mama and Papa went to the stars after I was born." The little voice reaches me, the *kiv* sitting up underneath the *frah*, far too intelligent eyes for a *kiv* her age looking back at me.

I don't know why I step closer. Or why there's some sort of relief in my bones.

I kneel at the side of the cot, taking my time to look at this little flower. So...Firespark has taken this *kiv*...is raising it...

"Your mor..."

"Mom takes care of me now." Eyes almost as dark as Estella's look back at me. "And Aunty Estella and Aunty Viv too." She studies me some more before rising higher. I see her moving, see her coming closer, and yet I remain still.

When her little hand reaches out, brushes lightly across my jaw, I somehow go still.

"You are different from the bad men."

I study her; my *ayahl* too. She is ill. So weak and in pain that it must be taking some huge effort from her to even sit up like this.

"What makes you think that, little one?"

Her fingers brush across my jaw to touch my nose before she touches the brim of my hat.

"I can tell," she says.

I don't know this *kiv*...so my *ayahl* shouldn't be heightening around me as if she's something of mine to protect. I try to reason with it. She belongs to Elsie. But that only makes it go haywire.

Shifting my focus back to the female who caught my attention in a seedy bar and hasn't relinquished it since, I find her paused in what she's doing, watching me interact with the *kiv* she's come to call her own.

"What about the males of this settlement? The ones still remaining. The ones supposed to protect you."

She swallows hard, pulling her attention from me and the *kiv* before pouring hot water into a receptacle and continuing with the food she is preparing.

"You saw one of them just outside. His name's James." I can see her shoulders are still stiff. There is tension here. And I'm only partially the cause of it. "They're too afraid to do anything. Many have died trying to...trying to protect us. Those that remain keep their heads down."

I don't know why that makes me growl and the *kiv* snatches her hand away from my hat, eyes wide.

I'm instantly regretful. Rising, I put some distance between me and the three females, walking till I reach the door.

Her species is soft. Beautiful. Little treasures. Just spending this short time with Elsie, I already know that. But the *kiv*. Seeing her sick, weak, and so fearful despite that she has the bravery of many more orbits...it does not sit right with me.

And that's why I need to do this job and leave. But I can do one thing before I go. I can make it so Firespark has a good life when I'm gone.

And I'll do my damnedest to do so.

I open the door, stepping out into the cool darkness. It closes quietly behind me shortly after and I get a moment of clarity.

I've never done this before. Never included my feelings into any job I've ever done. But this time, it's different.

My last job. I'll make it one to remember.

CHAPTER TWENTY

Elsie

The door closes quietly and we all watch it with some sort of expectation or just plain uncertainty.

"Is he gone?" Estella rises, moving to peek out the window. "Shit, did we scare him away?"

I huff a laugh through my nose. "Doubt it."

Estella stiffens and I know she's finally spotted him out there. Then she's leaning over the table, trying to peek through the curtains while remaining unseen.

"Estella!" I whisper to her harshly.

"He's walking around the cabin, Elsie." Her gaze darts back to me. "Do you trust him?"

I nod without even giving it a second thought. "I do."

She eyes me for a moment, before pacing the room then going over to pull Kiana into her arms. "Do you think this will work? Does he know what to do?"

My lips press into a line as I turn away from her and continue making the tea. It's made with a root we found while digging in the mines. The only thing that seems to soothe Kiana's aches.

"He doesn't want to know. He just knows that we need his help to frighten the Nirzoik away...and I think he's willing to give it."

"Give?" Estella shakes her head. "Nothing comes for free, my dear. All our credits are going into this plan. It better work."

"And more..."

I stir in some sweetener I'd saved up and bought, just to take the bitterness off the tea.

"More?" I can hear the incredulity in Estella's voice and know she's probably glaring at me wide-eyed. "What do you mean 'more'?"

I release a breath. She'd find out sooner or later. "I offered him triple what we had."

"*Elsie—*"

"I had to do it. I had no other choice."

She remains silent, and I'm glad she doesn't question my decision or my intelligence.

"This will work...right..." she says again after a few moments, and when I turn with the tea in my hand, I see the same fear I see reflected in my own eyes. The same fear reflected in all us settlers here in Comodre. The same fear I try to hide from Kiana.

I nod, giving Estella a smile. "He just has to scare them, right? Make them think we're not just here alone and defenseless. It will work." But even as I give them the tea and sit back on the chair, gaze on the slowly fluttering curtain by my window as it moves in the night air, I can't help that part of my heart that's filled with worry.

But it will work, right?

Morning comes and my eyes flutter open. Light's shining into the room and my body feels like I slept across the spokes of a broken cart.

I shift and almost fall out of the chair.

Estella grunts, curling in on herself and the little bundle snuggled beside her. Both she and Kiana knocked out after drinking the tea and I smile while looking at them, only a moment before a hard thud hits my ears and I jerk fully awake.

It happens again, louder this time and the house shakes. I didn't wake naturally. Whatever that is, it's what roused me from my slumber.

My heart thuds against my chest, gaze shooting to the door. Where's the Zamari?

I blink, forcing sleep from my eyes as I look around the cabin, but he's nowhere to be seen. He didn't come back inside last night. Did he sleep out in the cold?

Getting to my feet, I stagger a little before my hands close on the handle of the front door. It can't be the Nirzoik out there. They're not due to return for a while yet. But even though I know this, my heart still gives a heavy thud, relief crashing through me as I open the door and see no one there.

Squinting against the bright light of Ivuria, I step outside. She's already high in the sky. Just how long did I sleep for?

There's the thud again, coming from the back of my cabin, and James' door swings open. His gaze finds mine immediately and I lift my hand in stiff greeting as I step off my deck. He jerks his chin, eyes narrowed, gaze cold, but it's better than nothing.

When there's another thump, I step into the road, shielding

my eyes as I walk backward so I can take a proper look at my cabin. Another thud goes through my heart the next moment I spot him. There, on the roof covering the back side of the cabin, familiar bronze scales glisten in the sunlight.

The Zamari is shirtless, muscles stretching and flexing as he works, *ripping my roof apart.*

"Hey!" My words are drowned out by another crash and bang of wood as I pull up my skirt and hurry toward the back of my cabin. "What are you—" There, I stutter to a halt, my eyes widening at the piles and piles of wood now resting there. Wood that wasn't there the day before. Wood I don't own and wood I'm sure didn't come from my roof alone. There was a small mound at the back of the cabin, artificially created from me staking a few spare logs and a net into the ground to stop the sand and protect the back of the house from the wind. All of that is gone now. The ground cleared. A huge pit in its place, and posts standing tall, buried deep into the ground surrounding the same spot. My eyes dart back up to the Zamari. *"What are you doing?"*

I can't understand it. This amount of work would have taken me at least a few weeks to do on my own. He's done it in one night? Alone?

"I— Wh—" I struggle to find the words. Struggle to understand what I'm seeing.

And the Zamari doesn't stop working. There's a mallet in his mouth, his teeth gripping the handle as his gaze slides to me and my entire body heats with just that one look. He doesn't seem in the least surprised to see me standing there, and it tells me he's known of my presence from the moment I stepped outside.

"What are you doing?!" I hiss, my words coming out in a harsh whisper that I'm sure reaches him. I don't know whether to be confused, angry, or remain in shock.

The mallet drops from his lips and falls skillfully in his hand as he adjusts a board and nails it in.

"You need storage. A place to hide. Space."

My mouth opens and closes. Once. Two times.

He's right, of course. The shortcomings of my humble abode have always been on my mind. But with no one to do it for me, no time, and no spare credits to pay someone to make the changes, I've had to make do with what I have. The fact he noticed all that in the short time he spent inside the house makes me wonder what else he took in.

"I—" I stutter. "You're a carpenter?"

His gaze shifts to mine again. Heating me up. Scalding me. "I have many skills, Firespark."

I sputter again, clearing my throat as my thoughts shoot to more carnal, dangerous things. Skills indeed. "I don't have the credits to pay you for this. I—"

"No charge, Firespark. Complementary."

My cheeks heat.

Like the sex. Just like the sex.

Complementary.

I lick my lips, closing my mouth and biting down hard enough that my teeth hurt. The corners of his lips twitch almost as if he can read just where my mind has gone.

Looking around at the materials, I shake my head again. "Where did you get all this?" I point at the planks of wood, my finger swirling in a wide circle at all the resources he's amassed. "The wood. The tools. How..."

"Took it from the abandoned buildings." When my eyes widen, he continues, shoulders rising and falling in a shrug. "Brought them here."

My mouth opens, lips curling with a thousand unformed words that are going too fast for my tongue to form. "You *took* them?"

He slams another nail home before his gaze settles on mine again. Sure. Unreadable. "No one stopped me."

As I sputter, there's that slight quirk of his lips again. Of course, no one stopped him. They're scared shitless. And he's a mercenary. I can't have expected him to ask them nicely.

"Oh God," I groan.

"What's all this?" Estella appears at my back, eyebrows raised as she takes it all in. Her eyes grow wider, a mirror image of mine, till she looks up and spots the Zamari. "Well, I'll be damned."

I groan again.

"He did this all by himself?"

I nod.

"Where'd he get the materials from?"

I groan another time. "Lots of places in town with spare wood. He just decided to make use of them."

For a moment, Estella says nothing. And then she laughs. Laughs in a way I realize I've missed. Full. Hearty. So completely Estella that I remember all those times she used to steal snacks from storage on the mothership and we'd run down the corridor to our rooms cackling like the teens we were. It's a sound I never knew I missed.

I stare at her for a few moments, entranced before I release a breath, my mouth twitching into a smile as her laughter pulls me in.

"How am I going to explain this?"

She chokes on air, struggling to control herself, before she leans on one of the posts planted in the ground. "Better practice your speech, because you're going to need it about..." She pauses, eyes narrowing as she lifts one finger into the air as if waiting on something. And just like she knew it would happen, I hear my name piercing the air from the front of the cabin. Shouted loud. Full of barely withheld indignation.

"Miss Elsie Parks!"

"...now," Estella says.

"Shit."

Casting another glance at the Zamari, I take a deep breath and head back to the front.

The Outlaw

Human beings are noisy. Loud. Uncontrolled. Pushed by their emotions.

I work, ignoring the group that arrived as I finish adding the roof extension to Firespark's cabin. If I work all day and the next, I will complete the extension and then we can plan.

But even though I ignore the group that has called a meeting out in the open in front of her cabin, I can't ignore the stiffening of her shoulders, how she stands with her chin high, defending herself in front of what's obviously a group that she's at odds with.

Should I interfere? My *ayahl* says yes, already swirling around me and reaching in her direction. Fek. She said nothing about harming other humans, but this I cannot take. I will harm them if I must.

I scope them out without even turning around, my *ayahl* telling me everything I need to know.

"We don't take kindly to strangers, Ms. Parks. You know this." Male. Elsie's senior. Human of high standing in this settlement, judging from the way his garments seem of slightly better quality than the others surrounding him.

There are four others. Three females. One male.

"Who is this male that you have brought here to Comodre? Word says he arrived last night and has remained. He is not human. What is he?"

Firespark frowns. "Does it matter?"

The male she addresses fumes, cheeks growing red like Firespark's after she's been well and thoroughly pleasured. "You and I both know strangers are unwelcome here."

Firespark rolls her eyes. "He's not like the Nirzoik. He's here to *help* me. Help *us.* "

"Well, he's certainly helped himself." The male's focus shifts up to the cabin but I know he can't see me from where he stands. "Your *helper* ripped apart the walls of the saloon!"

Firespark's shoulders grow even more rigid. "What saloon? The building was ransacked. Torn apart." She takes a step forward, meeting the male face-to-face, and I feel a surge of pride. "The building hasn't been used for many orbits. We don't even have drinks to stock it. That means it's abandoned and every single resource in this settlement is for us all. A united world. Where we all share the spoils. Where no man is greater than the other." She lifts her chin higher, meeting his glare. "Isn't that the motto of our ancestors? The words that built Comodre?" Her gaze hardens. "I told him to take the planks. You have a problem with that...*mayor?*"

The way she says the word makes it sound like some sort of lofty title in this settlement. As if he's the one in charge. The one who makes the rules and enforces them.

Pity for him, I have a certain dislike for the law.

"Tread carefully, Ms. Parks," he says. "I would think that in your position, you would at least have some respect. I'm the only reason those brutes haven't taken you and your little friend," he gestures to the other human, Estella, "for their whores." He steps closer. "And you know it's happened before. It can happen again."

A growl is immediate in my chest. Setting my mallet down, I stretch the muscles in my neck as I shift from my position.

"Don't pretend what happened to Viv is something you have any right to speak about." Firespark's voice is so low, it almost sounds like she's growling. "You're not the fucking reason those brutes leave us alone. *We* are. We work ourselves to the bone just so they will leave us alone and I'm fucking tired of it. We're hardly surviving." She snarls, her words coming through clenched teeth. "And even then, they demand more. You think giving them what they want will stop them?" She takes another step forward, facing the male with zero fear. "*It won't*. I would have said this nicer, but you've come here being a dick like you own the place. Now, you can either *fuck* off and let me do what I want, or you can try to stop me. Fuck if I care what you do. Either way, I'm done playing by the rules."

His jaw ticks and in one swift movement, he grabs Firespark's wrist, pulling her against his chest. "What on Ivuria do you think you alone can do?" he hisses.

Thank the fekking gods. I was hoping he would do something stupid.

I'm off the roof in an instant, jumping from the slanted edge to land right behind Firespark with a thud.

Before the fool can react, my fist closes around the wrist he's dared to touch Firespark with and his light-colored eyes widen with immediate fear.

He grunts, trying to shake my hand off, even as his is still enclosed on her wrist. Tough luck. I squeeze harder, enough that I feel his feeble bones underneath his flesh. Know that if I squeeze any harder, they will crack.

"I hate males that touch what's not theirs," I rumble.

His mouth opens and closes, shock in his eyes as he suddenly releases his hold on Firespark. She glances at me, eyes wide, chest heaving, but there's an understanding that passes between us. No words need to be said as she steps away, even as my hand tightens some more on his wrist, twisting his arm till his body is bent awkwardly to relieve the pressure.

"You own the planks?" I ask, knowing fekking well he doesn't.

He sputters, gaze darting back at the others that accompanied him here. Coward beings. Especially the male that came along with this 'mayor'. He's retreated behind the females. All are watching me with a mixture of fear and anxiety. I can hear their life organs thumping hard in their chests.

The mayor squeezes his eyes tight, intent on not reacting to the pressure in his arm, before he forces them open out of pure pride. "No. But—"

"Then we have no trouble."

His mouth opens and closes. "Just...who are you?"

There's a chuckle and I catch Estella in my periphery, hands on her waist, legs apart in a wide stance, looking much prouder than she should. There's a twinkle in her eyes. "Can't tell ya, Marcus. He'll have to kill ya."

She learns fast.

Marcus' eyes widen even more, color draining from his face. "A—a mercenary then." Then there's pure panic in his eyes. "Elsie, you brought a *mercenary* to Comodre? Stupid bitch, *what were you thinking?!* He will rob us blind. Kill us all."

He squeals when I twist his arm tighter. Panting, he gasps for air, small dots of perspiration gathering on his brow. "I—I am the mayor of this settlement." He gulps, hardly able to meet my gaze. "You will do well to release me and not harm me."

I release a slight huff of a laugh through my nose, just loud enough for him to hear it before I lean in blocking my words from Firespark's view as I whisper into his ear.

"Harm is the least of your worries," I say. "Touch her again, and you might find yourself without a hand. Threaten her again, and you might find yourself no longer breathing. Right now, the only thing keeping you safe is the fact she hasn't ordered me to kill you."

He stops breathing. I hear the moment his lungs pause as I lean away from him and finally release his arm.

He pulls in a sharp intake of air, fiery eyes flashing to Elsie and then me as he shakes and stretches the muscles in his arm and backs away.

My *ayahl* writhes and sways. This male is a threat. Firespark might not realize it, but she has more than the Nirzoik to worry about.

I cast my focus her way and there's a hardness in her eyes.

Hmm. Maybe she does realize.

The mayor wipes his arm across his face, taking away fluid that had leaked from his snout. All the while his eyes shift from me to Firespark and back.

I study him a bit more. He and his entourage do not have the same haunting pain behind their eyes that I saw in Firespark's or even the *kiv*'s. Almost as if...life has not been as difficult for them.

And I bet I can guess why.

My jaw ticks as I regard them. A problem for another day.

"I'll be working on the cabin behind me." I turn to Firespark, the coolness of her blue eyes washing over me like a calming stream. "If anyone else has any objections, tell them to come see me."

CHAPTER TWENTY-ONE

Elsie

It's strange hearing all the sounds of work being done on the cabin and not being the one carrying it out.

For the first time in what feels like many orbits, I'm sitting on the chair on the deck, Kiana wrapped in a blanket in my arms, Ivuria shining down on us, and there's a sense of...peace.

The bangs and thuds that shook the cabin have now calmed. The roof's done. The walls of the back room are coming together. My cabin is suddenly bigger. And I can't believe any of it.

Wrapping Kiana tighter in my arms, I allow some of Ivuria's rays to hit her skin as I rock her slowly.

It's strange, this feeling.

For so long I've been working, letting every day go by with a tight knot of anxiety and uncertainty surrounding my every move. Just sitting for a few moments in peace seems almost criminal. Almost detrimental to my survival. As if, at any moment, my world will come falling down because of this one lapse in vigilance.

"One of us should have gone to the mines today," Estella says from where she's sitting on the deck itself, back braced against the wall. Her gaze is locked on the charred remains of her cabin, unmoving, as if images are passing before her eyes that I can't see.

"I know," I whisper after a few moments.

"Then why haven't either of us gone?"

I stare into the distance, not sure of the answer myself, and we lapse into the comfortable silence we've been nestled in since we came to sit on the deck.

"It's because of him, isn't it." Estella finally pulls her attention from the remains of her cabin to look at me. "After what he did with Marcus, I can see why you hired him." She tilts her head back and stares into the sky. "It felt fucking good seeing him put that asshole in his place."

"Estella..."

"No. It's true. He deserved it." She pauses, her finger tapping on the wood beneath her. "Especially after what he said about Viv."

I pull my gaze away from her, feeling my jaw tighten in the process. It's not like I can say anything to disagree. She's right, of course.

"Things are going to change around here," she whispers. "I can already feel it."

Staring up at the dim outline of Ivuria 11 in the heavens, a breath shudders from within me as I let her words settle in my mind. I sure hope she's right.

The dull sounds coming from the rear of the house pull me back and my thoughts go once more to the Zamari. I brought him water and offered him some of the little food that I have.

He accepted the water only. I tried to help him with the planks, too, and he refused.

For the greater part of the morning, I've watched him work. Unable to pull my gaze away from the muscles rippling in his back or the way his thighs bunched as he manipulated the large, heavy planks as if they weighed nothing. He's like a machine, doing the work of five men all on his own, and even as he puts my cabin together, it feels as if he's doing much more than that. It feels like he's also putting back together something deep inside me that was torn apart.

I shift with Kiana, looking down at her and once again wondering if I'm making the right decisions. Her little lips are rosy from the warmth and the effect of the medicine I gave her. Medicine we're almost out of.

She's so little. She doesn't deserve any of this.

I know the Zamari must be wondering why I've taken the place of her mother. Why I'm so attached to a child I didn't birth. And sometimes, I wonder if Kiana will grow up and look at me and think the same.

Maybe it's because I know what it's like to lose both my parents. Maybe it's because I don't want her to feel any of that. She was so young when her mother died, just a babe. She doesn't remember her at all. Like many others, the woman who birthed her was taken by the sickness. The strange illness that swept into our colony and remained.

No one knows where the sickness came from, or even what it really is. Some seem to fall prey to it, while others don't. I'm one of the lucky ones. And yet, I'd trade places just to not see her suffer.

Each day, watching Kiana brace against the intense muscle and joint aches, watching her struggle to eat and keep food down ...I wouldn't wish it on anyone. She will waste away without medicine or help, and for that, I need the Nirzoik gone. It takes mining for almost sixty days to gather enough *sansa* gems to even afford one dose of the medicine she needs, and with the Nirzoik tax, that time extends even more.

A heavy breath shudders through me as I watch her sleep. I wasn't lying when I faced Marcus. I told him the truth. I'm done living like this.

Something shifts in my periphery and I look up to see a figure stumbling down the sandy road. A large sack slung over her shoulder, Viv staggers as she moves. I can see the weariness pressed into her frame as if it was ironed in there.

"She's been gone since you left," Estella says. "Slept in the mines."

I force out another breath; a heaving sigh. A sort of pain I'm used to spreading through my chest as I watch my friend almost collapse on her deck.

She lifts her head then, turning it our way and I see the moment her gaze falls on us. See it in the way she perks up a little. She lifts a hand and waves and I reciprocate with the same motion.

"Sober?" I ask, the words only meant for Estella's ears.

"Yea," Estella responds. She eases up on her arms before she stands and stretches. "But not for long. She's going to need some company."

As if Kiana can sense Estella's movement, her eyes flutter open and she squints. There's a little smile when she catches me watching her before she looks towards Viv's cabin. "Aunt Viv?"

I smile at her. "That's right, Aunt Viv is back."

A smile spreads across her face as she tries to ease up enough so she can see.

"Gimme her here," Estella reaches for the child before

swinging her into her arms. "Let's go spend the night at Viv's." She grins. "You'd like that, wouldn't you my little *cagri* crystal."

Kiana giggles. "I'm not a cagri crystal!"

"Yes, you are! It's why I want to gobble you up." As Estella winks at me and heads off to Viv's, I can't help but smile as I watch them go. I wave again to Viv and she gives me a nod, but even from here, I can see the pain in her eyes. The strain. The pressure.

And yet still, she manages to smile as Kiana wriggles trying to get to her.

I stay there, watching them for a few more moments before my gaze falls to my hands. I feel like I should be doing something. Time's never been a luxury that I've ever had. At least, not since the crash.

Rising, I walk into the cabin and head to the back where there's now a door at the side of the kitchen. My eyes widen even though I've seen the progress he's made before. Still, the reality of all the work he's done is unbelievable. The roof's completely covered the new room I step into. The walls are all done; the flooring too. I turn slowly, taking in the new space and wondering if I'm possibly dreaming.

Quite possible. I've brushed death so many times in the last few days it's entirely plausible that I've died and this is all just the musings of a dying mind.

The thought doesn't scare me as much as it should.

When a sound catches my ear and my gaze flies to the ground at my feet, I frown a little. I hear it again and I shift, turning in a slow circle.

"Are you going to come in, Firespark? Or do I have to come get you?"

His voice does something to me that it shouldn't. Makes a deep tingling sensation travel from my fingertips to my toes and makes my lungs forget just how to make me breathe.

"Wh-where are you?"

I have to squint, but soon I see it. A section of the floor that's not as flat as the rest. And that's because it's lifted slightly. A secret door. My eyes widen some more as his hat emerges first and then I can see his face. In here, where there's hardly any light reaching from outside, those eyes of his draw me in like a moth to a flame. They light up the dark even as they pierce me and strip me bare.

"You made a hidey hole."

His brows shift slightly at my words before that same barely-there smile curves his lips. "For you and your *kiv*," he says. "You will need a proper hiding place when I'm gone."

And just like that, the bottom of my belly opens up and my stomach feels like it's hanging above a bottomless pit. Because he's leaving after all this. How foolish of me to forget.

I force a smile and nod. "Can I see it?"

He doesn't answer, just those eyes studying me for a moment before he disappears into the hole. And that's a yes. Funny how I understand him when he doesn't even speak. With one hand he keeps the trapdoor open, the other steadying me on a short flight of stairs as I descend into the darkness below.

I expected it to be small, just a crawl space, so when I step on the floor and I'm able to stand upright without my head touching the ceiling, I utter a little sound of surprise.

The space is as big as the room above it. It's lined with planks and well suited to storing grain—if I had any—and for hiding. Just like he said. I turn in a slow circle as the light is slowly extinguished as he closes the door.

"It's..."

"Perfect if they come and you can't fight. Get the *kiv*. Get your comrade. Hide here." His voice finds me in the dark, making me still. He's talking about the worst-case scenario.

"There was only enough *zyka* left to coat the planks surrounding this room. It will be safe if those fools decide to play with a fire cube and burn you to the ground." His voice wanes, as if he turns away. "There is a lock here on the inside. Use it. Lock yourself in. Do not attempt to fight the Nirzoik. Don't leave till they've gone away."

The lump that appears in my throat grows larger with each word he says. "You think it will come to that?"

There's silence between us, and then his voice appears right beside my ear. The heat of his body warming my spine. "It always does."

I push down the lump, willing that panic that always threatens to rise whenever I think of losing my home to those brutes. "You talk like you know them. The Nirzoik, I mean."

"I know what they are." His breath brushes against my skin, the tip of his nose like a faint shadow moving down my neck. I'm transported right back to that cave. To what he did to me. To what we shared. "If you're hiding here, they won't be able to tell. Their hearing lacks and the *zyka* will block your scent."

He...thought of everything.

"You used your zyka..." I force my words to sound as calm as I can make them, even though I'm anything but. "Isn't it expensive? How will I—"

"I can get more."

There's pressure in my chest at how much he's thought to put into this. *All* of this. When I didn't even ask him to. This... stranger. He's really done more for me in the short time I've met him than the very people I've lived with since crashing here on Ivuria 10.

It all comes crashing into me with such a huge wave I can't block it. The worry. The strain. The gratitude. The pain. My chest caves in a deep inhale that feels like it creates a vortex in my soul as I choke on my own emotions.

I don't mean to do it again. To be so vulnerable in front of him, wearing my emotions on my sleeve. But before I can try and hide it, strong arms encircle me and his touch makes the torrent churn over as if it wants to destroy me.

All the strength I've been riding on, forcing myself to see every waking day, pushing through, although deep down I am breaking apart inside—it all comes crashing through me like a raging storm that makes my knees buckle.

And he falls with me. Taking me to the floor with his arms still wrapped around me. Not saying a word. Allowing my tears to fall even though I try to hold them back. Not judging me for this weakness. Not asking why I'm breaking down like this.

I turn in his arms, desperate to see his face in the darkness. To see the disappointment. To see the disgust. But all I see are his glowing eyes and the fact that even in that gaze, there is nothing there vilifying me.

He doesn't say a word, and it's still like he understands it all.

This room. The hope it brings. The hope *he* brings. I never knew how much I needed it until now.

I lean myself against him even as his hand rises and cups my head in a way I'd have never expected from an outlaw. And yet, he does it just the same. He holds me there. Silently. His strength all that I need even though I should take none of it. Even though I know he's leaving soon and I will have to rely on myself all again.

But, for this moment, only for this moment, I want to be just a girl. Just a girl without all the responsibilities. Just a girl without all the weight on her shoulders. A girl who can play in the sands and enjoy the light of the star. Who can go to sleep under the twinkling lights that dot her night sky and not feel the fear that follows her every waking moment.

Just a girl.

And so I shudder in his grasp. For the first time, allowing myself to mourn something that I couldn't have changed for myself. Allowing myself to mourn the dream all the colonists had when they embarked on the Voyager Genesis 311. Allowing myself to mourn the fact that this paradise is anything but.

Something develops underneath my ear that's pressed into his chest. A sound. Like a deep purr vibrating from his throat. I shudder, my entire frame jerking in a tearless sob as that purr seeps into my bones like warm water loosening my aching muscles.

I collapse against him, only his strength holding me up as he continues to hold me tight. Allowing me to *feel*. Allowing me to just *be*.

I don't know how long he holds me like that. How long we stay there in the dark just experiencing this moment, but when he suddenly stiffens is the moment I know something is wrong.

"They're here."

Two words.

Two words that send a chill through my spine.

"Who?" I push away all the feelings churning in my chest to look up at him, dreading his answer. But he doesn't reply. I see the answer in his eyes. "The Nirzoik."

He pulls me up as he stands, turning and heading toward the trap door.

"Wait—" I stretch one hand toward him. "Something's wrong. They're not due here for at least a few more days."

I can tell that barely-there smile crosses his lips, just from the way he talks. "Good thing you brought me here early then."

And then he's gone. I don't get to stop him. Don't get to ask what his game plan is. Because there's only one plan. Scare them away...by any means possible.

This was the whole idea from the start. And yet, my heart's suddenly thudding too hard in my chest. What if we fail?

What if he gets hurt?

The thought makes another strange sort of pain throb in my chest and I pace a slow circle in the dark, biting my nails as I wait.

But I can't just wait here in the dark. I have to know what's going on out there.

The Nirzoik really shouldn't have arrived yet. This isn't normal. And whenever routine breaks, there's always one of us who pays the price.

Climbing the stairs, I push against the trap door.

It's heavy. Heavier than he made it seem and I bite back a grunt as I climb out of the space. Once on my feet, I creep toward the front door, ears perked for any sound.

I don't hear them. I don't hear anything. And the closer I get to the window, the curtain obscuring my view, the harder my heart thuds against my ribs.

I'm by the window, back pressed against the wall, listening for the slightest sound when I finally hear something.

Rocket bikes arriving outside my cabin. How many, I can't tell. My throat bobs as I hold my breath, waiting.

Heavy footfalls thud against the ground before growing louder as they step onto my deck. The wood groans under the weight, creaking with each step before a heavy fist slams into my front door, almost startling my soul from my being.

"Open up *kinchi!*"

I swallow hard, fingers digging into the wood behind me as I press my palms against the wall to keep me steady. I don't even feel the pain shooting from the wounds there. Don't even feel how my hand trembles against the planks.

There's a rumble of annoyance in the brute's throat and his fist lands two more times.

"You're sure this is the right one?" the Nirzoik growls.

"This is where they said he's hiding," another answers.

Another growl.

"You're harboring someone who doesn't belong, *kinchi...* and every resident must pay dues."

Dues? They came back all this way for just one person's dues? I doubt it.

When the fist slams into my door again, so hard the wall vibrates at my back, I can hardly breathe.

"Burn it down."

Those three words and my eyes widen. Three words and everything I feared would happen plays out right before my eyes. Only, I haven't even tried fighting back yet. I haven't even—

"You Nirzoik have always been so...hasty." The Zamari's voice cuts through the heavy footsteps of the Nirzoik as they step off my deck. Silences it. As if they've stopped walking, momentarily shocked by his appearance, and I wonder for a second where he was hiding that they didn't see him. But all that doesn't matter the moment I hear his voice. The moment an intense sense of relief crashes through me.

For a moment, no one speaks and I shift to the window, fingers trembling as I pull a bit of the curtain away just so I can peek. I see them immediately, so broad, their backs are all I can see. But then they shift spreading apart, almost as if they're covering more ground, spreading themselves out to deal with the threat suddenly before them.

Four Nirzoik. Four heartless brutes.

And then I see him and I realize just what they're doing.

The Zamari stands in the road, arms hanging weaponless at his sides, hat tipped low so they can hardly see his face. But I sense the moment he sees me. A slight movement of his eyes and our gazes lock. And in that moment, I know he's aware of every single thing happening around him. I become aware that things are about to get lethal. That I should run. Hide like he told me to. And yet, I cannot move.

They've created a circle around him and that pool of panic in my gut rises. He's surrounded. One against four and he hasn't even reached for his blaster.

"Who the *fek* are you?!" One of the Nirzoik says. He inhales loudly, loud enough that I hear. He twiddles a fire cube in his hand, the glow like a copy of the distant sunset. One flick of that thing and he could make my whole world come crashing down.

"I said..." The Nirzoik takes a step forward, shoulders bunching in a way that makes him look bigger. "Who...the fek... are *you?*"

The Zamari shifts his gaze from mine, meeting the Nirzoik's glare. "A warning."

His words drop on heavy silence before one of the Nirzoik laughs. Head thrown back, his shoulders shake with mirth as he glances at his colleagues. "Scouts weren't lying when they said they saw a stranger arriving." He stops the laugh so suddenly, I realize he wasn't really laughing at all. "A *Zamari*," he growls.

"Now what would a Zamari be doing in a place like this?"

When the Zamari doesn't answer, the Nirzoik takes another step closer. They're smart. Closing the distance to threaten him but not going close enough that he can reach them.

My pulse is a steady beat in my ears as I notice movement in the cabin window down the road. James' house. He's peeking just as I am. No doubt Estella and Viv are too. We all have bated breath, waiting to see what will happen. Waiting to see if this plan of ours will work.

"Silent, huh, Zamari? No words?" The Nirzoik's gaze slides to the comrade on his right, and my entire body readies as if I'm the one facing them out there. Because, even *I* can tell they're about to make a move. "Maybe you'll talk after this!"

The Nirzoik moves. Quickly, too quick for my brain to even realize what he's done, the Nirzoik swings a blaster into his palm and fires. A scream dies in my throat at the undeniable sound of the blaster fire, time slowing down as I see the red laser shoot through the air.

But just as quickly, time snaps back and it's the Nirzoik that falls. The thick scent of singed flesh reaches my nose as a soft breeze sweeps through the small clearing, kicking up sand and dust as I stare in shock.

The Nirzoik's on the ground, one clean shot to the center of his skull. And the Zamari...

My eyes widen as they settle on him. Blaster in his hand, still pointed in the direction of the downed Nirzoik. It doesn't take long for my brain to catch up.

How did he...when did he get his gun?

The other three Nirzoik are momentarily as stunned as I am, because they take too long to move. And then they're charging. All three at once. Roars on their lips, blades pulled from their straps.

The outlaw doesn't wait. He ducks, causing two to collide before he swings low with a kick that takes the third one down. He moves like air, gliding as he rights himself and presses one foot into the skull of the Nirzoik who's thrashing on the ground. His back is turned to the others and I want to scream for him to turn around just as they twist to face him, eyes filled with more rage than I've ever seen in their eyes before.

"Get him!" One screams.

I forget I'm supposed to be hiding. I stand, pulling away the curtain as I watch in a sort of disbelief that has me stunned.

Even with his back turned, the Zamari moves as if he can see the two brutes coming at him from behind. His blaster spins in one hand, completing a 360 before he points the barrel over his shoulder and fires.

The blast is so powerful, the Nirzoik it hits is thrust backward. His body goes limp. A searing wound in the center of his skull. My hand flies over my mouth, stifling what might have been a gasp if my throat could work.

Seeing his comrade being taken down so easily and with the Zamari's back still facing him, the other Nirzoik falters before an all-consuming rage lights up his soulless eyes. He launches into the air, the handle of his blade gripped with both hands as he aims for the Zamari's neck.

It's just a slight tilt of the weapon, but that's all he does. Just that slight tilt before the blaster goes off again, finding its target like a seeking missile.

There's a heavy thud as the Nirzoik falls to the ground and then the clatter of his blade as his lifeless fingers release it.

My whole body shakes with the effort it takes to measure my breathing, to breathe through the anxiety and panic, the adrenaline of what I just witnessed before my eyes.

The one squirming on the ground, no doubt being stifled by the sand his face is still being pressed into, reaches down, trying to grab his weapon from where it's holstered on his waist. Too late. The Zamari's blaster engages one more time. The target: the fool's hand. The Nirzoik's blaster is shot from its pouch and there's a muffled howl of pain as the Nirzoik snatches his hand back. Pulse still beating hard enough I have to focus to hear what's being said, I watch as the Zamari leans in, crouching so the brute can hear him.

"Now, for the warning..."

There are more muffled noises. Cursing. Indignation.

"Tell your chief, Comodre is off limits."

He waits a few more seconds, allowing the Nirzoik to squirm some more. When he finally lifts his boot off the Nirzoik's head and steps back, he allows the brute to rise. With heavy puffs, lips pulled back to reveal sharp teeth, the Nirzoik stands, gaze shifting to his downed comrades before going back to the Zamari.

"You should leave while your legs still work," the Zamari says. "And never return..." He slips his blaster back into its holster as if he doesn't need it anymore. "Or I mightn't be so generous the next time."

"Generous?" The Nirzoik spits. *You killed my brothers.*"

The Zamari's entire countenance is unreadable. "Good. You understand."

With that, he steps around the Nirzoik before pausing. "I really wouldn't want to turn around and still see you there." His fingers shift, as if itching for his blaster and I see the moment the Nirzoik picks up on the same movement. "Maybe your chief will get the message if *none* of you return."

He starts turning around when the Nirzoik's eyes widen and he hurries to his parked bike. One last hateful glance over his shoulder and he climbs on it, reaching for another of the parked ones.

The Zamari makes a sound in his throat. "Those are mine now." He pauses. "For the inconvenience."

The Nirzoik growls, teeth baring, before he turns, guns his engine, and shoots down the road. I watch the dust cloud follow him until he fades into the darkness of the incoming dusk, hardly believing everything that just happened.

When my gaze shifts back to the Zamari, he's looking right at me.

I can't...I can't tell what he's thinking, but I know the thought that's currently screaming in my head.

He did it! He scared the brute away!

He's much, much better than I thought he was...at *everything*. And suddenly I realize one glaring fact. He's not worth the credits I promised to give him. He's worth much, *much* more.

Really and truly, I can't afford him.

CHAPTER TWENTY-TWO

Elsie

I stand leaning against the wall near my front door as I watch Viv, Estella, James, and some of the others laugh and chatter around the small table they've parked in the clearing. The deck of cards is forgotten as they make jokes and share a few bottles of drink. They're so loud, I can't help but smile as I watch them.

It's a glimpse of life that I haven't seen in so many orbits, it's almost like I'm watching a movie.

Kiana's fast asleep at Viv's and I don't have to spend the night in the mines working to gather gems, because...we did it. Well, *he* did it.

The outlaw.

He stands leaning against his bike a few feet from me, watching the festivities like I am and yet still my skin prickles as if his entire attention is on me. And it is. Because the moment I look his way, his gaze shifts to mine and a deep warmth spreads all across my skin.

"Aren't you going to join in?" I smile. "It's a party for you."

His gaze narrows only slightly before he shakes his head. "Parties are not something I...do."

I breathe a soft laugh. Of course. After what I saw him do. After what we all saw him do, one thing's clear. He's no normal machine. And yet, he looks so different standing there right now. It's almost hard to reconcile that this same male before me is the one who took down four Nirzoik without even breaking a sweat.

Makes it almost laughable that we are so...*weak* compared to him.

"Hmm." I move closer till I'm standing at the edge of my deck. "What do you like to do?"

I don't expect him to answer. Since I've met this male, he's kept most of his secrets clutched tight. Something I understand, but at the same time, something that also tugs at a part of me I'm trying to ignore. Only, every second being around him makes that thing harder.

"Things that might bore a wild being like you, Firespark."

His nickname for me shouldn't make that warmth rise in my chest. It almost sounds like it's replaced my real name to him now.

"Like what? Lying on a blanket and staring up at the stars?"

There's a slight twitch of his lips. "Exactly like that." I'm momentarily surprised and then that warmth inside me increases so much I wonder if I might catch afire.

I can feel my cheeks heat. "Ok, uh...I'm going to head in. You're welcome to come in when you like. The bed's free." I lick my lips as I drag my focus back to the group still having fun before us. "You should go. Have fun. It's their way of saying thanks."

Those piercing eyes are still locked on me when I look back at him and the warmth inside me rises even more. With a slight nod, I turn and hurry inside, my heart beating harder than it should.

This is strange. This feeling.

It makes my skin tingle, a small knot of anxiety rolling in my gut as I walk slowly to the back of my cabin and enter the small washroom. There's a tub there and a waste removal system. Both scavenged but working well enough.

Stripping slowly, I remove my tunic and skirts as I stare at nothing in particular, my thoughts in a swirl.

He scared the Nirzoik away. We're...free.

It's almost too good to be true.

Filling up the tub, I dip my hands in it and let out a soft sigh. The water's still warm from the sun beating down on the sands, warming the pipes underneath. As I step inside, submerging myself, I can't help but release a low moan of relief. Releasing my braid, I lean back and rest my head against the edge, fully submersing the rest of my body. The wax-light set in the wall near the tub sends a warm glow across the water and my skin, and another unhindered moan leaves my lips as my muscles relax.

My fingers slide over my belly, moving up to my breasts, the tips going over my nipples and making them pebble. I bite back a gasp as I imagine him right before me.

Fuck. I'm so, so bad for this. Lusting after something, someone, who will never be mine. And yet still, I can't stop.

My fingers move lower till they're skirting over that dip between my thighs, slipping through the brush of hair to glide across my clit in a way that makes my legs tighten, trapping my hand there.

He's leaving soon. As soon as I pay him what I owe. And yet here I am wishing for...

Wishing for what? That he would stay?

The thought makes me pause and even though it should

scare me, I squeeze my thighs tighter, grinding against my hand, succumbing to a need that seems greater than even logic.

"Zamari," I whisper, my hips moving harder, that tight knot at the base of my belly growing even tighter, urging me toward release. "Zamari."

I want him more than I should. I need...

It's the sound of a deep growl that catches me first. One that makes me shudder from a strange sort of bliss. Makes my clit tighten and throb, my hand suddenly not enough.

Luminescent eyes meet mine as the Zamari steps into the room, filling the space, and I know I should feel some sort of embarrassment. He must know what I'm doing. Must have heard me. But where the embarrassment doesn't come, another emotion takes its place. Relief.

Maybe I wanted him to find me here. Maybe I wanted him to see me hot and shameless before him.

I watch as he walks to stand right behind me, my head tilting all the way back just so I can keep sight of him. And when he kneels so we're on eye level, one hand rising to trace the line of my throat, I swallow underneath his feather-light touch.

"What are you doing?" I whisper, my mind completely focused on the way his hands dip into the water, how they travel down my shoulders to curl around my breasts, forcing a strangled groan from me. How my core clenches hard on nothing, wanting more.

"You called me."

My cheeks heat and still, I don't remove my hand from between my thighs. I want this, whatever he's going to do, more than anything I've wanted in a long, long time.

The Zamari leans farther in, one hand trailing from my breast down my belly, tremors following the path of his touch until his hand closes around the one trapped between my thighs.

My breaths come in stuttered gasps as he pushes his fingers between mine, lacing our hands together before his fingers brush against my clit, making me writhe against it.

My eyes flutter closed when his lips meet mine. It's a slow, undemanding kiss. One that makes something inside me quiver as his hand replaces mine, fingers moving with expert precision. They slide through my folds, brushing over my clit and then stop there as I inhale through my mouth against his lips. There's only the soft tremor of a rumbling growl against my mouth as he rubs my clit, our breaths shared as I gasp and strain at the sudden onslaught of pleasure that shoots through me.

His fingers caress my heat, swirling, investigating, before venturing lower to my entrance. When he pushes one digit and then another inside, I whimper into his mouth, hips bucking against his palm.

"Sweet, Firespark," he growls. "You undo me."

My hips grind against his palm as he thrusts his fingers inside me, his tongue working wonders against mine while his other hand palms and squeezes my breast. I whimper again, the sensations almost too much. I can already feel that warmth ready to cascade right through me and my thighs tighten around his arm.

"That's it," he purrs. "Fek. You're the most beautiful thing I've seen in all of Ivuria."

His words are like a catalyst, driving me to the edge, and I pant his name again. "Zamari."

Another growl. "You tempt me, Firespark. To tell you my real name just so I can hear you moan it, just like that."

He takes my bottom lip between his teeth, nipping lightly, and my eyes flutter open to pitch black ones. Eyes that should make me so afraid and yet, still, do not.

"Your name..." I whisper, even though I know he won't let me know. Even though I know it's just more proof that I'm insane, falling for a male who will leave me in a few days. Falling for someone who can't even tell me who they really are because I am nothing to them.

And yet, the way he's looking at me. The way his fingers never stop, unrelenting in their assault as his dark gaze swallows me whole.

"I want nothing more than to tell you." That deep rumble of his voice, as if he's on the edge of his control, just like I am. "But I will not endanger you so."

"Danger..." A word that should make my juices stop flowing. One that should make me shiver and hide away. Instead, it makes my heart beat harder.

For he is danger. The most dangerous being I've ever known and yet, his touch, his attention... He dips his head again, kissing me so gently as his hand tightens on my breast, kneading as a grunt escapes his lips.

Dangerous. Yes. To everything I know. And yet still I'm attracted like metal to a magnet.

"A male like me can only bring misfortune." He whispers against my lips. "It's why we Zamari don't stick around. Stay around me long enough and you'll eventually reach harm. There are many males that wish to kill me, Firespark."

His fingers curl inside me, twisting with each stroke, and another surge of heat floods through my belly, making me clench. "I can take care of myself."

His voice is dark. His laugh darker. "Oh, Firespark. I know. That's why I'm slowly driven to madness." He breathes against my lips. "Why I want you so."

He wants me?

His fingers increase their relentless thrusting and my breaths come harder still.

"You want me..." I only manage to whisper.

His eyes seem to grow only darker. So dark that the wax-light reflects off them like they're shiny obsidian gems. He leans in, lips brushing against my ear before he runs his tongue along the edge. My eyes roll back as he fucks me harder with his hand. "Every bit of you."

A deep growl erupts from him at the same time that my eyes roll over again and my legs stiffen, pure intense pleasure crashing right through me.

"I want you too," I pant and he growls again, his strokes turning languid as his lips trail down from my ears to my neck. "If only for a little while."

His tongue moves against the skin there, sucking before I feel his teeth, almost as if he wants to bite me. But he resists. Pulls back at the same time that he slides his fingers from my core and brings them up through the water.

Feverish little tremors rock through me as I watch him bring those fingers to his lips. Eyes never leaving me, he wipes them clean with his tongue.

Finally, his gaze slides back to me. "Elsie..." he says, and my heart does a strange aching thing that makes me stiffen as I wait for him to reject me. But his gaze only searches mine for what feels like a moment in time where it's only him and me on this plane of existence.

And then he rises.

His hat comes off first. And then his vest. The tunic underneath is pulled out of his trouse, then the clasps unfastened and he lets it all fall to the floor.

His cock bobs right in front of my face, those swollen bands looking stretched and thicker than they did the first time.

He steps into the bath and even with my too-slack muscles, I manage to scoot over. It's too small for both of us. I end up sitting on his lap, his cock between my legs, pressing against my core. My already trembling folds settle against his hardness like a temptation for me to grind on him once again.

But the Zamari pulls me back against him, my back settling against his chest as he uses one arm to hold me there, the other to slowly run across my body as he washes me.

We sit like that in silence and peace, time ticking by but not bothering me in the way it usually does. There's no to-do list. I don't have to try and get as much work done as I possibly can. He forces me to relax. But I can't completely.

I will have to go back to the mines. It's our only source of income. And I owe him. I owe him a lot.

I tilt my head so I can look up at him.

His gaze is almost reverent. So intense, my breath catches. His eyes are still bled to black, but that is the only thing that tells me he's on edge. For his languid strokes as he washes me are gentle. The way his other arm holds me close? Gentle too.

"Why do your eyes do that?"

He stills, and I feel his gaze shift to mine even though I can't see his pupils. When he doesn't answer after a few beats, my lips press into a line. I understand. It's not like I don't. This —whatever this is between us—isn't ever going to develop into more. He already stated that much. This is all we will ever be. Two beings drawn to each other who will never be more than that.

"I can hear your life organ, Firespark." His arm slips from around me as he presses his palm against the center of my chest. "I can hear the lifeblood running through your veins." He trails a finger across my breast, higher, over my collarbone to my neck. "Hear it pulsing here."

And just his mention of it, I can suddenly hear it too. I shift on his lap, the movement causing my core to rub over his hardness, and we both suck in deep breaths.

"Your lifeblood calls to me just like your body does. For me to take it." He pauses and for the first time, he pulls his gaze away, staring at the entrance to the room as if some part of him is telling him he should leave. "Resisting you is torture."

My gaze flicks over his strong jaw, the way his teeth are clenched underneath, everything he's said repeating in my mind till it starts to make sense.

Slowly, I turn in his arms until I'm straddling him. His cock presses between us, heating my belly, and my core tightens at the sight of it. Taking a handful of the water in my hand, I run it over his shoulders, washing him in the same way he was washing me. For long moments, no words pass between us, because the puzzle pieces are slowly coming together.

The way he reacted each time he smelled my blood. How he'd licked my palms, numbing my wounds but taking in my blood at the same time. He is a being who is attracted to the very thing that keeps me alive.

It's enough for me to walk away. So why do I remain? Washing him. Grooming him in intimate slow strokes the same way his fingers rise and do the same at my back.

His hands dip into my hair, running the water through the strands as he undoes my braid and watches me.

"What did I taste like?" I whisper.

His throat moves, and when he opens his mouth to speak, I see the tips of his fangs. Sharp, pointed weapons. My skin would easily break if he decided to act on his urges.

The thought only makes my heart beat a little faster, and I run my tongue over my lower lip. He watches the movement, one of his hands coming around to trace my lips with his thumb.

His voice is guttural when he responds. "Like the sweetest nectar." His gaze travels over my face in that same way he does, as if he's scanning every detail. "I will never forget you."

Happiness all rolled up in a package wrapped with sadness. He will never forget me...

"You will leave once I get the rest of the credits I owe, won't you..."

I'm happy when he doesn't respond, just continues to wash my hair, because I know the answer.

He's not made to linger or attach. When the task is done, he will vanish like a mirage. Yet, the thought sits like a stone in my stomach. I want more time. I want to understand this male who kills without mercy, yet touches me with such care.

I lift my head slowly, eyes meeting his darkened gaze. Without a word, I rise on my knees, water streaming down my skin. He stills, the air crackling between us.

I know it then, like I knew what I had to do that day I left for Calanta. I don't want to regret what's left of our time. Breaking the intensity of his gaze, I look down between us.

His cock bobs as if it likes my attention and when I lower, pressing my heat against his tip, it jerks hard at the contact.

"Firespark..." The Zamari clenches his teeth as I lift my gaze back to his, forgetting about all else as I lower myself onto his tip.

It takes conscious effort to keep focused, to not let my eyes roll back at the feel of him pushing in. His cock is like smooth, hard silk, that milky pre-cum brimming from the tip to lubricate us as I slide down a little more.

My pussy clenches, greedy for more even as I pause to adjust to the sudden stretch. And then he's holding on to my hips with both hands, steadying me, allowing me to take him as much as I can before my pussy quivers with the strain.

Looking between us, I pant, eyes glazing over at the sight of him between my legs. I didn't take him all the last time. And this time, I'm only at the first band. It's slightly swollen this time and I reach between us to grip it with one hand.

His entire torso tightens, the muscles going rock hard as he inhales sharply. With my hand still gripping him, he pulls back and shunts forward, driving deep. My knees go weak and I release him, bracing on the bath as he takes the lead, his grasp on my hips holding me upright as he pulls back and drives upward again.

He leans forward, his eager lips meeting my breasts as he balances me on his cock, tongue swirling around the hardened nipple as a cry bubbles in my throat.

"Soft," he growls in response. "Your heat welcomes me so well, Firespark." He tightens his hold on my hips, lifting me up before driving me down again.

I grip his head, my fingers tight in his hair as I pant, leaning forward to rest my head on his as he licks and sucks on my nipple, his tongue adding to the pleasure of his heated cock incites in my core.

"Fuck me, Zamari."

He growls. "Fuck?" But he gets the meaning immediately. "I could fuck you all night."

Water sloshes and spills over the bath as he drives into me, holding me in place as his cock spreads and carves a path in my channel I know no other male will ever fit. I could weep, but the intensity of his thrusts is too much. My mouth opens in a soundless scream of pure, carnal bliss.

The orgasm that crashes through me makes me boneless. Makes me grip his head tight enough to leave a bruise. My whole body stiffens in his grasp as he drives deep, only stopping to savor the frantic throbs echoing through my core before he growls low in his chest. The sound like a warning to all that I am his and he is mine. And for a moment, I want to believe it. I want to believe it all.

I'm lost to the world as my body goes limp, the only thing keeping me there being his grip on me and his hard cock thrusting me into oblivion. I'm quivering at the edge of lucidity before he pulls all the way out before burying himself deep. He growls against my breast, the vibrations running over my nipple like little waves as he pulls out and thrusts deep again.

I can tell he's at the edge. But I want to push him over. It's madness, but I want to feel him become undone, just as he's made me feel. These emotions quickly taking over me? I want him to feel them, too.

A moan rushes from me as I push down on his next thrust, taking as much of him as I can. His hands tighten on my hips as I bear down, pussy quivering as I milk his thickness. And then I feel it. That first partially swollen band.

It's like a match is lit in some darkness in my mind and I know I want it.

I grind down, hard. Wrapping my arms around his neck, as he lifts his head, kisses and little nips peppering my clavicle to my shoulder.

I lift my hips an inch, making our juices spread before grinding down again. My head falls back, mouth open wide, my eyes staring at the roof but not seeing a thing. Only feeling. Only feeling *everything*.

There's a suddenness to it. An incredible stretch before that band suddenly slips into my heat. A deep, animalistic growl rolls from the pits of his being at the same moment. And then, there's pain.

Pain in my shoulder that brings me back from the void. I lift my head at the same time the Zamari freezes. When I look at him, he's staring at my shoulder like he's seeing a ghost. My gaze falls, and the twin lines of blood running down my clavicle meet my gaze. My blood.

It should alarm me. Should make me scream. But none of that happens. It all goes away when he lifts his dark gaze to mine, and even in those obsidian depths, I can see the utter horror. Horror at what he's done. Even as his cock jerks and tightens within me. Even as his fangs lengthen, his body telling me more than he will say out loud.

"Firespark." That deep, guttural growl only makes me quiver on him some more. "I am sorry, female. I—"

I shake my head, not wanting him to break the moment.

"I'm not sorry," I whisper. *Because I want this. And I'm a fool to want this, but I want it, anyway.* "Fuck me, Zamari."

There's a beat where he just stares at me, and then I feel his cock throb deep in my core. The stretch is almost impossible now and I wonder what it would feel like if I took all of him. If I had *both* of his bands within me. The Zamari growls as if he knows exactly what I'm thinking.

Gripping my hands with one of his, he holds my arms behind my back as he tilts me backward, mouth fastening to the wound on my shoulder as he licks and sucks it. Swallowing my blood and soothing my wound as his hips pull back and thrust forward.

He fucks me as if he knows what I want. This. Him. Everything he's made me dream of since he's come into my life. As if he, too, doesn't want this to end. As if he wants me and everything that comes along with it. He fucks me like there's no tomorrow, driving into my pussy until my cream coats his shaft. Until another orgasm meets me and rides through the entirety of his measured thrusts.

That thick band of muscle slides in and out of my pussy, spreading me for him, stretching me until I lose track of his thrusts and the way my body jerks and shunts. And then he stiffens. His hips surge forward, pinning me on his cock even as the hand on my hip holds me there.

I can feel it. Spurts and spurts of his spend bursting from his tip deep inside my channel. Some escape and falling into the water as he pulls back to drive home once, twice, three more times before he stills.

As the seconds tick by between us, he relaxes against the bath and I finally lean in, resting my head on his shoulder.

Because at the end of all this...I know I will never forget him, too.

CHAPTER TWENTY-THREE

Elsie

I stretch. My eyes flutter open to yet another morning, another new day where my heart doesn't immediately fly into my throat for fear of what awaits.

There's a sort of content, a laziness from having too-good sleep. I let out a small grunt of appreciation as I twist on my cot and turn toward the light streaming through the curtains at my window.

There's the shadow of warmth all around me, reminding me that for the first time in as long as I can remember, I'd been held all night. Curled up against the Zamari's chest. I don't remember when we left the bath and moved to the bed. But that utter feeling of safety remains.

Today, I feel like I'm finally starting to live.

I shift, pulling the blanket around me as I rise into a sitting position, my bare feet touching the floor as my gaze remains on the window. It smells like him. The blanket. That thick masculine scent that makes parts of me quiver. I breathe in deep, soaking it in, enjoying it for the moment while it lasts. Because soon, he will be gone. Soon his scent will fade. The shadows of his arms holding me tight will be but a memory.

Tilting my head so I can see my shoulder, I spot the two round pink dots there. They're already fading and when I brush a finger across them, there's no pain. Soon, they'll be gone too and just be a distant memory.

I sigh, my shoulders sagging.

He was hard all night. His cock pressing into my belly like a heated rod. And yet, he still held me close. Never moved. Demanded nothing. Just held me as if that's all he wanted.

Something like an ache goes through my heart at the thought.

Rising, I shrug off the blanket as I slip on my tunic over a set of trouse. Dressed, I open the front door and step out into the sun's light.

The sight before me has me stopping with one foot out the door.

Leaning against his bike, arms crossed, hat sitting low, is the focus of my every thought. The Zamari looks relaxed, almost bored, and I would have believed it if about a foot in front of him, Estella wasn't standing with both hands gripping her blaster with the business end pointed at him. Beside her, James stands doing the same. Same height as Estella, he's not a large man, but the fierce focus on his face is one I've never seen before. It almost looks threatening. As if he is ready to kill.

My eyes widen, heart thumping hard against my ribs as my gaze shoots back to the Zamari.

"What the hell's happening out here?" The door swings shut behind me and I take a step forward, almost colliding with Viv. She's sitting at the edge of my deck, Kiana in her lap, a rare smile on her freckled face.

Confusion makes my eyes grow even wider. "Viv?"

"Hey babe."

It's only her relaxed greeting that's calming what looks like a situation I should be worried about.

"Mom!" Kiana shifts, smiles up at me, and I reach down to rub her cheeks, my puzzled gaze shooting back to Viv. She only grins wider, her red hair blowing in the soft wind.

"What the hell's happening?" My whisper hisses past my lips as I try desperately to gauge the situation.

"Your boyfriend's teaching us how to fight." Viv's grin widens. "It's about time someone did." She laughs and snorts, and I have to look at her in wonder.

Viv doesn't laugh. Not anymore. Not since...

"Firespark." His voice makes my spine suddenly stiffen. Makes everything we shared the night before come flashing back through my mind at lightning speed. "Catch."

I turn just as something's thrown my way, and I catch it just on instinct. A blaster. My still-wide eyes move to the Zamari and his green gaze slices me from just under his hat.

"Come. We have little time."

I blink at him.

"Ooh," Viv's voice is a low whisper. "*Firespark*, huh."

My cheeks warm as I straighten and turn to the Zamari. "Don't have time for what?"

With his chin, he points toward Estella. "Go. Stand there." I move almost like a machine, without thinking. As soon as I'm in position, he continues. "I've calibrated that blaster to shoot to kill."

My eyes widen slightly. That's outlawed. Only officials from the Ivurian council know how to do that. I stare at him, thoughts flicking through my mind like rapid fire. He looks serious. Fuck, of course he'd know how to calibrate weapons to do that. I've seen him kill beings with one blow.

I guess I shouldn't be surprised. I didn't hire him because

he was lawful.

"From now on, whenever I hand you a weapon and you pull that trigger, prepare for whoever's on the other end to die."

I'm still staring at him, wondering where he's going with this. One glance at Viv and she only shrugs.

"Now...shoot me."

I blink a thousand times. "E-excuse me. What?"

His eyes bore into me. Cold. So, so cold. As if he's a different person than the one that fucked me like he never wanted to let me go. As if he's not the one that held me all night.

"Shoot."

I stare at him like he's gone crazy. He wants me to shoot him? With a blaster that's set to kill? What the hell is—

Before I can think, my hand snaps so hard the instant pain makes my fingers release the blaster. It flies, spinning to land in the sand about a foot away from me and I stare at it wide-eyed, not sure what just happened till I look up to see the Zamari's blaster pointed right at me.

I'm frozen as I stare at the barrel of that gun.

I raise my gaze slowly, pure shock probably screaming through my eyes as I lift my gaze back to his. He...he shot me. Well, *at* me. Shot the blaster from my hands even before I realized what he'd done. I never even saw him move. Never saw him reach for his weapon.

The pain in my hand stings and I can only stare at him, unable to understand what the fuck he's doing. And all the while knowing that if he'd wanted to kill me, he could have done so instead of shooting the blaster from my hand. I've seen him do it enough.

"Pick it up." Three words. Said so coldly, it's like we've never shared any warmth. As if last night didn't happen.

Foolish, foolish girl. I feel myself harden, pushing away any hurt or pain that's starting to grow. This is business. Only business. He's here for a job and I know this.

I fucking know it!

I just don't... Don't want to...

Aagh! I could scream at myself.

My jaws tighten, my hands falling to my side as I clench and unclench my fists. Still looking at me, his focus never waning, the Zamari jerks the barrel of his blaster at Estella and James. They both jump and James' blaster goes off, hitting the sand off to the side of the Zamari's bike. He ignores it as if the blaster fire is a mere annoyance.

"You two," he says. "Practice over there."

James glances at Estella, his cheeks red from his mistake, but they both move without a word, heading over to Estella's plot to aim at the thin strings of wood still left standing there.

In the seconds that pass between us, the Zamari's eyes seem to grow even colder. He doesn't say another word, simply waits for me to step forward and pick up the blaster, and when my fingers close around it and I stand again, that same cold gaze is following me still.

Little ice crystals form along my spine.

The blaster isn't one I've seen before and I wonder where he got it from. It's lighter than the one I had. Newer too.

"Fire," he commands, and I grip the weapon again. I don't know why my fingers tremble as I lift it and aim. Maybe because I don't want to shoot him!

"Do it," he says, as if he can read my mind.

I force a lump down my throat as I raise the weapon, looking right down the sights and straight at him. He doesn't expect me to—*FUCK!*

The blaster flies from my grip, pain shooting through my hand as it lands on the ground a few feet away from me again.

"What the *fuck?!*" I glare at him.

"Again," he growls, completely ignoring what I've said.

I fume, eyes never leaving him as I pick up the blaster once more.

My hand is aching because of the kickback of having a blaster shot from my grip *twice*. And it's making me seethe.

Lifting the blaster with both hands this time, I point it at him, a frown on my brow and my teeth clenched. He's so cold. What was I thinking yesterday? Why did I even imagine there was a chance that—

"This is why you needed me to protect you." His words fall like bricks. "Your colony. You will lose everything."

For a second, his words hit the very core of who I am, unveiling all my insecurities. Yes, we need his help. Yes, we haven't been able to defend ourselves. Yes, our whole lives depend on him.

But as I stare into those cold green eyes, that defiance I've always held deep down rears its head.

That may all be true, but he's wrong about one thing. The one thing he hasn't said, but I know he's thinking anyway.

"I'm not weak."

I see his finger move this time. The slightest shift and out of instinct, mine does too. I depress the trigger. For a moment, pure fear encapsulates me as I see the blaster fire exit the barrel. I've shot him.

My eyes widen as my mouth falls open in horror, but just like I've seen him do before, he dodges the blast as if he knew it was coming.

In the aftermath, I'm frozen in the reality of what I just did, just staring at him, and I realize everyone is staring at me too.

"Damn," Estella mutters off to the side.

In the corner of my eyes, I see Viv shaking her head with a soft laugh.

"He's only trying to teach you," she says. "Granted, his

methods are unconventional and *highly* traumatizing."

The Zamari's jaw ticks and before I know it, my hand's snapping as my blaster flies in the air and lands a few feet away from me once more.

FUCK!

"Again," he says.

My shoulders square and I march toward the gun. Grabbing it from the ground, I don't stop walking till I'm right in front of the handsome brute that slowly stole my heart while apparently still having the power to make me fume.

I lift the blaster, pressing it under his chin. "Do that again, and I really will shoot you," I whisper.

There. I saw it. That slight twist of his lips. That slight smile.

"There you are." A glint moves across the Zamari's eyes. "Firespark." He stares at me for a few moments, and I'm not sure what to do. My anger wanes and ebbs, only to be replaced by confusion and heat in my gut.

"You'll need that," he finally says, gaze never leaving mine, swallowing me whole, forcing my focus on him and only him. "That fire. When they come." I blink several times, easing the blaster down as I search his gaze. "What happened last rotation is just the start. They'll be back."

Ice forms along my spine before melting into an avalanche of frigid snow. I can suddenly hear my own breathing. Suddenly feel that knot of anxiety that has been my constant companion for far too long.

The Zamari leans off his bike.

"And when they come, you must be ready."

I'm frozen solid as he turns and addresses James as if they've known each other for years. He tells him to gather at least three more men who will be willing to accompany him. Where? I have no clue.

"Accompany you where?" I glance from James to the Zamari before James gives a slight nod before hurrying off on foot.

The Zamari turns to face me. "Supplies."

I blink at him as he turns to Estella next, telling her to collect as many weapons as she can. She nods before glancing my way. There's a shrug of her shoulders as she hurries off before I can say a word.

Turning slowly, I face the Zamari again.

"What is all this?" But I know what he's going to say. I just don't want to hear it.

"They won't give up your little colony. Not so easily. They'll be back. And this time, they'll be prepared." He steps closer. "You have to be prepared too, Firespark."

My breaths feel hot in my chest as I search his gaze. "But you killed three of them. We've never...we've never managed to ever kill any of them before. I thought..."

"That it would end there. That they would get scared and leave you all alone." He steps closer. "There's much more to this that you don't know, Firespark."

His words bring both terror and confusion, both emotions struggling for precedence and none winning. Throwing me from crushing anxiety to hope, then more fear and back.

"What do you mean?"

He goes still, only the air around him moving, and I suddenly get a strange feeling all across my skin. A bit like when my hairs stand up, only I'm not cold. His head turns in Viv's direction at the same time that I hear her pull in a deep inhale.

"E-Elsie?" Her voice quivers as she stands slowly, eyes wide as she stares down at Kiana, one hand on the child's chest. "*Elsie!*" Pure panic tears through her throat as she shakes Kiana. "She isn't breathing!"

CHAPTER TWENTY-FOUR

The Outlaw

I sense it just as it happens—the exact moment the *kiv's* lungs cease their rise and fall. When her tiny body went abruptly limp. My ayahl flared wildly, blasting around me, around Firespark, as the female named Viv rose, the lifeless *kiv* cradled in her arms.

"Elsie! She's not breathing!"

The words seem to still the air as I watch Firespark rush forward. Horror-filled eyes search the *kiv's* face as if to will this away. As if the suddenness of it means it's not real.

I expect her to wail. To fall to her knees in helplessness. But there is focus in her movements; a certain sort of rigidity to her spine that tells me she's pushing back the panic that's threatening at the edges of her consciousness. Solely because she refuses to believe.

Firespark snatches the *kiv's* slack form, breaths coming in ragged pants now. With laser-like focus, she presses a palm to the *kiv's* still chest, then brings her cheek to the *kiv's* snout, straining for even a wisp of breath. Finding none, she presses trembling fingers to the *kiv's* neck, then wrist—seeking, pleading for the beat of life.

The air grows heavy, stagnant, as if the sand holds its own breath. My muscles coil, ready to intervene, but hesitant to intrude on her desperation.

Come on, little one, I urge silently. *You must fight. Firespark needs you.*

"Oh gods," the one named Viv runs her hands into her hair, fingers clawed as she grips her skull. "She was alright just a second ago. She was smiling and then I thought she was sleeping and—I didn't—I don't know—" Her hands tremble as she pulls them from her hair. She reaches out to Firespark, helpless. Too filled with shock to know what to do.

Setting the *kiv* on the sandy ground, Firespark tilt's the *kiv*'s head back, forces open her mouth and breathes in. Palm pressed against the *kiv*'s chest, she pumps her hand once, twice, three times, before breathing into the *kiv*'s mouth again.

She is trying to revive the kiv, but I have witnessed this illness claim far too many lives. I know the merciless speed with which it steals the breath of even the most delicate souls.

This is a battle not meant for Firespark's hands—no matter how valiantly she fights against the inevitable. Fighting against what it's taking from her now. Her *kiv*. Her *heart*.

I watch her glassy eyes manage to withhold tears as she works on the *kiv*, unrelenting, not giving up, not even considering that the *kiv* might really be gone.

My ayahl still screams around me, reaching out to circle her, and I sense her pain, feel it as if it is mine, and the scene before me embeds in my mind. This is why I can never be with her. Never allow myself to fall to this intense pull that makes me want to keep her nestled in my arms. Because this pain, this searing pain of loss that's threatening to tear her apart...I never want her to be on her knees, my lifeless body beneath her, while she feels the same, trying to get me back because fate has taken me away.

I can't let that happen. I refuse to give her such pain. For her to be torn like this because of me...I cannot allow it. But I can help her now. I can help her here.

I move automatically, like something calling me to my mate's side to ease away her pain. I take the *kiv* and Firespark releases her almost as if in a daze. I see the tremor in her as her body shakes, that haunting look in her eyes as words stop in her throat. She watches me move toward the cabin and I'm almost inside it before her world seems to snap back in place and she hurries after me.

As I lay the *kiv* on the cot on which we spent the last oras together, I support her little head as I glance over my shoulder at Firespark.

"Your blade."

She gulps, frame still shuddering as she nods and heads over to where she prepares food. The blade clatters to the floor before she grasps it again and hurries back to me.

I could have used mine. Could have unsheathed it and done this all on my own, but I know Firespark needs this. Needs to assist. Needs to be a part of this as much as I would have if this *kiv* was mine.

There is that look in her eyes, the same look I saw back in that drinkery when she finally decided she had to trust me. She hands me the blade as I roll up my sleeve. Heavy footsteps sound as Viv enters the room behind us, her eyes wide and growing even wider as she spots the blade. The moment I rip open the *kiv's* tunic and place the blade to the center of her chest, Viv makes a strange sort of gut-wrenching scream.

She lunges at me and I allow her to grab my arm, fingers

like claws digging into my skin as she grips the blade with the other hand. "No! What are you doing?!"

I pause. Every second that we waste will make this more difficult. But it's Firespark that speaks next. It's Firespark whose hand closes over her friend's. Their gazes meet and something I don't understand passes between them. Some unspoken human exchange, the meaning lost on a Zamari like me.

"It's okay," Firespark says. "I trust him."

Her trust. I don't deserve it.

Her friend's hand trembles on mine, before it finally lifts.

"Do it." The same words she said back in that cave when I revealed my craving for her blood. When she allowed me to clean her wounds. The same trust.

Jerking my head in a nod, I dip the blade, slicing into the child's chest. There's a gasp, the one named Viv turning away while Firespark presses a hand over her mouth, the tears she's tried so hard to hold back brimming over her eyes as the *kiv*'s lifeblood spills.

My eyes bleed to black before I can even try to stop them. For a few moments, I remain still even as my chest heaves, the scent of the fresh lifeblood like a call to that primal thing inside me.

"You can do it." It's a whisper. An ever soft whisper close by my ear and I realize it's Firespark. "You're stronger than this," she says. "Please, do whatever you can to bring her back to me."

My jaws clench even as my fangs lengthen and ache. I have to lean into the sound of her voice, into her touch as she squeezes my shoulder.

Such utter trust.

Before my primal can surge, I slice through my arm, dark liquid brimming from my skin. The pain is negligible. I don't even feel it. But yet I struggle. Struggle because I am once again at the edge of control.

I need to drink. I need to drink soon.

Leaning over the wound I made in the child's chest, I let my lifeblood drip. My cells mixing with hers, lifeblood to lifeblood. It covers the *kiv's* wound, seeping under her skin, going into her vessels, straight to her life organ. Enough that her entire wound is covered with more of my lifeblood than hers. Only then do I pull away, ripping a part of my tunic to wrap around my arm.

When I glance behind me, Viv's eyes are large pools, both hands pressing over her nose and mouth, her back flat against the wall as she stares at the *kiv* in horror.

I'm reminded why we Zamari never do this outside trying to save our own kind. It is too much for most others to understand. I can already feel my wound stitching back together in my arm. Already know my cells are doing the same to the *kiv*, forcing her body to respond.

And then there's the fact that, in opening another being, the scent of lifeblood is far too strong. What's the use if you end up killing the thing you're trying to save?

"What now?" Firespark's voice wheedles into the shadows pulling against my mind.

"Need to...put pressure. Continue your...life support."

I stagger back, my gaze shifting to hers. I can no longer see the details of her face, only the heat map of her form. My gaze shifts to the *kiv* and then to Viv and it is the same. There's that urge to hunt. To claim.

To *drink*.

I am losing...control.

I cannot be here when I do.

My steps are unsteady as I shake my head, trying to give myself some clarity. My fangs lengthen as I put distance between us, staggering across the room to Firespark's food preparation area. I grab a receptacle there. With a grunt, I let my fangs bleed venom into the receptacle, easing some of the ache, but not enough.

Never enough.

This is bad. I haven't been this affected by the urge since I reached matehood. And as I set the receptacle down, gaze finding Firespark again. I know it's because of her. Because of that urge to have her. And because I tasted her lifeblood.

"What you just did…" There's a tremor in her voice. Her hands are on the *kiv's* chest. Her fingers covered with my lifeblood mixed in with the *kiv's* as she puts pressure on the wound. "What will happen now?"

"Atrophy." My words are strangled. "The sickness. Reached her life organ. My lifeblood will help. The cells will…heal it."

"Continue the chest pushes," I continue. "And when she breathes, give her the medicine you have."

Firespark's eyes shoot to Viv and the other woman gives a shaky nod before hurrying up to the loft. As Firespark continues breathing into the *kiv's* mouth as she pumps her palm against the *kiv's* chest, Viv returns with the little vial of medicine. I stagger back some more, and when my gaze meets Firespark's again. I see it in her eyes. She knows.

She understands.

"Go," she says.

It's like I needed that permission to leave. And as I stagger from her cabin, my primal almost ripping through my *ayahl*, her pained wail is the last thing I hear before my bike heads off into the plains.

Elsie

I don't stop pumping Kiana's little chest, don't stop breathing into her mouth and performing the chest compressions, even when minutes pass and there's no change.

I can hear Viv behind me, hear when she slides down the wall to collapse on the floor. I don't need to turn around to see the horror in her eyes. I can feel it. It surrounds me like a dark shroud. Only pure desperation and strangled hope push me to continue in a sort of panicked daze.

Breathe. Pump. Pump. Pump. Pump. Breathe. Pump. Pump. Pump.

Please, Kiana. But my plea is wordless. My hands ache, whether through tiredness or the pain of loss slowly seeping into my soul, but I continue anyway.

"Come on, Kiana." I say it aloud this time, forcing the words through my clenched teeth. Because even though I knew this day would come, even though I've seen it happen to her mother and others before her, I refuse to believe it's happening now.

That...and because of what he did. The Zamari. Whatever he did will work. I just know it.

Wherever this blind hope and trust stemmed from concerning that male, it spurs me on now. Whatever he did will work! And so I continue. I continue the chest compressions. I don't stop.

"Viv," I croak. "Get the medicine ready."

Because she's going to need it when she starts breathing again. That's what he said and I believe him. I believe she will breathe again.

Kiana's first breath makes blood gush against my fingers as her little heart contracts and pumps. And then the blood keeps flowing. For a moment, my hands freeze on her chest, a pained cry leaving my lips that doesn't sound like it comes from my voice at all.

"*Viv!*" My call is strangled and I hear her scrambling toward me. Hear when she inhales sharply. "The medicine!"

I put pressure on the wound, blinking away tears that make my vision blurry as I try to stop the blood running from the wound in Kiana's chest.

Short little inhales lift her chest, blood spurting, as if her lungs can't do much more than that. But she's breathing. She's alive. And it's all because of *him*.

"Oh my God," Viv whispers, eyes tortured and hands shaking as she opens the vial and sticks the needle in. "Oh my God."

"That's it." My voice shudders with emotion. "Breathe, darling." I turn my head to my sleeve to wipe away the tears. "There you go. Breathe. You're such a fighter."

I give a nod to Viv as she sticks the needle into Kiana's arm and administers what's left of the medicine. All of it. There's none left now, and that sends a sort of panic through me. Another day. I'll deal with that worry another day. After Kiana is breathing properly again. Right now, I'll focus on getting her there. Getting her awake. For despite that she's breathing, her eyes are still closed. A mercy, because the wound in her chest is still wide open.

"Here." I sniff, gesturing to Viv with my chin. "Put pressure here."

Viv's still shaking as she takes my spot, putting pressure on the wound as I hurry away, climbing up to the loft. I hear her whispering encouragement to the child as I search underneath the baskets there for the little med kit I have.

There's nothing left in it except empty vials, a sewing needle, and some thread.

I grab the needle and thread, hurrying back down the short flight of stairs to the room below.

My hands are a bloody red, his blood and hers, and my heart cramps at the sight as I take my spot back at Kiana's side. Threading the needle, I set it down before switching spots with Viv.

Lifting my gaze, I gesture to Viv. "Get that for me?" I use my chin to point at the cup the Zamari had set down, all the while cognizant of each stuttered inhale in Kiana's chest.

He saved her. With his blood. It's the only reason…

I swallow hard, forcing the thought from my mind as I lift one hand for Viv to put the cup in. The clear fluid settled inside it is unassuming. But I know the miracle that it is. My heart aches some more. Tipping the cup, I let the Zamari's venom seep over Kiana's wound, hoping it will do for her what it did for me. Numb the incision. Take away her pain. Then I dip the needle and thread in it, too.

Viv watches silently at my back, but I can tell she's panicking even though she's standing still.

With a heavy breath, I turn back to Kiana, squaring my shoulders. I can do this.

She's breathing. The Zamari did all the hard work. Now, I just have to finish what he did to ensure she survives.

The now empty vial lies on the cot beside Kiana, open and vulnerable, just like my heart. Tightening the last stitch, I set down what's left of the needle and thread, hands trembling.

"She's breathing," Viv croaks. Collapsed on the floor beside me, her eyes are as clouded and teary as mine. "How...how did it work?"

My throat aches, words unable to come forth, too many emotions holding them back. I'm only happy she's still unconscious and can't feel a thing. But that will all change once she wakes.

Sniffling, I pull on the strength that has carried me this far as I use my fingers to massage what's left of the venom into the wound. Each little shudder of her chest is like a tincture for my soul. I obsess over every breath, counting the seconds in between, my heart thudding at each interval, afraid that she will stop breathing again.

Viv wipes her eyes and yet more tears continue streaming down.

"I'm so useless," she mutters. "If you weren't here...I..."

I shake my head. "We knew this would happen... eventually. It's how they always go. Quietly and suddenly." I pause, looking down at Kiana. Her face is so peaceful. As if she's just been sleeping all along. "I just thought..." *I thought we had more time.* And then it's *my* tears that are brimming again. Because maybe we do. The Zamari has given us more time with her.

Hands still shaking, I rest my head beside Kiana's. I can hear my own breaths shuddering through my chest, feel a sort of fever going right through me, as if my muscles have separated from my bones. As if I was just at the brink of being torn apart.

The sobs come softly at first, and then they shake me, disappearing into the pillow as they grow louder. It happened so quickly. One moment she was smiling up at Viv and the next...

I don't even want to think about it.

When an arm wraps around my shoulder, Viv leaning against me, my tears come even harder. This world's so fucking broken. How can I ever think that one day it would all come together? That one day this peace I've felt since the Zamari arrived will become the norm? This terror, this heartache, this pain, the constant loss, that's my normal. It's like the universe is reminding me, telling me I shouldn't forget.

We stay like that for a long time, even after Estella returns and sees the terrifying scene. I'm numb as Viv explains everything. I can't even move. I don't know how long I remain like that with Kiana, every breath I take dependent on the ones she pulls in and releases. Every slight movement of her chest telling me she's still there, still hanging on, because of *him*.

The day passes until Ivuria sets and darkness settles across Comodre, and still I stay. Still I wait. I just want to hear her voice again. Just want to know that she'll really be okay.

I hear Viv and Estella talking, *arguing* over bringing Marcus here. Those years he spent in the lab aboard the mothership, following his father around, are the only reason he is the mayor of this sad little colony. And the only reason we "preserve" him. Marcus doesn't have to mine sansa gems. The little he knows about medicine makes him too precious. He's the closest thing we have to a doctor in Comodre.

But Viv doesn't trust him, and who's blaming her? He watched as those brutes forced themselves onto her in front of everyone. He did *nothing* to stop them.

The door slams shut as Estella leaves and still, I don't budge. We hate the fucking brute, but, as much as I hate to admit it, we need him. We need his help.

Kiana needs his help.

Cupping her head, I gently stroke her hair, words of love and affection stuck in my throat. I can only look at her, hoping she knows that we're here. Hoping she knows how much she's loved.

It's so slight, I don't see it at first. That flutter of her lids.

But then her body heaves and she coughs. I jump, my hands freezing above her as I stare at her wide-eyed.

When she coughs again, my vision goes blurry. "Kiana?"

My fingers tremble as they travel over her cheeks, cupping her little face so I can look down at her. She takes a deep inhale, her eyes fluttering open to little slits and her brows furrowing. I'm at once frightened of the pain she must be feeling.

"Kiana, darling?"

Viv's presence looms behind me as she clenches and unclenches her fists in distress.

"Kiana?" I repeat, my voice cracking as the child squints.

"Mom?"

Relief I can't describe crashes right through me and I almost grip her to my chest too tight.

"Oh gods, Kiana." I rock her in my arms. "My darling Kiana, how are you feeling? Can you breathe?"

She gasps a little, her breathing still abnormal. Sharp inhales with smoother exhales. But she's awake. She's awake, she's alive, and she's breathing.

She nods at me, and I watch as a little confused smile stretches her lips. This ever-brave girl. "Why are you crying?" she whispers. "Did I make you sad?"

I sob-laugh, choking on my own heart as I pull her tighter against me.

Behind me, the door flies open, an out-of-breath Estella rushing in with wide eyes.

"Kiana," she croaks. Behind her, Marcus steps in, his gaze finding mine immediately. For a few moments, we just stare at each other, but I can't find it in me to summon any hatred. Any animosity.

Estella rushes forward, collapsing at the floor by the side of the cot. Wrapping her hands around Kiana and me.

"Oh my baby..." she moans.

Marcus walks over, rolling his sleeves up as he takes Kiana in. "Let me see her."

Reluctantly, and only because I know this is for the best, I release Kiana, allowing him to see her.

His gaze flicks over her and then to Estella. "You said she stopped breathing." The tone is almost accusatory, as if he thinks Estella lied and has wasted his time.

"She *did*." Estella frowns. "I called you over here so you could help us. She's obviously still not breathing properly."

Kiana's little huffs of air fill the suddenly silent space like a testament.

"Seems like Elsie here has it all under control," Marcus finally says. "She's administered the medicine, and...it worked..." His frown deepens.

"Anybody can fucking administer medicine, Marcus!" Estella screams. "You're the *medic*. The only one we have. Surely you can do something more! What if she's in pain? What if she stops breathing again?!"

His mouth slams shut, and even though he's a fucking dickhead, I see the shadow of regret in his gaze. "We don't have enough medicine to waste on regular aches and pains, Estella. We haven't had enough medicine in a long..." His shoulders rise and fall with a sigh. "You know we can only make her comfortable. Once she stops breathing...the sickness...it's..." His voice trails off before his brows knit even more. I sense when he zones in on the edge of the telling wound in the center of Kiana's chest. "Are you sure she stopped breathing? Once they do—"

I pull the blanket over Kiana and stand, forcing Marcus to step back. "She'll be fine now. As you said, there's nothing you could have done to help, anyway."

His face is a concoction of confusion and simmering anger. His gaze shoots to the loft, then flicks around my room and I'm suddenly reminded that this male is not my friend. We may have come to this world together. We may have survived this long together. But that's where our loyalties end.

"Where is the stranger?"

My chest tightens at his question as I reach for my poncho and throw it over my head. Now that Kiana's awake and Estella and Viv are both here, I know she's in good hands, and I can finally focus on that bit of me that's been clawing for attention. That part of my heart that's fallen for a certain Zamari.

Because he's gone, and in my grief, I could ignore that look I saw in his eyes before he left. That *pain*. But now I know she's going to be okay, I can't ignore it so much anymore.

Slipping the poncho over my head, I move and grab the knife I'd handed to the Zamari. The blade is still soaked with his blood, but I don't even clean it. There's no time.

Heading back to the cot, I give Kiana a kiss on the forehead before turning back to face Marcus. His jaw ticks with having to wait for my response.

"That's none of your business and really not what you should be concerned with right now." The voice that leaves my throat is so icy, it doesn't sound like mine. I step forward, forcing him back. "Let me make this clear. The only reason I'm leaving you here in my home is because Kiana might need your help while I'm gone. Got that?"

His jaw ticks, but he's the mayor and the only medic we have. "The only other medical care is all the way in Calanta." I lift the knife, something far too raw and powerful controlling my actions. "Kiana needs you, Marcus, so for the love of all the gods, put whatever assumptions you have about me and the Zamari behind you and focus on *her*, or so help me..."

His jaw ticks, but then his gaze shifts back to Kiana and I see the change in his eyes. For he knows I speak the truth. He needs to focus on keeping her alive. As far as we know, we're the only humans left in all of existence. Losing another of our people...losing Kiana...it's too much to bear.

"Fine," he grunts.

Estella turns, tortured eyes shifting to me, and our gazes meet. I hold her gaze for a few moments before shifting my focus to Viv. They're both looking back at me with fear, relief, but also a sort of knowledge in their eyes. A lump forms in my throat before Estella gives me a nod. There's no need to ask. They both know where I'm going. Where I *have* to go.

I swallow the lump in my throat, before my gaze shifts back to Viv. With tears in her eyes, she gives me a nod too and I release the breath I'd been holding.

"She'll be safe with us," Estella says, and I know she's right. I just needed one of them to say it out loud. To make some part of my brain come to peace with the fact that I have to leave. Because there's someone else who needs my help right now, too.

CHAPTER TWENTY-FIVE

The Outlaw

My bike lies abandoned as I lean against the sand drift.

Light diminishes quickly; Ivuria a setting star on the horizon.

I lean my back against the hot sand, willing myself to calm. For how long have I stayed here, hoping this urge will go away? Oras. All that happens is that it grows stronger still.

Fek.

Snapping my navigator from a pocket in my trouse, I lift it so I can see. I should head to Calanta. Find some female that's looking for credits in exchange for pleasure. Pay her to let me drink, and an extra satchel of credits for her silence. But I can't bring myself to do it. Can't bring myself to go.

And so I'm sitting alone in the middle of the sands. Out in the fekking open where I'm vulnerable. Because I can't go. Not when the female I want is back in that little town named Comodre.

Fek.

The thought of drinking from someone other than her has my *ayahl* writhing with such agitation it's more like a disruptive wave. It makes my skull ache, my fangs aching harder. Everything inside me wants to hop on my bike, turn around, and go back to her.

Pressing back against the sand, I force myself to breathe.

I can overcome this. I have done it before. Only, it's never ever been quite this bad.

And that means I'm weak. It means that even when I return to Comodre, I'll be vulnerable. And that will only put my Firespark at risk.

I'm compromised.

With a grunt, my hand dips into another pocket to retrieve my communication pod. I stare at it for a few moments. I hardly use the thing. And there's a reason for that. There's only one being I can call and he's an uncertainty. I grunt a painful laugh. Things are dire when your only 'friend' is literally worlds away.

Only, I have no choice but to contact him.

I type in the message quickly, selecting the contact as soon as I finish, my finger hovering over the button that will send the message to the only maniac I know will be fit for the job I might not be able to finish. For if the Nirzoik come, and they will come, Firespark will need someone not as crazed as I am to finish the job.

Would you like to send this message? The comm pod blinks before me.

No. No, I *wouldn't* fekking like to. Asking that vagabond to come here is a mistake. But I *have* to.

Before I can reconsider and talk myself out of it, I hit send. The message shoots off to the stars. He might not come. But if he does, there's still hope I can have success in what's about to come next.

Stuffing the comm pod and navigator back into my pocket, I release a shuddering breath. I shift, the hot sand scalding the scales at my back, until I realize it isn't the sand that's hot. It's me. I'm the one burning up, as if my blood is boiling and only one thing can cool it.

I shift again, digging my claws into the sand beneath me, my eyes on Ivuria setting in the distance. It's so utterly quiet out here, so utterly peaceful, that the chaos within me seems almost misplaced. Right here, right now, without my own body turning against me, I could sit and watch that star for oras.

But the further it disappears beyond the horizon, the more glaring the fact that my thirst is not ebbing.

I glance back at my bike, wondering if I might have any synth blood hidden somewhere within it. But I already know the answer to that. Because I already checked.

It's been a long time since I've needed to drink. A long time since the need has ever gotten this demanding. I try to breathe through it, to clench my teeth till my fangs pierce my flesh, but nothing stops the urge.

I want her.

Firespark is the only thing I need.

And this isn't just about her lifeblood.

Pressing my head back, I breathe deep. Oras tick by as the little light left diminishes into nothing. Sitting in the dark, only torment as company, I wonder how much longer this will last.

And that's when I hear it. Like the sound of an insect buzzing in my ear. I freeze, knowing exactly what that sound is. The soft brush of a hoverbike shooting across the plain. Claw reaching for my blaster, the grip is tight against my palm as I turn slowly and shift higher against the sand drift's sloped edge. Just enough that I see over the top.

I spot it immediately. Not because it's coming my way, but because there's a huge beam shooting on either side of the thing. Either this person is new to Ivuria, traveling with such a beacon in these dangerous plains, or they're looking for something. Or *someone*.

I track the bike as it nears, blaster still tight against my palm as the vessel draws closer. The light swoops over me and I duck as the bike zooms past, but not before I see the golden strands whipping in the wind at the traveler's back.

No.

My *ayahl* rises and goes haywire.

Firespark.

For a second, my whole world stops, and then all my focus, all these urges, the dissatisfaction of my *ayahl*, it all explodes like a raging storm. Remaining behind the sand drift, I breathe hard, trying to control myself, trying to keep still so I don't go after the one thing I've been aching for.

What is she doing out here?

Gaze shifting back to my bike, I know I'll have to hop on and head after her. Whether I like it or not, I will have to reveal myself. No way I'm letting her continue on her way out here all alone. I might be dangerous right now, but there are far other dangerous things out on these plains and I won't let her come to harm.

I'll just have to fight this for a bit longer. For long enough until I get her back to safety.

But it's neither of those things that make a strange feeling settle in my chest.

It's because I know *why* she's out here. It's because I know that just like before when that sandworm attacked, she's come looking for me.

There's a strange ache in my chest; so much that I have to clutch the spot.

I have to go after her.

But as if she felt the call of my *ayahl*, the sound of her bike grows louder again. She's turned around.

It takes longer for her bike to come close to the drift this time. She's going slower. Still hidden behind the drift, I fight myself as I listen. *She's heading back.* But I know that's just foolish hope.

And then her engine dies. The light she's carrying sweeps over the top of the drift and I clench my teeth. I hear the moment she hops off the vessel; the slight crunch of sand under her boots.

The light she's carrying swings closer, and closer still, until it sweeps over my bike. I'd dropped it a few lengths away where I'd left it abandoned in the sands, staggered off it, and I threw myself against the drift.

The moment her light touches it, the beam remains in that spot for a few seconds. And then she's running. My Firespark is running across the sands to the abandoned vessel.

I watch her with an ache in my life organ. Knowing I deserve none of her goodness. Knowing that a male like me can only bring something as perfect and untouched as her to ruin.

"Zamari?" Her light swings when she reaches the bike, the beam frantic as soon as she realizes I'm not there. "Zamari?" A little louder, and that ache in my chest increases.

To hear her call the name of my people and not my own designation. To know I haven't been able to reveal it is reason enough of why I should stay away.

But what a treacherous male I am.

Watching her now, I want nothing but to have her writhing on my cock while my fangs are buried in her neck. I want to hear her scream as my knot spreads her, locking us together while I drink, giving her more pleasure than she can ever perceive and giving me everything I want.

Her.

Every bit of *her*.

She has no clue what my bands are. That every time I slid into her heat, I fought between temptation and duty. Every single time I've wanted to knot her and make her mine.

Her light swings again as she spins, the beam passing right over me before it swings back.

I see the look in her eyes then. The desperation. The shock. And then the utter relief. She staggers across the sand, the loose grains preventing her from moving as quickly as she wants to, but soon she's right before me.

She kills the light, plunging us into only the light of the stars above us as she falls to her knees beside me.

Her hands tremble as she brings them close and I grit my teeth harder. I can still scent the lifeblood staining her fingers. And even though it did not come from her, it's *hers* that I want.

"I found you," she whispers. She leans in, throwing her arms around my neck as her entire frame shudders with relief. "I thought I wouldn't. I was so worried."

Gods, what are you doing to me? What temptation is this?

She leans back, gaze desperately searching my face in the shadows. "Are you alright?" Those soft hands of hers cradle my jaw and I stare at this *enyati* before me. For that is exactly what she is. A creature made by the gods. I wouldn't be surprised if she sprouted wings. Then she could do what's best and fly away from me.

"You shouldn't have come."

She's already shaking her head before I can finish. "No. Don't say that. I needed to come. And I know you need my help."

I growl, fangs baring. A sight that should terrify her, but she doesn't even startle. Instead, she releases me and suddenly stretches her arms high, shrugging off the strange outer layer she wore the first time I saw her. Her chest rises and falls as she looks at me. With a deft swing of one leg, she straddles me and another growl escapes. Tilting her head to the side, hair cascading over her shoulders, Firespark does something I never imagined she would ever do.

She offers her neck to me.

"Go ahead. You have my approval. Drink."

Fek. Her offering is so sudden, I'm unable to restrain myself. To react appropriately. The very thing I've been dreaming of. Offered to me on a platter. I growl and it rumbles low, vibrating through the air between us so much that I see tiny bumps speckle her arms.

"Take as much as you need." Her throat moves as she waits, neck bared, head dipped in submission. My cock grows painfully harder.

"*How do you know what I need?*" My voice is so distorted, it hardly sounds like words, and Firespark shivers at the sound. And yet, even with that shiver, she doesn't seem afraid.

Her gaze flicks to mine. "I'm only guessing." Even in the dark, her skin grows warmer, and she averts her gaze once more. "Am I wrong?"

Another growl erupts from my chest.

But I was already at the edge before she arrived. Now that she's here, her sweet scent is clouding my mind. There is no resistance.

I grip her thighs, claws spreading around the round curve of her ass as I pull her tighter against me. Her sharp, surprised inhale only makes my cock throb harder.

So. Fekking. Perfect.

Instinct is all that takes over as I tug on the waist of her trouse, my claws gripping the fabric and the thin undergarment underneath, sliding them down till they can go no further.

Without questioning what I'm doing, or why I'm undressing her, Firespark's chest rises and falls as she stands and shrugs out of the bothersome garments. Her creamy skin is a beauty in the star's light. Her scent like a present from the gods.

Before she can sit again, I pull her into me, my face notching in the perfect center of her thighs as if it's a seat made for her. She inhales again, sharp, as my breath tickles the dusting of hair there.

Gods save me. The thick musk of her sex. I growl against the little bud nestled between her folds that she likes so much, and she shudders against my lips.

I am starved. I thirst. But first I will drink from this.

She's the sweetest, softest thing as I thrust my tongue into her tight little hole, a growl erupting from me as her sex clenches me tight. Pure pleasure rocks through me at the taste of her, enough to make me growl again as I close my lips over her mound.

"Oh, fuck." She pulls my hat off, depositing it in the sand as her fingers claw into my filaments, pulling tight before she tugs me harder against her.

"Yes, Firespark," I growl against her bud before taking it into my mouth again. "Just like that."

My tongue thrums within her, thrusting, scooping, taking, her juices filling my lips but not nearly enough. There's a sensation chasing me. Something like death and complete insanity. Something that's telling me that I need more of this feeling. More of *her*. Or my simple existence will be worth nothing at all.

I grip her tighter, spreading her round cheeks, pulling her harder against me until my tongue hits the very end of her channel and a soft little thing there. The moment I touch it, my *ayahl* rises like a tormented cloud around me.

The entrance to her womb. Suddenly, the thought of filling

her with my seed till her belly swells makes me growl like a rabid beast.

And Firespark trembles, her legs shaking as she holds on to me tight.

Her reaction, her little moans, the wet sound of her pussy in my mouth, it's all driving me insane. Sliding my arms down, I force her knees to bend as I lean off the sand drift, lifting her as I do. She settles on my shoulders, the exact place she's meant to be, and I give her exactly what she wants.

She whimpers, entire body shaking the harder I nibble and suck on her folds. She writhes as if my tongue buried deep inside her is a sweet torment that's slowly driving her mad. She pushes and pulls against me, her body stiffening as it reaches mini peaks before coming back down, only to rise again, and a dark chuckle rumbles through my chest.

"Sweet, Firespark," I growl. "You shouldn't have come."

Her eyes flutter open and the raw need inside them makes my cock throb so hard, my restrictive trouse becomes a prison.

"If you don't stop, you're going to make me—"

I thrust my tongue deeper, harder, and she lets out a deep moan. Her fingers claw against my scalp as her hips buck, grinding her pussy against my lips, and I can sense the moment she's about to reach her peak. Know that I need it as much as she does.

"There, my sweet female. Give it to me. I want your release on my tongue." I dig deeper, taking her all in, not allowing her to pull away as her entire body shudders, her legs trembling on my shoulders before she bites down hard enough I scent lifeblood in her mouth.

Fek.

When her body seizes and bucks, I take it all like the hungry beast I am. Every last drop, I lap up her arousal and every drop of her release until there is no more. And yet, I still crave.

Firespark breathes hard as she slides off my shoulders to straddle me again, her fingers moving to the fastener on my trouse and I lick my lips slowly, taking in the last remainder of her juices as I watch her wrestle with the fasteners.

Grasping her by the chin, I pull her forward, crushing her lips against mine.

I taste it, the sweet nectar of her lifeblood, and I groan against her mouth, knowing I'm way past the edge of tolerance. Still, she fumbles with my trouse, even as she whimpers against my lips with every thrust of my tongue.

I am lost for a few moments in the universe that is Elsie Parks. The human who caught my primal's attention. The one I know I should let go.

The sound of the fastener opening breaks through my clouded thoughts as Firespark tugs impatiently on my trouse. With a growl, my hand closes around her wrist.

"What do you think you're doing?"

Blue eyes meet mine. "Giving you exactly what you've given me."

Eyes still locked with mine, her hand reaches down, closing around my cock as a groan escapes me. Her hand is cool against my flaming skin as she tugs it free from its prison and it stands. Tall and throbbing, her fingers feel like silk against its heat.

"Fuck," she breathes. "You seem much bigger than the last time."

I open my mouth to answer. To tell her that she's the reason. That I've been aching for her for so long. But I don't get the chance to. Firespark dips, that sweet mouth of hers closing around my tip, the heat underneath my skin cooled by her moist tongue.

I buck, feel a shot of preseed shoot through the tip, hear her moan of appreciation as she swallows it down, and know there is no hope of stopping myself this time.

And yet, I try.

Planting my claws into the sand, I grit my teeth hard as her tongue swirls around me. Another growl erupts as I plant my claws harder. Nothing prepared me for this. Nothing has ever felt this good. And when her gaze locks with mine again, my hips thrust forward on their own accord, forcing my cock deeper past her lips.

I freeze, struggling for control, but Firespark only moans, one hand sliding down to my secondary knot and making my head fall back against the drift.

She moans harder, taking me deeper as her tongue swirls, her jaws contracting as she sucks. The sight is mesmerizing. Even more so as her other hand disappears between her legs.

The breath in my chest stutters so hard I feel I have lost the knowledge of how to breathe.

She moans harder as she rubs that bud between her soft folds, all while her eyes flutter closed as she sucks on my cock. I am lost at the sight of it.

My hips buck again and again and Firespark moans in tune, taking as much of me as she can before I burst.

"Firespark!" I try to jerk back, to not blast the coming storm into her mouth, but her gaze is locked with mine, a grunt over my cock that vibrates against the surface as she urges me on. Seed shoots up through my shaft, making it stand impossibly harder as my spend fills her mouth. I see her gulp, her eyes watering with the pure demand, but then she's swallowing, her tongue swirling around me as she doesn't let even a drop escape.

This female will be my undoing.

Licking her lips, she slides my cock from between them, still stroking the still-hard rod with slow deliberate slides of her hand as she rises and straddles me again. I jerk in her hand and her eyes grow more intense as she slides me across her folds and to her center.

Firespark leans in, lips brushing against mine, the scent of my spend on her tongue and the knowledge that she took it all in making me crazed all over again.

"Fuck me," she whispers, and then her voice cracks. "Please."

Only the sound of her breaking apart pulls me from that pure, selfish need. I pull my hands from the sand and wrap them around her, staring into those beautiful eyes that are right before me. My nose presses against hers as I grip her, trying to read these new emotions flitting across her eyes, too fast for me to hold on to a single one.

"Fuck me," she whispers again. "Like you mean it. Don't hold back. I can take it. I *need* it."

And I know immediately what she means. What she really needs.

I tell myself I'm doing this because she's asked me to. That as my cock slides against her core that I'm doing it because she's begged. It's all a lie.

My cock pierces her with a single thrust and she sinks on me with a cry, sliding all the way to my secondary knot. There, I pump, letting her get used to the stretch, letting her get used to me as her walls become slippery with her juices, her body begging for more.

And I will give it to her. Because my Firespark has faced death today. Someone she loved was almost taken away from her. I know the *kiv* survived. Otherwise, she wouldn't be here. But now, she needs to *feel*. Needs to be reminded that life is more than fear or tragedy.

She needs *me*.

For the first time in all my existence, there is a being who does both. A being who not only *wants* me, but *needs* me.

I thrust into her, hardly holding back as my cock slides into her hot channel. She whimpers, back arching as I impale her and force deeper into her, that first band on my cock, my *kholo*, sliding past her entrance, spreading her from the inside out.

"Yes," she pants," give it to me. Give me everything."

I want nothing more than to do exactly just that, but her heat clenches around me, holding me tight. It's like sweet torture as I stiffen, allowing her to adjust to the stretch, allowing her muscles to tighten and relax around me until neither of us can take it anymore.

Firespark arches toward me, spine curving, and I capture her lips in mine as she lifts her hips and grinds down, pulling a deep rumble from my chest as her cunt accepts every bit of me, one inch at a time.

I can't hold it any longer. Gripping her hips, I steady her as I pull back, just at the base of where that first knot will swell before sliding forward again. I work her on my cock, each thrust letting her take all of me. Every inch, until she's sitting at the base of the second *kholo*.

And then I fuck her. I pull back, and I fuck her hard. Each thrust making her body rise and fall solely on my accord. There is nothing for her to hold on to except for me. Nothing for her to feel except the stretch of my cock and the heat it brings. I fuck her like I won't see her again. I fuck her like I want to consume her. And she lets me. Firespark doesn't resist. She opens her body to me. Her soul. And even in my treachery, I fall into it. Into her.

The pressure on my cock is almost too much, the tightness, her cunt like an addictive vice as she takes me in.

Chest heaving, our gazes meet as she tilts her head back,

baring her neck again, and my fangs leak venom just looking at her tender skin.

"Now," she whispers, her cunt clenching on the word.

With a growl, I lunge forward, cradling her by the nape as my lips brush against her soft skin.

"*Are you sure?*" I don't know how enough sanity reaches me to ask, for only a beast lies underneath my skin. Hardly controlled, already at the end of his leash.

"Yes," she pants.

My fangs ache so hard, I close my eyes for a moment before doing the unthinkable.

CHAPTER TWENTY-SIX

Elsie

It's a sharp pain; one that feels like two thin nails instantly sink into the curve of my neck. I *feel* the venom, like thick, hot fluid flooding into my veins.

The Zamari shudders and groans, then goes incredibly still. My chest heaves, the force of his cock spreading me apart plus his nearness all collide with his bite. A whimper passes my lips as I grip him tighter, hands gripping his shoulders right before the unexpected happens.

I knew it would hurt. Had prepared myself for the pain. But the moment he shudders again and a new sensation shoots through my veins I know nothing could have prepared me for this.

I feel my blood moving like liquid being pulled up through a straw. Such an odd sensation, but one that quickly makes my knees go weak. I go dizzy as the Zamari inhales and begins to suck me dry.

He growls. An unholy sound as his hips pull back and he

thrusts deeper inside my tight channel. A moan bubbles past my lips as indescribable pleasure shoots through me. As if fed by the very fangs buried into my skin, the pleasure shoots through my core like a thick, warm thread of pure sugar.

One arm grips my hips as he holds me steady, pulling back before burying himself deep. And then again. Again. Until I can no longer count. My pussy heats and weeps as he thrusts harder and harder while holding me still, his lips fastened on my neck while he drinks.

Drinks from me.

My eyes roll back, head lolling as my body goes limp. I can feel my energy waning. Feel my life force ebbing with each gulp he takes. With each hard thrust. With each second we're joined like this. I shudder against him; the only thing I can do is hold on as he takes every bit of me.

I see the stars above us, a soundless scream of bliss leaving my lips as my body quakes under his assault. So spent, the orgasm that crashes through me makes my body jerk in surprise. I feel my cunt choke, the muscles tightening, releasing, then swallowing him some more and the Zamari rumbles again, his relentless thrusts never ceasing.

I keep my grip on him. A slave to the pleasure shooting through me, I'm no longer sure whether my eyes are open or shut. Whether the darkness surrounding me is a result of awareness or if bliss has rendered me unconscious.

The Zamari growls and shudders, a deep groan against my neck as he pulls back and gives one final hard thrust, pulling me down on his cock till all of it is buried deep.

I don't feel it at first, but then it is all that I *can* feel. The swell. The feel of his cock growing thicker, impossibly thicker, locking us together. The pressure is so much, the lock so tight, that I gasp, my whole body stiffening as I inhale through the stretch.

The Zamari growls, his fangs sliding from my neck as his tongue licks the wound with languid strokes.

"Don't fight it, Firespark. I won't hurt you." His growl is primal, like he's a different male from the one I've been traveling with. "Let your sweet cunt take me in."

I hold my breath, fighting to do what he's asking, but the stretch is almost too much. "What—what's happening?"

He growls again, lips traveling up my neck to my ear where he licks the lobe.

"It's my knots." He growls again. "I tried not to. I am sorry, Firespark. I have taken more than you have offered."

His knots?

So that's what those—

My eyes roll back as I feel his hand between my legs, fingers brushing through my folds to find my center. His finger trails along the seam where we're joined, a possessive growl rumbling in his throat, before he trails that same finger higher, searching through my folds. I gasp as he brushes over my clit and he stops there. Easing back so he's looking at me, his eyes are pitch black as he thrums my clit.

I'm lost.

Sitting on his swollen cock, my whole body trembles as he works my clit, pushing me toward another peak.

"I can't," I breathe. Any strength I have is just enough to keep me awake, but he responds with another growl, head dipping once more to my neck where he kisses me there, tongue licking the wound as he still thrums on my clit.

I rise and crash again, pleasure shooting through me.

This being...he has taken me places I have never been.

The stars above me are the last I see.

The Outlaw

I cradle Firespark in my arms, reaching for the thick garment she's discarded and wrapping it around her as I tuck her tightly in my arms.

Her breaths are steady, her life organ beating uninterrupted thumps in her chest, but her eyes are closed. Spent from the intensity of my bloodlust.

My cock tightens, throbbing deep inside her channel where we're still joined and I grit my teeth against the surges of pleasure still going through me.

Lifting a hand, I brush away a lock of her pale strands, so I can see her face.

She looks so peaceful now. So...relaxed. No worry in her eyes. Completely at ease.

I shift, taking her with me as I settle back against the drift, able, for the first time since riding away from Comodre, to think clearly.

A satisfied purr rises in my chest as I lick my lips, the taste of her lifeblood still on my tongue. I brush a finger over the marks on her neck, tracing the two dots. I tried not to take too much. I hope I did not.

It is hard to determine just how much her body can take in a first drinking.

Pulling her tighter against me, her cunt pulses around my cock and my jaw clenches again. I had best keep still.

Leaning in, I press my face into her filaments, reveling in her pure scent. Running my fingers through them as we'd washed together had been one of the most intimate things I've done with any female. With Firespark, it had felt only natural.

Her body shudders, the growing cold of the dark sands creeping across her skin.

We cannot stay here for long.

Urging myself to calm, I force myself to think of other things. Like the potential group of Nirzoik that will descend on her little settlement all too soon. But my cock has other ideas. It throbs within her, reveling in her tightness. Reveling in her heat.

She shudders again, a slight moan leaving her lips as she shifts, fingers curling and digging into my arms before her eyes fly open.

"Hello, beautiful."

I don't know why I hold my breath. As if now, after the fact, she will regret what we have just done. Regret the fact she let me feed. Worse, that she will despise that my cock is still swollen within her. I can already tell the males of her kind do no such thing. She was surprised by it. Scared even.

She shifts, lifting her body before she stiffens and inhales deeply, only to release the breath with a moan. The look in her eyes changes from sudden confusion of having regained consciousness to pure pleasure.

"Fuck," she murmurs, shifting her hips in a way that makes me hiss. "You're really stuck in there." Her gaze lifts to mine, one hand moving to trace a line across my brow then curve around my jaw. "A knot."

"It shouldn't hurt—" I hiss again when her hips shift once more and I see a twinkle pass through her eyes. She...likes it?

"So, you're stuck with me?" There's a slight twist of her lips that turns into a fully fledged smile before she leans in, her whisper against my lips as she presses her pelvis into mine. "You're so fucking big. It feels like..." She utters such a delicious groan that, instead of my knots loosening, they swell thicker. "It feels like you're stretching me past my limit." She groans again before she takes my lower lips between her teeth, biting gently. "Is it bad that I don't want it to stop?"

Now it's my turn to growl, my cock throbbing at her words. "You shouldn't say those things."

Firespark giggles, sucking on my lip before releasing it. "Why?"

"Because," I growl, "it only makes me want to mount you harder."

She smiles, releasing a pleased laugh through her nose before she leans in, resting her head on my shoulder. With one hand, she traces the wound on her neck.

"Does it hurt?" I tense, waiting for her answer.

She shakes her head. "I can't feel it."

"Good."

With a smile, she settles against me and once again I wonder why the universe is tempting me so. We sit there, wrapped up together in silence; Firespark tracing an invisible pattern where her fingers rest on my chest, and a soft cool desert breeze brushing past us.

"How's the *kiv*?"

She inhales deeply, eyes unfocusing as she stares out into the void. "Thank you," she says after a few moments. "You have no idea how much what you did means to me." A deep sigh lifts and falls from her shoulders. "I think Kiana will be okay. For now."

I remain silent, running a finger through her strands. She's thanking me as if what I did wasn't the honorable thing to do. The right thing. The *kiv* needed my help. But who am I to speak about honor?

"You know..." She says after a few moments. "This is nice."

I stare up at the stars above us, soaking in the expanse of the universe. Of her.

She's right. It is nice. There is nowhere I'd rather be than here, at this very moment.

"It's not a lot of times that I get to just...enjoy Ivuria 10 like this," she whispers. "Out here, with you, the world almost seems...right."

My gaze lowers with her words, my focus falling on nothing. For she's right about that too. With her in my arms... nothing else seems important.

And that's why I have to protect her.

For a while now, this hasn't been about completing my final mission. It's been about *her*.

"Firespark..."

She stiffens. Head tucked against my chest, I feel her warm breath on my skin as she speaks. "I know..."

More silence falls between us. The type that's heavy with words unsaid.

"When do you think they'll come?" she asks.

"Soon."

She nods again. "Do you think we'll be ready?"

My arms tighten around her as I stare into the distance. For there's only one suitable answer to that question.

"Yes."

I'll make sure of it.

CHAPTER TWENTY-SEVEN

Elsie

As the pressure lessens, the trapped juices leak out as he pulls himself from within me. I almost whine at the loss, only catching myself when I pout.

What's wrong with me? We need to return to Comodre. I can't stay forever in this moment of peace.

The Zamari groans as his cock throbs between us, still slightly hard even now and it's a conscious effort not to lick my lips. Does he even know what he tastes like? His pre-cum is sweet, like sucking on cagri crystals, his cum even sweeter. I resist a moan just thinking about it.

Clearing my throat, I shift in his arms and his hold on me slackens, allowing me to rise on shaky legs. He stands immediately, steadying me with one hand as he pushes the thick meat of his cock back into his trouse. Grabbing and setting his hat on his head next, he still keeps me steady as he reaches down for my trouse.

"Brace on me." His luminous eyes only flick on me for a

second before he's crouching at my feet, spreading my panties so I can step into them.

It's a strange feeling seeing him crouched there. It makes something stutter through my heart and I grasp at the feeling, a slight shiver going through me as I step into the underwear. My trouse is next, and he holds them open the same way, allowing me to step into them while steadying myself against him.

When I'm finally dressed, he stands, gaze flicking over me before he reaches for my poncho and helps me into that, too.

"Come," he says, and I nod.

I'm a little woozy as I grab the beacon-light I'd been traveling with, and his steady arm grasps me the moment I turn around.

"It's okay, I'm alright. Just a little—"

He lets out a soft growl and suddenly my chin is held in a gentle grasp as he forces me to look at him. Those piercing eyes study me for far too long.

"I really am." I smile.

"I must have taken too much," he murmurs. "Your body isn't used to being drained."

I smile again, a soft laugh breathing through my nose. "It's not something we humans do." The look on his face is suddenly so easy to read. Passing by in a split second before his face returns to the unreadable mask he usually wears.

Fear. Regret. Shame.

For a moment, I'm too startled to speak. "B-but, it's fine. We give blood for like hospitals all the time. I will be all right."

He's so still, so silent, I'm not sure what he's thinking. So, I do the first thing that comes to my mind.

Going on my tiptoes, I plant a kiss on his lips, a laugh bubbling in my throat when I hear a resulting rumble in his chest.

"I'll be okay," I whisper against his lips. "I only wanted to help you... I helped, right?"

I search his gaze, noting that it's not bled to black anymore. He's better.

"More than you know, Firespark."

Something warm floods through me as he leans in, breath brushing over my lips before he places the sweetest softest kiss on my mouth.

"We should go," he breathes, pulling away. "It is not safe here and we've already stayed too long." I nod, pulling my poncho against me as I step toward where I'd abandoned my bike. But the Zamari steers me the other way.

We reach his bike shortly after and he activates it, the thrusters engaging as the bike hums happily above the sand. He climbs on, still steadying me with one arm before his gaze meets mine again.

"Your turn, Firespark." He shifts, putting space between him and the back of the bike seat as he waits. Space just the right size for me to fit.

"I can—"

He's already shaking his head. "No way I'm letting you ride after you've just had my fangs in your neck."

My cheeks warm, but I don't have the willpower to protest. I nod and he reaches for me, hands closing around my waist as he lifts me onto the bike, pulling my arms to wrap around his waist as if that's exactly where I'm meant to be.

"Ready?"

Head resting against his hard back, I nod, and he fires up the engine, guiding the bike slowly over to where I'd discarded mine. It's a newer model, better than the one I had before. One of those he'd gotten from his run-in with the Nirzoik.

Activating the control panel, he taps in some command and the bike fires up on its own. There's a soft, comforting squeeze on the back of my hand before we shoot off, the unmanned bike trailing us as we head back toward Comodre.

As the wind whips around us, the sky above us peaceful and clear, I keep my cheek pressed against him.

Knowing I will have to say goodbye when this is all done is only getting harder and harder to accept.

This...*stranger* that I met in a bar is the only person who makes my soul sing in a way I'm not sure I want to let go of. The only person who has made me feel whole in a long time.

The moment we pull into Comodre, I sense the change as if there is something different in the air itself. My chest tightens as the Zamari turns down my street, my heart doing a weird unsteady thud as I near my cabin and spot the group of people waiting on the street.

"Humans," he says. But I already knew that. The Nirzoik are bigger. Even in the shadows, their form is terrifying compared to a human's. But regardless that I know it's my people, my heart does not simmer down.

What do they want? And why are they here?

I make out four people before we slow down to a stop. One has a lantern and they step forward. James. He jerks his chin at the Zamari before his gaze shifts to me and then back. Behind him is the only other male living down this little offshoot—Craig—and two females from farther in town. They're all staring at the Zamari as if they expect him to cut their throats, yet hoping he won't.

Again, I wonder what they're doing here. And when it's not immediately obvious, my worry calms down a bit. If they were here to argue or make a fight, they'd have started by now.

"They want to help," James says. "Me, Craig, Sasha, and Thalia will ride with you on those bikes you got from the Nirzoik. We'll ride to Calanta, get the grain and supplies—"

"That's not happening," the Zamari cuts him off, taking his time to brace his legs on the sandy road as the bike steadies. "I'm here to protect her. I'm not leaving."

It's clear who he's referring to because their gazes all shift to me. A flutter goes through my belly while James blinks a few times, as if thrown off course. "I thought—"

The Zamari shrugs. "You go to Calanta. There are four of you. You should be safe enough. Stick together. Get the supplies. Return."

"This is bullshit." Craig speaks up from the back. "It's far too dangerous to travel to Calanta with such a small party and with..." He trails off, his gaze shifting to the two women beside him.

"And with what?" One of them, Thalia, frowns.

"With *women*," he finishes, spitting the words as he shifts his gaze back to the Zamari.

There's a tense silence and I release my hold on the Zamari, almost groaning with the loss of heat as I climb off the bike. He reaches back with one arm immediately, steadying me as I get off, and another warm feeling spreads through my chest.

"Come on, James," Craig continues, hands on his hips as his brows dive. "Back me up here." When James doesn't say a thing, I can almost see Craig's anger rise. "The only reason I agreed to do this is because *you* said *he*—" he jams a finger in the Zamari's direction "—would come with us. It's a death wish going across the plains alone and all the way to Calanta, man!"

His words, of course, don't just fly by me. They hit me hard. I'd thought the same when I'd headed to Calanta all alone. But somehow, I'd made it.

"You won't be *alone*," Thalia says, frowning. "There'd be

four of us, as the outlaw says." Her gaze shifts to the Zamari before averting just as quickly.

"Two *women* and one other man aren't exactly what I would call the greatest odds for such a journey, *Thalia*." He says her name with utter disdain. With a big sigh, he tilts his head to look up at the night sky, running his hands through his hair to grip his skull in unhidden distress.

This has nothing to do with me, so I decide to take my leave.

"I'll see you inside," I whisper to the Zamari, giving James a slight nod as I step onto my deck. I'm only two steps toward my door when Craig's words make me falter.

"We're not all fucking fools like *Elsie* here. Going all the way to Calanta alone. Stupid. Reckless. No common sense—"

There's movement. Air against my skin even though there isn't a gust. It whips past me at the same time that there's a dull thud and a pained grunt.

I turn to see Craig on the ground, a heavy knee pressed into his chest and a blade at the center of his throat, the slightest pressure meaning certain death.

Sasha and Thalia gasp and instinctively grab on to each other while James stands wide-eyed, arms extended outward in alarm, his Adam's apple frozen high in his throat. It happened so quickly, I don't think any of us breathed.

The Zamari's voice is a bone-chilling growl. "*Elsie* braved those fekking plains alone for *me*. Your only flicker of hope stands right here." He sneers, his gaze piercing into a stunned and trembling Craig. "And you dare undermine her strength. *Show some respect*...or find out just how unforgiving these wastelands can be."

Craig's hands wave in the air above his head. "I-I'm sorry, man. I—"

He grunts when he's suddenly gripped by the throat and

pulled to his feet before the Zamari forces him to face me, pushing him down on his knees in front of me. Trembling, Craig looks up at the Zamari and I find I'm staring at the Zamari too.

But he's not focused on me. That snarl on his face reveals the sharp line of his bared teeth, violence flowing around him like a wave. He's not doing this because he thinks I want him to. Neither is he doing it because it's what I've paid him to do.

He's pissed. Annoyed. He's looking at Craig with a mixture of disappointment in Craig's existence matched with utter disgust. And all because Craig's spoken about me like I wasn't even standing right here to hear every single word.

We've never been friends. Even with our cabins so close, we've hardly spoken. I had no illusions that this male liked me. But to hear him rip into me so...

Hands still gripping the man's throat, the Zamari leans in. "Make it better."

Mild confusion flashes through Craig's eyes before his focus shifts to me. "S-sorry, Elsie." I can see the tension in his entire face as the Zamari's fist tightens, forcing his words to distort. "I di'n mean en'thin' by'it."

The Zamari releases him so suddenly he falls on his hands and knees, wheezing and coughing as he tries to pull air into his lungs. I stare at him, wondering why I feel no pity. Why looking at my fellow species being manhandled doesn't bring me any pain.

Maybe because it's people like him, too scared to fight, too scared to die, that's led us to this situation in the first place. People like him who would rather live like slaves than fight for their freedom.

Movement and the Zamari comes to the edge of the deck, cleaning the tip of his blade with his fingers, before his gaze lifts to mine. "I'm sorry you had to hear that, Firespark."

My smile is soft as I stare at him. Stare into those cold eyes. Eyes that should chill me, and yet, all I can feel is warmth. I nod before glancing at the others. I offer them a slight smile too, before heading inside without saying a word. Because there's nothing to be said. He said it all for me.

I'm not weak. I'm not a fool. Reckless, yes. Daring? Maybe too much. But I risked my life to travel those plains, to bring back some hope, and I'll be damned if that risk doesn't result in some changes around here.

As I shut the door quietly behind me, I turn to face Viv and Estella, who are there waiting for me.

Kiana is asleep, her breaths steadier, and I lean against the door in a strange sort of space as Viv and Estella update on her progress. All the while thinking that the world outside these walls is cold, vicious, and lonely.

Viv and Estella? They aren't just my friends. They're my family.

I listen to them and accept their embrace before I sit by the cot beside Kiana, my eyes on the door and the mumblings of conversation filtering in from outside.

The others are planning—apparently without Craig—and I can't help but wonder just how many more of my people will give up before we've even begun.

CHAPTER TWENTY-EIGHT

Elsie

The days after Kiana's recovery blur together. I wake each morning with Ivuria starting her trip across the cloudless sky with a haze of wariness surrounding me. This morning is no different and I rise and stretch, bones aching from restless sleep. Eyes still blurry with slumber, I smooth back Kiana's hair and check her breathing, needing the reassurance of that soft brush of air against my skin. I take a few moments to just watch her breathe before rising and heading to the bathroom to wash up. Once done, I put the kettle on to prepare Kiana's tea.

The door opens softly at my back and my skin prickles with awareness as I hear it close just as quietly. I don't have to turn around to know who it is. He's the only person who can make my heart beat hard like this with just his presence alone.

"Morning," I whisper, voice low enough that it won't disturb the sleeping child. He doesn't answer and I don't expect him to. His silence is a constant in this turbulent world, and despite everything, despite the heaviness in my soul, I smile.

This is our routine. The one that's been keeping me sane the past few days while that wariness lies in the air, hanging over Comodre like an invisible cloud. The Zamari's warning has made us all alert. The threat of the Nirzoik returning has made every day I wake feel like a big question as to what will happen next.

I try to pay it no mind as the tea comes to a boil and I pour it into two mugs. One I bring near my lips, blowing away the steam, and the other I lift, taking it with me as I turn around.

Those luminous green eyes make my heart stutter. Something blooms around me like a cloud as I continue blowing on the tea while bringing the other mug to him.

He takes it with one hand, eyes never leaving me.

"You know you can sleep in here. With us. It's not much in terms of space but—"

"I know, Firespark. Believe me, I would much rather stay in here with you than out in the cold Ivurian sands."

"Then..." But I stop short. I stop because my words are replaced with a soft smile of knowing. Because I know what he's going to say. He's said it many times before. It's the same conversation every morning.

"Out there, I can protect you. In here, you are safe."

We stare at each other for a few moments, his eyes never leaving mine and mine not able to pull away from his as I continue cooling the tea. Looking into his eyes like this, it feels as if he's saying more. Only when I turn to rouse the little bundle wrapped up in the blanket on my cot does my gaze shift.

Kiana stirs, only to dutifully swallow the spoonfuls I place on her tongue before she falls back asleep. I tuck her in before rising, immediately feeling the warmth at my back. The hardness of his chest. The soft growl in his throat.

"Firespark..." The Zamari snakes one arm around me as he

takes the mug from my fingers with the other. I hear him pull air into his lungs as he dips his nose into my hair. "The night was cold and dull without you."

That soft smile that seems to only be present when he's around widens and I lean into him, the curve of my spine fitting against his chest. The roundness of my ass notching right where I want it to be. I feel his hardness as I shift and that soft growl in his throat grows deeper.

"Maybe you should have come in," I whisper, knowing I'm tempting the beast but unable to stop myself. My body complies as he steers me away from the cot. Leaving the empty mugs on the small kitchen table, he guides me toward the backroom, and there, as the darkness envelops us, he presses me into the wall.

It's like striking a match, heat and passion instantly igniting. His kiss is searing. His touch. His...*everything*. My head falls back against the wall, neck baring as he licks and sucks in my skin, fangs grazing over me as if he wishes to devour me whole. But he doesn't bite. Never bites. He *worships*.

In this momentary spot of reality where it is only him and me together, he doesn't use words to tell me I am beautiful. Or perfect. Or safe. I feel it like a mantra whispered over my skin with every kiss. Every caress. Every touch. His hands grope and squeeze every inch of me, as if he is unseeing and he needs his fingers to tell him everything there is to know about me. To paint a picture in his mind that he will hold forever.

And when he spreads my legs with one thigh, lifting my skirts as his hard length finds my entrance, I am lost to this world. Lost every time he takes me. Lost knowing that every day that passes, I want him so much. Too much.

Lost knowing that this will all end.

And that's why we ignite. Why this passion blazes so high.

I grip onto him as he thrusts, moans muffled against him as he brings us both to a peak. I open up to him and the pleasure coursing through me, all while wishing things were different. That maybe the next morning won't be our last together. Because I never know when will be our last. And that terrifies me.

By the time my breaths settle enough for me to calm and my legs are no longer weak from the force of my peak, the Zamari sets me down on my feet.

He leans into me, bending so that our foreheads touch, and in those luminous eyes, I see more than he thinks I see. I see that this is hard for him, too.

"I—"

I stop the three words that constantly want to bubble past my lips. They keep coming. Every morning they do. And every morning I stop them in my throat because I don't want to spoil this. For however much longer it will last, I want to have it all.

I love him. But it's insane to say that out loud when I know where this is going. So I clear my throat. "Do you need to drink?"

My gaze searches his. Sees when something strange passes through his eyes. But just as he does every morning, he presses closer, inhaling me softly before shaking his head.

"You tempt me, Firespark."

And I want to. I *want* to tempt him. To make him abandon whatever is holding him back. I want him to just...take me. Damn the consequences.

But such thoughts are selfish. Foolish. I'm not the only one who will be affected by my choices. And so, I do the right thing. I tilt my chin, planting a kiss on his surprisingly soft lips.

Time to start another long day.

We're out of medicine. Out of credits. And the Nirzoik will come again.

Monitoring Kiana becomes a full-time task. One of us—me, Estella, or Viv—stays with her during the day, while the others go to the mines, trying to get enough gems to save up for her treatment. Despite the Zamari's obvious disapproval, it's the only way I know I can get the credits we need. And though his jaw clenches every time I set out, as if he's holding back the urge to order me not to go, I know the gems are our only chance. And so, we mine. In the nights when we return, we take turns, one person staying with Kiana. All routine, all while the world is turning around us.

The next several days pass in the same manner. The only indications of time's progression are Kiana's gradual strengthening and the steady activity I observe around town. My people are becoming braver. There's a light at the end of this long tunnel. Along with some others, we carry blasters now. Proudly strapped against my hip for quick removal. Just in case.

When the Nirzoik miss their usual collection date, there's a sort of nervous hope in the air that even I dare to soak in.

Supplies are brought in. The cellar the Zamari built slowly filled with more food than I've seen since before the mothership crashed. And weapons too. The entire town's stash is collected, surveyed, and tested. Daily blaster practice begins in the town center at the *endolo* tree, more and more humans getting the courage to bear arms. *Because of him.*

His ruthlessness is a charm that brings hope that we can actually do this.

But the days are long and tiring. I only catch glimpses of him as we go about our tasks. But every time I do, he is watching me.

It becomes a game. Whenever I walk through town on my way to the mines, I walk knowing he'll be waiting for me. And, as usual, he is. Standing at the same spot. Never failing.

Between what was supposed to be the schoolhouse and what's now the general store, he leans against the wall, arms crossed, hat pulled so low I can barely see his eyes; but I know he's watching me. Watching as I hurry on my way. And he's always there when I'm heading back.

The increased activity in the colony simply because of the hope he brings causes the streets to no longer be empty and dead. People move about. The street gets busy enough that I have to look where I'm going so I don't bump into anyone. Comodre has life again and it all makes a hesitant ball of excitement grow in my chest.

Late, while Kiana sleeps and I slip into the bath, he appears at the door. The same time every evening. He settles behind me, water warming us both as he brushes and washes my hair before allowing me to do the same for him. Then he'll use his fingers or his tongue until I shudder before he takes me, thrusting deep into my heat until we're both consumed.

Afterward, he takes me to bed and tucks me in, wrapping me in the blanket as I hold Kiana in my arms and he circles us both. Without fail, he holds us like that till he believes I sleep. And then he rises, quietly disappearing into the darkness as he leaves us to go keep watch.

Late one night, when Kiana stirs and whispers that she's thirsty, I rise. After fetching her water, I find the Zamari filling the doorway. The air stills between us. Silently, he enters and crouches by the cot. Clawed hand impossibly gentle, he brushes her hair back. My breath catches at the display of affection. He stays by her side, watching as I fetch the cup and bring it to her lips. Kiana drinks and drifts off again, and still he remains.

When luminous eyes meet mine over her sleeping form, I feel that invisible tether between us strain against circumstance, pulling tighter...

I...don't want this to end.

But there is always the calm before the storm.

And it comes raging one day. One day when the sky above Ivuria 10 is covered in dark clouds.

I should have known it was an omen. Known it meant my life was about to be changed forever.

Known it meant that these good times were over.

CHAPTER TWENTY-NINE

Elsie

The wind whips cold, plastering tendrils of my hair against my face as I exit the mine.

The first thing that hits me is the shadows. Above us, heavy dark clouds hover and roll, blocking out the sun.

I pause, mouth falling open as I stare at the ominous sight. I don't even remember Estella is exiting the mine behind me until she bumps into my back.

"Whoa." She stops short too, wide eyes staring up at the sky. "Rain? Already?"

Shaking my head, my brows furrow. "It shouldn't be. The rainy season...isn't due yet..." But it *is* going to rain. I can feel it, as if the drops are forming in the air right before me.

My words trail off as my gaze shifts to the silhouettes of cabins in the distance. Comodre.

"Hey, if that's the case, I'm not complaining." Estella heaves her sack filled with gems over her shoulder before stepping by my side. "We should hurry back. Set the barrels—"

Her words are cut off as she winces, widened gaze flashing my way when I suddenly grip her arm so hard my fingers dig into her skin. "Elsie, what the he—"

But I'm not looking at her. I can't pull my gaze away from the thing that's caught my attention. I sense when she turns her puzzled gaze from me, her body tightening with the sudden terror she must feel coming from mine. For she sees what I see. And I know she does, because she stiffens in my grasp.

"That's—"

As if her single utterance is all I needed to convince myself I'm not seeing things, I release her arm and set off in a run. Fear pushes my body to move, even as the distant toll of the town bell reaches my ears.

At first, I'm not sure what I'm seeing. Lights in the distance, high in a darkened sky. The haunting sound of the bell grows the closer I get, piercing the air as the cold wind whips around me, chilling me from the outside in.

I hear it next. The rumbling. The sound of metal smashing together. Under the toll of the bell, it echoes across the town, shaking the sands at my feet. Shaking the very foundations that we've built. My heart stutters in my chest, my surroundings disappearing around me as I stare at the behemoth hovering in the air. Because I know this. This rumbling. This terror. I've heard and seen it before.

A scraper ship. The Beh'ni'nites. They're here? But why?

I stop breathing as I come to a sudden halt, my gaze fixing on a plume of smoke rising from the center of town.

Something is burning, something big, and there could only be one cause for that. It's not the Beh'ni'nites.

"What the fuck is that?" Estella heaves in huge breaths as she stares in horror at the beast in the sky.

"A scraper ship."

"But...those don't come near settlements, right? It'll tear the cabins apart. Surely they see us!"

"It's the Nirzoik." The words are whispered on my lips. I don't know how I know it's them. Maybe it's the fire. The faint scent of smoke rising to us on the wind.

They like to burn us down. Scorch everything we have; turn it all to ashes.

My free hand reaches for the handle of the blaster holstered on my waist.

"How did the Nirzoik get a scraper ship?!" Estella's panic is clear. It's the only reason I manage to hold back my own.

My legs start moving again, my gaze hardening as I push through the sand displacing around my boots. Each step makes me sink a little as I head toward the town. Each grain working to make my progress slow and threatening to pull me down even as I force my legs to move.

A strange sort of panic rises inside my chest the closer I get to Comodre. One that has me resolute even as terror settles at the base of my spine. I sling the sack of gems over my shoulder, holding it tight with one hand, while the other stretches before me in a strange sort of balancing act as I slide down the final sand mound that leads down into the settlement.

The moment I enter the outskirts of Comodre, the chaos hits me full-on. People are screaming, running, trying to find cover. There is blaster fire with no indication of where it's coming from. Cries for mercy pierce the air mixing with the distinct crackle of fire eating through timber.

I almost collapse to my knees.

Comodre...is falling.

Up above us, the huge ships casts a shadow that blends in with the coming storm, the dark clouds projecting eerie shadows on the worn-down cabins, making everything look ominous. A sudden crack of lightning lights up the massive ship making its way over us.

"Shit," Estella says as she comes to a stop beside me. "I saw them," she breathes, "in the ship." She swallows hard, and I look up at the vessel above us. Its wide mouth is open, as if it's about to devour us all. "I saw them. More than I can count and they've got weapons too."

"Comodre isn't worth all that manpower," I whisper, not to her but more to myself. But the words are just my mind swirling around the fact that *I* brought them here. I'm the reason this is happening. Because I hired the Zamari. Because I pushed back. "We can't fight off that many."

My limbs suddenly feel weak as the reality of what's happening sinks in my soul. My world is shattering and I don't know how to mend it.

The thunder that follows next rumbles and rolls, breaking through the air around us and fading into the sound of tearing metal that grows louder with each second. There's a roar of many voices that echoes all around us.

The Nirzoik are storming in.

Fuck.

The smoke hits me next, its stench chalky as it fills my nose.

Fear fills my soul, holding me still. Making me unable to move. The same fear that had settled and taken residence when the Nirzoik rode into our little colony orbits ago. The same fear that has threatened to overcome me at every turn.

It's too familiar. Almost as if, all this time since the Zamari's arrival, it had never once left. Only lay dormant. Waiting. It threatens to pull me down now, even as I push myself to move as I hurry past the first few rickety buildings, my chest heaving with labored breaths.

Kiana. Viv. The Zamari. I have to get to them. Warn them that the Nirzoik are here. *I need to get home.* But there's no way for me to do that without going straight through the town. It's the only way.

My jaw tightens as I lift my head, facing the way ahead. Guess that's what I have to do.

Dodging frightened humans running for cover and somewhere to hide, I head straight into the chaos. My feet thump hard against the sand as I run, all the while trying not to collide with my own people who are doing the same.

The first Nirzoik I see almost makes me stumble at the very sight of him on the ground. He catches a fleeing woman, one claw deftly closing around her throat, halting her movement, while his other fist slams into her belly. She doubles over, body curling in to stop the pain, before he throws her down as if she's just a sack of cloth. His gaze meets mine next.

Shit.

Go! I scream for Estella to keep up when my heart does a sudden thump. Alarm floods through my veins as I crash into solid metal. The force is so strong, it throws me backward and I land on my spine, the bag with the gems loosening from my grip to scatter its contents across the sandy road.

"Shit!" Estella skids to a halt, her eyes wide as she looks up at the Nirzoik who's suddenly before us. Smoke chokes the air, the wind sending a blast of it straight at us and I cough, forcing myself to breathe as I squint to see his face.

"Shit!" Estella utters again, gripping me by the arm as she tries to pull me upright, all while her wide eyes stay focused on the threat looming over us.

He's armored. Wearing a chest plate and helmet that cover his vital organs. And what's utterly terrifying is that this Nirzoik doesn't react. Doesn't knock us down. Doesn't immobilize us so he can move on to his next target. He simply watches me from a single good eye in that metal helmet—the other just a darkened hole filled with twisted scars. As I scramble to rise, his sharp teeth glint through his helmet's mouth slit as he pulls his lips back in a grin.

I'm standing now, chest heaving, panic in my veins as every possible scenario runs through my mind.

I'm too late. They're already at my cabin. The Zamari would have been there finishing preparations and Viv would have been there too, watching over Kiana. There's a sudden regret in my gut that I'm not there with them. That I *would* have been if I hadn't insisted on going to the mines today. But I need the gems. For Kiana's medicine. And I need them to pay him what I owe. But if he's at my cabin, I can only hope he managed to defend Viv and Kiana before these fiends got too close. I can only hope...

My thoughts snap to the Nirzoik before us as he takes a sudden step forward. He's bigger than the others that slink from the shadows with him. Some snagging fleeing humans, their fists slamming into them, downing them in an instant. I swallow hard as I try to keep this big one in my focus all while seeking a way out. A way to get past him. But more Nirzoik appear at his back.

At least a foot taller than usual, he towers over his companions. There's something *wrong* about him. Maybe it's his sheer size. Maybe it's because of the scars on his face. Apart from the one seeing eye, deep grooves mar his features in every spot I can see. Scars that are dark and old, as if they've been there for a very long time.

This one is a hardened warrior. A fighter.

Weighing my options, I wait for him to react. The blaster still strapped to my waist is no use now with him so close. But maybe I can create a distraction. Even in the corner of my eye, I can see Estella slowly reaching for the blaster she has tucked into the back of her trouse.

A distraction...I can do that.

I just have to keep him focused on me. And I need to do it quickly. The rumbling of the ship above us is growing closer. We don't have much time.

"This the one?" One-Eye asks, and I blink at him, shoulders tightening. He doesn't speak like the others do. His accent isn't from Calanta or anywhere on this side of Ivuria 10. He's an off-worlder. A Nirzoik I've never met before.

"Does it matter?" Another Nirzoik appears from behind the cabin to our right and I shift backward slightly, my focused gaze taking in them both. While the others were creating havoc, these ones were hiding. What were they waiting for? "They all look alike."

There's another scream from down the road and the distinct sound of fire eating fresh wood. Another cabin goes up in flames, the sound mixing with the screech of scraping metal still approaching.

Echoing all around Comodre, I can hear more Nirzoik. Their roars. The screams of my people. Even with the Zamari's training, we're no match for them, and that thought makes a ball of guilt and fear swell in my chest.

How did I ever make myself so disillusioned to think we could ever win against these fiends? We can never win. Not like this.

The Nirzoik before us leans in, so close I see the scarred flesh of that unseeing eye in too great of a detail. The skin is twisted, gnarly, as if that eye was taken out by fire.

"Fuck." Estella mutters, face twisting in disgust as she takes a step back at the same time that I do. My boots press hard against a few of the gems that had scattered, and I freeze when I hear sand crunch behind me. A quick glance and I spot two more Nirzoik a few feet that way, too. We're surrounded, and the streets are growing filled with wounded humans.

"Where the fuck is your man?" Estella whispers.

I gulp, not in the least bit thinking about the fact she's referring to the Zamari as mine. "With Kiana and Viv, I think." *I hope.*

The big Nirzoik before us rolls his shoulders, gaze snapping to me and I realize he heard Estella's whisper, even though her voice was so low, I almost didn't hear her.

"*This one?*" One-Eye growls, eyes sharpening on me. "We need the right one. No use if I don't have the one he wants."

Who 'he' wants? This isn't a normal raid. They have some kind of plan. And that means we need to do something before it's too late for us to do anything at all. I glance at Estella, but she's staring at the Nirzoik. She's panicking. I can see the vein throbbing in her neck and her hand halfway paused to her blaster. But we can get out of this together. One of us, at least.

I wait for her to look at me, but the terror is causing her to stare at the Nirzoik instead, her gaze shifting to the ship above then back as the realities sink in. But I want her to look at me. *Need* her to. Need to give her a signal that I'm about to do something stupid so she can run away and go get the Zamari.

"It's that one." The words cut through the sound of the rolling thunder and scraping metal. "That *kinchi.*"

My gaze snaps to the one that spoke, a Nirzoik off to the side, breath stopping in my nose when I see he's pointing a blaster right at my skull. I recognize him and a part of my gut sinks. He's the one the Zamari let free. The one he sent with a message to their leader. It takes every ounce of bravery as I shift my gaze from the weapon pointed at my skull to the one-eyed behemoth before me. My chest tightens as soon as I do.

There is no indication of anything in One-Eye's gaze as he looks at me, and I'm reminded that these aren't regular beings. He's aware of every single thing happening around him right now. Of the ship above us. Of every grunt and whimper of my people at their feet. Aware that my hand is hovering just a second away from grabbing my blaster. Aware that I'm wanting to make a move.

And his utter stillness makes that terror settling on my spine rise and grow, seeping into my bones.

"So..." he finally says. "You're the one the Zamari protects."

Under the complete focus of that singular eye, I don't move. I don't even breathe. As if the slightest thing will let him know the truth.

Behind him, there's another scream and a deep grunt as a Nirzoik exits one of the cabins a few doors down. A struggling Thalia is gripped by the throat, her kicks and punches doing nothing to stop him as he throws her into the road. Her body hits the ground hard, her chest heaving as she grips her throat and coughs, pulling deep lungfuls of air into her chest.

More Nirzoik exit other cabins, thrusting more people from their hiding places into the road, some wheezing from the lack of air, some with their hands up pleading for mercy as blasters are pointed at their heads.

A sort of growing pain clenches around my heart as I stare at the scene before me.

"*Where is he?*" One-Eye growls. "I know he is here." He takes a step forward and I take one back. "For many orbits, I've tracked his kind across Ivuria, and each one I found turned out to be the wrong one." He moves forward, closing the little distance I put between us in just one step. "Tell me...where the Outlaw of the Plains is." He sniffs, inhaling deep as his gaze slides down my body in a way that makes my skin crawl. "*You've mated with him.*"

The utterance makes me go still.

The Nirzoik releases a laugh that sounds eerily like the scraping metal that sounds far too close now. "So...it's true about you humans..."

When I don't respond, he continues. "Only females with

great resilience can handle a Zamari without chancing death."
He inhales again and I step back in horror, realizing that, in
some perverted way, he's trying to catch a scent of what's
between my legs. "My comrades say human cunts are soft and
eager...that they suck on a Nirzoik's cock even when you
scream and pretend you wish it to end." He pauses, cold eye
meeting mine once more. "Did you let that Zamari knot you,
human? Is that why he is here in this desolate place?"

My jaw clenches and his gaze shifts to the motion. I see the
faintest hint that my non-response is getting on his nerves when
his lips pull back over those sharp teeth.

He tilts his head, a glint of what can only be the
manifestation of evil lighting his eye. "That red-furred one
fought like fire, didn't she?" He pierces me with that glint of
malice. "Even while her cunt still gripped and *sucked* on us."

"Son of a bitch." The words leave my mouth in a whisper
that slides from between my clenched teeth as I pull my blaster
without thinking, the barrel pointing at his skull only a second
later. He stiffens, but that's the only reaction I get. Beside me,
Estella steps forward and I know she's thinking exactly what I
am. That he's talking about Viv. That what happened to her is
replaying in her mind just as it is in mine. We weren't there, but
we heard her screams. Heard how she fought while these beasts
did the unthinkable.

One-Eye snorts, his eye narrowing for a moment. With one arm
he forces the Nirzoik at his side to lower his weapon, even though I
still have mine raised. "Is that what you did, little human? Pay the
Zamari with your cunt? Is that why he promised to help you?"

I swallow hard, realization hitting me that even with my
blaster at the center of his skull, this fiend is not afraid. And it
has nothing to do with his armor. My gaze shifts to all the
Nirzoik standing still around us.

If I try to kill him now, I will die a second later. I'm sure of it.

My breaths make my shoulders rise and fall as I refuse to say a word. Refuse to give him any information at all. But it seems my silence is enough. It seems it's everything he needs because he snorts again.

"He'll want more than that, *kinchi*. You humans aren't worth more than a few matings. You *break* too easily." He says the words with enough venom it would feel like a slap to the face if it wasn't coming from the likes of him.

"He's still a better male than you will ever be." The words barely leave my lips before my neck snaps to the side, the Nirzoik's fist connecting with my jaw. I stagger back, just as one of the others moves almost immediately and kicks the blaster in my hand. The force sends my wrist back, and my hand opens, releasing my hold on the weapon so my bone doesn't snap.

It flies into the sand a few steps behind me just as Estella grabs for me, supporting my body as her fiery gaze flies to One-Eye.

"You fucking pieces of shit!" she screams and for a moment, I fear he'll attack her too. "You're *scum*! Pure rotten *scum*. When you go to bed tonight, jerk off to the sound of me telling you to FUCK OFF. Fucking loser."

I grip her arm, squeezing tightly. "It's okay, Estella," I whisper, widening and closing my eyes to get rid of the sudden dizziness that makes it hard to concentrate. I stretch my jaw, pushing through the pain as I shift my gaze back to One-Eye. "He's just a big bad Nirzoik who's trying to prove a point...by beating on someone weaker than he is. That make you feel stronger, big guy?"

I sneer at him even though I can feel the blood in my

mouth. I'm goading him. Will probably regret it later. But something tells me I need to draw this out. We need time.

He lifts one hand, and I clench my jaw, bracing myself to duck in case he swings again. But he doesn't move to strike me. He simply does a strange motion with his fist. A signal.

Suddenly, the rumbling, the shaking, stops. The deep, thrumming sound around us slowly dies as the ship above pauses midair, floating in the center of the storm building in the skies. Time seems to still.

His cronies snigger, the ones closest to us leaning against the beams of the cabin next to us, shoulders relaxing as if there is nothing to fear.

The sight makes my chest tighten. Is there something I'm missing here? Maybe I'm not the one playing a game, trying to gain borrowed time. Is this all some kind of joke when they've already taken the Zamari down?

Something deep in the center of my chest aches. I can't consider that. I don't *want* to consider it. Because some part of me knows it can't be true. Some foolish part of me feels like I would *know*, deep down, if they'd killed him. He's still alive. Fighting. Protecting Viv and Kiana. I just have to get there. I have to get to them.

One-Eye sneers. "You think fekking a Zamari gives you guts, foolish female?" He spits through that mouth slit and the thick blob of his saliva falls to the sand by my feet as he sneers. "You are nothing but a seed bucket."

I swallow hard, still keeping my mouth shut as I wipe away the streak of blood on my cheek. He takes another step forward, boots pressing the gems I gathered into the sand. His gaze skips down to one and he crouches and takes the red gem between his claws, turning it as he examines it in the low light.

My eyes narrow as I slip my arm from Estella's grasp and take a step toward the brute. It's me he wants. That's clear. He knows about the Zamari. Knows I'm the one who brought him here. Estella doesn't need to be a part of this.

"Elsie—" she starts, but I lift my hand, telling her it's alright.

One-Eye watches me, and I can see the evil growing in his eyes like some kind of darkness eating him from the inside out. "Tenacious," he says. "I can see why he stays." His gaze shifts around the colony for just a second. "Or, from the look of things, perhaps he abandoned you already."

More sniggering, but for a moment, his words give me hope. My fingers twitch from where my arms hang at my side. He's talking as if he knows the Zamari personally. But what's more than that, he doesn't know *where* the Zamari is...and that can only mean he's still alive somewhere.

"You humans have always been foolish prey animals not prepared for the dangers of Ivuria," he says, rising to his full height as he lifts the gem higher so it catches more light. "We had a good thing going here, human. You mine the gems, we take a cut of the spoils. Nothing too much. A few credits here and there. It's how things work in these wastelands. All we've shown you," his gaze shifts to me, "is kindness."

One-Eye's sudden grin is filled with so much malice, I feel it like a sword in my gut. But that does it. His words snap me out of whatever daze I'm in.

"Kindness?" I hiss back, pushing past the pain in my jaw. I jerk my hand at the humans writhing in pain just behind him. At the desolation around us. "What the fuck do you know about kindness?"

He snarls, the words affecting him more than I thought they would. And just as quickly, his whole expression shifts.

He laughs. He towers over us as he looks down at me with that full-mouthed grin that shows off his serrated teeth through the slit in his helmet.

A lump hardens in my throat as I stare at him. This Nirzoik isn't like a low-level grunt. He's smart. Speaks like he actually thinks instead of simply follows orders. Of all the times they have come to us, this time feels the most uncertain. My gaze shifts as I count how many of his men I can see. At least ten in my periphery, then there's the ship hovering above us, the distant screams and roars I still hear.

We're in a terrible spot.

Far behind One-Eye, a woman screams as a Nirzoik throws her from wherever she'd been hiding. My gaze snaps to the sound to see it's Sasha. She lands on her belly and the Nirzoik chasing her kneels in her back, pulling on her hair and bending her neck back toward him. My pulse picks up at the sight. We're losing time. When my gaze goes back to the monster before me, I prickle when I find that single eye boring into me with focused intensity.

He knows this is hard. Knows I want to make this stop. And he's going to use that against me.

"That monster you brought here, do you even know what he is?" One-Eye tilts his head, watching me. "We Nirzoik have protected you." I scowl at his words but he's not finished. "He will abandon you and your pathetic colony."

"He won't."

In just a second, there's the smooth shink of metal against leather as he unsheathes twin swords from his sides. He rotates them in his claws, all the while staring at me. And somehow, I'm not afraid. I stare right back at him. "Tell me where he's hiding...and we will end this slaughter. We will go back to normal and not hold this...lack of judgment against you humans." He pauses. "We will let you live."

As if I would ever believe that. "Fuck you." My chest tightens as I say the words, knowing the humans lying still on the ground nearby can hear me. Knowing they must feel I am dooming them and myself. But I can't turn on the Zamari.

He wouldn't turn on me.

I take a step back, eyes on those blades that seem to extend far too long, their sharp tips so pointed they're undoubtedly made to skewer. But the Nirzoik follows me.

"First rule of the plains, little one...never trust an outlaw. Just before you hired him...that Zamari eradicated a whole settlement. Their lifeblood still stains the sands. *Not one being was left alive.*" He growls the last sentence with enough rage that I see it in his eye.

His words make a strange sort of cold wash over me and my throat tightens even more.

"You don't even know him," I whisper, even as the image of a whole town left with only bodies dead on the ground rises in my mind. It's a scene that has appeared in my nightmares over and over. Comodre completely devastated. Exactly as it is now. And he's saying the Zamari did this same thing somewhere else? *My* Zamari?

Another step back. "I don't believe it."

Only a snarl is left on One-Eye's lips now, and I can feel the threat coming off him in waves. "The Outlaw of the Plains spares no one."

A scream echoes in the air from where Sasha and Thalia lie, and I know it's now or never. I have to do *something*.

"Kill her." One-Eye suddenly says, lifting one arm with a signal, and my heart stops.

I react automatically, those lessons with the Zamari coming to me as if they knew they'd be called. There is no fear, no hesitation as I dive for my blaster. My palm closes around the grip when a sudden red line of fire shoots straight across One-Eye's shoulder. It paints our visions red for but a moment, eating through the air before it hits the Nirzoik far down the road. The one pressing his knee into Sasha's spine. The one forcing her neck back with a blade right at her throat. The moment that red blast finds its target, the blade falls and Sasha's head snaps forward. The sudden release in pressure on her scalp is instant as the Nirzoik above her drops dead.

It hits me then that One-Eye wasn't ordering for *my* death; he had ordered *hers*. Why? Probably to scare me into telling him what he wants.

And that single red blaster fire? My heart does one singular thump as I roll to my feet. Desperation mixes with uncontrollable relief as I grip my blaster.

No more running now. "You want to know where he is, you fucker?" I growl. "*He's here.*"

CHAPTER THIRTY

Elsie

White-hot light pierces from the barrel of my weapon as I press the trigger, but One-Eye is fast. The brute shifts to the side and the blast hits against his armor, burning a hole that doesn't go far enough before he's suddenly on me. Pain shoots through my shoulder as he pulls my arm backward. My spine is suddenly against his chest as a blade appears at my neck, halting any efforts to get away. I still, my blaster still gripped in my hand but with the barrel pointing upward, useless. My wide eyes flick to Estella as she grips her weapon before me, pointing at the Nirzoik who' holding on to me.

"*Finally.*" One-Eye growls. "I've been waiting for you, Zamari. Show yourself!"

For a moment, the entire town center is quiet. Only the distant crackling of wood and the swirling gusts of smoke, sand, and air fill the space. Above us, the sky grows darker, almost swallowing the shape of the ship still hovering there like a predator waiting for its next kill.

I meet Estella's frightened gaze, silently begging her to run, to save herself. But she stands firm, blaster unwavering in her grip. She shakes her head as she looks at me and I know she's too good of a friend.

"Let her go," Estella's voice wavers but her hands don't. Both squeeze her grip as she holds her blaster steady.

One-Eye laughs, the sound grating against my ears. "Foolish human. She will be the bait to draw him out. Once his lifeblood coats my blades, only then will I be satisfied. Then we will decide on your punishment for trying to defy us." His grip tightens on me as he yells again into the empty town.

"I have waited long for this. Face me, Zamari! Or do you care nothing for these pathetic creatures you defend?" The sand plays around us, forming fleeting figures in the air before dissipating in the wind. All the while, my heart thumps an unsteady beat.

Don't come out, I want to scream. *Don't come out. It's a trap!*

But then, he speaks. His voice reaches my ears as if he was right beside me. As if he was standing right in front of us.

"I always thought you were foolish." The Zamari's voice is like a fresh wave of hope I didn't know I still needed. My gaze flies around, trying to spot him in the swirling gusts and it's clear I'm not the only one trying to see him either.

One-Eye spins with me still in his grasp, turning one way and then the next. That threatening aura that had surrounded him is suddenly gone. All that fills him is uncertainty as he shifts, desperate to find the source of that deep timbre.

"I'm not as ruthless as you say." His voice is suddenly directly behind us and One-Eye spins to face him. My heart swells a thousand times when my gaze lands on the Zamari a few feet away. Shrouded in the swirling sand, he stands tall. No fear. No panic. Nothing but focus as he stands facing the Nirzoik holding me captive. "I'm worse."

He smiles, but there isn't a hint of humor. His eyes are stone cold. "Long time no see, Farkruul. How's the eye?"

One-Eye growls, hands tightening on me. "One more step, Zamari..."

My pulse is an unsteady thing in my ears that almost makes it difficult to hear. With each breath, I can feel the sharp edge of the blade at my throat. As if, should I even cough, I'd end my own life.

I stop breathing as I stare at the Zamari. I almost want to tell him to run. If he wasn't standing so self-assuredly I might have tried. Because we're surrounded. And even thinking that, I wonder why no Nirzoik has shot at him yet.

What are they waiting for?

But as the sand thins, I see the Zamari's weapon is pointed at the Nirzoik holding me. Straight at his head. One move of his finger and I have no doubt he's skilled enough to shoot him straight through that eye hole. He'll kill him.

One-Eye's grip on me tightens, his ragged breaths hot on my neck as if he knows the same. And, as if they can hear my thoughts, the Nirzoik that had scrambled at the sudden death of one of their own fan out, weapons trained on the Zamari.

I've seen him take out four Nirzoik...but this many? I know it won't happen the same as before.

"You're surrounded, Zamari," One-Eye snarls. "Maybe I'll take *your* eye this time. Even the score."

The Zamari's stare remains icy, unmoved until it shifts to me. I don't know how I see it. I *feel* it. The air chills as his focus zones in on my jaw and then the blade at my throat. Those green orbs of his bleed to black before our very eyes. "Release her." His finger shifts against the trigger and I feel One-Eye swallow, the movement travels even through his armor pressed against my back.

I know the Zamari can probably shoot this brute before he has a chance to harm me. But he's not taking the chance. Because the slightest wrong move and my head will no longer be attached to the rest of me. It's the reason I go impossibly still, and One-Eye knows this, too.

One-Eye scoffs. "You die either way, Zamari. Shoot me, and my comrades will shoot you. One move and I will make your seed bucket's lifeblood stain these sands before I die." The Zamari doesn't react but I do. I try not to breathe but I shudder anyway. "*For ten orbits, I have hunted you.*" One-Eye grips me tighter. "And I find you here. In some washed-up wasteland colony." Still, the Zamari doesn't react, and it only seems to make One-Eye angrier. "You took *everything* from me, Zamari. And now you halt the growth of the Moxtron? Even a Zamari like you can die. It's only fair I take everything from you, too."

The Moxtron? It doesn't ring a bell, but his words chill me anyway. This goes way deeper than pure disgruntlement at their operation being disrupted. This is about revenge.

I stare at the Zamari, those words he said to me repeating in my head. When he tried to tell me that being around him is too dangerous. Was this what he was talking about? That he has enemies that will come find him? If that's the case, if he thought something like this would scare me away, he's mistaken. For this danger wasn't just brought by him alone. The Nirzoik are here because of me too. Because they can't relinquish the power they want to wield over us. Because they just won't give up!

But One-Eye is right about one thing. There are about fifteen of them, and only one Zamari. He's going to get shot, probably several times, and I don't want to see that happen.

The Zamari's gaze shifts to me, and in that one look, I tell him all I need to. That he should abandon this mission. Prevent what's about to happen to him if he can. That maybe this is the end for me, but I need him to leave if we can't survive together. That he should protect the others. Save Estella. Save Viv. Keep them safe so they can care for Kiana.

That I never should have gotten him involved in this from the start. That...that even though I tried not to, I've fallen in love with him, and I don't want to see him die.

And with all those thoughts bleeding through my gaze, I see the understanding in his as if he can read my mind. His understanding...and his stark rejection of everything I said.

"Firespark," he shakes his head. "Don't you dare."

I sense the strange sort of confusion that goes through the Nirzoik that still has his grip on me.

"Estella," the Zamari says, eyes never shifting from mine. Estella's gaze snaps to his, her body unmoving as if should she breathe, the slight movement will make all hell break loose. "Run."

Her eyes widen slightly before they lock with mine and I see a million thoughts pass through her eyes. But most of all, I see that she's going to put her trust in him. She turns, legs pumping as she dashes in the opposite direction. No Nirzoik try to stop her, but One-Eye does something with his free hand. A signal and the earth starts shaking again. The ship. Fuck.

Everything happens at once.

At the same time that the Zamari fires, I expect the brute to slit my throat. He doesn't. Self-preservation is too much of an automatic reaction. Instead of slicing my neck, he shoves me forward as a shield. I duck, the force with which he pushed me causing me to hit the dirt, sand chafing the upper layer of my skin. Pain shoots through my entire body, even as my shoulder aches, blood finally flooding through my arm from being released. I don't think as I land. I turn immediately as I swing my arm down, spinning in the sand as I release a shot from my blaster that sears the air, hitting One-Eye in what I hope is the nuts.

But he can't even howl in pain. He's already falling to his knees from the Zamari's bullet before he collapses face-first into the sand. I hear a scream at the same time that energy blasts light up the air from all sides.

The Zamari is a blur. Bullets slice the air past him as he moves, lasers leaving his blaster and no doubt finding their targets. He moves with such deadly proficiency that even in this life-or-death moment, I'm in awe of his skill.

Rising to my knees, I spin, blaster ready. But before me is chaos. Swirling sand. Too many moving bodies. Humans rising from the ground to stagger to safety are suddenly indistinguishable from Nirzoik as blaster fire bursts all around me. But something makes my gaze snap to the side. I see a Nirzoik aim at me before I twist and fire in his direction. The blast hits him in the arm and his weapon flies from his hand, just as the Zamari somersaults in the air, blaster going off at incredible speed as he spins.

I look up, his dark form silhouetted against a sharp crack of lightning and the ship that's almost completely covered us now, before he lands at my side. His red laser shot sears through the Nirzoik I wounded before the brute can scramble for the weapon he dropped. His lifeless body drops with a thud amidst more blaster fire that burns through the air. I need to take cover. I have to run.

My gaze shifts to the nearest cabin and I spin in the sand, ready to make my way there when the Zamari's solid weight is suddenly crashing down over me. He pins me to the ground, dark gaze meeting mine as his entire form suddenly stiffens with a jolt. He snarls, teeth baring to reveal his fangs as the acrid stench of scorched flesh sears my nose.

Everything stills for the span of a single heartbeat. Unwillingness to believe roots me in place as I stare into his eyes. When he grunts, chest heaving with a slight lurch, reality comes crashing down.

"Sorry I took so long, Firespark." With a grunt, he rises, lifting me in his arms with a feral snarl, and there, marring his vest, is a smoking, seeping blaster wound.

Eyes widening, my heart seizes. That shot had been meant for me.

I jerk in his grasp, hand reaching for the wound. "Why would you…" I choke out through the horror clamping my throat. He says nothing. And then I'm thrust inside the cabin I'd been heading toward. His dark gaze meets mine again for a single moment before the door slams, plunging me into darkness. I stare at the door in momentary shock.

But then I'm moving.

"Zamari!" I race to the door, fingers trembling with too much adrenaline and fear as I push against it. It doesn't budge. He blocked it with something on the other side. Locked me in.

Breaths coming in unsteady pulls of air into my nose, I scramble onto the table by the window, forcing the broken pane of glass to open. But it's stuck! All the while, the sound and streaks of blaster fire light up the town before me.

"—*sie! ELSIE!*" My ears ring as I turn around to realize I'm not alone in this broken-down cabin. Estella is behind me, eyes wide, chest heaving.

"Help me," I say and she nods, rushing toward the window. Even with our combined efforts, the thing won't budge.

The shadows move and we freeze at the same time, wide eyes focused on what's happening on the outside. Heavy footfalls beat on the sandy road as more Nirzoik stream into town. Jumping down from the heavy ship above. One massive one passes right before us, unaware that we are so close, and more follow after him. Their cries light up the shadows as they begin their assault and a pit opens up at the bottom of my gut.

One stops right in front of the cabin and I stop breathing. He's huge, shoulders rising and falling with bulk that looks like it can squash me with just one slam of his fist. Even from where we hide, his shark-like grin chills my bones as if he's looking right at me. Clad in metal armor, topped with a metal helmet just like One-Eye, two sharp blades are grasped in each hand as he braces back and roars, the sound splitting my eardrums.

We're overrun. There's no way—

Estella meets my gaze. "We can't stay here. We have to get far away from this place."

She's right. They'll find us in here. Kill us. But when my gaze meets hers I know she can already tell her plan isn't the one that's currently racing across my mind.

"Elsie—"

"We have to help him." My chest heaves with heavy breaths. "I brought him here. I caused all this. *I* have to help him."

Both of our gazes snap back to the window the moment a searing red light pierces the growing darkness.

It hits the Nirzoik standing outside the cabin, right through a small gap in the center of his armor. He roars again before another shot fires, hitting him in another exposed spot on his arm. He staggers back, tries to lift himself up, before his body goes limp.

I stare at the sight before relief and hope shoots through me. He's still out there.

"The Zamari..." Estella breathes.

I can't see where he is, but knowing he's still out there gives a sense of renewed determination. "I have to do something. He's the only one fighting for us. He can't do it alone!"

I sense Estella's agreement even through the fear in her

eyes. That she wants to run. That though she wants to fight, there's also the need to save herself and, as our gazes lock, I hope she can see in mine that I won't hold it against her if she does. I love her too much to lose her too.

Swallowing hard, I pull my friend into my arms, giving her a tight hug and knowing it might be the last time I ever see her again. Nerves tight, I turn my attention upward, spotting the remains of a loft. There's a hole above it, big enough for me to fit through. I'm moving before Estella even realizes.

Climbing up to the loft, I spread my arms to balance, more than one shout from a Nirzoik outside making me tremble enough to almost fall. The boards up here are untrustworthy. Weak from being exposed to the elements for so long. But they hold my weight enough that I reach the hole in the roof.

One glance at Estella down below and she gives me a nod.

With a grunt, I ease up on my elbows as I push myself through the hole to climb up on the slanted roof. Wind whips around me like a manifestation of the terror of seeing the scraper ship from this point of view. It's a monstrous thing hovering over our colony and my whole world stalls when I see the net hanging from its mouth. It trails far behind the vessel, pulling the metal and all other things it's caught in its web. Far out, near the edge of town, I see sand rise as one building collapses. And then another. They're trawling. Destroying the cabins, our homes, gathering them up like they're scraps. Ripping people's lives apart.

We can't let them win. There will be nothing left if we do.

Flattening myself on the roof as I crawl to the gable at the top, I take care not to put my weight on the dead spots over rotten wood where nails once were. Areas where I'll most likely end up with my ass in the foundations if I'm not careful. Grunting, I move to straddle the gable as I look over the edge.

I see a Nirzoik immediately. One not wearing armor like

that other one. Aiming, the blaster warms up and I press the trigger. White light beams from the barrel, splitting the air to hit the Nirzoik in the shoulder.

He growls, turning in my direction and my stomach drops, wishing all at once that I had better aim. I need a shot that can kill the fucker.

Tightening my fist, I fire again, and again, pulling on the emotion the Zamari had forced me to feel. All that frustration. I stop thinking and simply pull the trigger.

Three shots later, and the Nirzoik collapses on the ground. But not before one of his comrades spots me. I barely manage to duck before he unloads blaster fire my way.

Gripping the gable, I spot him storming toward the building and I shout down below.

"Estella! Incoming!"

As the brute slams himself into the door and the boards bend inward, I spot the sack filled with gems swinging. It collides with his head before Estella uses her blaster to finish the job. But it's not enough to stop him. I'm about to fire when red blaster fire hits him in the back of the head. His body goes still before he collapses.

The Zamari. My breaths come heavy and hard as my gaze flicks around the buildings. I don't see him. But I know he's there. Protecting us. That's good enough for me.

Estella kicks at the lifeless body as she tries to pull the door shut just as another Nirzoik slams into it so hard, his sudden appearance makes a scream die in my throat.

Estella screams too, but she's quick with the blaster, firing three shots into the Nirzoik's chest. He falls on top of the other body by the door.

Good woman.

Turning my focus back to the streets, I take out two more Nirzoik, all the while that red blaster fire continues to appear. I don't know where he's hiding. It's as if he's everywhere. Keeping them confused. Not letting them get close.

I see him a second later, blaster firing as he leaps from the roof of one building. The darkness of those eyes finds me as he lands and rolls, taking cover behind the slumped, unmoving frame of a Nirzoik. Bodies drop as he takes them down. There's a moment when he pauses before rolling out from behind the cover just as blaster fire hits the point where he was. The scent of burnt flesh fills the air before I spot him again. Streaks from his weapon seem to ricochet with how fast he pulls the trigger.

But there are too many. They keep coming from the ship. And there's the fact the ship is still moving.

I have to stop that ship. But how? The rumbling gets almost deafening, and my gaze shoots back to the Zamari.

He's standing now, walking forward out in the open and I want to scream for him to take cover. Only, he looks at me, and I understand immediately what he's doing. Underneath the scream of crumpled metal, underneath the rumbling of the sand, I can hear my people in pain. Screams. Raw terror. Comodre being decimated.

I grip the gable tighter as my breath comes in hot spurts through my nose, watching as the Zamari walks forward. Drawing the Nirzoik's attention. Pulling their focus away from us.

I see his body jerk as a shot pierces through his chest, right at the site of the first wound. His body twists with the force of the blast, but he doesn't stop moving. Doesn't stop going forward. Doesn't stop firing.

Like a deadly machine, he spots the Nirzoik, even the ones hiding in the shadows. His blaster engages, fires in sync with his movements, and then there's the undeniable thud of bodies hitting the ground.

But he's wounded. Bleeding. And the sight tears at some wound deep inside me.

Another blaster shot hits him just as two Nirzoik storm from opposite directions. He manages to take one down but the other throws his entire body weight on him.

No.

They crash into the ground and my eyes widen as I see the Zamari's blaster skating through the sand. The tussle kicks up so much sand that my heart lodges in my throat as I wait, fingers gripping the gable so hard they hurt.

Please. Come on. Please.

Rising to my feet, I'm about to find a way down when the roof suddenly shakes *hard.* I fight for balance, forgetting how to breathe when I turn to see a Nirzoik has landed on the roof behind me. He's one of the armor-clad ones. Twin blades grasped in his fists.

Shit.

The Nirzoik before me growls before he stalks forward and I take an automatic step back. The roof shudders with his approach and I lift my blaster, not sure how I will shoot him when he's covered in impenetrable armor not even blaster fire will pierce. I fire anyway, but it's useless; his armor blocks my attempts.

Gulping hard, I take another step back as I look over my shoulder at the drop below. It's a long way down. But if I fall, I won't die. It'll be painful though. I will definitely break some bones.

Injury or death? The choice is obvious.

One more glance and some of the pressure on my heart lifts when I spot the Zamari. He's gained the upper hand on the ground, kneeling in the Nirzoik's chest, fist clenched as he lands a powerful blow in the brute's skull.

Clenching my teeth, I turn back to the Nirzoik's standing before me, a plan hatching in my mind.

"What are you waiting for, you big oaf? Scared of a little human like me?" My insides shudder as I say the words, and the Nirzoik's resultant roar only chills the swirling air around me. He charges, his weight shaking the roof, and I know I only have a split second.

"Zamari! Catch!"

It all happens too quickly and yet I see every detail as if time has slowed down for me to document it.

I throw the blaster over the side, watching it sail through the air toward the Zamari as the Nirzoik heads for me. I see the Zamari turn, see his gaze lock with mine as he reaches for the weapon with one hand, spinning under the swipe of a sword at the same time that he catches it.

As my focus snaps back to the threat before me, two blaster shots go off on the ground as the Zamari uses my blaster to take down the closest threat, just as the Nirzoik on the roof before me lunges. I sway backward, my widened gaze falling to the Nirzoik's feet, praying that I didn't miscalculate this. I see the moment sudden confusion puzzles his gaze. There's a roar as one of his boots pierces through an unstable part of the roof, sending him off balance as his leg slides into a hole of his own making. Bingo. Momentary celebration as I fight to regain my balance. I sway on my foothold as the Nirzoik makes a wild swipe at me, his sword coming too close to my ankle for comfort. But even though he's caught in the roof, the whole thing shakes and I realize it's about to cave in.

"Estella! Get out of there!" My world tilts, a scream leaving my lips as everything suddenly goes off balance.

I see when the Zamari turns at the sound of my scream. Horror in his eyes as he moves in my direction and there's that split second when my heart rises in my chest, blood rushing upward in my entire body, as I fall.

I twist, arms flailing, desperate to grasp on to something, *anything* as I go over the side of the collapsing roof, the idea of crashing into the ground not so great now that it's actually happening. Somehow, by the mercy of the gods, my fingers close around some jutting wood of a barebone deck roof. I hold on to it for dear life, only able to pull air into my lungs as my other organs fall through that pit in my belly. But as I swing there, as I turn with the momentum, my whole world stops.

There's a spark of lightning. It comes down as if from the ship itself, a straight beam that cracks the air, lighting up Comodre before it finds its target.

The Zamari.

He suddenly freezes, as the lightning connects, the scales across his body going completely blue. The shock of energy immobilizes him as his body does a strange gulping movement that wrenches my heart right through me.

That...wasn't lightning. That was a weapon.

Terror makes my gaze shift to the ship above us. To the figure that's standing there at the mouth of the vessel. One I didn't see before, but one that I can't miss now. He stands tall, though cast in shadow. Only the glowing cannon in his hand, sparking white energy, giving shape to his form.

Even in the shadows, I sense the brute's gaze. Feel the evil. The malice, as he stands there looking down at us.

So, One-Eye wasn't the one in charge. He wasn't their leader. Whoever that shadowed brute is, it's him. He's the one doing all this.

Pain shoots through my heart as my focus finds the Zamari. His gaze is still locked with mine only now a sort of clarity swoops in, chasing away the darkness and leaving only his green pits as a blade suddenly appears at the center of his chest. A guttural, deep wail-like scream leaves my lips.

One-Eye. He's alive somehow. Blood coating his face, his clothing. Blood everywhere. But he's alive. And his blade has sunk to the hilt.

Time slows down as I swing there, watching the male I love fall to his knees before me. Watching dark fluid sprout around the wound in his chest, soaking through his tunic and vest like a fountain of wine underneath his skin.

I *love* him.

I know that now. Because the sight before me feels like my soul's being ripped from my very being. Like something is tearing me apart from the inside out. Like that blade coated with his blood has pierced *my* heart.

A pained cry that doesn't seem like it originated from my lips barrels from my throat, breaking the stillness underneath the sound of the imposing vessel above us.

My fingers let go and I fall the rest of the way, collapsing on the ground before I scramble to my feet. The Nirzoik still standing before me, blade in the Zamari's chest...the ship above me that's slowly ripping my colony apart...everything fades into the background.

All I can see is how those green eyes keep their focus on me, never swaying even when his body chokes the moment the Nirzoik pulls his blade back.

I run the short distance to collapse on my knees before him, hands automatically pressing against his chest, the thick fluid immediately staining my skin, making that wound in my heart yawn and get even bigger. There's too much blood. Far too much blood.

I'm dimly aware of blaster fire coming from behind me. Dimly aware Estella is screaming my name as she fires two more shots, none of them doing any damage to the armor-clad brute before us.

There's a dark chuckle as One-Eye laughs. "Fekking Zamari," he mutters, his words garbled like he's speaking underwater, choking on his own blood. "Looks like I finally won."

I look up as he lifts his weapon, ready to finish the job. Where his scarred eye should be is just a cavernous, bloody hole. I can see the life seeping away from him. And yet, he still wishes to kill us all.

The anger that floods through me is unlike anything that's ever channeled through me before.

I roar. I *roar* at him. A terrifying cry. My lips pull back, my eyes blaze with fire, and I ROAR. One full of pain and loss and frustration. At the same time, the Zamari chokes, blood brimming from the corners of his mouth as his lips curl into a smile.

"There you are," he whispers. "Hello, my Firespark."

That only makes more pain shoot through me.

He twists, his arm lifting as he fires from the blaster still in his hand before he collapses in my arms. The bullet grazes right through the hole in One-Eye's helmet, searing right across his seeing eye, blinding him and leaving behind charred flesh and blood.

The Nirzoik staggers back, a roar on his lips as reaches up to touch the wound.

My gaze flies back to the Zamari.

"Run," he says.

I shake my head. "And what? Leave you here to die?" I can't.

I can't run away from you.

Keeping one hand on the wound in his chest, I reach for the blaster he's holding with the other hand.

I don't manage to touch it.

There's a clang. A deep, vibrating clang and the Nirzoik staggers a few more steps away. I look up to see James with a metal rod in his hand. His eyes are wide with terror, arms trembling but he attacks again while the Nirzoik is stunned, hitting the metal rod against the brute's helmet.

More people appear, seemingly from the shadows. Some grab the swords of the fallen Nirzoik and jab the brute wherever they can find a gap in his armor. He swats at them, his movements jerky and uncoordinated as he stumbles and sways, his roars echoing below the sound of the ship still making its way toward us.

My people have finally found their courage. And yet, it brings no happiness. Because my love is dying in my arms.

I look down at the blood coating my fingers, how his chest rises and falls with great effort, the blood in his mouth, and find that his gaze is still on me.

"I'm sorry," I whisper, a sob lodging in my throat, my eyes getting so blurry I can no longer see. "I'm so, so sorry."

When his gaze shifts away from me, the blaster in his hand rising slowly as he focuses on the stunned Nirzoik, I watch him do the last thing he can to protect me. To protect my people. Even while he's bleeding to death.

His hand steadies for a few moments before he presses the trigger and the shot eats through the air. It hits One-Eye dead center in his remaining socket and for a moment, the brute just stops moving, arms falling limp to his side before his entire frame falls forward.

Estella collapses on the ground at my side, her hands hovering over mine, her terrified gaze on the wound and the blood.

"Shit," her voice shakes as she stares at the blood. I can see it in her eyes as her gaze shifts to mine, almost as if she doesn't want to say it in front of him. We don't have enough resources to tend to a wound like this.

"Looks like I needed his help after all," the Zamari croaks, shoulders rising and falling with a laugh.

I shake my head, not understanding what he means or how he can find any humor at a time like this. I can only focus on the blood. Focus on the fact he's bleeding out and there's nothing we can do.

Using my teeth, I rip my tunic, tearing off a greater part of my top. Rolling the frayed fabric into a ball, I press it against his chest.

"Marcus," I choke. "Where's Marcus?!"

Estella lifts her head, gaze locking with James, before she shakes it. But I already know. Marcus, that fucking coward, is probably hiding somewhere. Or maybe he left the moment he saw that scraper ship in the sky.

"Fire," the Zamari croaks, and my breaths stutter.

Yes, he's right. I nod, my head bobbing as I stutter. "Y-yes. We need to cauterize the wound. That will help, right? And then you will heal? You can heal from this." I say it as if I'm sure. As if I'm forcing it to be true, and there's a strange look in his eyes that I notice even behind the pain he must be feeling.

"Fire," he repeats. "For the ropes." He struggles with the pocket of his trouse before he takes something into his palm. A fire cube. I stare at the thing before Estella grasps it.

Rising, she shouts. "Swords! Grab swords and follow me! We need to burn those ropes and cut them free!" She points to the ship, but I don't even lift my gaze to it. I can't. My one priority now is to get the Zamari to my cabin. To get him to safety.

Those standing around us go into motion. Rushing with Estella toward the trawling net. As they hurry to save what's left of Comodre, my hand trembles on the now-soaked piece of cloth against my palm.

I look down at the blood coating my fingers, at how his chest rises and falls with great effort, at the blood staining his lips, and find that my world is crumbling.

"I'm sorry," I whisper again, a sob lodging in my throat, my eyes getting so blurry I can no longer see. This is all because of me. Because I brought him here.

When his gaze shifts away from me, the blaster in his hand rises slowly as he focuses somewhere to my left. His hand steadies for a few moments before he presses the trigger and the shot eats through the air. It hits a Nirzoik who was heading away on a rocket bike; the blast going dead center in the side of the head and for a moment, the brute just stops moving, arms falling to his side before his entire frame falls backward off the rocket bike before the machine stutters and stalls.

My gaze shifts back to the Zamari as he looks at me again and a sob lurches in my throat.

"You can't die now. You've done the job and I haven't fucking paid you yet."

Despite his waning energy, his lips twist in a smile. "Complementary, Firespark."

My heart swells and aches again. "Like the sex?"

His lashes dip before he forces his eyes open once more. "No. Not like that. My time with you was never about the job."

Tears well in my eyes as I can only stare at him and wish things were different right now.

"Search," the Zamari croaks, and my breaths stutter. "Have your people search the cabins for more Nirzoik. Some might be hiding—"

I shake my head, suddenly not caring about any of the Nirzoik. They can fucking go to hell. "I shouldn't have let

Estella take the fire cube. If I'd cauterized the wound, then I could've stopped the bleeding."

His blood is like magic. I just have to help him. Surely he can heal. Please, gods, he has to. He *must*.

He shakes his head. "Would scar." He coughs and blood appears on his lips, sending more alarm through me. "Need you to..."

I grip him tighter, leaning in, my chest heaving with heavy breaths I can't control. "What do you need me to do?"

"Search, Firespark," he repeats. "Leave me, and go."

"Please," I whisper. "Tell me what to do." My hands are shaking so much I can't even feel the wetness of the blood on his chest anymore. "This is my fault. If you didn't come here...if I didn't hire you..."

"This isn't your fault, Firespark. None of this is."

"There's so much blood. It's like it went through your heart."

I know it makes no sense. I know *I* make no sense. But talking, keeping him talking, is giving me hope.

"Only one of them." He coughs and more blood spurts at his lips.

"But you can heal. You helped Kiana. Surely—" I swallow hard, my mind a chaos-filled swirl, before my eyes widen in a light-bulb moment. "If you drink from me, will it help?"

I search his gaze as he looks up at me, that strange look growing in his eyes. He lifts his hand then, his fingers closing around my jaw so gently that another sob lodges in my chest. It feels like goodbye. I'm not ready to say goodbye.

Tears run down my face as I shake my head. "No. You can't. I'm not ready yet. I'm not ready to say goodbye. And not like this. I'm—" The words tumble from my lips so quickly, I don't have time to think about what I'm saying. "I didn't tell you how I feel. I wasn't ready. Didn't want this to end so I didn't say a word. I didn't tell you...that I'm falling for—that I *have* fallen for you. Even though I know I shouldn't. Even though I know your time here is short and I'm just a temporary attraction. Zamari, I—"

"Vy'syn," he says, and I swallow the rest of my words as he leans forward, forehead pressing into mine, gaze swallowing me whole. "Vy'syn."

I blink at him, not daring to believe what I just heard. For even though that sound should mean nothing to me, somehow I know exactly what it is that he just said.

"My name," he clarifies, and my heart does another painful lurch.

A sob-stained chuckle lodges in my throat. He's telling me his name?

"*No*," I manage to get out, despite the tightening in my throat. Because I know what this means. The only way he's telling me his name is if one of us dies. And I'm not the one currently bleeding out. "You're going to survive this. You *have* to."

His other hand reaches for the one I have pressed against his wound. He lifts it, moving it a few inches to the other side of his chest. It takes me a moment, but there, I feel the steady beat of his heart. Strong. Unfaltering. The only consolation that he might yet overcome this.

"Vy'syn...Vykla'methion...of...Kelon 4. Some call me the Outlaw of the Plains. Some call me the Traveler of the Void." He inhales deeply, his heart thumping hard under my hand as more tears stream down my face. "I am all of those. But most of all...I am the male who wants to be your mate."

I choke on another sob. "My w-what?"

"I'm not leaving Comodre, Firespark. I can't even if I wanted to. Not unless you're coming with me. From now on, where you go, I go, too. Where you stay, I stay." He pauses, gaze studying my face in that way he often does. "You are my light. The thing my Zamari hearts have been searching for. I would like to stay...if you will give me the pleasure of protecting you. I would like to be something more than the outlaw you hired. I would like to be something for *you*."

His words are like holy incantations I didn't think I'd ever be blessed with. A sob bursts from me as I laugh and cry at the same time. Because I can't believe it.

"Vy'syn," I whisper. My whole body shakes with the weight of it all, and the utter relief. I lean forward, placing a kiss on his lips even as my tears mix in with the blood there. "I love you. Did you know that? I fell in love with you and now you're telling me your name and everything I've wanted to hear you say. But you're bleeding out, Vy'syn, and I'm afraid this is all just a dream or maybe you're delirious from the blood loss." I sniff, then pull air into my lungs. "How can I stop the bleeding?" I press harder on the wound, afraid that if I let go, he'll leave me here, and this conversation is the last I'll have with him. "*Tell me how.*"

It is only then that I realize his breaths are labored, too.

"It will heal. Slowly. But I will live."

I keep the pressure on his chest but ease back enough that I can look at him, knowing my eyes are swollen with tears, but not caring. "Don't lie to me."

"Never have, Firespark." His lips twist in a slight smile. "Never will."

Beneath the sound of the storm building above us is the shout of many voices rejoicing.

I turn to see a figure running through the shadows cast across the colony.

"They're cut," Estella comes to a halt, her body out of breath. "We did it."

I grip the Zamari tighter, as my gaze shifts to the ship

passing over us, its net now hanging free and useless. It trails over the cabins and sand as the ship makes its way across and I hold the Zamari closer, knowing that without him, we wouldn't have gotten this far.

"Here, let me help," Estella says, taking the bloodied rag from my trembling fingers. I hear the crack of thunder as she unrolls it. The first raindrop hits me in the forehead as she helps wrap the band tight around the Zamari's chest, covering the wounds and adding pressure from both sides.

Vy'syn's lips twist in another weak smile. "Rest, Firespark. I will not leave you until you drive me away."

Another raindrop hits us and he looks up too, and then we all are. All the people that returned from cutting the ropes, me, Estella, Vy'syn...we all look up as the heavens open and the rain begins to fall.

I tilt my face to it, letting the cool drops soak me completely, aware that other people who were too afraid until this point are also coming out from their hiding places to look up at this miracle.

The laugh that bubbles in my throat is a strange one. One of disbelief and complete gratitude.

We survived.

And now, I have even more to look forward to.

CHAPTER THIRTY-ONE

Elsie

Walking back to the cabin, Vy'syn barely leans on me as we go, even though I know he needs to. Up ahead, I can hardly see Estella and James through the heavy rain that beats down on us, only the glint of the new weapons—fresh new blasters and swords—grasped in their hands.

"I should have run back for the bike," I whisper. "You're in no condition to walk."

I just didn't want to leave him...and I think he knows.

The dark stain in the center of his chest makes my heart ache every time I look at it. It hasn't stopped bleeding, only slowed down.

Vy'syn grunts. "I don't deserve the way you care for me, Firespark."

I squint up at him through the heavy rainfall, not sure what he means. "Why? All heroes deserve love and care."

That green gaze of his slides from my eyes to my lips, making something heat in my core that I try to brush away.

He's injured. Now is not the time.

"I've killed many beings, Firespark. All deserved a blast from my weapon. Regardless...I am no hero." I can sense there's more he wants to say. More he's holding back. "What Farkruul said...about that town..."

I shake my head. "I don't need you to explain. You're not a bad person, Vy'syn. Whatever you did, I know you did it because you had to."

He stops walking, the rain soaking us both as we stand still in it. Those eyes of his engulf me as he studies my face, as if wanting to know if my words are true.

One arm lifts as he brushes a finger over my bruised jaw. "I'm sorry, Firespark. I was too late."

I huff a soft laugh through my nose. "You came just in time."

"Viv and the *kiv*..." he murmurs. "I had to make sure they were safe. I know...they are important to you... I went to the mines first. I thought you were still there."

I nod, smiling slightly as I lift my hand to brush my fingers against his jaw.

"Farkruul spoke the truth," he continues. "I killed everyone in an entire settlement. One just like yours. None survived."

I'm about to stop him again, but he continues. "They were Nirzoik, Firespark. They had..." He pauses, studying me some more. "They had slaves. Some were only *kivs*."

The way he hesitates tells me there's more. More he's protecting me from as if the details are too much for me to bear and I blink up at him through the rain.

"Is that what you were afraid of? That I would fall for you even though you're an outlaw that does what outlaws do?" I turn, guiding him with me until we reach my cabin. "Too late for that." I grin.

"Too late." He growls in his throat and the hairs along my

arms stand on end. But it's not fear I feel. Just the distinct sensation of soft silk running across my skin. "I fell for you the moment I saw you, Firespark. My *ayahl* is finally content."

"Your *ay-all*?"

His lips twitch, a chuckle rising in his chest, before he winces from the pain. "It knows you well. Aches to touch you all the time. Call it my sixth sense given form."

I quirk my brows, hand tightening in his as I turn toward the cabin. "Six senses, huh? That some kind of Zamari ability?"

"We have seven," he growls, and my brows shoot up. Before I can respond, he releases my hand and drops to one knee. I'm about to ask why when a small body crashes into his.

"Papa!" Kiana cries, wrapping her little arms around his neck.

The Zamari doesn't even flinch, just cradles her close, a gentle hand cupping her head. He glances up at my shocked face.

"What?" A hint of a smirk. "I told you. Seven senses."

"Aren't you just full of surprises," I whisper, heart swelling at this display of quiet affection between the two most important people in my world. He levels me with a simmering look that promises I've only scratched the surface.

I'm only pulled away by the sight of Viv walking toward us, her gaze shifting to James still standing in the rain then to Estella who'd no doubt been the one to fetch them from the hiding spot.

"You guys did it," she breathes. She presses a smile on her face that doesn't reach her eyes before there's a sob as she throws herself into my arms. It's barely a hug before her eyes widen and she suddenly pulls away.

"Blood." She looks at my arms and then down at me. "You're hurt."

I shake my head. "Not me, but..."

"Look, Mom! Papa has a boo-boo just like I do!" Kiana pokes at Vy'syn's bloody chest before touching where the scar is on her own, and he makes a soft purr in his throat.

"He sure...does..." Viv blanches, her queasiness at the sight of the blood evident as she discreetly shifts Kiana away. "You should go tend to him. Kiana and I will be in my cabin."

I nod.

"And I'm gonna help James and the others search the cabins. Assess the damage," Estella says, with James tagging behind. His gaze shifts to me and he gives me a curt nod that I return. There's respect in his eyes. As if he's seeing me for the first time since our mothership fell.

"Look, Aunt Viv! It's raining!"

I smile as Viv grips Kiana and runs off the deck, spinning with her in the rain.

I watch them go, noting that as the sounds die down, leaving only the downpour of the rain, it's only me and the Zamari here now. Alone. I've never been as nervous alone with him since those first days together. Now, my nerves have settled back in the center of my chest.

"Come in." My gaze lifts to meet his as he rises. "I should clean you up."

The warm water trickles down Vy'syn's chest before I squeeze the piece of linen into the small bowl I have stationed near the cot. Turning back to him, I continue drying his skin. Swaying wax-light gives the room a warm glow while the sound of thunder and rain surrounds us.

We remain in silence, only the sound of my ministrations breaking the air between us.

Wiping away as much of the blood as I can, I'm happy to see it's already clotting.

"You heal quickly."

He grunts and when I glance at him, the air I pull into my nose feels like a long extended one. He's so focused on me. Watching me intently as I tend to him. And his eyes have bled to black again.

He's been watching me like that ever since I forced him to lie down. Even as I hurried around the cabin, trying to find everything I needed, which wasn't much, his focus never faltered. I boiled that root I usually give Kiana to drink for the pain, soaked it in the warm water I'm using to clean the wound. Put an extra pillow underneath his head. Tried to be gentle with every touch.

I don't know if it's helping, but he isn't complaining. Just watching me with that intensity that makes my heart flutter in my chest.

"Why do you do that?" I whisper.

"Mm?"

My gaze shifts to his, only for my cheeks to heat a little more. Inhaling, my chest rises with a warm sigh as I turn to dip, rinse, and wring the piece of linen again.

"Like it's the first time you're ever seeing me." I glance at him once more, but his gaze doesn't change. Doesn't shift.

The wax-light plays across the contours of his face, making it hard to look away. It's cozy in here, as if this was the place he was always meant to be.

"That's simple, Firespark." His voice is that deep, silky timbre that sends little vibrations unbidden across my skin. "You are the most beautiful treasure I have ever set my sights on."

"Treasure?" I give a small laugh, even though his words warm me from the inside out.

"Treasure." He repeats.

Silence descends between us once more as I continue tending to him. I take my time, making sure I get every grain of sand that flew into the wound. Making sure I tend to it the best I can so he can get well.

"You weren't just kidding, right?" I whisper. "When you said you would stay. It wasn't the chattering of a dying man. You weren't delirious?"

I don't know why I hold my breath, waiting for him to answer.

"I'm staying, Firespark."

I finally breathe, a shy glance reaching him before I continue working.

"Do you think we did it? Think we liberated Comodre?"

For a few seconds, he doesn't respond. "No."

I bite my lip, a part of me sinking before I nod, pushing the thoughts away. Because, for the first time, I'm not scared if they come. We faced the worst today, and I hope the others realize that, too.

"I called a...friend..." He says after a few moments, those dark eyes not shifting as I look up at him. "In a moment of weakness. I...worried I might not be able to protect you. It is... good he did not come."

I focus on tending to his wound as I mull his words over in my mind. He'd called someone to help us? Before I even realized, he'd been committed to making sure we got out of this alive.

It had never been about the credits. It had always been about us.

"Why is that?" I glance at him again and for the first time since he's rested here, his gaze shifts from mine to the roof.

"Krynn is...not as gentle as I am."

I almost choke on air as a chuckle rises in my throat. "I don't think 'gentle' is what people would call you."

There's a purr in his throat as those dark eyes slide to me again. "I try to be gentle with you."

My cheeks heat.

"I can be even gentler next time..."

Next time...

I clear my throat and resist the urge to lick my lips.

It takes over an ora before I'm done and I rise with a smile, feeling his gaze on my back as I lift the bowl and piece of linen and take them to the washroom. When I return, I head to the loft to get a fresh skirt from where my clothes are packed away.

He watches me rip the layers into thick, long shreds before I lay them out on his lap.

"Can you sit up?"

He nods, doing what I ask without a word. And as I lean in close, wrapping each layer of fabric around his back and bringing it around his front in a tight bandage, I can feel his attention, feel *him* so, so close to me. So close that every breath I take and every breath I release is air we both share. When I'm finally done, I can't move. Something has me frozen as I glance up at him. Some unseen force that demands I stay close.

"Firespark," he murmurs before I'm suddenly pulled against him. "You shouldn't have tried to help me."

"You were alone. Fighting a war you shouldn't even be a part of."

"I was fighting for you."

"And I couldn't bear to see you do that and die. I couldn't—"

His lips crash into mine with an intensity that leaves me breathless. When he lifts me so I straddle him on the cot, I barely manage to protest before he growls on my lips.

"Sweet Elsie..."

"We shouldn't do this. You're in pain..."

"Not enough," he whispers back.

Little shivers go through me as he rips what's left of my tunic away, the thunder and lightning cracking outside in harmony with the crashing beat of my heart. We strip, shredding the clothing as if the garments burn, and when we're finally naked, skin to skin, it's like my whole being lights up.

Vy'syn kisses me as if he will go out of breath if my lips are not on his. His hands trail along my spine, gripping my hips, my ass, touching me everywhere as he pulls me up against him, sliding my wet center over his already thick shaft.

A breath shudders from us both at the contact. Like electricity sparking straight through my core as his head dips and he takes a nipple into his mouth.

My back arches, my hips rocking automatically as he leans back, taking me down with him, forcing me to grind on him as my core heats and throbs, begging to be filled.

"I know you need it," I whisper as I lean in, nipping the edge of his ear. The pointed tip flutters at my words and I run my tongue over it. "I know you need to drink."

He growls against me, both hands on my hips as he pulls me up against his shaft then forces me back down, sliding his shaft through my folds, forcing that tiny bud to grind against him.

I whimper in his ear, unable to control the words that spill from my lips.

"Please," I whisper. "I want your cock. Want you deep inside me while you drink till you're full." My pussy jumps then clenches as my own words make me grow impossibly wetter.

Vy'syn growls again.

"I will knot you again, Firespark. My control is weak. Are you sure—"

"Yes." It's my turn to growl. "You say it as if it inconveniences me," I pant. "I want your knots every time. *All the time. Fucking knot me while you fuck me hard. I need it, Vy'syn. I need *you*."

I don't care that I sound desperate. Don't care about the fact that I'm now grinding myself on him, spreading my juices all along his shaft as if I'm marking him as mine. The thought of him swelling inside me, joining us together, only makes me throb and clench harder. Patience be damned.

There's another shuddering growl in his chest before he grabs my hips and lifts me high enough that his cock bobs underneath me. I reach for him, hand sliding over his smooth head as he shudders at the contact, a deep moan vibrating through him.

Lining him up with my entrance, I ease myself down, spreading my legs as I brace on my knees. My hips rotate as I lift them before sliding down on him again, the sensations almost too indescribable to be real.

Taking as much of him as I can, I lean forward, allowing him to guide my hips as he slams upward. His tempo is merciless, fingers gripping me tight as he fucks me hard. It feels like my brain is vibrating to the back of my skull and my eyes roll back, lost to the desire as I collapse on him, giving full control as I bare my neck to him.

He growls so hard that he brings me down hard, sliding that first swollen section in. The moan that barrels through me rivals the sound of the thunder outside. The stretch makes me whimper in a language that doesn't exist as he pulls back and continues thrusting in long, deep strokes, working me inch by inch as his cock gets wider and wider until I feel where the second knot will be.

Please, Vy'syn, I want it more than anything.

I must whimper those exact words because he growls again

before I feel my pussy stretching to accommodate him. He licks my neck then, his tongue like a warm textured cloth, the only warning before I feel the sharp prick of his fangs.

I cry out as the two warring sensations collide. The stretch. The pain from his fangs. And then the explosion of pure sugar in my veins. The pain in my neck disappears, leaving behind only pure goodness. The feel of him drinking, of his knot spreading me wide—it's all too much. I scream with the pressure of the orgasm that crashes through me.

Shuddering, I'm unable to control the strength of the feelings he causes to rise within me, and he grips me tighter, his hold shifting to the curves of my ass as a moan rumbles through him.

I come far too quickly. An intense peak that makes me go buttery in his grasp. My pussy clenches on his thick rod, clenching hard as I scream through the torrent of pleasure taking me over. His peak is just as intense as mine because he shudders too, his cock pulsing, pulling back and pushing forward as it empties itself within me, until it can't move anymore, his knots swelling so much, fitting me so tightly that his hips have to still.

Vy'syn's fangs retract, slipping from my neck, and through hazy eyes, I catch when he licks a stray drop of blood from his lips. Leaning in again, he runs his tongue over the wound, making sweet little tremors pass through my shoulders.

"Can't run, Firespark," he growls. "You're stuck with me now."

I breathe a laugh before settling against him, content with the stretch within my core, knowing that we're tied together until it releases us.

"I wouldn't dare run," I whisper. "You'd surely catch me."

Another growl. "I would."

I smile as he shifts and reaches for the blanket before

pulling it over my body. I snuggle into the warmth, eyes closing slowly to the sound of the rain outside.

"You do know, though," I murmur. "I'm a package deal. There's Kiana and—"

"And she's mine now too."

I lift my head, breath catching in my throat. "Vy'syn, you don't have to—"

"Firespark." He stops me right there. "I would want it no other way."

EPILOGUE

Vy'syn

Following the fight with the Nirzoik, much of Comodre was destroyed. Several humans have become homeless and I watch them scramble for someone to blame. I *wait* for them to blame my Firespark for bringing me here; for causing this change in their lives. But none do.

Maybe because they see me watching. Maybe because they are afraid.

But there has been a change in some. Those who tilt their heads in respect whenever we are close. Those who watch me with awe in their eyes.

Some call me their liberator.

Would they still think the same if they knew I only did this for one reason? For her?

Will they think the same when they realize it's not over yet?

The Nirzoik were here for a reason. The fact they came back for war tells me more than these humans realize. Their little colony was not just an unfortunate recipient of those thugs' attention. There is more going on...only, I don't know what. Not yet.

I will have to wait and see. Until then, I will remain here. I will do everything in my power to protect her. Protect *them*.

The two beings that make my ayahl sing.

At the town meeting with the skeevy one they call Marcus, the remaining residents of this little colony spoke up. For the first time, I saw a little light of my Firespark's beam in their eyes. Saw that whatever pushes her to fight for this little civilization has finally infected them too.

Some lost family. Friends. The human casualties were few, but it hit them hard anyway. They ask where they will go from here. What will happen to them now, and I wonder if Firespark hates that I tell them the truth. That I give them no hope. But when my gaze turns to her, she always gives that supportive jerk of her chin. Firespark trusts me. Leans on my word. Trusts that I will lead her people in the right direction.

So, I tell them they will have to fight if they want to survive. That the Nirzoik will return. That if they want a life, any life at all, they should prepare to die for it. To do more than they did last time or they should give up on this place and try to make a life somewhere else in the plains.

And I tell them that I will fight too. For Elsie. For our *kiv*, Kiana.

My gaze shifts to them now and Firespark looks up from where she sits mending clothing for the *kiv*. Almost at the same time, the *kiv* does the same.

They both smile and my *ayahl* warms.

Shifting my gaze, I glance around at the changes already made to the cabin. A bigger cot has been moved into the back room that is now our private quarters. *Ours.* A word I never thought I'd ever use in relation to any female. Yet, here I am.

Kiana's toys lie stacked neatly in a box, some scattered across the floor. Firespark's medical herbs hang to dry, infusing the rooms with earthy scents, and mixing with the freshness of the rain coming in through the window.

It's still rough, but it feels...right. Firespark makes it feel right, and I find myself wishing to contribute something more to this space we will share. I want to provide more than just physical defenses here.

When she realizes my focus is still on them, Kiana shuffles off the cot and limps over to me. My gaze automatically moves to the fresh vials of medicine stacked on the table. I traveled in the rains to Calanta to get them. A dangerous journey, but the little *kiv's* smile makes it worth it. Firespark's relief made it necessary. The *kiv* already had her daily dose, but this day appears to be a bad one for her. One in which she struggles more than usual.

"Papa?" she says, and my *ayahl* immediately warms again. The human word for progenitor. A precious title she has bestowed upon a brute like me. Reaching down, I lift her onto my lap. "Can you tell me one of your stories?"

Stories of worlds I have seen. Stories of beings I have met. This *kiv* is insatiable. And even when I try to leave out the details, her little mind becomes filled with questions. She is a smart little thing. One with a sense of justice that rivals many.

"Mm," I hum in my chest. "Which should I tell you about this time?"

"The one about the brave queen who battled the sandworm to save the king!"

I grin, fangs baring, but my little, fearless *kiv* only grins back, baring her blunt teeth at me. A rumble of approval vibrates in my chest.

"That one is your favorite."

"It is! One day, *I* want to battle a sandworm!"

A deep laugh bubbles from my lips. "I'm sure it would shudder in fear from your terrifying *roar!*"

Kiana tilts her head back, creating claws with her little hands as she roars, and more laughter rises within me.

Happiness. Peace.

I have never longed for this. Only because I could never imagine it for a male like me. But now that I have it, I know I can never let it go.

My gaze lifts in time to catch a strange look in Firespark's eyes before she smiles and looks away. I see it every time I'm with the *kiv*; how she watches us when she thinks I'm not aware. There is pure joy in her eyes and her features grow soft. My Firespark is happy. Content.

Is this what my people have forgotten? Is this why we travel the stars, searching for something, searching for that one thing that will make everything else make sense?

I guess I'm one of the lucky ones.

A Zamari who is finally content.

For I have found what so many are searching for.

EPILOGUE 2

Elsie

I awake slowly, cocooned in warmth beneath the thick quilts. The still-dark, rainy skies outside tempt me to not move an inch, and I stretch just as strong arms tighten around me, pulling me closer.

Every morning I wake like this, in his arms, and every morning I take a moment to just lie here, enjoying the feel of him.

Vy'syn rumbles a growl in his chest as I try to rise. Pulling me closer, he tucks me against his chest. "The skies still weep, Firespark. Where are you going?" That sleepy, growly voice only makes me want to stay in bed more.

"I have to go start breakfast."

He growls again. "I'll do it."

Momentary panic makes my eyes widen. I've been hiding the ingredients for a while. Stuff we got from Calanta after I forced Vy'syn to let me accompany him despite the downpours. The vendor promised me it's food from the Zamari homeworld called Kelon 4, even sold me a recipe, and I'm sure I can pull off at least one meal. But it's a surprise.

"Um, no, you can't today. I have to make something for Kiana." I hate the white lie but it's the best I can do.

"I'll make it." He turns with me, pulling me onto his chest as he rests on his back. Green eyes open to slits as he looks at me.

"I...don't think you know how."

He actually scowls a little and I can't help but giggle. "The *kiv* likes the meals I make."

A warm feeling spreads over me, and I lean in to press a kiss against his lips. "So she does."

Seeing the way he interacts with Kiana, adopting her in much the same way I have, warms my heart every day. I giggle again as his gaze shifts to the closed door on the other side of our room. Another extension, a room made specifically for Kiana. Even in the pouring rain, he's worked to make sure we're comfortable.

"I'm sure she won't mind if I'm the one doing breakfast today."

I see the moment he softens, his shoulders slumping a little before he looks back at me. His gaze travels over my face before landing on my lips and I push back at the warmth starting between the center of my thighs.

"No," I push at him. "I have to get up."

Vy'syn growls, and for a moment his arms slacken and I think he's letting me rise, only for his hands to tighten on my hips as he lifts me and brings me higher against him. I wriggle, another giggle bubbling through me before he seats me on his face. The heat of his breath against my bare cunt makes me shudder with sudden need.

"Vy'syn," I groan.

He gets to work immediately, tongue sliding out to brush

through my folds. I shudder again, the thin linen dress I wore to bed little more than a scrap that's now ridden up above my waist.

I shift against him, pleasure warring with duty, but that only makes him moan into my pussy.

"If you're going to leave me here, at least let me eat first," he growls. Another swipe of his tongue and my eyes flutter closed. He allows me to grip his hair as I grind on his face, that warm tongue of his rolling around my clit before thrusting deep inside me.

"Elsie," he rumbles, his words a sweet vibration. "My Elsie. My Firespark."

It doesn't take long for me to come, my hips bucking against his lips as he takes every drop of my arousal, licking me clean. When I finally rise, his eyes are half-closed, a pleased sort of look on his face as he rests back against the bed.

"You're such a naughty boy."

"Boy?" He eases up slightly and I giggle as I shuffle off of him. Giving him a kiss, I dodge out of the way as he swipes at me. "Why don't you come back here and test that theory, little human?"

I flush, hurrying out of the room before I forget my whole plan and spend the morning riding him instead.

Stepping into the room that's now solely open plan for cooking, eating, and entertaining guests, I unwrap the precious packages of alien spices and foods I'd transported back hidden in my poncho. The aromas are strange yet enticing, and slight nervousness makes me second guess even trying. Closing my eyes, I take a deep breath. I hope I can reproduce the dishes properly.

Braiding my hair back, I hurry to the bathroom, wash up and change into a short, red linen dress I found at the Calantian market before stepping back out to start the meal. As

I chop and stir, the kitchen transforms into a realm of utterly foreign scents.

Following the recipes, I mix odd purple vegetables with beans for a fragrant stew. Thinly cut pieces of meat are then added in such a way that the meat soaks up the flavors. A taste test and a bite into a meat roll presents a burst of fluid into my mouth filled with flavor. If I had fangs, it would be like sinking my teeth into prey. I can see why it's a Zamari dish. Closing my eyes, I breathe out slowly, savoring the taste.

By mid-morning, the dish is complete. I glance at the bedroom door, eager for Vy'syn and Kiana to wake. This is the most ambitious meal of my life and I pace—walking to the front door to look out the window to coming back to the table and making a mental note of everything laid out on it.

Right on routine, I hear Kiana as she wakes. Soon, she comes into view. My gaze shifts to the scar on her chest. A mark that tells a story of faith and miracles. The mark that brought my girl back to me. She grins and there's no hesitation. She moves as fast as her body will allow, all the while chattering excitedly about the new smells. Vy'syn follows at a slower pace, stopping short at the table.

His gaze shifts to me, taking in my dress, before something passes behind his eyes that I cannot read. Immediately, I wonder if I've done everything wrong. Did I mess up the meal? Does he not like the look of it?

"I, well...I wanted to make you something special, so I tried a traditional Zamari dish." I gesture at the table. "If it's wrong or if it doesn't taste good, I'm—"

"Firespark." His single utterance makes the words die on my lips. Vy'syn stands frozen, that strange look still in his eyes. He blinks hard before walking over to me. I don't know what to expect, my gaze searching his for a hint of what he's thinking.

When he sweeps me into his arms, a surprised yelp and giggle leave my lips.

"You made all this...for me?" His gravelly voice is hushed with emotion. I nod, throat suddenly tight at his reaction. Bringing me over to the table, he pulls out a chair and sits with me in his lap. Picking up a carved fork, he takes a tentative bite of the stew.

His eyes drift shut, a rumbling sound like a purr rising from his chest. "I remember this," he murmurs. "It has been so long."

He eats some more. After each bite he takes, he lifts the spoon and puts some into my mouth as well. Kiana giggles, thinking it's funny.

"Mama is a baby!"

She almost makes me choke on a laugh but the joy is quickly ripped away when there's a knock at the door. The sound echoes sharp and hard in the room, making my spine stiffen, momentarily drowning out the soft sound of the rain outside.

The Nirzoik.

For a moment, terror fills me. My breath stills. My chest tightens up.

"It's Estella," Vy'syn murmurs, hand stroking the small of my back, almost as if he can sense my distress. "And Viv." How does he know it's them? I don't know. "And they are hungry."

"Coming!" I shout, but Kiana's already sliding off her chair. Movements still jerky, she walks to and opens the door, grinning when her aunts are suddenly swooping her up in their arms.

"Well, what the fuck is this? A party and I wasn't invited?" Estella quirks a brow.

I roll my eyes in mock annoyance. "Only because you'd eat everything."

"Damn right." She's at the table shortly after, shrugging off her wet outer layer and hanging it behind her. Another sort of warmth fills me as Viv joins too and we all settle in and eat together. Like the old times. Like a family.

My gaze shifts to Vy'syn, watching him savor every bite even as he makes sure that I get my fill.

Later, when we're all full and the others have gone, he insists on assisting me with clean-up duty. Strong arms wrap around me from behind. He leans into me, moments ticking between us that I don't want to end.

"Thank you, Firespark," he whispers against my hair. "You are everything I've craved."

I lean back against him, cherishing his closeness.

"No," I whisper. "Thank *you.*"

Because now I have a family, and I realize it's what I'd thought I lost back on the mothership. But he's given it all back to me again.

And I accept it, closing my eyes and allowing myself to breathe.

It's not over yet. Comodre still has a lot more battles to win, but life isn't so bleak anymore.

Finally, I feel like I'm living again.

ABOUT THE AUTHOR

A. G. Wilde is an avid reader, a gamer, a lover of all things space, alien, and sci-fi.

She is addicted to intense romance, irresistible heroes, and deliciously naughty things.

facebook.com/agwilde

x.com/authoragwilde

instagram.com/authoragwilde

amazon.com/author/agwilde

AFTERWORD

♥ This concludes *Outlaw* ♥

You've reached the end of the book! Now, I have one question.

Do you want a Zamari of your own? (I do.)

So happy you've read Elsie and ~~Vy'syn~~, ahem, I mean **the Zamari's** story (oh my God, almost put my life on the line there). I loved writing them so much. From Elsie's will to power through anything to the Zamari's no nonsense badassitude.

Revealing bits about Ivuria and her orbiting planets, I kept imagining what it would be like to live there. I decided halfway through that Elsie was a star and I am quite fine living here on Earth, snuggled in my Oodie and drinking tea. But hey, I'm all for adventure! :D

As you can imagine, the story doesn't end with Elsie. If I recall, a certain Zamari sent a message to someone in space and one day, it will be answered.

Till then, see you and happy reading!

♥ A.G.

Scan the QR code below if you want to ☞ Join my mailing list, ☞ Find me on Facebook

NEXT IN THE SERIES

VAGABOND

ALSO BY AG WILDE

Xul: Captured by Aliens Book One
Athena wakes up in hell.
Well...it's an alien slave ship, but it might as well be hell because she only has three choices.
Mate. Become a sex slave. Or be killed.
Great options.
Desperate for freedom, a chance for survival is presented in the handsome rogue alien called Xul.
But Xul is caught up in problems of his own and a mission he cannot afford to let fail—one that could be easily compromised if he dared open his heart.
That doesn't leave her with many options and it doesn't help that she finds him utterly frustrating...
...and strong, hot, irresistible...
She shouldn't really be thinking about him like that.
Should she?

Other books in the series: Crex, Yce, Kyris, Kyro

Riv's Sanctuary: Riv's Sanctuary Book One
Abducted from Earth over a year ago, Lauren spent most of that time getting accustomed to her new life as one of the "animals" in an alien zoo.
When she's sold by the zookeeper, her life takes a turn she wasn't expecting. She has no idea where she'll end up till she's

brought to a sanctuary owned by a tall blue hunk of an alien called Riv.

Riv's life is quiet and peaceful in a place as far away from civilization as he can manage. So when an annoying chatterbox of a human ends up on his doorstep, he's less than pleased. The human disrupts his life and his solitude and he can't wait to get rid of her.

He's not interested in helping her, and he's definitely not interested in love.

Except...she's managed to wheedle her way in and suddenly those barriers around his heart don't seem so strong anymore.

He has two options: Let her go.

Or let her in.

Other books in the series: Sohut's Protection, Ka'Cit's Haven

---

Ajos: The Restitution Book One

She didn't move to the big city just to be kidnapped by aliens.

That wasn't even possible...

Right?

WRONG.

When Kerena wakes up, she's not on Earth anymore.

Heck, she's not even in the same galaxy, and the face hovering so close she can make out every detail? That face is definitely...not...human.

But before she can really figure out what's going on, Kerena realizes she's caught in the middle of a war—one she was thrust into as soon as she was ripped from Earth.

She's surrounded by aliens in a rebellion, but there's one—the one with the strange golden eyes, minty-teal skin, and rippling muscles—that holds her attention.

His presence is magnetic and his heated gaze makes something stir deep within her.

He's battling something that has nothing to do with the war and his warning that she should stay away does not go unheeded.
He's a dangerous rebel fighter. She gets that. So...why is he still hovering so close? And why is he growling at everyone that so much as looks in her direction?
Most of all, why does he keep looking at her like she belongs to ... HIM?

Other books in the series: V'Alen

Arrival: Captured Earth Book One

ADIRA
The machines came, and they trampled us all.
I have nothing left. No family. No friends. No home.
They harvest us. They breed us. They feed from us...
There is no hope...Not until one fateful moment when my eyes open and I see something streaking across the skies.
What appears is like a demon before my eyes...
But can they be worse than the evil already upon us?
I will just have to wait and see.

FER'RO
Sailing across the stars for what feels like eons...we have followed our enemy to a little blue planet.
We had wanted to arrive before them...now I think we may be too late.
But when we kill the first Scrit and I see the being drowning within its depths, I know I have to save it.
And *it*...turns out to be a *her*. **A female.**
This planet has hope yet. I will save her and her kind.

...Little do I know...she's the one who ends up saving me instead.

Dark. Steamy. Gritty. A thrilling romance intertwined in a plot that will give you chills.

Other books in the series: Base Zero, Cataclysm, War

Claiming His Mate
Fated Mates of the Atari

When I get a once-in-a-lifetime chance to go on a luxury space cruise, I jump at it.
This cruise is the beginning of something amazing, and nothing is going to stop me from going.
But when things go wrong shortly after departure, it's clear I have made a mistake.
Suddenly thrown into a world where I have no way of defending myself, the last thing I expect is an Atari warrior coming to my rescue.
This cruise has been full of surprises...but the Atari is the biggest one of all.
He's tall, growly, possessive, and he sends my pulse into overdrive with just the slightest look.
Why the heck is my body reacting this way to this stranger?
And did he just declare that I am his mate?

Other books in the series: Craving His Mate, Fighting for His Mate, Guarding His Mate

---

Scan the QR code to view all books